PRAISE FOR The Nautical Chart

"What a lovely, well-rounded and distinctive novel to lure us from troubled shores. In *The Nautical Chart*, Spain's best-selling author Arturo Pérez-Reverte has composed a contemporary and thoughtful suspense story of a seaman's happenstance, a woman's obsession and a desperate voyage by Jesuits that started 232 years earlier." —*Los Angeles Times Book Review*

"Irresistibly juicy." —*Newsday*

"Ingenious." —*The New York Times Book Review*

"Engrossing and often beautiful . . . In *The Nautical Chart*, the author has crafted a work whose intentional, delicious, and old-fashioned blurring of the distinction between high literature and pop entertainment entitles it to a space of its own in that library—and in yours." —*New York Magazine*

"There's nothing like treasure to get the blood up. In fictions as diverse as *Treasure Island* and *Treasure of the Sierra Madre*, a common fable emerges, one of grasping ambition meeting well-deserved come-uppance. *The Nautical Chart*, the latest historical thriller by Spanish novelist Arturo Pérez-Reverte, fits neatly into this tradition. . . . While the swashbuckling tale of mystery cruises along on a breeze freshened with gusts of Melville, Conrad and Stevenson, Pérez-Reverte's real debt is to Dashiell Hammett's Maltese Falcon." —*The Washington Post Book World*

"With his chess-like plots and mysterious characters, Arturo Pérez-Reverte has established himself as the master of the intellectual thriller, a reputation again confirmed with *The Nautical Chart*. . . .

Pérez-Reverte is [also] a master of conveying ambiguity, particularly in regard to relationships, and this trip across the sea with all its inherent dangers and promise becomes a powerful vehicle for its expression." —*Chicago Tribune*

"A novel that combines the best traditions of plot-driven mystery/suspense fiction with complex characters and a graceful, atmospheric narrative style." —*Houston Chronicle*

"Through four novels, Pérez-Reverte has established himself as a master of the literary thriller. . . . Pérez-Reverte takes his genre-bending to another level this time by merging the swashbuckling spirit of the best sea adventures with an introspective, philosophical meditation on the idea of navigation." —*Booklist* (starred)

"This marvelous thriller is the fifth (and best) fiction in English translation yet from the very popular Spanish author. . . . Dazzling, ends up smashingly . . . In a virtually perfect fusion of absorbing action and precise, intricate characterization, Pérez-Reverte magically sustains the tension and suspense over a span of almost 500 pages. A classic of its genre, equal to the best of Eric Ambler and Patrick O'Brian." —*Kirkus Reviews* (starred)

"The imagery is rich, both from a historical perspective and in the vivid scenes of port towns and oceangoing vessels. Pérez-Reverte's love of the sea and everything related to it is palpable. *The Nautical Chart* is a pleasure voyage for anyone who shares that love."

—*The Boston Globe*

"Fascinating and increasingly thrilling." —*The Baltimore Sun*

The Nautical Chart

Also by Arturo Pérez-Reverte

The Flanders Panel

The Club Dumas

The Seville Communion

The Fencing Master

Arturo Pérez-Reverte

The Nautical Chart

Translated from the Spanish by
Margaret Sayers Peden

A HARVEST BOOK
HARCOURT, INC.
San Diego New York London

www.HarcourtBooks.com

This is a translation of *La carta esferica*

Library of Congress Cataloging-in-Publication Data
Pérez-Reverte, Arturo.
[Carta esferica. English]
The nautical chart/Arturo Pérez-Reverte;
translated from the Spanish by Margaret Sayers Peden.—1st U.S. ed.
p. cm.
"A novel of suspense"—Cover.
ISBN 0-15-100534-6
ISBN 0-15-601305-3 (pbk.)
I. Peden, Margaret Sayers. II. Title.
PQ6666.E765 C3813 2001
863'.64—dc21 2001039446

Text set in Dante MT
Designed by Cathy Riggs
Printed in the United States of America

First Harvest edition 2002
A C E G I K J H F D B

A nautical chart is much more than an indispensable instrument for getting from one place to another; it is an engraving, a page of history, at times a novel of adventure.

—*Jacques Dupuet*

CONTENTS

The Nautical Chart

LET us observe the night. It is nearly perfect, with Polaris visible in its prescribed location, to the right and five times the distance of the line formed between Merak and Dubhe. Polaris will remain in that exact place for the next twenty thousand years, and any sailor watching it will be comforted by seeing it overhead. It is, after all, reassuring to know that something somewhere is immutable, as precise people set a course on a nautical chart or on the blurred landscape of a life. If we continue perusing the stars, we will have no difficulty finding Orion, and then Perseus and the Pleiades. That will be easy because the night is so clear, not a cloud in the sky, not a hint of a breeze. The wind from the southwest eased at sunset, and the harbor is a black mirror reflecting the lights of the cranes in the port, the lighted castles high on the mountains, and the flashes—green on one side and red on the other—from the lighthouses of San Pedro and Navidad.

Now let us turn to the man. He stands motionless, leaning against the coping of the wall. He is looking at the sky, which appears darker in the east, and thinking that in the morning the easterly will be blowing, raising a swell out beyond the harbor. He also seems to be smiling a strange smile. Lighted from below by the glow of the port, his face is less hopeful than most, and perhaps even bitter. But we know the reason. We know that during the last weeks, at sea and a few miles from here, wind and waves have been decisive in this man's life. Although now they have no importance at all.

Let us not lose sight of him, because we are going to tell his story. As we look over the port with him, we can make out the lights of a ship moving slowly away from the dock. The sound of her engines is muffled by distance and the sounds of the city, along with the throb of propellers churning the black water as the crew hauls in the final length of mooring line. And as he watches from the wall, the man feels two different types of pain. In the pit of his stomach is a pain born of the sadness evident in the grimace that resembles—soon we will understand that it merely resembles—a smile. But there is a second pain, sharper and more precise, that comes and goes on his right side, there where a cold moistness makes his shirt stick to his body as blood seeps down toward his hip, soaking the inside of his trousers with each beat of his heart and each pulse of his veins.

Fortunately, the man thinks, my heart is beating very slowly tonight.

I

Lot 307

I have swum through oceans and sailed through libraries.

—Herman Melville, Moby Dick

We could call him Ishmael, but in truth his name is Coy. I met him in the next-to-last act of this story, when he was on the verge of becoming just one more shipwrecked sailor floating on his coffin as the whaler *Rachel* looked for lost sons. By then he had already been drifting some, including the afternoon when he came to the Claymore auction gallery in Barcelona with the intention of killing time. He had a small sum of money in his pocket and, in a room in a boardinghouse near the Ramblas, a few books, a sextant, and a pilot's license that four months earlier the head office of the Merchant Marine had suspended for two years, after the *Isla Negra,* a forty-thousand-ton container ship, had run aground in the Indian Ocean at 04:20 hours . . . on his watch.

Coy liked auctions of naval objects, although in his present situation he was in no position to bid. But Claymore's, located on a first floor on calle Consell de Cent, was air-conditioned and served drinks at the end of the auction, and besides, the young woman at the reception desk had long legs and a pretty smile. As for the items to be sold, he enjoyed looking at them and imagining the stranded sailors who had been carrying them here and there until they were washed up on this final beach. All through the session, sitting with his hands in the pockets of his dark-blue wool jacket, he kept track of the buyers who carried off his favorites. Often this pastime was disillusioning. A magnificent diving suit, whose dented and gloriously scarred copper helmet made him think of shipwrecks, banks of sponges and Negulesco's films with giant squid and Sophia Loren emerging from the water with her wet blouse plastered to her body, was acquired by an antique dealer whose pulse never missed a beat as he raised his numbered paddle. And a very old Browne & Son handheld compass, in good condition and in its original box, for which Coy would have given his soul during his days as an apprentice, was awarded, without any change in the opening price, to an individual who looked as if he knew absolutely nothing about the sea; that piece would sell for ten times its value if it were displayed in the window of any maritime sporting-goods shop.

The fact is, that afternoon the auctioneer hammered down lot 306—a Ulysse Nardin chronometer used in the Italian Regia Marina—at the opening price, consulting his notes as he pushed up his glasses with his index finger. He was suave, and was wearing a salmon-colored shirt and a rather dashing necktie. Between bids he took small sips of a glass of water.

"Next lot: *Atlas Marítimo de las Costas de España,* the work of Urrutia Salcedo. Number three oh seven."

He accompanied the announcement with a discreet smile saved for pieces whose importance he meant to highlight. An eighteenth-century jewel of cartography, he added after a significant pause, emphasizing the word "jewel" as if it pained him to release it. His assistant, a young man in a blue smock, held up the large folio volume so it could be seen from the floor, and Coy looked at it with a stab of sadness. According to the Claymore catalogue, it was rare to find this edition for sale, since most of the copies were in libraries and museums. This one was in perfect condition. Most likely it had never been on a ship, where humidity, penciled notations, and natural wear and tear left their irreparable traces on navigational charts.

The auctioneer was opening the bidding at a price that would have allowed Coy to live for a year in relative comfort. A man with broad shoulders, a clear brow, and long gray hair pulled back into a ponytail, who was sitting in the first row and whose cell phone had rung three times, to the irritation of others in the room, held up his paddle, number 11. Other hands went up as the auctioneer, small wooden gavel in hand, turned his attention from one to another, his modulated voice repeating each offer and suggesting the next with professional monotony. The opening price was about to be doubled, and prospective buyers of lot 307 began dropping by the wayside. Joining the corpulent individual with the gray ponytail in the battle was another man, lean and bearded, a woman—of whom Coy could see only the back of a head of short blond hair and the hand raising her paddle—and a very well-dressed bald man. When the woman doubled the initial price, gray ponytail half-turned to send a miffed glance in her direction, and Coy glimpsed green eyes, an aggressive profile, a large nose, and an arrogant expression. The hand holding his paddle bore several gold rings. The man gave the appearance of not being accustomed to competition, and he turned to his right brusquely, where a dark-haired, heavily made-up young woman who had been murmuring into the phone every time it rang was now suffering the consequences of his bad humor. He rebuked her harshly in a low voice.

"Do I hear a bid?"

Gray ponytail raised his hand, and the blonde woman immediately counterattacked, lifting her paddle, number 74. That caused a stir in the room. The lean bearded man decided to withdraw, and after two new raises the bald, well-dressed man began to waver.

Gray ponytail raised the bidding, and caused new frowns in his vicinity when his phone rang once again. He took it from the hand of his secretary and clamped it between his shoulder and his ear; at the same time his free hand shot up to respond to the bid the blonde had just made. At this point in the contest, the entire room was clearly on the side of the blonde, hoping that ponytail would run out of either money or phone batteries. The Urrutia was now at triple the opening price, and Coy exchanged an amused glance with the man in the next seat, a small dark-haired man with a thick mustache and hair slicked back with gel. His neighbor returned the look with a courteous smile, placidly crossing his hands in his lap and twirling his thumbs. He was small and fastidious, almost prissy, and had melancholy, appealing, slightly bulging eyes, like frogs in fairy tales. He wore a red polka-dot bow tie and a hybrid, half Prince of Wales, half Scots tartan jacket that gave him the outlandishly British air of a Turk dressed by Burberry.

"Do I have a higher bid?"

The auctioneer held his gavel high, his inquisitive eyes focused on gray ponytail, who had handed the cell phone back to his secretary and was staring at him with annoyance. His latest bid, exactly three times the original price, had been covered by the blonde, whose face Coy, more and more curious, could not see no matter how hard he tried to peer between the heads in front of him. It was difficult to guess whether it was the bump in the bidding that was perturbing ponytail or the woman's brassy competitiveness.

"Ladies and gentlemen, is this the last bid?" asked the auctioneer, with great equanimity.

He was looking at ponytail, without eliciting a response. Everyone in the room was looking expectantly in the same direction. Including Coy.

"Then at the current price, going once. . . . At this price, going twice. . . ."

Gray ponytail thrust up his paddle in a violent gesture, as if he were brandishing a weapon. As a murmur spread through the room, Coy again looked to the blonde. Her paddle was already up, topping his bid. Once again the tension built, and for the next two minutes everyone in the room followed the rapid duel's intense pace as if watching a fight to the death. Paddle number 11 was no sooner down than 74 was up. Not even the auctioneer could keep up; he had to pause a couple of times to sip from the glass of water sitting on the lectern.

"Do I have a further bid?"

Urrutia's *Atlas* was at five times its opening price when number 11 committed an error. Perhaps his nerve faltered, although the error might have been his secretary's; her phone rang insistently and she passed it to him at a critical moment, just as the auctioneer was holding the gavel high in expectation of a new bid, and gray ponytail hesitated as if reconsidering. The error, if that is what it was, might also have been the fault of the auctioneer, who may have interpreted the sudden movement, the turn toward the secretary, as a capitulation and an end to the bidding. Or perhaps there was no error at all, because auctioneers, like other human beings, have their hang-ups and their phobias, and this one might have been inclined to favor ponytail's opponent. Whatever the case, three seconds were all that were needed for the gavel to bang down on the lectern. Urrutia's *Atlas* was awarded to the blonde woman whose face Coy still hadn't seen.

LOT 307 was one of the last, and the rest of the session proceeded without emotion or drama, except that the man with the ponytail did not bid on any other item, and before the end of the auction he stood up and left the room, followed by the hastily tapping heels of the secretary—not, however, without first directing a furious glare at the blonde. Nor did she lift her paddle again. The thin, bearded individual ended up in possession of a very handsome marine telescope, and a gentleman with a stern expression and dirty fingernails, sitting in front of Coy, obtained for only slightly more than the opening price a model of the *San Juan Nepomuceno* that was almost a meter long and in quite good condition. The last lot, a set of old charts from the British Admiralty, remained unsold. The auctioneer called an end to the session, and everyone got up and moved to the small salon where Claymore treated its clients to champagne.

Coy looked for the blond woman. In other circumstances, he would have devoted more attention to the smile of the young receptionist, who came up to him with a trayful of goblets. The receptionist recognized him from other auctions. She knew that he never bid on anything, and was undoubtedly aware of the faded jeans and white sneakers he wore as a complement to the dark navy-blue jacket with two parallel rows of buttons that at one time had been gold and bearing the anchor of the Merchant Marine, but now were a more discreet plain black. The cuffs showed the marks of the officer's stripes they had once sported. Coy was very fond of the jacket—when he wore it he felt connected with the sea. Especially at dusk when he made the rounds of the port district, dreaming of the days when just calling at hiring offices you could pick up a ship to sign on to, times when there were remote islands that were a man's haven, reasonable republics that knew nothing of two-year suspensions, and where arrest warrants and subpoenas from naval tribunals never arrived. He had the jacket made to order fifteen years earlier, with regulation trousers and cap, at the tailor shop of Sucesores de Rafael Valls. After he passed the examination for second officer, he would sail everywhere with it, wearing it on the ever rarer occasions in the life of a Merchant Marine officer when it was obligatory to wear correct attire. He called that ancient treasure his Lord Jim jacket—still very appropriate to his present situation—because it dated from the beginning of what he, an assiduous reader of seafaring literature, defined as his Conrad period. In that vein, Coy had previously lived a Stevenson period and a Melville period. Of the three, around which he ordered his life whenever he decided to take a glance back at the wake that every man leaves behind him, this one was the least happy. He had just turned thirty-eight, and was facing twenty months on suspension and a captain's examination that had been postponed without a set date. He was stranded on land, burdened by a court action that drew a frown from the hiring officer of any shipping company whose door he darkened, and the boarding-house near the Ramblas and his meals at Teresa's were mercilessly devouring his savings. A couple of weeks more and he would have to accept a berth as an ordinary seaman aboard some rusting freighter with a Ukrainian crew, Greek captain, and Antillean registry, the kind that shipowners scuttle for the insurance from time to time, often with a bogus cargo and no time to pack your seabag. Either that or give up the sea and look for a job on dry land. The mere idea nauseated him, because Coy—even though it had been of little use aboard the *Isla Negra*—possessed the principal virtue of every sailor: a certain sense of insecurity that took the form of mistrust, something comprehensible only to someone who has seen a barometer drop five millibars in three hours on the Bay of Biscay, or has found himself being overtaken by a half-million-ton, quarter-mile-long oil tanker in the Strait of Hormuz, in closer and closer quarters. It was the same vague sensation, or sixth sense, that waked you at night when there was a distinct throb of the engines, that raised apprehension at the sight of a black cloud on the far horizon, or when unexpectedly, and for no real reason, the captain appeared on the bridge to give a look around, as if he had nothing particular in mind. A feeling that was normal, on the other hand, in a profession in which the usual procedure when standing guard was to make minute by minute comparisons between the gyroscopic and magnetic compasses; or, to put it another way, to verify a false north by means of another north that itself was not true. And as was the case with Coy, that sense of insecurity was paradoxically accentuated as soon as his feet touched the deck of a ship. He had the misfortune, or the good luck, to be one of those men who was happiest ten miles from the nearest coast.

He drank a sip from the glass the receptionist had just offered him with a flirtatious glance. He wasn't good-looking. His less than average height exaggerated the width of his brawny shoulders, and he had wide, hard hands bequeathed him by a businessman father who had no naval credentials and who in lieu of money had left him the rolling, almost clumsy stride of someone not convinced that the earth he is treading on can be trusted. The harsh lines of his wide mouth and large, aggressive nose were softened by the tranquil, dark, soft eyes that recalled certain hunting dogs when they look at their masters. He also had a timid, sincere, almost childlike smile that came often to his lips, reinforcing the impression of that loyal, slightly sad gaze, a look rewarded by the champagne and friendly overtures from the receptionist, who was walking away through the clients now, de rigueur short skirt switching above the shapely legs she believed were holding Coy's eyes.

Believed. Because at that moment, even as he lifted the glass to his lips, he was looking around for the blonde woman. For an instant his eyes lighted on the short man with the melancholy eyes and checked jacket, who nodded courteously. Coy kept searching the room until he sighted her through the crowd. Again her back was to him, and she was standing holding a glass of champagne. She was wearing a suede jacket, dark skirt, and low-heeled shoes. Gradually, he made his way toward her, curious, studying her smooth gold hair, cut high at the nape of the neck and falling on each side toward her chin in two perfect diagonal, though asymmetrical, lines. As she talked, her hair swung softly, the tips brushing cheeks Coy could appreciate only from a foreshortened perspective. And after crossing two thirds of the distance between them, he saw that the naked line of her neck was covered with freckles, hundreds of tiny little specks barely darker than the pigment of her skin, which was not terribly fair despite the blond hair—a tone that indicated sun, open skies, and outdoor life. And then, when he was but two steps away and starting to move around her casually in order to see her face, she said good-bye to the auctioneer and turned, pausing a couple of seconds in front of Coy, just long enough to set her glass on a table, sidestep him with a lithe movement of her shoulders and waist, and walk away. Their glances had crossed in that brief instant, and he had time to notice that her unusual eyes were dark, with glints of blue. Or maybe it was the other way round, blue eyes with dark glints, navy-blue pupils that slid over Coy without noticing him, as he confirmed that she also had freckles on her forehead and cheeks and throat and hands. That she was covered with freckles, and that they lent her a singular, attractive, almost adolescent look, even though she must be well into her twenties. He could see that she wore a large, masculine, stainless-steel watch with a black dial on her right wrist. And that she was a few inches taller than he, and very pretty.

Coy left five minutes later. The glow from the city reflected on clouds scudding through dark skies toward the southeast, and he knew that the wind was going to shift and that it might rain that night. He stood in the doorway with his hands in the pockets of his jacket while deciding whether to head left or right, which involved a choice between a light snack in a nearby bar or a walk to the Plaza Real and two Bombay Sapphire gins with a lot of tonic. Or maybe one, he corrected himself quickly, after recalling the lamentable state of his wallet. There was very little traffic, and through the leaves on the trees, as far as he could see, a long line of stoplights was sequentially changing from yellow to red. After deliberating for ten seconds, just as the last light turned red and the nearest changed back to green, he started walking to his right. That was the first mistake of the night.

LNAM: Law of Non-Accidental Meetings. Based on Murphy's well-known law—one that had several serious confirmations recently—Coy had the habit of establishing, for private consumption, a series of colorful laws he baptized with absolute technical solemnity. LADWU: Law of Always Dance With the Ugliest, for example; or LBTAFFD: Law of Buttered Toast Always Falls Face Down, and other principles more or less applicable to the recent miserable state of his life. These laws didn't accomplish anything, of course, except to occasion a smile from time to time. At his own expense. No matter, Coy was convinced that in the strange order of the Universe, as in jazz—he was a great jazz fan—chance played a large role, like improvisations so mathematical that you had to ask yourself if they weren't written somewhere. And it was right here that his recently formulated LNAM was proved. As he approached the corner he saw a large silver-gray car parked at the curb, with one of its doors standing open. Then, near a streetlight a little farther away, he could see a man talking with a woman. He first recognized the man, who was facing him, and after a few steps, when he could see how angry he was, Coy realized that the man was arguing with a woman. Now visible in the light from overhead, she was blond, with hair cut high on the nape of her neck. She was wearing a suede jacket and a dark skirt. He felt a tingling in his stomach. Sometimes, he told himself, life becomes predictable by nature of its pure unpredictability. He hesitated a minute before adding, or vice versa. Then he reckoned direction and drift. If there was one thing he was capable of, it was instinctively to calculate these situations, although the last time he had determined a route—a rout would be much closer to fact—it had led directly to a naval tribunal. At any rate, he altered his course by ten degrees in order to pass as close as possible to the couple. That was his second mistake. It was at odds with any sailor's common sense, which counseled maintaining sea room at any cost, or danger ahead.

THE man with the gray ponytail looked furious. At first Coy couldn't hear what he was saying because he was talking in a low voice. He did, however, observe that one hand was raised, with a finger pointing at the woman, who was standing stock-still, facing him. Then the finger moved, jabbing her shoulder with more anger than violence, and she retreated a step, as if frightened.

"... the consequences," Coy heard ponytail say. "You understand? All the consequences."

Again the finger was poised to jab her shoulder, and she took another step back. Now the man seemed to think better of it, and instead he grabbed her arm, not so much in a violent way as to convince or intimidate. She jumped, startled, and again moved back, shaking free. Ponytail made a move toward her arm again, but found himself blocked by Coy, who had slipped between them and was staring him straight in the face. Ponytail's hand froze, its rings glittering in the light, his mouth open to say something to the woman ... or maybe because he didn't know where this character in the navy-blue jacket and sneakers had come from, with his sturdy shoulders and wide, hard hands hanging at either side with feigned casualness, fingers at the side seams of his well-worn jeans.

"Pardon?" said the man with the ponytail.

He had a slight, unrecognizable accent, something between Andalusian and foreign. He stared at Coy, surprised and curious, as if trying unsuccessfully to place him. His expression had changed; he was stunned, especially once he realized that he didn't know the intruder. Ponytail was taller than Coy—almost everyone that night was—and Coy saw him glance over his head toward the woman, as if expecting a clarification regarding this change in the program. Coy couldn't see her. She was behind him, and hadn't moved or spoken a word.

"What the hell . . ." began ponytail, but he cut himself short, his face bleak as if he had just been given bad news. Standing there before him, mouth closed and hands at his sides, Coy calculated the possibilities. Even though he was furious, the man kept his cool. He was dressed in an expensive jacket and tie, elegant shoes, and on his left wrist, above the hand with the rings, shone a very heavy, ultramodern gold watch. This guy lifts twenty pounds of gold every time he knots his tie, thought Coy. The total effect was attractive. He had good shoulders and an athletic build. But he isn't the kind, Coy concluded, to pick a fistfight in the middle of the street, not right in front of the Claymore auction gallery.

Coy still couldn't see the woman, although he could sense her eyes on him. I hope at least, he told himself, that she doesn't go running off, that she'll take time to say thank you—if I don't get my face bashed in, that is. For his part, ponytail had turned to his left and was staring at the window of a boutique as if expecting someone to step out carrying an explanation in an Armani handbag. In the light from the shop window, Coy could see that the man's eyes were brown. That surprised him a little, since he had remembered them being green in the auction house. But when the man turned in the opposite direction, toward the street, Coy could see that he had one eye of each color. The right one was brown, the left green, starboard and port. He also saw something more disturbing than the color of the man's eyes. The open door of the car, which was an enormous Audi, lighted the interior, where the secretary sat witnessing the scene and smoking a cigarette. It also lighted the coat-and-tie-clad chauffeur, a hulk with very curly hair, who was getting out of the car. The chauffeur was not elegant, nor did he look as if he would have ponytail's refined voice. His nose was flattened like a boxer's, and his face seemed to have been stitched and restitched a half dozen times, losing a few pieces in the process. He had a sallow, somewhat Berberish cast to his skin. Coy remembered having seen rough guys who looked like him working as doormen in whorehouses in Beirut and dance halls in Panama. They often carried a switchblade hidden in their right sock.

This was not going to turn out well, he reflected with resignation. LTLGVL: Law of Takes a Lot and Gives Very Little. Those two were going to break a couple of indispensable bones, and in the meantime the girl would run away like Cinderella or Snow White—Coy always got those two stories mixed up, because they didn't have ships in them—and he would never see her again. But for the moment she was still there, and he took note of the blue eyes with dark glints; or maybe, he remembered, it was dark with blue glints. He felt them on his back. He didn't miss the twisted humor in the fact he was about to get the holy shit beat out of him over a woman whose face he had seen for only two seconds.

"Why are you sticking your nose in something that's none of your business?" asked the man with the ponytail.

It was a good question. Ponytail's tone was focused, calm, but also curious. At least that's how it sounded to Coy, who was keeping the chauffeur in sight out of the corner of his eye.

"This is... Oh, for God's sake," ponytail blurted when Coy didn't answer. "Just... get out of here."

I bet she's wishing the same thing, Coy thought. She's agreeing with this guy and saying, Who asked you to hold a candle at this funeral? Move along, and don't butt in where you're not invited. And you mumble an apology, your ears burning; you walk away, turn the corner, and slit your wrists for being a complete idiot. Now she's leaving and saying....

But she didn't say anything. She was as silent as Coy himself. Coy stood there between them, staring into the bicolored eyes opposite him, a step away and a foot above his. He couldn't actually think of anything else to do, and if he spoke he was going to lose what small advantage he had. He knew from experience that a man who keeps his mouth shut is more intimidating than one who doesn't, because it's difficult to guess what he has in mind. Maybe ponytail was of the same opinion, because he was looking at Coy thoughtfully. Finally Coy saw a glimmer of uncertainty in those eyes that reminded him of a dog he had known, a Dalmatian.

"Well, well," ponytail said. "Look what we have here. A hero from a B movie."

Coy kept staring, not uttering a word. If I move quickly, he thought, I could land a kick to his midsection before taking on the Berber. The question is the girl. I wonder what the fuck she'll do.

Suddenly ponytail exhaled, with a sigh that sounded like a sour, exaggerated laugh.

"This is ridiculous," he said.

He sounded sincerely confused by the situation. Coy slowly lifted his left hand to scratch his nose, which was itching. That always happened when he was thinking. Give him the knee, he mused. I'll say something to distract him, he thought, and before he answers I'll knee him in the balls. Then the problem will be the other guy, who will be warned. And not in the best of moods.

An ambulance passed by, flashing orange lights. Thinking that soon he was going to need one himself, Coy ventured a quick look around, without seeing anything he could use for a weapon. So he eased his fingers toward the pocket of his jeans, his thumb passing lightly over his keys to the boardinghouse. He could always try to slash the chauffeur's face with the keys, as he had once done to a drunk German at the door of the Club Mamma Silvana de La Spezia—hello, good-bye—when he saw him ready to jump him. Because, as sure as sin, that's what this sonofabitch was going to do.

The man facing him ran a hand across his forehead and down the back of his head, as if he wanted to smooth the already smooth hair pulled into a ponytail, then wagged his head sideways. He had a strange, pained smile on his lips, and Coy decided he liked him much better when he was serious.

"You'll be hearing from me," he told the woman over Coy's shoulder. "You can count on that."

In the same instant he looked toward the chauffeur, who had taken a few steps in their direction. As if that was an order, he stopped. Coy, who had glimpsed the movement and felt his muscles tense with adrenaline, relaxed with concealed relief. Ponytail again took a long look at Coy, as if he wanted to engrave him in his memory, with subtitles for emphasis. He raised the hand with the rings and pointed his index finger at Coy's chest, just as he had earlier with the woman, but he didn't jab him. He just held the finger there, pointed like a threat, then turned and walked away as if he had just remembered a pressing engagement.

After that came a brief succession of images: a look from the secretary in the back seat of the car, the arc of her cigarette as it fell to the sidewalk, the door slamming on ponytail's side of the car after he got in beside her, and the last black look from the chauffeur standing at the curb—a long, foreboding glare more eloquent than his boss's—just before the slam of the second car door and the smooth purr as the motor started. With just what that car burns as it takes off, Coy thought sadly, I could eat like a king for two days.

"Thank you," said a woman's voice from behind him.

DESPITE appearances, Coy was not a pessimist. For that it's essential to have lost all faith in the human condition, and he had been born without any to lose. He simply viewed life on land as an unreliable, lamentable, and unavoidable spectacle, and his one desire was to stay as far away as necessary to keep the damage to a minimum. Despite everything, he still had a certain innocence in those days, a partial innocence related to things and areas outside his calling. Four months in the dry dock had not been enough to wear away a candor more suited to the world of the sea, the absorbed, slightly absent distancing sailors often maintain when dealing with people who feel solid ground beneath their feet. At that time he still looked at some things from afar, or from outside, with a naive capacity for surprise not unlike what he had felt as a boy when he was taken to press his nose against the toy-shop windows on Christmas Eve. But now there was also the certainty—as much a relief as it was disillusion—that none of those exciting marvels was destined for him. In his case, knowing he was outside that perimeter, and that his name was not on the list of good boys to receive presents, was calming. It was good not to expect anything from anyone, for his seabag to be light enough that he could sling it over his shoulder and walk to the nearest port, without regret for what he was leaving behind. Welcome aboard. For thousands of years, even before Homer's concave ships set sail for Troy, there were men with wrinkles around their mouths and rainy November hearts, men whose nature leads them sooner or later to look with interest into the black hole of a pistol barrel, men for whom the sea was a solution and who always sensed when it was time to make an exit. Even before he knew it, Coy was one of them, by vocation and by instinct. Once, in a cantina in Veracruz, a woman—it was always women who phrased this kind of question—had asked him why he was a sailor and not a lawyer or a dentist. He could only shrug his shoulders, and after a long pause, when she was no longer expecting an answer, he said, "The sea is clean." And it was true. At sea the air was fresh, wounds healed more quickly, and the silence became so intense that it made unanswerable questions bearable and justified silence itself. On a different occasion, in the Sunderland restaurant in Rosario, Argentina, Coy had met the sole survivor of a shipwreck, one of nineteen men. Three o'clock in the morning, anchored in mid-river, a leak, all men asleep, and the ship on the bottom in five minutes. What most impressed Coy about the survivor was how quiet he was. Someone asked him how that was possible—eighteen men going down with their ship, without any warning. The man had looked at him, silent and uncomfortable, as if it was all so obvious it wasn't worth the trouble to explain, and then raised his glass of beer and drank. City sidewalks filled with people and brightly lit shop windows made Coy uneasy. He felt clumsy and out of place, like a fish out of water, or like that sailor in Rosario, who was almost as silent as the eighteen men who had been lost. The world was a very complex structure that could bear contemplation only from the sea, and terra firma took on soothing proportions only at night, while on watch, when the helmsman was a mute shadow and you could feel the soft throbbing of the engines issuing from the belly of the ship. When cities were reduced to tiny lines of lights in the distance, and land was the shimmering radiance of a beacon glimpsed on the swell. Flashes that alerted you, repeating again and again: careful, attention, keep your distance, danger. *Danger.*

He didn't see any warning flashes in the woman's eyes as he returned to her with a drink in each hand in the crowded Boadas bar. That was his third error of the night. There are no handbooks on lighthouses and perils and signals for navigating on land. No prescribed routes, no updated charts, no outlines of shoals measured in feet or fathoms, no markers at such and such a cape, no red, green, or yellow buoys, no conventions for boarding, no clear horizons for calculating latitude. On land you have to navigate by blind reckoning, and you are aware of reefs only when you hear their roar a cable's length from the bow, when you see darkness grow light in the froth of the sea breaking on a reef just below the surface. Or when you hear the unexpected rock—all sailors know there's one waiting for them somewhere—scraping the hull with a murderous screech that makes the bulkheads shudder, in that terrible moment when any man at the helm of a ship would rather be dead.

"You were quick," she said.

"I'm always quick in a bar."

She watched him with curiosity, amused, as he cleared a path through the people clustered around the bar with the decisiveness of a small, compact tugboat. He had ordered a Bombay Sapphire gin and tonic for himself and a dry martini for her, carrying them back with a skillful, pendular motion of his hands, without spilling a drop—a feat that deserved no little credit in the Boadas at that hour.

Then she looked at him through her drink, her eyes indigo blue.

"And what do you do in life, besides move well through bars, go to maritime auctions, and help defenseless women?"

"I'm a sailor."

"Ah."

"A sailor without a ship."

"Ah."

A half hour earlier, after the man with the gray ponytail climbed into the Audi, she had said "Thank you," and he had turned to look at her closely for the first time. Standing there on the sidewalk, he reasoned that the easy part was behind him, that now it wasn't his move, but that of the woman whose thoughtful and vaguely surprised gaze was checking him over from head to toe, as if she were trying to catalogue him with one of the species of man she knew. There was nothing for him to do but try a modest, restrained smile, the same smile you give the captain when you sign on to a new ship, at that initial moment when words mean nothing and both parties know there will be time to sort things out. But for Coy the problem was precisely that he had no guarantee they would have the necessary time, that there was nothing to keep her from thanking him once more and marching off in the most natural way, disappearing forever. He bore the ten long seconds of scrutiny silently and motionlessly. LUF: Law of the Unzipped Fly. I hope to God it's zipped, he thought. He watched as she tilted her head to one side, just enough so the left side of her smooth blond hair, cut asymmetrically with the precision of a surgeon's scalpel, brushed her freckled cheek. After that, no smile, no words, she just walked slowly along the sidewalk, up the street, hands in the pockets of her suede jacket.

She was carrying a large leather shoulder bag that she tucked close to her side with her elbow. Her nose was not as pretty seen in profile. It was a little irregular, as if it had once been broken. That didn't diminish her attractiveness, Coy decided, it gave her a touch of unexpected toughness. She walked with her eyes to the ground and focused a little to the left, as if offering him the opportunity to occupy that space. Together they walked in silence, a certain distance apart, without exchanging glances or explanations or commentary, until she stopped at the corner, and Coy understood that this was the moment either for good-byes or for words. She held out a hand and he took it in his large, clumsy one, feeling a firm, bony grasp that belied the juvenile freckles and was more in line with the calm expression of her eyes, which he had finally decided were navy blue.

And then Coy spoke. He spoke with the spontaneous shyness that was his usual way with people he didn't know, bunching his shoulders with a simplicity and accompanying his words with a smile that, although he didn't know it, lighted his face and took the edge off his roughness. He spoke, touched his nose, and spoke again, with no idea whether someone was waiting for her somewhere, or whether she was from this city or from out of town. He said what he thought he had to say and then stood there, moving nervously and holding his breath, like a child who had just recited a lesson and was waiting, without much hope, for the teacher's verdict. She looked him over for another ten seconds, and again tilted her head so that her hair brushed her cheek. And then she said yes, why not, she too felt like having a drink. They walked toward the Plaza de Cataluña, and then toward the Ramblas and calle Tallers. When he held the door of the Boadas for her he caught her aroma for the first time, vague and subtle, a scent that came not from cologne or perfume but from skin dotted in tones of gold, skin he imagined to be smooth and warm, with the texture of a peach. As they headed for the bar against the wall he noticed that all the men and women in the place looked first at her and then at him, and he wondered at how men and women always look first at a beautiful woman and then shift their gaze toward her companion in an inquiring way, to see who that fellow might be. As if to decide whether he deserves her, whether he's up to the test.

"AND what does a sailor without a ship do in Barcelona?"

She was sitting on a tall bar stool with her bag across her knees, her back against the wood bar that ran the length of the wall beneath framed photographs and bar souvenirs. She wore two small gold balls on her ears, and not a single ring on her fingers. Almost no makeup. At the open neck of her white shirt, which revealed hundreds of freckles, Coy caught the gleam of a silver chain.

"Wait," he said. Then he took a sip of gin and noticed that she was studying his old jacket, that she may have hesitated at the darker lines on his cuffs, where the missing stripes had been. "Wait for better times."

"A sailor ought to sail."

"Not everyone agrees."

"Did you do something bad?"

He nodded, with a sad half-smile. She opened her bag and took out a pack of English cigarettes. Her fingernails were short and wide, not carefully filed. She must have bitten her nails at one time, he was sure. Maybe she still did. One cigarette was left in the box, and she lit it with a match from a pack that bore the logo of a Belgian shipping line he was familiar with, Zeeland. She protected the flame in the hollow of her hands in an almost masculine manner.

"Was it your fault?"

"Legally, yes. It happened on my watch."

"You ran afoul of another ship?"

"I touched bottom. A rock that wasn't on the charts."

It was true. A sailor never said "I hit a rock," or "I ran aground." The common verb was "touched." I touched bottom, I touched the dock. If you cut another ship in half and sank it in the midst of the Baltic fog, you said, "We touched a ship." At any rate, he noted that she had used the marine term "ran afoul," instead of "accident" or "collision." The cigarette box was lying open on the bar and Coy looked at it—the head of a sailor framed by a life buoy, and two ships. It had been a long time since he'd seen a pack of unfiltered Players, cigarettes he'd seen his whole lifetime. They weren't easy to find, and he hadn't known they were still producing them in the white cardboard box. It was funny that she was smoking that brand. The auction of naval memorabilia, the Urrutia, he himself. LAC: Law of Amazing Coincidences.

"Do you know the story?"

He pointed to the box. She looked at it and then looked up.

"What story?"

"The one about Hero."

"Who's Hero?"

He told her. He told her about the name on the ribbon of the cap worn by the sailor with the blond beard, about his youthful years on the sailing ship that appeared on one side of the picture, and about the other ship, the ironclad that was his last berth. About how the elder Player and his sons had bought his portrait to put on their cigarette boxes. Then he sat while she smoked—the cigarette had been burning down between her fingers—and looked at it.

"That's a good story," she said after a while.

"It isn't mine. Domino Vitale tells that story to James Bond in *Thunderball.* I sailed on a tanker that had all of Ian Fleming's novels."

He also remembered that the ship, the *Palestine,* had spent a month and a half blockaded off Ras Tanura, in the midst of an international crisis, with the planks of the deck burning beneath a vicious sun and the crew flat in their bunks, suffocated by heat and boredom. The *Palestine* was a bad luck ship, one of those where the men turn hostile and hate each other and lines get tangled. The chief engineer grumbled deliriously in a corner—they'd hidden the key to the bar but on the sly he was drinking methyl alcohol from the infirmary mixed with orange soda—and the first officer wouldn't speak to the captain, not even if the ship was about to run aground. Coy had had more than enough time to read those novels, and many more, on his floating prison during those interminable days when the scorching air that filtered in through the portholes made him gasp like a fish out of water, and every time he got out of his bunk he left the sweat-imprinted silhouette of his naked body on the dirty, wrinkled sheet. A Greek tanker three miles away had been hit by a bomb from an airplane, and for two days he could see the column of black smoke rising straight to the sky, and the glow that stained the horizon red and outlined the dark, vulnerable silhouettes of the anchored ships at night. During that time, he often woke up terrified, dreaming he was swimming in a sea of flames.

"Do you read much?"

"Some." Coy touched his nose. "I read some. But always about the sea."

"There are other interesting books."

"Could be. But those are the only ones that interest me."

The woman stared at him, and he shrugged his shoulders and rocked back and forth on his feet. They hadn't said a word about the guy with the gray ponytail, he realized, or about what she was doing there. He didn't even know her name.

THREE days later, Coy was lying in bed in his rented room in La Marítima, staring at a mildew stain on the ceiling while he listened to "Kind of Blue" on his Walkman. After "So What," in which the bass had been sliding sweetly, the trumpet of Miles Davis came in with his historic two-note solo—the second an octave lower than the first—and Coy, suspended in that empty space, was waiting for the liberating release, the unique percussion beat, the reverberation of the cymbal and the drumrolls smoothing the slow, inevitable, amazing path for the trumpet.

He thought of himself as nearly illiterate in music, but he loved jazz, its insolence and ingenuity. He had fallen in love with it during long watches on the bridge, when he was sailing as third officer aboard the *Fedallah,* a fruit carrier of the Zoe line whose first officer, a Galician they called Gallego Neira, had the five tapes of the Smithsonian Collection of Classic Jazz. They included musicians from Scott Joplin and Bix Beiderbecke to Thelonious Monk and Ornette Coleman, passing through Armstrong, Ellington, Art Tatum, Billie Holiday, Charlie Parker, and others. Hours and hours of jazz with a cup of coffee in his hands, nights beneath the stars huddled on the flying bridge, staring at the sea. The chief engineer, Gorostiola, who came from Bilbao and was better known as the Tucumán Torpedoman, was another passionate fan of that music, and the three of them—later they went on together to the *Tashtego,* a sister ship in the Zoe line—had shared jazz and friendship for six years, following the rectangle the *Fedallah* cut as she carried cargoes of fruit and grain between Spain, the Caribbean, northern Europe, and the southern United States. That was a happy time in Coy's life.

From the floor below came the sound of the radio belonging to the landlady's daughter, who usually stayed up late studying. She was a sullen, graceless girl at whom he smiled courteously without ever receiving a greeting or a look in return. La Marítima had been a bathhouse—built in 1844 it said above the door facing the calle Arc del Teatre—and was later converted into a cheap rooming house for sailors. It straddled a rise between the old port and the Chinese quarter, and no doubt the girl's mother, a hard-faced woman with dyed red hair, had alerted the girl from an early age to the inherent dangers of her clientele, rough unscrupulous men who collected women in every port, hitting land with a raging thirst for alcohol, drugs, and more or less virgin girls.

Through the window, and blending with the jazz on his Walkman, he could hear every note of Noel Soto singing "*Noche de samba en Puerto España.*" Coy turned up the volume. He was naked except for his shorts; on his stomach, open and face down, lay the Spanish edition of Patrick O'Brian's *Master and Commander.* His mind, however, was miles away from the nautical feats of Captain Aubrey and Dr. Maturin. The stain on the ceiling resembled the outline of a coast, complete with capes and coves, and Coy followed an imaginary course between two extremes of the yellowish sea on the smooth ceiling.

It was raining when they left the Boadas. A fine rain slicked the asphalt and sidewalks with glimmering lights and misted halos around automobile headlights. She didn't seem to care that her suede jacket was getting wet, and they walked along the central paseo between newspaper kiosks and flower stands just beginning to close. A mime, stoic beneath the drizzle trickling down the white paint on his petrified face, followed passersby with sad eyes after she bent down to leave a coin in his top hat. She walked on exactly as before, a little ahead of him and looking to her left, as if leaving to Coy the choice of occupying that space or discreetly fading away. He stole a glance at the hard profile behind smooth hair that rippled as she walked, and the dark-blue eyes occasionally turned toward him as the prelude to a thoughtful look or a smile.

There weren't many people in the Schilling. Again he ordered a Sapphire gin and tonic and she settled for tonic alone. Eva, the Brazilian waitress, poured their drinks while staring at Coy's companion, then arched an eyebrow toward him, drumming on the counter with the same long green-polished fingernails that had been conscientiously digging into his naked back three dawns before. But Coy ran his hand over his wet hair and smiled his inalterable smile, very sweet and tranquil, until the waitress muttered "bastard," smiled in return, and even refused to charge for his drink. Coy and the woman sat at a table facing the large mirror reflecting rows of bottles along the wall. There they continued their intermittent conversation. She was not talkative; at this point she had told him only that she worked in a museum. Five minutes later he learned that it was the Museo Naval in Madrid. He deduced that she had studied history, and that someone, maybe her father, was career military. He didn't know whether that had anything to do with her well-brought-up-girl look. He had also glimpsed a contained strength, an internal, discreet self-confidence that he found intimidating.

Coy did not bring up the guy with the gray ponytail until later, when they were walking beneath the arcades on the Plaza Real. She had confirmed that the Urrutia was a valuable if not unique piece, but it wasn't clear whether she had acquired it for the museum or for herself. It's an important maritime atlas, she commented evasively when he alluded to the scene on calle Consell de Cent, and there's always someone who's interested in that kind of thing. Collectors, she had added after a minute. People like that. Then she dipped her head a little and asked what his life was like in Barcelona, making it obvious that she wanted to change the subject. Coy told her about La Marítima, about his walks through the port, and about the sunny mornings on the terrace of the Universal bar opposite the headquarters of the Merchant Marine, where he could sit for three or four hours with a book and his Walkman for the price of a beer. He also told her about the long weeks he had ahead of him, about the frustration of finding himself ashore, without work and money. At that moment he thought he saw, at the far end of the arcade, the short, mustached individual with the brilliantined hair and checked jacket who had been at the auction house that evening. He watched him a minute to be sure, and turned to the girl to ask whether she had recognized him too, but her eyes were empty of expression, as if she'd noticed nothing in particular. When Coy looked back, the little man was still there, strolling with his hands clasped behind his back, casual as you please.

By now they were at the door of the Club de la Pipa. Coy quickly calculated how much he had left in his wallet and decided that he could invite her for another drink, and that in the worst case Roger, the manager, would run a tab for him. The girl seemed surprised by the look of the place, the bell at the door, the ancient stairs, and the room on the second floor with its curious bar, sofa, and engravings of Sherlock Holmes on the walls. There was no jazz that night, and they stood at the deserted counter while Roger worked a crossword puzzle at the other end. She wanted to try the Sapphire gin because she liked the smell. She declared her enchantment with the place, adding that she never would have imagined there was anything like it in Barcelona. Coy said it was going to be closed down because the neighbors complained of the noise and the music; a ship soon to be scrapped, one might say. She had a drop of gin and tonic at a corner of her mouth, and he thought of how fortunate he was to have only three drinks in his belly, because with a couple more he would have reached out and wiped that drop off with his fingers, and she didn't seem the kind who would let anything be wiped away by some sailor she had just met and whom she studied with a mixture of reserve, courtesy, and gratitude. Finally he asked her name and she smiled again—this time after a few beats, as if she had pushed herself to do it—and her eyes met Coy's for a long, intense second before she spoke her name. It was a name as unique as her look, he thought, and he pronounced it once aloud, slowly, before the distant smile was erased entirely from her lips. Afterward Coy asked Roger for a cigarette to offer her, but she didn't want to smoke anymore. She raised the glass to her lips and he saw her white teeth through the glass, and heard the ice tapping against them with a moist clicking. His eyes traveled to the silver chain quietly gleaming at the open neck of her shirt, on skin that in that light seemed warmer, and he wondered whether anyone had ever counted those freckles all the way to Finisterre. Whether they had been counted one by one, on a southerly heading, just as he longed to do. It was then, when he raised his eyes, that it was evident she had sensed his look, and he felt his heart skip a beat when he heard her say it was time to go.

ON the landlady's daughter's radio the same voice was now launching into "*La reina del barrio chino.*" Coy turned off his Walkman—Miles Davis was soloing "*Saeta,*" the fourth theme on "Sketches of Spain"—and stopped staring at the stain on the ceiling. The book and headphones fell to the bed when he stood up and walked across the narrow room, about the size of the cell he had occupied for two days in La Guaira that time the Torpedoman, Gallego Neira, and he, fed up with eating fruit, had left the ship to buy fish to make a bouillabaisse. Neira had said, "Have a cup of coffee and wait for me, just fifteen minutes for a quickie and I'll be back." After a while they'd heard him call for help through the window, and had run inside and busted up the bar, busted everything—tables, bottles, and the ribs of the thug who'd taken the Galician's wallet. Captain don Matías Noreña, mad as hell, had to get them out by bribing the Venezuelan police with a handful of dollars he then systematically deducted, down to the last penny, from their pay.

Coy felt a tug of nostalgia, remembering all that. The mirror over the sink reflected his muscular shoulders and weary, unshaven face. He let the water run until it was good and cold and then splashed it over his face and the back of his neck, snorting and shaking his head like a dog in the rain. He toweled himself vigorously and stood for a while studying his face: strong nose, dark eyes, rugged features, as if he were scoring points in his favor. *Zero,* he concluded. *This bird is not going to be feasting on a peach.*

He pulled the dresser drawer out and felt behind it until his fingers found the envelope where he kept his money. There wasn't much, and in the last few days it had dwindled dangerously. He stood rooted there for a moment, mulling over his idea, and finally he went to the closet and took out the bag containing his meager belongings: a few dog-eared books, his officer's bars, on which the gold was beginning to verge toward a mossy green, jazz tapes, a wallet-size photo album—the training ship *Estrella del Sur,* hauling wind, Torpedoman and Gallego Neira at the counter of a bar in Rotterdam, Coy himself wearing a first officer's stripes, leaning on the rail of the *Isla Negra* in New York harbor—and the wooden box in which he kept his sextant. It was a good sextant, a Weems & Plath with seven filters, black metal and a gilt arc, that Coy had bought in installments, beginning with his first salary after earning his pilot's certificate. Satellite positioning systems had sounded the death knell for that instrument, but any sailor worth his salt knew its reliability—as a guard against electronic failures—in establishing the midday latitude, when the sun reached its highest point in the sky. Even at night, using a star low on the horizon, there were the nautical ephemerides, tables, and three minutes of calculations. In the same way that military men clean and coddle their weapons, Coy had kept the sextant free of saline corrosion and dirt over all those years, cleaning its mirrors and testing for possible lateral and index errors. Even now, without a ship beneath his feet, he often carried it on his walks along the coast, to sit on a rock with the horizon of the open sea before him and calculate angles. That custom dated from the time he was sailing as a student on the *Monte Pequeño,* his third ship if you counted the *Estrella del Sur. Monte Pequeño* was a 275,000-ton tanker owned by Enpetrol, and her captain, don Agustín de la Guerra, liked to solemnify the stroke of midday by inviting his officers to a tot of sherry after they and the young midshipmen had compared calculations made on the flying bridge, the captain with watch in hand and they shooting the sun's tangent on the horizon through the smoked filters of their instruments. He was a captain of the old school; a little behind the times but an excellent sailor from the days when large tankers, ballasted, steamed to the Persian Gulf through the Suez Canal and returned laden with cargo around Africa, past Cape Town. Once he had thrown a steward down the ladder because he lacked respect. When the union complained, he replied that the steward was a lucky man, because a century and a half before he would have been hanged from the mainmast. On my ship, he had told Coy once, you're either in agreement with the captain or you keep your mouth shut. That was during a Christmas dinner on the Mediterranean, sailing into terrible weather—a hard, force 10 wind that obliged them to cut back the engines at Cape Bon. Coy, an apprentice seaman, had disagreed with some banal remark by the captain, who had thrown his napkin on the table and ordered Coy to stand watch outside, on the starboard flying bridge, where Coy passed the next four hours in darkness, whipped by the wind, rain, and spray breaking over the tanker. Don Agustín de la Guerra was a rare survivor from other times, despotic and hard on board, but when a Panamanian cargo ship with a drunken Russian watch officer had rammed de la Guerra's stern one night, when rain and sleet saturated radars in the English Channel, he'd been able to keep the tanker afloat and steer her into Dover without losing a drop of crude, saving the company the cost of tugs. Any knothead, he said, can sail around the world these days by pressing buttons. But if the electronics go down or the Americans decide to black out their damn satellites—the devil's own invention—or some Bolshevik sonofabitch runs up your ass, a good sextant, a compass, and a chronometer will still get you anywhere. So practice, my boy. Practice. Obedient, Coy had practiced tirelessly for days and months and years; later too, and with that same sextant, he had performed more difficult observations on cloudy, dangerous nights, or in the middle of strong storms racing across the Atlantic, clinging, soaked, to the gunnel while the bow slammed down like a machete and he, glued to the eyepiece, awaited a glimpse of the faint gold disk among clouds driven by a northwesterly wind.

He felt a quiet melancholy as he hefted the familiar weight of the sextant in his hands, sliding the index arm and hearing it tick along the toothed arc that marked from 1 to 120 the degrees on any terrestrial meridian. He computed how much he could get for it from Sergi Solàns, who had been admiring the instrument for years. After all, Sergi would say when they were raising a glass at the Schilling, they weren't making sextants like that anymore. Sergi was a good kid who had been buying almost all the drinks since Coy found himself ashore and out of money; nor did he hold a grudge because Coy had gone to bed with Eva the night the Brazilian beauty was wearing a T-shirt diabolically clinging to the size 40 breasts that never saw a bra and Sergi was too drunk to fight for her. He had also studied sailing with Coy, and shared a ship for a few months when both were midshipmen on the *Migalota,* a Ro-Ro owned by Rodríguez & Saulnier. Now he was studying for his captain's exam as first officer on a Trans-Mediterranean ferry that plowed the Barcelona-Palma line twice a week. It's like driving a bus, he said. But with a sextant like that in your cabin, you'd feel like a real sailor.

Coy centered the arm in the middle of the arc and carefully returned the Weems & Plath to its case. Then he went to the dresser, opened his wallet, and took out the card the woman had given him three days earlier when she said good-bye at the corner of the Ramblas. No address, no telephone number, nothing but the two parts of her name: Tánger Soto. Below, in a rounded, precise hand, with a small circle dotting the *i,* she had written the address of the Museo Naval in Madrid.

After he closed the cover of the sextant, Coy was whistling *"Noche de samba en Puerto España."*

II

The Trafalgar Showcase

There are nothing but problems on land.

—Dietrich von Haeften, HOW TO COPE WITH STORMS

Later he learned what it meant to leap into the void, a unique experience for Coy, who could not remember having made a precipitous move in his life. He was the kind of person who took all the time he needed to plot a meticulous route on the nautical chart. Before he found himself on mandatory shore leave, that had been a source of satisfaction in a profession where accomplishing safe passage between two points situated at far-spread geographical latitudes and longitudes was essential. There were few pleasures comparable to deliberating over calculations of course, drift, and speed, or predicting that such and such a cape, or this or that lighthouse, would come into view two days later at six in the morning and at approximately thirty degrees off the port bow, then waiting at that hour by a gunnel slick with early-morning dew, binoculars to your eyes, until you see, at exactly the predicted place, the gray silhouette or the intermittent light that—once the frequency of flashes or occultations is measured by chronometer—confirms the precision of those assessments. When that moment came, Coy always allowed himself an internal smile, serene and satisfied. Taking pleasure in the confirmation of the certainty achieved through mathematics, the on-board instruments, and his professional competence, he would prop himself in one corner of the bridge, near the mute shadow of the helmsman, and pour himself a lukewarm coffee from a thermos, content that he was on a good ship, rather than in that other, uncomfortable world, the one on dry land, now reduced by good fortune to a faint radiance beyond the horizon.

But such rigor in plotting a vector on the nautical charts that regulated his life had not shielded him from error or failure. Saying "land ho!" and then physically corroborating the presence of terra firma and its consequences did not always occur in that sequence. The land was there, whether it was on the charts or had popped up unexpectedly, as such things tend to do, piercing the fragile refuge—that little dot of iron floating on an enormous ocean—where Coy felt completely safe. Six hours before the *Isla Negra,* a container ship of the Mínguez Escudero company, split open her hull halfway between Cape Town and the Mozambique Channel, Coy, the first officer, had warned the captain that the British Admiralty chart corresponding to that area called attention, in a special box, to certain imprecisions in the surveys. But the captain was in a hurry, and besides, he'd been sailing those waters for twenty-five years using the same charts, without a problem. He was also two days behind schedule because of bad weather in the Gulf of Guinea, and because he'd had to evacuate by helicopter a crew member who had broken his back when he slipped down a ladder near the Skeleton Coast. English charts, he had said during mess, are so meticulous they handled them with kid gloves. The route is clear: two hundred forty fathoms at the highest shoal and not a flyspeck on the paper. So we'll pass straight between Terson and Mowett Grave. That was what he'd said: kid gloves, flyspeck, and straight between the islands. The captain, don Gabriel Moa, was a sixty-plus-year-old Galician, small, with a ruddy forehead and gray hair. In addition to his blind trust in the Admiralty charts, he wore four decades at sea in the wrinkles on his face, and in all that time no one had ever seen him lose his composure; not even in the early nineties, it was said, when he'd sailed a day and a half listing twenty degrees after losing eleven containers in an Atlantic storm. He was one of those captains for whom owners and subordinates would put their hands in the fire—curt on the bridge, serious in his cabin, invisible ashore. He was an old-time captain, the kind who addressed officers and midshipmen formally, and whom no one could imagine making an error. And that was why Coy held to the course on the English chart that pointed out imprecisions in the surveys; and that was also why, twenty minutes into his watch, he had heard the steel hull of the *Isla Negra* screech on rock, shuddering beneath his feet, before he recovered from his shock and rushed to the engine-order telegraph to call "Stop the engines!" Captain Moa appeared on the bridge in his pajamas, his hair every which way, and stared into the darkness outside with a stupid expression Coy had never seen on his face. He had stammered, "It can't be," three times in succession, and then, as if he wasn't entirely awake, had murmured a weak "Stop the engines," after the engines had been stopped for five minutes and the helmsman was standing motionless with his hands on the wheel, looking first at the captain and then at Coy. And Coy, with the terrible certainty of someone who has to his misfortune received an unexpected revelation, could not take his eyes off the honored superior whose orders he would have followed without a second's hesitation up to now, even if that meant steering through the Molucca Passage with no radar, and who, taken by surprise and with no time to put on the mask of his reputation, or maybe—men do change with the years and in their hearts—the mask of the efficient sailor he once had been, was showing his true stripes. He was a dazed old man in pajamas now, overwhelmed by events, incapable of issuing an intelligent order; a poor frightened man who suddenly saw his retirement pension fading away after forty years of service.

The warning on the English chart was not without justification. There was at least one unmarked needle in the channel between Terson and Mowett Grave, and somewhere in the universe some joker had to be bellowing with laughter because that one isolated rock in a vast ocean had set itself expressly in the path of the *Isla Negra,* as expressly as the famous iceberg was in the way of the *Titanic,* and on the watch of first officer Manuel Coy. In any case, both men, captain and first officer, had paid for it. The investigating tribunal, composed of a company inspector and two men from the Merchant Marine, had taken Captain Moa's record into account and resolved his case with a discreet early retirement. As for Coy, that Admiralty chart had led him far from the sea.

He was now in Madrid, becalmed beside a stone fountain in the shape of a child with a heretical smile strangling a dolphin, and looking like a shipwreck survivor who had washed up on a noisy beach in high season. Hands in his pockets, in the midst of the crush of automobiles and the racket of blaring horns, he was observing from afar the bronze galleon over the entrance to number 5 Paseo del Prado. He had no way to judge the precision of the hydrographic surveys of the course he was proposing to follow, but in his mind he was already far beyond the point at which it is still possible to steer a different course. The Weems & Plath sextant, which his friend Sergi Solàns had acquired at a reasonable price, had paid for a Barcelona-Madrid train ticket, and ensured sufficient funds to keep him afloat for two weeks. A hefty roll of banknotes was in the right pocket of his jeans, the remainder in the canvas bag in storage at Atocha station. It was now 12:45 on a sunny spring day. Traffic was moving noisily in the direction of the general headquarters of the Navy and the offices of the Museo Naval. A half hour earlier Coy had paid a visit to the headquarters of the

Merchant Marine a couple of streets away to see how his appeal was progressing. The woman in charge, mature, with a pleasant smile, and a flowerpot with a geranium on her desk, had stopped smiling after Coy's record appeared on her computer screen. Appeal denied, she reported in an impersonal tone. He would receive written notification. She dismissed him, turning back to more important matters. Maybe from that office, which was some one hundred seventy nautical miles away from the nearest coast, the woman entertained a romantic notion of the sea, and did not respect sailors who ran their ships aground. Or perhaps to the contrary she was an objective, dispassionate bureaucrat for whom a grounded ship in the Indian Ocean was no different from a wreck on the highway, and a sailor without a berth and on the outfitters' black list seemed like any individual deprived of his driving license by a strict judge. The bad thing was, Coy had reflected as he descended the stairs to the street, the woman probably wasn't all that wrong. At a time when satellites marked routes and waypoints, the cell phone had swept captains capable of making decisions off the bridge, and any executive could direct transatlantic cargo ships or a hundred-thousand-ton tanker from his office, there was little distinction between a sailor who beached his ship and a driver who drove off the road because his brakes failed or he was driving drunk.

Coy paused, concentrating on what steps to take next, until all bitter thoughts were left behind, adrift on the blue. Then, standing beneath a chestnut tree sprouting new leaves, he made his decision. Looking left and right, he waited for a nearby light to change, then set off with conviction. He crossed the street and marched up to the door of the museum, where two servicemen with white belts and helmets and red stripes down their pants stared with curiosity at his double-breasted jacket before letting him pass through the arch of the metal detector. His stomach was aflutter as he climbed the broad stairway, turned right on the landing, and found himself in the lobby, next to the huge double wheel of the corvette *Nautilus.* To his left was the door to administration and information, and to the right the entrance to the exhibition halls. A uniformed man with a bored expression sat behind a desk, and a civilian stood behind a counter where museum books, prints, and souvenirs were sold. Coy licked his lips; suddenly he felt a horrendous thirst. He spoke to the civilian.

"I'm looking for Señorita Soto."

His voice was hoarse. He glanced toward the door on the left, afraid he would find her surprised or uncomfortable. What in the world are you doing here? And so on and so on. He hadn't slept the night before. His head pressed against his reflection in the train window, he'd pondered what he was going to say, but now everything was wiped from his brain, as slick as the wake at the stern. Repressing the impulse to turn and walk out, he shifted his weight from one leg to the other, watched by the man at the counter. He was middle aged, with thick glasses and an amiable expression.

"Tánger Soto?"

Coy nodded. It was strange, he thought, to hear that name in the mouth of a third person. Well, apparently she has a real life after all. There are people who say hello to her, good-bye, all those things.

"That's right," he said.

No, he thought, this trip wasn't strange, it was absurd, as was the fact that his seabag was checked at the station. And now he was here to meet a woman whom he had seen only one night for a couple of hours. A woman who wasn't even expecting him.

"Is she expecting you?"

He shrugged.

"Maybe."

The man repeated that "maybe," his air pensive as he looked at Coy suspiciously. Coy was sorry he hadn't had a chance to clean up that morning; the beard he'd shaved the night before, just as he left for the Sants station, had reappeared as dark stubble. He raised his hand to finger his chin, but interrupted the gesture mid-course.

"Señora Soto has gone out," the man said.

Almost relieved, Coy nodded. Out of the corner of his eye he saw that the man at the desk, leaning forward over a magazine, was checking out his shoes and threadbare jeans. Good thing, Coy thought, he had changed his white sneakers for some old deck shoes with rubber soles.

"Will she be back today?"

The man's eyes were on Coy's jacket, trying to decide whether that dark wool guaranteed the respectability of the person he was speaking with.

"She may be," he said, after brief consideration. "We don't close until one-thirty."

Coy looked at his watch, then pointed toward the nearest hall. Large portraits of Alfonso XII and Isabel II were hung on either side of a door through which he could see display cases, ship models, and guns.

"Then I'll wait in there."

"As you please."

"Will you tell her when she comes back? My name is Coy."

He smiled, an exhausted, sincere smile, the result of six hours on the train and six cups of coffee, and the man behind the counter seemed to relax.

"Of course," he said.

Coy crossed through the hall, his footsteps on the wood floor deadened by his rubber soles. The terror that had gripped his gut gave way to an uneasy uncertainty, not unlike the feeling you get when a ship lurches and you reach for something to hold on to, but it isn't there, so he tried to settle his nerves by looking at the objects around him. He walked past a large painting of Columbus and his men on shore—a cross, pennants in the background, and the blue Caribbean, with natives bowing before the discoverer, innocent of what lay ahead for them—and turned to his right, pausing before display cases filled with nautical instruments. It was a stupendous collection, and he admired the forestaffs, the quadrants, the Arnold chronometers, and the extraordinary collection of eighteenth- and nineteenth-century astrolabes, octants, and sextants, for which someone would undoubtedly be prepared to pay much more than he had received for his modest Weems & Plath.

There were few visitors in the museum, which was larger and brighter than he remembered it. An old man was studying a large rectangular map of Gibraltar, a young couple, probably tourists, were looking into glass cases in the Hall of Discoveries, and a group of schoolchildren was listening to a teacher's explanations in the room dedicated to the rescue of the galleon *San Diego.* The noontime brightness poured through large skylights and illuminated Coy as he wandered through the central patio. Had he not been obsessed with thoughts of the woman he was there to see, he truly would have enjoyed the models of frigates and ships-of-the-line displayed in their entirety or in cross section, showing their complex internal structure. Coy hadn't seen them since his last visit to the museum, twenty years before, when the entrance had been from calle Montalbán and he was still a naval student. Despite the years that had gone by, he was thrilled to immediately recognize his favorite—a model of an eighteenth-century ship-of-the-line nearly ten feet long, with three decks and a hundred and fifty guns, housed in a gigantic glass case. It was a ship that had never breasted the waves, because she had never been built. Those were real sailors, he said to himself, as he had so many other times, studying the rigging, the sails, and the masts and yards of the model, admiring the deep topsails along which rugged, desperate men had to maneuver, keeping their balance on precarious foot ropes, clinging to the canvas during storms and battles, with wind and shot whistling and below them the deck quivering beneath the masts and the implacable ocean. Coy let himself sail with the ship for a moment, lost in a daydream of a long chase at the first light of dawn, of fleeing sails on the horizon. When there was no such thing as radar or satellites or sonar, ships were little dice cups dancing at the mouth of hell, and the sea was a mortal peril, but also an unassailable refuge from all things—lives lived or yet to be lived, deaths looming or already accomplished, but all of it left behind on land. "We come too late to a world too old," he had read in some book. Of course we come too late. We come to ships and ports and seas that are too old, when dying dolphins peel away from the bows of ships, and when Conrad has written *The Shadow-Line* twenty times, Long John Silver is a brand of whiskey, and Moby Dick has become the good whale in an animated film.

Near a full-scale replica of a section of the *Santa Ana*'s mast, Coy passed an officer in the impeccable uniform of the nation's Navy, an impressive-looking man whose cuffs boasted the special loop in the third gold stripe that meant Frigate Captain. He stared hard at Coy, who held his gaze until the officer looked away and walked off toward the back of the hall.

Twenty minutes went by. At least once every minute Coy tried to concentrate on what he was going to say when she appeared, if in fact she ever did, and all twenty times he was tongue-tied, unable to string together a coherent phrase, his mouth half open as if she were actually there before him. He was in the hall devoted to the battle of Trafalgar, standing beneath an oil painting of the scene of an engagement between the *Santa Ana* and the *Royal Sovereign,* when again he was aware of the nerves in the pit of his stomach, like needles—yes, that was the exact word—needling him to get out of there. Up anchor, idiot, he told himself, and with that he seemed to wake from a dream, aghast. He felt the urge to scramble down the stairs, stick his head under cold water, and shake it until he cleared his mind. Damn fool, he berated himself. Damn fool, in spades. *Señora* Soto. I don't even know if she's living with someone or married.

He turned, stepping back in confusion. His eyes lighted on the inscription of a showcase: "Boarding sword worn during the battle of Trafalgar. . . ." He looked up and there was Tánger Soto, reflected in the glass. He hadn't heard her arrive, but she was there, motionless and silent, watching him with an expression between surprise and curiosity, as unreal as she had been the first time. As vague as a shadow locked inside the glass case, a shadow that wasn't hers.

Coy was not a sociable man. As already noted, that factor, along with a few books and a precociously lucid vision of the dark corners of the human soul, had early led him to sea. Nevertheless, this was not entirely incompatible with a candor that occasionally surfaced in his attitudes, in the way he would look at others without moving or speaking, in the rather awkward way he behaved on dry land, or in his sincere, confused, nearly shy smile. He had shipped out driven more by intuition than by conviction. But life does not advance with the precision of a good ship, and gradually his mooring lines slipped into the sea, sometimes fouled in the propellers or dragging along consequences. There were women, of course. A couple of them had got under his skin, into flesh and blood and mind, effecting the pertinent physical and chemical procedures, the analgesic balms and prescribed havoc. LPPP: Law of Pay the Price Punctually. At this point, that trail was faint, vague pangs of regret in the memory of a sailor without a ship. Precise, but also indifferent, memories closer to melancholy for the long-gone years—it had been eight or nine since the last woman who was important to Coy—than to a feeling of material loss, or absence. Deep down, those shadows were anchored in his memory only because they belonged to a time when everything was a beginning for him—new stripes on a brand-new Navy jacket, new bars on the epaulets of his shirts, and long periods of time admiring them in the same way he admired the body of a naked woman, times when life was a crackling new nautical chart with all navigational notices updated, its smooth white surface as yet untouched by pencil and eraser. Days when he himself, sighting the profile of land against the horizon, still felt a vague attraction to persons or things awaiting him there. All the rest—pain, betrayal, reproaches, interminable nights lying awake beside backs turned in silence—were in those days simply submerged rocks, murderous shoals awaiting the inevitable moment, without any chart to give warning of their presence. The fact is that he did not really miss those female shadows; he missed himself, or missed the man he had been then. Maybe that was why those women, or those shadows, the last known ports in his life, surfaced at times, hazy in the outlines of memory, for ghostly rendezvous in Barcelona, at dusk, when he was taking long walks by the sea. Or when he was climbing the wooden bridge of the old port as the setting sun spread its crimson across the heights of Montjuich, the tower of Jaime I, and the piers and gangplanks of the TransMediterranean, or was searching the old docks and mooring stones for scars left on stone and iron by thousands of hawsers and steel cables, by ships sunk or cut up for scrap decades before. At times he thought about those women when he walked out beyond the city center and the Maremagnum theaters among other solitary, isolated men and women absorbed in the dusk, dozing on benches or dreaming as they stared out to sea, as gulls glided above the sterns of fishing vessels cutting through the sun-red waters beneath the clock tower. Not far from the clock tower was an ancient schooner stripped of sails and rigging that he remembered being forever in that same place, its timbers cracked and weathered by the wind, sun, rain, and time. And that often led him to think that ships and men ought to disappear when their hour came, to sink to the bottom out in the open sea instead of being left high and dry to rot ashore.

Now Coy had been talking for five minutes, almost uninterruptedly. He was sitting beside a window on the first floor of the

Museo Naval. He let words flow the way one fills a void that grows uncomfortable if the silences are too prolonged. He spoke slowly, in a calm tone, and smiled faintly when he paused. Sometimes he shifted his gaze outdoors, to the tender green of the chestnut trees lining the Paseo del Prado down to the Neptune fountain, then turned back to the woman. Some business in Madrid, he said. An official errand, a friend. By chance, the museum was around the corner. He said anything that came to mind, just as he had that time in Barcelona, with the candid shyness so typical of him, and she listened, her head tilted and the tips of her blond hair brushing her chin. Those dark eyes with the glints that again seemed navy blue were fixed on Coy, on the faint, sincere smile that belied the casualness of his words.

"That tells it all," he concluded.

That told nothing, for as yet they were merely easing toward the harbor with great care, engines throttled back, waiting for the harbor pilot to come aboard. *That* told nothing, and Tánger Soto knew it as well as he.

"Well," she said.

She was leaning against the edge of the table in her office, arms crossed, looking at him thoughtfully with that same intensity, but this time she was smiling a little, as if she wanted to reward his effort, or his calm, or the manner in which he met her eyes, without boasting or evasion. As if she appreciated the way he had presented himself, justified his presence, and then, not attempting to deceive her or deceive himself, awaited her verdict.

Now it was she who talked. She talked without taking her eyes off him, as if to measure the effect of her words, or maybe of the tone in which she was saying them. She talked naturally and with a hint of either affection or gratitude. She talked about that strange night in Barcelona, about how pleased she was to see him again. And then, as if everything that was possible to say had already been said, they simply observed each other. Coy recognized that once again the time had come for him to leave, or else look for some reason, some pretext, some damn thing that would allow him to prolong the moment. Either that or she would walk him to the door and thank him for the visit. Slowly, he got to his feet.

"I hope that fellow won't be bothering you again."

"Who?"

She had taken a second longer than necessary to answer.

"The one with the ponytail, and the two different color eyes." He touched his face, indicating his own. "The Dalmatian."

"Oh, him."

She didn't immediately add anything, but the lines around her mouth hardened.

"Him," she repeated.

She could either be thinking about the man or gaining time to go off on some tangent. Coy stuck his hands in his jacket pockets and looked around. The office was small and brightly lit, with a discreet sign: SECTION IV. T. SOTO. RESEARCH AND ACQUISITIONS. There was an antique print of a seascape on the wall and a large corkboard on an easel covered with prints, plans, and nautical charts. There was also a large glass case filled with books and files, document folders on her worktable, and a computer whose screen was circled with little notes written in a round, good-little-schoolgirl hand that Coy easily identified—he had her card in his pocket—by the large circles dotting the "*i*"s.

"He hasn't bothered me again," she said finally, as if she'd needed time to remember.

"He didn't seem happy about losing the Urrutia."

Her eyes narrowed, her mouth still hard.

"He'll find another."

Coy looked at the line of her throat descending toward the bone-colored shirt. Open at the neck. The silver chain still gleamed there, and he wondered what hung on that chain. If it was metal, he thought, it would be devilishly warm.

"I still don't know," he said, "if the atlas was for the museum or for you. The fact is that that auction was . . ."

He stopped short as he caught sight of the Urrutia. It was with other large-format books in the glass case. He easily recognized its leather cover and gold tooling.

"It was for the museum," she replied, and after a second added, "Naturally."

She followed Coy's eyes to the atlas. The light from the window outlined the contours of her freckled profile.

"And that's what you do? Acquire things?"

She bent forward slightly, her hair swinging. She was wearing a gray wool jacket, unbuttoned, a full dark skirt and flat-heeled black shoes, with black stockings that made her seem taller and more slender than she was. A well-bred girl, he mused, appreciating her in the natural light. Strong hands and a well-bred voice. Wholesome, proper, calm. At least in outward appearance, he thought, scanning those telltale fingernails.

"Yes, in a way that is my job," she agreed. "Check auction catalogues, oversee purchases of antiques, visit other museums, and travel when something interesting shows up. Then I make a report, and my superiors decide. The board provides limited funds for research and new acquisitions, and I try to see that the money is invested in the most appropriate way."

Coy grimaced. He remembered the hard-nosed duel in the Claymore auction gallery.

"Well, your friend the Dalmatian got his shot off before he went down. The Urrutia cost you an arm and a leg."

She sighed, sounding both fatalistic and amused, then nodded, turning up her palms to indicate she had blown her last penny. As she gestured, Coy again noted the unexpectedly masculine stainless-steel watch on her right wrist. Nothing more, no rings, no bracelets. She wasn't even wearing the small gold earrings he'd seen three days before in Barcelona.

"It did cost us. We don't usually spend that much. . . . Especially since we already have a lot of eighteenth-century cartography in this museum."

"It's that important?"

Again she leaned forward from the edge of the table, and for a brief instant stayed like that, head down, before looking up with a different expression on her face. Once more the light played up the gold of her freckles, and it crossed Coy's mind that if he took just one step forward he might, perhaps, decipher the aroma of that enigmatic, speckled geography.

"It was printed in 1751 by the geographer and mariner Ignacio Urrutia Salcedo," she was explaining. "After five years of toil. It was the best aid for navigators until the appearance of Tofiño's much more precise *Atlas Hidrográfico* in 1789. There are very few copies in good condition, and the Museo Naval didn't have one."

She opened the glass door of the case, took out the heavy volume, and opened it on the table. Coy moved closer. They studied it together, and at last he confirmed what he had thought from the moment he met her. Not a trace of cologne or perfume. Only the scent of clean, warm skin.

"It's a fine copy," she said. "Among rare book dealers and antiquarians there are plenty of unscrupulous people, and when they find one of these they take it apart and sell the individual plates. But this one is intact."

She turned the large pages carefully, and the thick white paper, well preserved despite the two and a half centuries since it was printed, whispered between her fingers. *Atlas Marítimo de las Costas de España,* Coy read on the title page, beautifully engraved with a seascape, a lion between columns bearing the legend *Plus Ultra,* and various nautical instruments. *Divided into sixteen spherical charts and twelve plans, from Bayonne in France to Cape Creus.* The navigation charts and maps of ports were printed in large format and bound to facilitate their preservation and handling. The volume was open to the chart that embraced the sector between Gibraltar and Cape Saint Vincent. It was drawn in extensive detail, and included soundings measured in fathoms and a meticulous key to indications, references, and dangers. Coy followed the coastline between Ceuta and Cape Spartel with his finger, stopping at the place marked with the name of the woman beside him, Tangier. Then he followed it north, to Punta de Tarifa, and continued to the northwest, pausing again on the shoals of La Aceitera, which were much better defined, with little crosses marking danger spots, than the passage between Terson and Mowett Grave islands in the modern surveys of the British Admiralty. He knew the charts for the Strait of Gibraltar well, and everything was remarkably exact. He had to admire the rigor of the plotting; it was more than he would have expected from the hydrographics of the period, so long before the satellite image, or even the technical advances of the end of the eighteenth century. He observed that each chart had scales for latitude and longitude detailed in degrees and minutes—the former on the left and right sides of the engraving and the latter graduated four times in accord with the four different meridians: Paris and Tenerife in the upper portion, Cádiz and Cartagena in the lower. At that time, Coy recalled, the Greenwich meridian hadn't yet been adopted as the universal reference.

"It's very well preserved," he said.

"It's perfect. This atlas was never used for navigation."

Coy turned a few pages: *Nautical chart of the coast of Spain from Águilas and Monte Cope to the Herradora or Horadada tower, with all shoals, points, and coves. . . .* He also remembered that section, the coast of his childhood. It was steep and hostile, with narrow, rocky inlets and reefs between the low cliffs. He traced the distances on the heavy paper: Cabo Tiñoso, Escombreras, Cabo de Agua . . . It was almost as perfectly plotted as the chart of the Strait.

"Here's an error," he said suddenly.

She looked at him, more curious than surprised.

"You're sure?"

"Yes, I am."

"You know that coast?"

"I was born there. I've even dived there, brought up amphoras and artifacts from the bottom."

"You're a diver too?"

Coy made a dismissive sound, shaking his head.

"Not professionally," he said, apologetically. "A summer job, vacation time."

"But you have experience . . ."

"Well," he said, "maybe as a kid. But it's been a long time since I've been in the water."

She looked at him thoughtfully. Then she looked back to the place his finger was pointing to on the chart.

"And what's the error?"

He told her. Urrutia's survey situated Cabo de Palos two or three minutes farther south on the meridian than it actually was. Coy had rounded that point so many times that he clearly remembered its location on the charts. 37°38′ true latitude—he couldn't at this point be exact about the seconds—was converted on the chart to 37°36′, more or less. It had undoubtedly been corrected on subsequent, more detailed charts, using better instruments. At any rate, he added, a couple of nautical miles' difference was not major on a 1751 chart.

She said nothing, her eyes on the engraving. Coy shrugged. "I suppose those flaws make it appealing. Did you have a limit in Barcelona, or could you have gone on bidding?"

She was beside him, leaning with both hands on the table, seemingly absorbed, and was slow to answer.

"There was a limit, of course," she said finally. "The Museo Naval isn't the Bank of Spain. Fortunately, the price was within it."

Coy laughed a little, quietly, and she looked up.

"At the auction," he said, "I thought it was something personal. You were so dogged in your bidding."

"Of course it was personal." Now she seemed irritated. She turned back to the chart as if something there was demanding her attention. "It's my job." She shook her head, as if to clear it of some thought she hadn't expressed. "I'm the one who recommended the acquisition of the Urrutia."

"And what will you and museum do with it?"

"Once it's been completely reviewed and catalogued, I'll get reproductions for internal use. Then it will go to the museum's historical library, like everything else."

They were interrupted by a discreet rap at the door; standing there was the frigate captain Coy had passed in the exhibition hall. Tánger Soto excused herself and followed the captain into the hallway, where the two talked a few minutes in low voices. The new arrival was middle-aged and good-looking, and the gold buttons and stripes lent him distinction. Occasionally he would look at Coy with a curiosity not entirely free of suspicion. Coy did not appreciate the looks, or the broad smile with which the officer blessed the conversation. Like many members of the Merchant Marine, Coy was not fond of career Navy men. They seemed too arrogant, and they were forever inbreeding, marrying the daughters of other officers; they crammed into church on Sundays, and tended to spawn too many children. Besides, there were no battles now, no enemy ships to board, and they stayed home in bad weather.

"I have to leave you for a few minutes," she said. "Wait for me."

She went down the hall with the captain, who shot Coy a last glance before he left. Coy sat in her office, looking around; there was Urrutia's chart again, and then the other objects on the table, the print on the wall—"4th View of the battle of Tolón"—and the contents of the glass case. He was about to sit down when, next to the table, his eyes caught the large easel with the thumbtacked documents, plans, and photographs. He walked over, with nothing in mind but to kill some time, and discovered that protruding from beneath the prints pinned to the upper half of the panel were plans of sailing ships—all were brigantines, he saw after glancing at the rigging. Below them were aerial photographs of coastal waters, and reproductions of antique nautical charts, as well as one modern chart. It was number 463A from the Naval Hydrographic Institute—Cabo de Gata to Cabo de Palos, which corresponded in part to the one in the open atlas on the table. What a coincidence, Coy thought.

A MINUTE later she was back. My boss, she said. High-level consultations about vacation schedules. All very top secret.

"So you work for the Navy?"

"As you see."

He was amused. "That makes you some kind of servicewoman, then."

"Not at all." The golden hair swished from side to side as she shook her head. "I'm classified as a civil servant. I took an examination after I got my degree in history. I've been here four years."

She turned pensive and looked out the window. Then, as if she had something on her mind she couldn't dismiss, she went to the table very slowly, closed the atlas, and put it back in the case.

"My father, though, was in the service," she added.

There was a note of defiance, or perhaps of pride, in her words. That confirmed a number of things Coy had noticed: a certain way she had of moving, a gesture here and there, and the serene, slightly haughty self-discipline that seemed to take over at times.

"Career Navy?"

"Army. He retired as a colonel, after spending most of his life in Africa."

"Is he still alive?"

"No."

She spoke without a trace of emotion. It was impossible to know if it upset her to talk about it. Coy studied the navy-blue irises, and she bore his scrutiny with no expression.

"Which is why your name is Tánger. For Tangier."

"Which is why my name is Tánger."

THEY walked past the Museo del Prado and along the botanical garden in no hurry, then turned left and started up Claudio Moyano hill, leaving the noisy traffic and pollution of the Atocha traffic circle behind them. The sun shone on the gray booths and stalls stair-stepped up the street.

"Why did you come to Madrid?"

He stared at the ground. He had answered that question at the museum, before she had even asked. All the commonplaces and easy pretexts had been exhausted, so he took a few more steps before responding.

"I came to see you."

She did not seem surprised, or curious for that matter. She was wearing the light wool jacket, and before they left her office she had knotted a silk scarf of autumnal colors around her neck. Half turning, Coy observed her impassive face.

"Why?" was all she asked.

"I don't know."

They walked on a bit in silence. Finally they stopped before a stall piled with detective novels strewn about like flotsam washed up on a beach. Coy's eyes slid over the worn volumes without paying much attention: Agatha Christie, George Harmon Coxe, Ellery Queen, Leslie Charteris. Tánger picked up a copy of *She Was a Lady,* looked at it absently, and put it back.

"You're mad," she said.

They walked on. People were strolling among the stands, picking up books, leafing through them. The booksellers kept a sharp eye on them from behind their counters or standing in the doorways of the booths. Most were wearing dusters, sweatshirts, or pea coats, their skin tanned by years in the sun and wind, like sailors in some impossible port, stranded among reefs of paper and ink. Some were reading, unaware of passersby, sitting among mountains of used books. Two young sellers greeted Tánger, who answered them by name. Hello, Alberto. See you, Boris. A boy with a hussar's locks and a checked shirt was playing the flute, and she placed a coin in the cap at his feet, just as Coy had seen her do on the Ramblas, when she'd stopped before the mime whose white-face was streaked by the rain.

"I come by here every day on my way home. Isn't it strange what happens with old books? They choose you. They reach out to their buyer—Hello, here I am, take me with you. It's as if they were alive."

A few steps farther on she paused to look at *The Alexandria Quartet,* four volumes with tattered covers, marked down.

"Have you read Durrell?" she asked.

Coy shook his head. He'd never seen any of these books. North American, he supposed. Or English.

"Is there anything about the sea in them?" he asked, more to be courteous than out of interest.

"No, not that I know. Although Alexandria *is* still a port."

Coy had been there, and he didn't recall anything special. Heat, days of dead air, deck cranes, stevedores lying prostrate in the shade of the containers, filthy water lapping between the hull and the dock, and cockroaches you stepped on as you came ashore at night. A port like any other, except when wind from the south carried clouds of reddish dust that sifted into everything. Nothing to justify four volumes. Tánger touched the first with her finger, and he read the title: *Justine.*

"Every intelligent woman I know," she said, "has at some time wanted to be Justine."

Coy looked at the book with a perplexed expression, wondering if he ought to buy it, and if the bookseller would make him buy all four. The books that had caught his attention were others nearby: *The Death Ship,* by one B. Traven, and the Bounty trilogy, *Mutiny on the Bounty, Men against the Sea,* and *Pitcairn's Island,* all in a single volume. But she was moving on. He saw her smile again, take a few more steps, and distractedly leaf through another mistreated paperback. *The Good Soldier,* he read. Ford Madox Ford did sound familiar, because he had collaborated with Joseph Conrad on *The Inheritors.* Finally Tánger whirled around and looked at him, hard.

"You're mad," she repeated.

He touched his nose and said nothing.

"You don't know me," she added a moment later, a hint of harshness in her voice. "You know nothing at all about me."

Curiously, Coy didn't feel intimidated or out of place. He had come to see her, doing what he thought he had to do. He would have given anything to be an elegant man, easy with words and with something to offer, even if just enough money to buy the four volumes of the *Quartet* and take her to dinner that night in an expensive restaurant, calling her Justine or whatever she wanted him to call her. But that wasn't the case. So he kept quiet, and stood there with all the openness he could muster, at once sincere and neutral, almost shy. It wasn't much, but it was everything.

"You don't have any right to show up like this. To stand there with that good-little-boy face. . . . I already thanked you for what you did in Barcelona. What do you want me to do now? Take you home like one of these books?"

"Sirens," he said suddenly.

She looked at him with surprise.

"What about sirens?"

Coy lifted his hands and let them drop.

"I don't know. They sang, Homer said. They called to the sailors, isn't that right? And the sailors couldn't help themselves."

"Because they were idiots. They ran right onto the reefs, destroying their ships."

"I've been *there.*" Coy's expression had darkened. "I've been on the reefs, and I don't have a ship. It will be some time before I have one again, and now I don't have anything better to do."

She turned toward him brusquely, opening her mouth as if to say something disagreeable. Her eyes sparked aggressively. That lasted a moment, and in that space of time Coy mentally said so long to her freckled skin and to the whole crazy daydream that had led him to her. Maybe he should have bought that book about Justine, he thought sadly. But at least you gave it a shot, sailor. Too bad about the sextant. Then he gathered himself. I'll smile. I'll smile in any case, say what she will, until she tells me to go to hell. At least that will be the last thing she'll remember about me. I'd like to smile like her boss, that frigate captain with his shiny buttons. I hope my smile doesn't come off too edgy.

"For the love of God," she said. "You're not even handsome."

III

The Lost Ship

You can do everything right, strictly according to procedure, on the ocean, and it'll still kill you, but if you're a good navigator, at least you'll know where you were when you died.

—Justin Scott, THE SHIPKILLER

He detested coffee. He had drunk thousands of hot and cold cups in endless pre-dawn watches, during difficult or decisive maneuvers, in dead hours between loading and unloading in ports, in times of boredom, tension, or danger, but he disliked that bitter taste so much that he could bear it only when cut with milk and sugar. In truth, he used it as a stimulant, the way others take a drink or light a cigarette. He hadn't smoked for a long time. As for drinking, only rarely had he tasted alcohol on board a ship, and on land he never went past the Plimsoll mark, his cargo line of a couple of Sapphire gins. He drank deliberately and conscientiously only when the circumstances, the company, or the place called for massive doses. In those cases, like most of the sailors he knew, he was capable of ingesting extraordinary quantities of anything within reach, with consequences that entailed husbands guarding their wives' virtue, police maintaining public order, and nightclub bouncers making sure that clients toed the line and didn't leave before paying.

That was not the case tonight. The ports, the sea, and the rest of his previous life seemed far from the table near the door of an inn on the Plaza de Santa Ana, where he was sitting watching people strolling on the sidewalk or chatting on the bar terraces. He had asked for a gin and tonic to erase the taste of the syrupy cup of coffee before him—he always spilled it clumsily when he stirred—and was leaning back in his chair, hands jammed into his jacket pockets, legs stretched out beneath the table. He was tired, but he was putting off going to bed. I'll call you, she'd said. I'll call you tonight or tomorrow. Let me think a little. Tánger had an appointment she couldn't break that afternoon, and a dinner date in the evening, so he would have to wait to see her again. That was what she told him at noon, after he had walked with her to the intersection of Alfonso XII and Paseo Infanta Isabel; and she said good-bye right there, not letting him see her to her door. She offered the strong hand he remembered so well, in a vigorous handshake. Coy had asked how the devil she thought she could call him, since he had no home, no telephone, no nothing in Madrid, and his seabag was checked at the station. Then he saw Tánger laugh for the first time since he'd known her. It was a generous laugh that encircled her eyes with tiny wrinkles, making her, paradoxically, look much younger, more beautiful. Then she asked him to forgive her stupidity, and for a couple of seconds looked at him, his hand in hers, the last trace of laughter fading from her lips. She gave him the name of an inn on the Plaza de Santa Ana, across from the Teatro Español, where she had lived for two years when she was a student. A clean, cheap place. I'll call you, she said. I'll call you today or tomorrow. You have my word.

And there he was, staring at his coffee and wetting his lips with the gin and tonic—they didn't have Sapphire blue in the bar—the waitress had just set before him. Waiting for her to call. He hadn't moved all afternoon, and had eaten dinner there, a bit of overcooked beef and a bottle of mineral water. It was possible she might come in person, he thought, and that possibility made him keep an eye on the plaza, not to miss her approaching along calle de las Huertas, or any of the streets leading up from the Paseo del Prado.

Between the benches on the plaza, some beggars were talking loudly and passing around a bottle of wine. They had begged for money at the tables on the terraces and now were counting up the night's take. Three men, a woman, and a little dog. From the door of the Hotel Victoria, a guard costumed as RoboCop watched them like a hawk, hands crossed behind his back, legs spread apart, standing exactly where he had ejected the female beggar shortly before. Chased off by RoboCop, she had zigzagged among the tables to where Coy was sitting. Give me something, friend, she'd said in a listless voice, staring straight ahead. Give me something. She was still young, he thought as he watched her counting the take with her buddies and the mongrel. Despite the blemished skin, the dirty blond hair and vacant eyes, there were traces of a former beauty in her well-defined lips, the curve of her jaw, her figure, and the red, chapped hands with long dirty fingernails. Terra firma rots people, he thought once again. It overpowers and devours them. He searched his own hands, resting on his thighs, for the first symptoms of aging that accompany the inevitable leprosy of city pollution, the deceptively solid ground beneath your feet, contact with people, air with the salt sucked out of it. I hope I find another ship soon, he told himself. I hope I find something that floats so I can climb aboard and be carried far away while there's still time. Before I contract the virus that corrodes hearts, disrupts their compass, and drives them rudderless onto a lee shore.

"There's a call for you."

He leapt from the chair with an alacrity that left the waitress wide-eyed and bounded down the hallway leading to the lobby. One, two . . . he counted to five before answering, to slow his pulse. Three, four, five. Hello. She was there, her calm, well-bred voice apologizing for calling so late. No, he replied, it wasn't late at all.

He'd been waiting for her call. Just a bite out on the terrace, and he was about to have his gin. As good a time as any, he insisted. Then a brief silence at the other end of the line. Coy laid a broad, square hand on the counter, contemplating its rough network of tendons, nerves, and short, strong, widespread fingers and waited for her to say something. She's relaxed on a sofa, he thought. She's sitting in a chair. Lying on a bed. She's dressed, she's naked, in her pajamas, in a nightgown. She's barefoot, with an open book in her lap, or she's watching TV. She's lying on her back, or on her stomach, and the lamplight is picking up the gold of her freckled skin.

"I have an idea," she said finally. "I have an idea that might interest you, a proposition. And I thought maybe you could come to my place. Now."

ONCE, sailing as third officer, Coy had crossed paths with a woman on a boat. The encounter lasted a couple of minutes, the exact time it took the yacht—she was aft, sunbathing—to pass the *Otago,* where Coy was standing on the flying bridge, looking out to sea. Along the deck he could hear a monotonous clanging as sailors hammered the hull to remove rust before going over it with coats of red lead and paint. The merchant ship was anchored between Malamocco and Punta Sabbioni. On the other side of the Lido the sun was brilliant on the Lagoon of Venice, and on the campanile and cupolas of San Marco three miles away. The tiled roofs of the city were shimmering in the light. A soft west wind was blowing at eight or ten knots, rippling the flat sea and swinging the bows of anchored ships toward the beaches dotted with umbrellas and multicolored cabanas. That same breeze brought the yacht from the canal, tacking to starboard with all the white elegance of her unfurled sails, slipping by the ship at a half cable's length from Coy. He needed his binoculars to see her better, to admire her sleek, varnished wood hull, the thrust of her bow, her rigging, and her brass gleaming in the sun. A man was at the tiller, and behind him, near the taffrail, a woman sat reading a book. He turned the binoculars on her. Her blond hair was knotted at the back at her neck, and something about her evoked the white-gowned women one could easily picture in that place, or on the French Riviera, at the turn of the century. Beautiful, indolent women protected by the broad brim of a hat or a parasol. Sphinxes who gazed at the sea through half-closed eyes, or read, or just sat. Coy avidly focused the twin circles of the Zeiss lenses on that face, studying the tucked chin, the lowered eyes concentrating on the book. In other times, he thought, men killed or squandered their fortunes and reputations for such women. He was curious about the person who might deserve that woman, and he swung his glasses to focus on the man at the wheel. He was facing in the other direction, however, and all Coy could make out was a short figure, gray hair, and bronzed skin. The yacht passed on by and, fearful of losing the last instants, Coy again focused on the woman. One second later she lifted her head and looked into the binoculars, at Coy, through the lenses and across that distance, straight into his eyes. She sent him a look that was neither fleeting nor lingering, neither curious nor indifferent. So serene and sure of herself she seemed almost inhuman. Coy wondered how many generations of women were necessary to produce that gaze. He lowered the binoculars, dazed by having observed her at such close range. Then he realized the woman was too far away to be looking at him, and the beam he had felt bore into his gut was nothing but a casual, distracted glance toward the anchored ship the yacht was leaving behind as she sailed into the Adriatic. Coy stood there, leaning against the wing bridge, watching her go. And when he held up the binoculars again, all he could see was the upper stern and the name of the vessel painted in black letters on a ribbon of teak: *Riddle*.

Coy was in no way intellectual. He read a lot, but only about the sea. Even so, he had spent his childhood among grandmothers, aunts, and cousins on the shores of another ancient, enclosed sea, in one of those Mediterranean cities where for thousands of years mourning-clad women gathered at dusk to talk in low tones and watch their men in silence. That had left him with a certain atavistic fatalism, a rational idea or two, and strong intuition. And now, facing Tánger Soto, he thought about the woman on the yacht. After all, he said to himself, they might be one and the same, and men's lives always turn around a single woman, the one in whom all the women in the world are summed up, the vortex of all mysteries and the key to all answers. The one who employs silence like no other, perhaps because silence is a language she has spoken to perfection for centuries. The woman who possesses the knowing lucidity of luminous mornings, red sunsets, and cobalt-blue seas, one tempered with stoicism, infinite sadness, and a fatigue for which—Coy had this curious certainty—one lifetime is not enough. In addition, and above all else, you had to be female, a woman, to achieve that blend of boredom, wisdom, and weariness in your gaze. To demonstrate a shrewdness as keen as a steel blade, inimitable and born of the long genetic memory of countless ancestors stowed like booty in the holds of black, concave ships, thighs bloodied amid smoking ruins and corpses, weaving and ripping out tapestries through countless winters, giving birth to men for new Troys and awaiting the return of exhausted heroes, of gods with feet of clay whom they at times loved, often feared, and nearly always, sooner or later, scorned.

"Would you like more ice?" she asked.

He shook his head. There are women, he concluded with a shiver of fear, who have that gaze from the day they're born. Who look at you the way she was looking at him that moment in the small sitting room whose windows were open to the Paseo Infanta Isabel and the illuminated brick-and-glass building of Atocha station. I am going to tell you a story, she had said as soon as she opened the door and led him to the sitting room, escorted by a shorthaired golden Lab that lay down close by, its dark, sad eyes fixed on Coy. I am going to tell you a story about shipwrecks and lost ships. I'm sure you like that kind of story, and you are not going to open your mouth until I finish telling it. You will not ask me whether it's real or invented, and you will sit quietly and drink tonic without gin, because I am sorry to inform you I don't have gin in my house, not Sapphire blue or any color. Afterward I will ask you three questions, and you may answer yes or no. Then I will let you ask me a question, just one, which will be enough for tonight, before you go back to the inn and to bed. That will be all. Do we have a deal?

Coy had answered without hesitation, a little surprised but with reasonable sangfroid. We have a deal. Then he sat down where she indicated, on a beige upholstered sofa. They were in a sitting room with white walls, a desk, a small Moorish-style table with a lamp on it, a television with a VCR, a pair of chairs, a framed photograph, a table with a computer next to a bookcase filled with books and papers, and a cabinet for tapes and CDs with speakers from which the voice of Pavarotti—or maybe it wasn't Pavarotti—issued, sounding something like Caruso. Coy read the spines of a few of the books: *Los jesuitas y el motín de Esquilache, Historia del arte y ciencia de navegar, Los ministros de Carlos III, Aplicaciones de Cartografía Histórica, Mediterranean Spain Pilot, Espejos de una biblioteca, Navegantes y naufragios, Catálogo de Cartografía Histórica de España del Museo Naval, Derrotero de las costas de España en el Mediterráneo.* There were numerous references to cartography, shipwrecks, and navigation. There were also novels and literature in general: Dinesen, Lampedusa, Nabokov, Durrell—the *Quartet* fellow from Moyano hill—something titled *Green Fire* by Peter William Rainer, Joseph Conrad's *The Mirror of the Sea,* and a number of others. Coy had not read one of those books, with the exception of the Conrad. His eye lighted on a book in English that had the same title as a movie—*The Maltese Falcon.* It was an old dog-eared copy, and on its yellow cover were a black falcon and a woman's hand holding coins and jewels.

"It's a first edition," Tánger said when she saw him pause at that title. "Published in the United States on Valentine's Day, 1930, at the price of two dollars."

Coy touched the book. "By Dashiell Hammett," it said on the cover. "Author of *The Dain Curse.*"

"I saw the movie."

"Of course you saw it. Everyone's seen it." Tánger pointed to a shelf. "Sam Spade is the reason I became unfaithful to Captain Haddock."

On a shelf, a little apart from the other books, was what looked like a complete set of *The Adventures of Tintin.* Beside the cloth spines of those tall, slim volumes he saw a small, dented silver cup and a postcard. He recognized the port of Antwerp, with the cathedral in the distance. The cup was missing a handle.

"Did you read those when you were a boy?"

He was still looking at the silver cup. "Junior Swimming Championship, 19 . . ." It was difficult to read the date.

"No," he said. "I recognize them, and I think I may have looked through one. A meteor falls into the ocean."

"*The Shooting Star.*"

"That must have been it."

The apartment was not luxurious, but it was nicer than average, with expensive leather cushions, tasteful curtains at the two windows overlooking the street, and a good painting on the wall. It was an antique oil in an oval frame, a landscape with a river and a pretty good ship—even though, in his opinion, she was not carrying enough sail for that river and that wind. The kitchen, from which she'd brought the ice and tonic and a couple of glasses, seemed clean and bright; he could see a microwave, a refrigerator, and a table and stools of dark wood. She was dressed in a light cotton sweater in place of the morning's blouse, and she had slipped out of her shoes. Her black-stockinged feet moved noiselessly, like those of a ballerina, with the Lab tagging along. People don't learn to move like that, Coy thought. You move or you don't move, one way or the other. A woman sits, talks, walks, tilts her head, or lights a cigarette in a certain way. Some things you learn, some you don't. No one can surpass predetermined limits, try as she may, if she doesn't have it inside. Predetermined behavior, gestures, and manners.

"Do you know anything about shipwrecks?"

The question changed his line of thought, and he smothered a laugh in his glass.

"I've never actually been shipwrecked, if that's what you mean. But give me time."

She frowned, ignoring the sarcasm.

"I'm talking about ancient shipwrecks." She kept looking into his eyes. "About ships that went down a long time ago."

He touched his nose before answering. Not much. He'd read things, of course. And dived at some of the sites. He also knew the kinds of stories sailors often tell among themselves.

"Have you ever heard of the *Dei Gloria*?"

He searched his memory. It wasn't a name that was familiar to him.

"A ten-gun merchant ship," she added. "She went down off the southeast coast of Spain on February 4, 1767."

Coy set his glass on the low table, and the movement caused the dog to come lick his hand.

"Here, Zas," said Tánger. "Don't be a pest."

The dog didn't move a hair. He stood right by Coy, licking him and barking, and she thought it necessary to apologize. Actually the dog wasn't hers, she said. He belonged to her roommate, but because of a job her friend had moved to another city two months before. Tánger had inherited her half of the apartment, and Zas.

"It's fine," Coy intervened. "I like dogs."

It was true. Especially hunting dogs, which tended to be loyal and quiet. As a child he had owned a cinnamon-colored setter that had the same loyal eyes as this dog, and there had also been a mongrel that had come aboard the *Daggoo IV* in Malaga, staying on until he was swept overboard near Cape Bojador. Coy absentmindedly rubbed Zas behind the ears, and the dog leaned into his hand, happily wagging his tail.

Then Tánger told him the story of the lost ship.

THE *Dei Gloria* was a brigantine. She had sailed out of Havana on January 1, 1767, with twenty-nine crew and two passengers. The cargo manifest listed cotton, tobacco, and sugar, and the destination was the port of Valencia. Although officially she belonged to a man named Luis Fornet Palau, the *Dei Gloria* was the property of the Society of Jesus. As was later confirmed, this Fornet Palau was a figurehead for the Jesuits, who maintained a small merchant fleet to assure the traffic of passengers and commerce that the Society, extremely powerful at that time, conducted with its missions, settlements, and interests in the colonies. The *Dei Gloria* was the best ship in that fleet, the swiftest and best-armed against threats by English and Algerian pirates. She was under the command of a reliable captain by the name of Juan Bautista Elezcano from Biscay, who was experienced, and closely connected with the Jesuits. In fact, his brother, Padre Salvador Elezcano, was one of the principal assistants to the general of the Order in Rome.

After the first few days, tacking into an unfavorable east wind, the brigantine found winds from the south- and northwest, which sped her across the Atlantic through heavy cloudbursts and squalls. The wind freshened southwest of the Azores, gradually increasing until it turned into a storm that caused damage to the rigging and made it necessary to man the pumps continually. That was the state of the *Dei Gloria* when she reached the 35th parallel and continued east without incident. Then she tacked in the direction of the Gulf of Cádiz, with the aim of sheltering from the easterlies of the Strait, and without touching port she found herself beyond Gibraltar on the second of February. The next day she rounded Cabo de Gata, sailing north within sight of the coast.

From this point on, things grew a little more complicated. On the afternoon of February 3, a sail was sighted off the brigantine's stern. The ship was approaching rapidly, taking advantage of the southwesterly wind. Soon identified as a xebec, it was quickly gaining on them. Captain Elezcano maintained the *Dei Gloria*'s pace, sailing under jib and courses, but when the xebec was within a little over a mile, he observed something suspicious in her actions, and he put on more sail. In response, the other ship lowered her Spanish colors and, revealing herself as a corsair, openly gave chase. As was common in those waters, it was a ship licensed in Algeria; from time to time she changed her colors and used Gibraltar as a base. It was later established that her name was the *Chergui,* and that she was commanded by a former officer of the Royal Navy, a man named Slyne, also known as Captain Mizen, or Misián.

In those waters, the pirate ship had a triple advantage. One, she made better time than the brigantine, which, because of the damage suffered to her masts and rigging, had limited speed. Two, the *Chergui* was sailing with the wind in her favor, keeping to windward of her prey and between her and the coast. Three, and most decisive, this was a vessel fitted for war. She was superior in size to the *Dei Gloria,* and had at least twelve guns and a large crew trained to fight compared to the brigantine's ten guns and crew of merchant seamen. Even so, the unequal chase lasted the rest of the day and that night. By all indications, the captain of the *Dei Gloria* was unable to gain the protection of Águilas because the *Chergui* had cut off that course, so he tried to reach Mazarrón or Cartagena, running for the protection of the guns of the forts there, or hoping to meet a Spanish warship that would come to his aid. What happened, however, was that by dawn the brigantine had lost a topmast, had the corsair upon her, and had no choice but to strike her flag or fight.

Captain Elezcano was a tough seaman. Instead of surrendering, the *Dei Gloria* opened fire as soon as the corsair sailed within range. The gun duel took place a few miles southwest of Cabo Tiñoso; it was brief and violent, nearly yardarm to yardarm, and the crew of the brigantine, though not trained in war, fought with resolve. One lucky shot started a fire aboard the *Chergui,* but the *Dei Gloria* had now lost her foremast, and the corsair was prepared to board. The *Chergui*'s guns had inflicted serious damage to the brigantine, which with her many dead and wounded was taking on water fast. At that moment, by one of those chance occurrences that happen at sea, the *Chergui,* almost alongside her prey and with her men ready to leap onto the enemy deck, blew wide open, from bow to stern. The explosion killed all her crew and toppled the brigantine's remaining mast, speeding her downward plunge. And with the debris of the corsair still steaming on the waves, the *Dei Gloria* sank to the bottom like a stone.

"LIKE a stone," Tánger repeated.

She had told the story precisely, without shadings or adornment. Her tone, thought Coy, was as neutral as a television commentator's. It did not escape him that she had followed the thread of the narrative unhesitatingly, relating the details without a single doubt, not even when it came to dates. The description of the pursuit of the *Dei Gloria* was technically correct, so it was clear, whatever the reason, this was a lesson well learned.

"There were no survivors from the corsair," she continued. "As for the *Dei Gloria,* the water was cold and the coast distant. Only a fifteen-year-old ship's boy managed to swim to a skiff that had been lowered before the battle. Without oars, he drifted, propelled southeast by wind and currents, and was rescued a day later, five or six miles south of Cartagena."

Tánger paused to look for her Players. Coy watched her carefully open the wrapping and put a cigarette in her mouth. She offered him one, and he refused with a gesture.

"Taken to Cartagena"—she bent over to light her cigarette from a box of matches, again protecting the flame in the hollow of her hands—"the survivor recounted the events to the harbor authorities. But he didn't have much to tell, he was badly shaken from the battle and the shipwreck. They were to interrogate him again the next day, but the boy had disappeared. At any rate, he had given important clues to clarifying what had happened. In addition, he pinpointed the place the ship had gone down, for the captain of the *Dei Gloria* had ordered a position reading at dawn, and this very boy had been charged with noting it in the log. He actually had the page in the pocket of his long coat, the paper where he had written the latitude and longitude. He also told them that the charts on which the ship's pilot had worked out his calculations from the time they came within sight of the Spanish coast were Urrutia's."

She paused as she exhaled, one hand cupping the elbow of the other arm, hand uplifted, cigarette between her fingers. It was as if she wanted to give Coy time to measure the import of that last bit of information, told in a tone as dispassionate as all the rest. He touched his nose without comment. So that was what was behind the story, he thought, a sunken ship and a map. He shook his head and nearly laughed, not from disbelief—such stories could contain as much truth as chimera, with one not excluding the other—but from pure and simple pleasure. The sensation was almost physical. A mystery at sea. A beautiful woman telling him all this as if it were nothing, and he sitting there listening. Whether or not the story of the *Dei Gloria* was what she believed was the least of it. For Coy it was a different matter, a feeling that made him warm inside, as if suddenly this strange woman had lifted a corner of a veil, an opening through which a little of that wondrous matter dreams are woven from escaped. Maybe that had a lot to do with her and her intentions—he wasn't sure—but it certainly had a great deal to do with him, with what makes certain men put one foot before the other and travel roads that lead to the sea, and wander through ports as they dream of finding sanctuary beyond the horizon. Coy smiled but said none of that. She had half-closed her eyes, as if the cigarette smoke was irritating, but he knew that what was disturbing her was precisely his smile. So he wasn't an intellectual or a charmer, and he wasn't good at expressing himself. Also, he was conscious of his burly physique, his rough hands and manners. But he would have stood up at that moment, touched her face, kissed her eyes, her lips, her hands, had he not assumed that his action would have been greatly misinterpreted. He would have sunk with her to the rug, put his lips to her ear, and whispered his thanks for having made him smile the way he used to when he was a boy. For being a beautiful woman, and for being so fascinating. For reminding him that there was always a sunken ship, an island, a refuge, an adventure, a place somewhere on the other side of the ocean, on that hazy boundary where dreams blend into the horizon.

"This morning," she said, "you told me you knew that coast well. Is that true?"

She looked at him questioningly, one hand still cupping an elbow, the cigarette held high between her fingers. I would like to know, he thought, how she gets that hair cut to be so asymmetrical and so perfect at the same time. I would like to know how the hell she does that.

"Is that the first of the three questions?"

"Yes."

He lifted his shoulders slightly. "Of course it's true. When I was a boy I swam in those coves, and later I sailed that shore hundreds of times, both very close and farther out to sea."

"Would you be able to determine a location using old charts?"

Practical. That was the word. This was a practical woman, with her feet on the ground. One might say, he considered with amusement, that she was about to offer him a job.

"If you mean the Urrutia, every miscalculation of a minute in latitude or longitude can translate to an error of a mile." He raised his hand and moved it before him, as if referring to an imaginary chart. "At sea everything is always relative, but I can try."

He sat mulling over what she had said. Things were beginning to fall in place, at least some of them. Zas again gave him a big lick when he reached for the glass on the small table.

"After all"—he took a sip—"that's my profession."

She had crossed her legs, and was swinging one of her black-stockinged feet. Her head was to one side, and she was looking at him. By now Coy knew that this posture indicated reflection, or calculation.

"Would you work for us?" she asked, watching him intently through the smoke of her cigarette. "I mean, we'd pay you, of course."

He opened his mouth and counted four seconds.

"You mean the museum and you?"

"That's right."

He set down the glass, contemplated Zas's loyal eyes, then glanced around the room. Outside, on the far side of the Repsol gas station and Atocha terminal, he could see, lighted at intervals, the complex of tracks.

"You seem unsure," she murmured, before smiling with disdain. "What a shame."

She bent down to flick ash into an ashtray, and the motion tightened her sweater, molding her body. God in heaven, thought Coy. It almost hurts to look at her. I wonder if she has freckles on her tits, too.

"It isn't that," he said. "It's just that I'm amazed." His lip curled. "I didn't think that captain, your boss . . ."

"This is my game," she interrupted. "I can choose the players."

"I can't imagine that the Navy is short on players. Competent people who don't ground their ships."

He watched her reaction closely, and said to himself: This is as far as you go, mate. Get up and button your jacket, because the lady is going to give you the bum's rush. And you deserve it, for being a clown and a big mouth. For being short on brains, an imbecile.

"Listen, Coy." It was the first time she had spoken his name, and he liked hearing it from her mouth. "I have a problem. I've done the research, it's my theory, I have the data. But I don't have what it takes to carry it out. The sea is something I know through books, movies, going to the beach.... Through my work. And there are pages, ideas, that can be as intense as having lived through a storm on the high seas, or having been with Nelson at the Nile or Trafalgar.... But for this I need someone with me. Someone who can give me practical support. A link to reality."

"I understand what you're saying. Wouldn't it be easier, though, for you to ask the Navy for what you need?"

"But I am asking you. You're a civilian and you have no ties." She studied him through the smoke spirals. "You offer many advantages. If I hire you, I control you. I'm in command. You understand?"

"I understand."

"With military people that would be impossible."

Coy nodded. That much was obvious. She had no stripes on her cuff, only a period every twenty-eight days. Because naturally she was one of those. Not one day more or less. You only had to see her—a blonde in permanent high gear. For her, two and two always made four.

"Even so," he said, "I imagine you will have to give them an accounting."

"Of course. But in the meantime I have autonomy, three months' time, and a little money for expenses. It isn't much, but it's enough."

Again Coy focused on the view outside. Below, in the distance, a train was approaching the station like a long serpent of tiny lighted windows. He was thinking about the frigate captain, about how Tánger had looked at him as she was now looking at Coy, convincing him, with that array of silences and expressions she used so well, to intercede with the admiral in charge. An interesting project, sir. Competent girl. Daughter, you know, of Colonel So-and-So. Pretty thing, I might mention in passing. One of our own. Coy wondered how many people with a degree in history, museum employees by dint of examination, were given carte blanche to search for a lost ship, just like that.

"Why not," he said finally.

He had leaned back in the chair and was again rubbing Zas behind the ears, entertained by the situation. All things considered, three months with this woman would be a magnificent return on the Weems & Plath sextant.

"After all," he added, as if reflecting, "I don't have anything better to do."

Tánger seemed neither satisfied nor disenchanted. She just dipped her head a little lower, as he had seen her do before, and the tips of her hair once again brushed her face. The eyes on Coy were taking in every detail.

"Thanks."

Finally she'd said it, just as he was beginning to wonder why she wasn't saying it.

"You're welcome." Coy touched his nose. "And now it's my turn. You promised me a question and an answer. . . . What is it exactly you're looking for?"

"You already know that. We're searching for the *Dei Gloria.*"

"That much is obvious. My question is why. I'm asking what *you're* looking for."

"Museo Naval aside?"

"Museo Naval aside."

The light from the lamp fell obliquely on her freckled face, intensifying the effect of the fading whorls of cigarette smoke. The play of light and shadow turned her hair to shades of matte gold.

"I've been obsessed with this ship for some time. And now I think I know where she is."

So that was it. Coy felt like smacking himself on the forehead for being so stupid. He looked at the framed photograph: Tánger as a teenager, light hair, freckles and a T-shirt loose over bare, brown thighs. She was leaning against the chest of a tan middle-aged man in a white shirt, with short hair. About fifty, he estimated. And she, maybe fourteen. Behind them was the ocean and a beach, and he also noted an obvious resemblance between the girl and the man. The shape of the forehead, the willful chin. Tánger was smiling into the camera, and the expression in her eyes was much more luminous and open than any he had seen. She looked expectant, on the verge of discovering something, a present or a surprise. Coy remembered. LDS: Law of the Diminishing Smile. Maybe you smile at life like that when you're fourteen, and then with time your lips grow chill.

"Go easy. There aren't any more sunken treasures."

"You're wrong." She scowled at him. "Sometimes there are."

To convince him, she talked a while about treasure hunters. There were people like that, obsessed with old maps and secrets, and they searched for things hidden at the bottom of the sea. You could see them in Seville, in the Archivo de Indias, the New World archives, bent over old files, or casually dropping by museums and wandering through ports, attempting to wheedle information without giving away clues or raising suspicions. She had seen several come by number 5 Paseo del Prado on the trail of a piece of evidence, asking if they could look something up in the archives or consult old sea charts, sowing a patch of false information to camouflage their true objectives. One of them, an Italian and a very pleasant man, had gone so far as to woo one of her fellow employees in order to gain access to classified documents. These were unique, interesting people, adventurers in their way, dreamy or ambitious. Most of them looked like bookish library mice, fat, bespectacled, not even remotely like the muscular, tanned types with tattoos you saw in movies and television documentaries. Nine out of ten followed impossible dreams, and only one out of a thousand ever fulfilled his ambition.

Coy kept petting Zas, contemplating the dog's faithful eyes. He felt Zas's appreciative breath on his wrist. Moist.

"That ship wasn't carrying treasure, unless you didn't tell me the whole story. Cotton, tobacco, sugar, you said."

"That's correct."

"And you also said one in a thousand, didn't you?"

She nodded through the smoke, took another puff of her cigarette and nodded again. She was looking at Coy as if she didn't see him.

"The *Dei Gloria* was also carrying a mystery on board," she said. "Those two passengers, the interception by the corsair. You understand? There's something more. I read the survivor's statement, it's in the naval archives. There are pieces that don't fit together. And then his sudden disappearance. Pouf! Vanished into thin air."

She had put out her cigarette, crushing it until the last little ember was extinguished. She is one tenacious girl, Coy said to himself. No one who wasn't would have got this far, nor would she have those poker-player eyes, or crush the life out of cigarettes as if she were murdering them. This babe knows exactly what she wants. And I, for good or for ill, am standing right in her path.

"There are treasures," she said, "that don't have a price."

Coy took another quick glance toward the train tracks illuminated in the distance, and a look at the service station across the street, halfway between the door to this building and the terminal. A man was standing in front of the station, and he seemed to be looking up, although from the fifth floor that was difficult to determine. Something in his attitude or his appearance, however, seemed familiar.

"Are you expecting anyone?" Coy asked.

She turned to him, surprised. She said nothing, but slowly walked toward him, focused on him, not the window. When she got there, she looked down. As she leaned forward her hair fanned across her chin, hiding her face. She raised a hand to brush it back, and Coy studied that profile hardened by the broken nose, lit by the glow from the street. She seemed preoccupied.

"That man's been there a while," he said.

Tánger was holding her breath, then finally released it like a groan or a sob of irritation. Her expression had turned somber.

"You know him?" Coy asked.

Administrative silence. Sphinx, Venetian domino, Aztec mask. Mute as the ghosts of the *Chergui* and the *Dei Gloria*.

"Who was that man with the ponytail? Why were you arguing with him that night in Barcelona?"

Zas's eyes were shifting from one to the other, tail wagging with glee. Tánger stood there quietly a few seconds more, as if she hadn't heard the question, and placed her hand on the windowpane, leaving the mark of her fingerprints. She was very close, and Coy again breathed in the scent of warm, clean flesh. A gentle erection began to press against the left pocket of his jeans. He imagined her naked, leaning against that same window, the illumination from outside lighting her skin. He imagined tearing off her clothes and turning her toward him. He imagined picking her up in his arms and carrying her to the sofa, or to the bed in the next room, with Zas affectionately wagging his tail from the doorway. He imagined that he went mad and followed her through wind and storm to the lighthouse at the end of the world. He imagined that she wanted more from him than just to use his skills. He imagined all that and much more in a sequence of quick scenes, moving through them rapidly, ardently, desperately, until suddenly he realized that she was scrutinizing him, and that the expression in her eyes was exactly that of the woman on the yacht near Venice, the time he had spied her through the binoculars and believed that despite the distance he was penetrating her thoughts.

"I promised you one answer," she said finally. "There've been enough for tonight. The rest will have to wait."

He wanted to go to bed with that woman, he thought, as he ran down the stairs two at a time. He wanted to go to bed with her not once, but an infinite number of times. He wanted to count every golden freckle with his fingers and his tongue, and then lay her back, gently part her thighs, enter her, and kiss her mouth as he moved in her. Kiss her slowly, taking his time, tirelessly, until, as the sea molds a rock, he softened those hard lines that made her seem so distant. He wanted to put sparks of light and surprise in her navy-blue eyes, to change the rhythm of her breathing, and cause her flesh to throb and shiver. And then in the darkness, like a patient sniper, he would watch for that moment, that brief, fleeting moment of self-centered intensity, when a woman is absorbed in herself and her face contains the faces of all women ever born and yet to be born.

That was Coy's state of mind as he stepped out into the street well past midnight, his erection retreating woefully to its cold bachelor's nest. That was why he found nothing strange in the fact that instead of following the sidewalk downhill to his right, he should look both ways at the Paseo Infanta Isabel, cross at a red stoplight, and walk straight in the direction of the man standing by a light in front of the service station. At heart, and in body, Coy did not like to fight. On the wildest of his shore leaves, during the happy time when he had ships from which to go ashore, he had played the part of involuntary actor, chorus, and comrade. He was one of those guys who goes along with friends and then, when the atmosphere heats up and things come to a boil, he is suddenly punching and taking punches without being responsible for any of it. That happened especially in the days of the Torpedero—the Tucumán Torpedoman—and Crew Sanders, when Coy would often return to the ship with an eye black as a widow's weeds, the collar of his jacket turned up in the cold of dawn, walking along wet docks reflecting yellow light from the sheds and the cranes and the dark silhouettes of moored ships. Three, four, ten staggering men, sometimes with the arms of a drunken buddy over their shoulders, feet dragging, and always some laggard on the edge of alcohol coma who followed farther behind, weaving dangerous "s"s past the mooring stones at the edge of the water. Jan Sanders was the man who drew the humorous illustrations for the Sigma naval calendars peopled with a crew of plastered, whoring, trouble-making sailors who despised their captain, a petty little tyrant with a huge mustache, and who shared catastrophes, scraps, and shipwrecks across all the seas and through all the whorehouses of the world. Independent of the calendars, Crew Sanders had been composed of Coy, Gallego Neira, and chief engineer Gorostiola, alias the Tucumán Torpedoman, when the three sailed on Zoe ships between Central America and northern Europe, and were just as likely to be broiling in anchorages and ports with tropical Caribbean rhythms as shivering with cold when an icy wind swept the deck and the bridge and the mercury dropped off the thermometers in New York, Hamburg, or Rotterdam. These three were the basic Crew, the standard models, although others were added depending on the port. Neira was six feet five and weighed two hundred and ten pounds, and the Torpedoman was a shade shorter and a few pounds heavier. That was useful, even reassuring, in places like Panama, where they were advised to go no farther than the duty-free shop at the end of the wharf, because any farther and there were always pistols and knives waiting for you. Between those two wild men, Coy looked like a dwarf. They had arms like twenty-inch hawsers, hands like propeller blades, and a marked inclination to break things—bottles, bars, faces—after the fifth whiskey. Where those two walked—with Coy in tow—the grass never grew again. In a bar in Copenhagen, for example, filled with blond men and blonde women who in the end turned out to be more blond men, the Torpedoman got riled because when he copped a feel he found a handful of something he hadn't expected. After a brief skirmish he and Neira grabbed Coy, one by each arm, and took off with his feet dangling between them, back to the port and the ship with a half-dozen police—also, inevitably, blond—hot on their heels. "I swear to God I thought he was a bimbo," the Torpedoman kept repeating. Neira was making fun of the Torpedoman's questionable eye for women, and even Coy was in stitches—something his newly split lip could have used—while the Torpedoman was shooting glances at them out of the corner of his eye, highly offended. "Now don't you tell anyone, you hear? Don't even think of it. Assholes."

The man at the service station was just standing there, watching Coy bearing down on him. Coy zeroed in, hands in his jacket pockets, feeling an intense inner energy, a vital exuberance that made him want to shout at the top of his lungs, or pick a fight—with or without Crew Sanders. He was a puppy dog in love. He was aware of it, and yet instead of feeling miserable, he felt stimulated. From his point of view, the sailors with Ulysses who had sealed their ears with wax in order not to hear the sirens' song would never know what they'd missed. Everyone knows the old saw: Any sailor who has nothing to do, looks for a ship, but a woman too. And that justification was as good as any. This adventure, or whatever the devil it turned out to be, included in the same package a ship—albeit a sunken one—and a woman. As for the consequences—the blows and fighting that the ship, the woman, and his own state of mind might generate—he didn't give a rat's ass.

Once at the service station, Coy walked straight toward the stranger standing guard by the light and the closer he got the stronger was the feeling of familiarity he'd had looking down from the window. When he was almost upon him, and his target was watching him with obvious suspicion, Coy began to coil his line, recognizing the short individual from the auction, the same one he thought he'd seen beneath the arcades on the Plaza Real, and who now, no question about it, was right there before him in his green country-estate car coat, looking as if he were dressed for a parody of a morning hunt in Sussex. The parody bit accentuated his short stature, as well as the bulging eyes and melancholy expression Coy remembered so clearly. The English apparel was laughably at odds with his Mediterranean appearance—black eyes and mustache, brilliantined hair gleaming at the temples, and sallow, southern European skin.

"What the fuck are you doing here?"

Coy approached his quarry at an angle just in case, hands held a little away from his body, muscles tensed, because more than once he had seen pint-sized guys leap forward and sink their teeth into fellows the size of a refrigerator, or palm a knife and bury it in a man's thigh before you could say Hail Mary. At any rate, the man was not about to show Coy his profile, maybe because in that getup he was a strange hybrid of formal and grotesque, a kind of cross between Danny DeVito and Peter Lorre decked out for a rainy-day turn about the English countryside.

"Sorry?"

The man smiled, sadly. Coy thought he heard a vague South American accent. Argentine, maybe. Or Uruguayan.

"One meeting might be chance," Coy said. "Two, a coincidence. Three, my balls tell me . . ."

The little man seemed to consider his comment. Coy noted the meticulously knotted bow tie, the impeccably shined dark-brown shoes.

"I don't know what you're talking about," he said finally.

His smile grew a little wider. A courteous, slightly pained smile.

He had the face of a decent fellow, a pleasant man whose mustache made him look old. His bulging eyes were focused on Coy.

"I'm talking," Coy replied, "about being fed up with seeing you everywhere I go."

"And I repeat, I don't know what you are referring to." The composed expression did not alter. "In any case, if I have offended you, believe me, I regret that."

"You'll regret it even more if you don't tell me what you're doing here."

The little man raised his eyebrows, as if surprised. He seemed sincerely wounded by the threat. This cannot be, his face said. It isn't seemly for a nice young man like you to be saying such things.

"Let us negotiate instead," he said.

"What the hell does that mean?"

"I mean, my good sir, let us be civilized."

His accent again suggested Argentina. He's putting me on, thought Coy. This sonofabitch is laughing in my face. He debated for an instant whether to punch him in the nose, right where he stood, or push him into a corner and search his pockets to see who he was. Coy was about to make his move when he saw the service-station attendant stepping out of his booth, watching them. Am I headed for trouble, Coy asked himself. Do I raise a ruckus and then face trying to undo the damage? He looked up to the windows on the top floor. All the lights were out. She wanted nothing to do with it. Or was she there, with the lights turned out to keep from being seen? Coy was unsure. This was a fine kettle of fish. Then he saw that the melancholy dwarf had sidled a little toward the curb and was hailing a taxi. Smooth as a chess pawn sliding from one square to another.

Coy stood a while in front of the service station, contemplating the dark windows of the fifth floor. Someone is pulling my strings, he thought. Has me on a stage complete with audience and stage crew. And I'm letting myself be shanghaied like a drunk Ukrainian. He supposed that Tánger was still upstairs, watching from the dark, but he couldn't perceive the least movement. Even so, he stayed a while, looking up, sure that she had seen everything, fighting the impulse to go back upstairs and ask for an explanation. Two smacks with the back of his hand, and she, fallen back against the sofa. I can explain everything, and besides, I love you. Then tears, and a good fuck. Forgive me for taking you for a fool, et cetera, et cetera. Blah, blah, blah.

He came back to reality with a sigh that was close to a moan. There must be rules for all this. Rules I don't know and she does. Or maybe rules she makes up as she goes. And maybe the rules of the moment for going ahead or cutting out are as follows: Goodbye, great evening, and turn out the light as you go, but don't say we didn't warn you, sailor. Or maybe someone was even being truthful with him.

He was so puzzled that he headed toward the nearby traffic circle and then slowly walked up calle Atocha. In the first bar that was open—they didn't have Sapphire gin there either—he stood quietly at the counter, looking at his drink without touching it. The place was an old saloon with a zinc counter, Formica chairs, a television, and photos of the famous matador Rayo Vallecano on the wall. There was no one there but the waiter, a skinny man with a tattoo on the back of one hand. His grease-spotted shirt and contemptuous expression did not invite confidence as he swept the sawdust from a floor scattered with crumpled napkins and shrimp shells. Coy was sitting facing a mirror with the printed logo of San Miguel beer, and his face was reflected over the list of snacks and food written in white script. His eyes were precisely at the level of "pork roast with tomato sauce" and "squid à la vinaigrette," which was not a thing to raise anyone's spirits. He studied his image with uncertainty, asking it what steps he should take in the next hours.

"I want to go to bed with her," he told the waiter.

"We all want that," was his philosophical reply, as he continued to sweep.

Coy nodded, then lifted the glass to his lips. He drank a little, looked at himself in the mirror, and made a face.

"The problem," he said, "is that she doesn't play fair."

"They never do."

"But she's beautiful. The bitch."

"They all are."

The waiter had deposited the broom in a corner, and once back behind the bar, served himself a beer. Coy watched him slowly drink half the glass without taking a breath; then he examined every photo of El Rayo, ending with a poster of a bullfight in Las Ventas seven years before. He unbuttoned his jacket and dug into his pants pockets. He pulled out three coins, laid them on the counter, and began trying to slip one between the other two without moving or touching either.

"I'm headed for trouble."

This time the waiter did not immediately reply. He stared at the foam on the rim of his glass.

"Well, she may be worth it," he said after a moment.

"I don't know yet." Coy shrugged. "There's a sunken ship, just like a movie. . . . And I think there are even some bad guys."

For the first time, the waiter looked at Coy. He seemed vaguely interested.

"Dangerous?"

"I don't even know."

A long silence. Coy kept playing with the coins, and took a couple of sips while the waiter, leaning on the end of the bar, finished his beer, took a package of cigarettes from beneath the counter, and lit one. His tattooed hand included four blue dots between the knuckles of his thumb and index finger—a typical jailbird. He was young, so he couldn't have been there long. Two or three years, Coy calculated. Maybe four or five.

"I think," said Coy, "that I'm going to go ahead with it."

The waiter nodded slowly, but said nothing. Coy left two coins on the counter, pocketed the other, and left.

IV
Latitude and Longitude

". . . but then I wonder what Latitude or Longitude I've got to?" (Alice had not the slightest idea what Latitude was, or Longitude either, but she thought they were nice grand words to say.)

—Lewis Carroll, ALICE'S ADVENTURES IN WONDERLAND

Zas was stretched out on the floor, tail wagging, his head on Coy's shoe. A ray of sunlight was falling obliquely through the window, making the Labrador's gold hair gleam, as well as the compass, the parallel rulers, and the protractor on the table, purchased that morning at the Robinson bookstore. The rulers and protractor were Blundell Harling, and the compass a W & HC of brass and stainless steel, a model Coy had expressly asked for. There were also two soft-lead pencils, a gum eraser, a graph-paper notebook, the latest edition of the book of lighthouses, and the number 2 chart put out by the Naval Hydrographic Institute, corresponding to the Spanish Mediterranean coastline. Tánger Soto had paid for everything with her credit card, and now it was all on the table in the sitting room of the apartment on Paseo Infanta Isabel. Urrutia's *Atlas* was also there, opened to chart number 12, and Coy was running his fingertips across the slightly textured surface of the thick, white paper, perfectly preserved after two hundred and fifty years of wars, catastrophes, fires, and shipwrecks. *From Monte Cope to the Herradora or Horadada tower.* The survey embraced sixty miles of coast: on the horizontal, east to Cabo de Palos, and from there, on the vertical, north, like two sides of a rectangle, including the saltwater lake of the Mar Menor, separated from the Mediterranean by the narrow sand spit of La Manga. Except for the error he had noted the first time he saw the chart—Palos was a couple of minutes to the south of its true latitude—the plotting of the coast was meticulous for its epoch. The wide, sandy bay of Mazarrón west of Cabo Tiñoso, the rocky coast and cove of Portús to the east, the port of Cartagena with the menacing little cross that marked the shoal of the island of Escombreras in the inlet, then more rocks to Palos point and the sinister Hormigas islands and their only shelter, the bay of Portman, which the chart showed still free of the mud from the mines that clogged it years later. The engraving was of an extraordinary quality, with light dots and fine lines to mark the various geographical features. And like the rest of the illustrations in the atlas, it had a beautiful inset in the upper left corner: "Presented to our Sovereign King by his Excellency Sr. D. Zenón de Somodevilla, Marqués de la Ensenada, and executed by naval captain Don Ignacio Urrutia Salcedo." Besides the date—"the year 1751"—the inset also had the notation, "The numbers for the Soundings are Fathoms of two Spanish *varas.*" Coy's finger paused at that line, and he looked questioningly at Tánger.

"A Spanish *vara,*" she said, "was made up of three of the so-called Burgos feet. That was eighty-three and a half centimeters. Half of what you sailors call fathoms. Six feet made one Spanish *braza.*"

"One meter sixty-seven centimeters."

"That's correct."

Coy nodded, turning back to the chart to study the small numbers that marked the elevation of sandbanks in the vicinity of anchorages, capes, and reefs. Soundings were electronic now, and in a half second they provided the exact relief of the bottom of the sea. In the mid-eighteenth century, however, that data could be obtained only through the laborious task of sounding by hand, with a long cord ending in a lead weight. If the depths marked on the Urrutia chart were in fathoms, he would have to transpose each of these measurements into feet, to make them conform to contemporary Spanish charts. Every two units on Urrutia's chart would therefore convert into approximately eleven feet.

Two empty coffee cups sat at one side of the table, beside the pencils and gum eraser. There was also a clean ashtray and English cigarettes. Music was coming from the tape player—something old and very pleasant, perhaps French or Italian, a melody that made Coy think of gardens with geometrically trimmed hedges, stone fountains, and palaces at the end of straight allées. He studied her face as she bent over the chart. It went with her, he thought. That music was as appropriate as the casual khaki shirt she was wearing open over a white T-shirt, a man's shirt, military, with large pockets. Informal clothes looked as good on her as more formal ones, the jeans with slight wrinkles at the groin and knee, the bare ankles—also covered with freckles, he had discovered with stupefied delight—and sneakers.

Focusing again on the chart, Coy studied the scales of latitude and longitude. Ever since the Phoenicians began to cross the Mediterranean, all nautical science had been directed toward making it easier for the sailor to identify his position. Once his position was established, it became possible to know what course to follow and what its dangers were. The charts and atlases were more than mere guides, they were manuals for applying astronomic, geographic, and chronometric calculations, which allowed the sailor, either directly or by reckoning, to ascertain his location on the meridians—latitude north or south in relation to the equator—and on the parallels—longitude east or west in relation to the corresponding meridian. Latitude and longitude helped the seaman situate himself on a hydrographic chart, using the scales in the margins. On modern charts these scales are detailed in degrees, minutes, and tenths, of which each minute is equal to a conventional nautical mile of 6,076 feet. Position on the parallels was established by using the scale that appeared on the upper and lower borders of each chart, and the position on the meridians through those on the left and right. Then with the aid of a compass and parallel rulers you extended the lines of each position and the ship would be at their intersection—if the calculations had been correctly done. The matter was complicated by additional factors such as magnetic declination, ocean currents, and other elements that required complementary calculations. There also was a great difference between navigating when using the flat charts of the ancients, on which meridians and parallels measured the same on paper, and the nautical charts that were more representative of the true shape of the earth, with distances between meridians shortening as you approached the poles. From Ptolemy to Mercator, the transition had been long and complex, and hydrographic surveys did not begin to reach perfection until the end of the eighteenth century and the application of the marine chronometer for determining longitude. As for latitude, that had been established since ancient times through observation and astronomic declination—the forestaff, the octant, the modern sextant.

"What was the *Dei Gloria*'s position when she went down?"

"Four degrees and fifty-one minutes east longitude . . . The latitude was thirty-seven degrees and thirty-two minutes north."

She had answered without stumbling. Coy nodded and bent over to establish those coordinates on the chart spread out on the table. As he felt Coy move, Zas lifted his head, then again rested it on Coy's shoe.

"They must have established their position by taking bearings on the land," said Coy. "That's most likely if they were sailing within sight of the coast. I can't imagine them shooting the sun with an octant in the midst of being chased down. The question is whether they set their location by reckoning. That's always relative. You calculate speed, direction, drift, and miles sailed. Errors can be very great. In the era of sail, they called a location obtained by reckoning the 'point of fantasy.'"

She looked at him. Serious, reflective. Attentive to every word.

"Have you sailed much?"

"Yes. Especially when I was young. For one year I was a student aboard the *Estrella del Sur,* a fore-topsail schooner turned into a training ship. I also spent a lot of time on the *Carpanta,* a friend's sailboat. . . . And I read books, of course. Novels. History."

"Always about the sea?"

"Always."

"And dry land?"

"I preferred to have land twenty miles behind me."

Tánger nodded, as if those words confirmed something.

"The battle was after dawn," she said finally. "They had light."

"Then it's most likely they took land references. Bearings. All they would have to do is cross two to find their position. I suppose you know how that's done."

"More or less." She smiled uncertainly. "Though I've never seen a real sailor do it."

Coy picked up the protractor, a clear plastic circle that had 360 degrees of circumference numbered in tens around the edge of the arc. That allowed direction to be calculated with precision by transferring indications on the ship's magnetic needle to the paper of a nautical chart.

"It's easy. You look for a cape or something you can identify." He placed the gum eraser on the chart, representing an imaginary ship, and moved the protractor toward the nearest coast. "Then you correlate it with your onboard compass, the needle, and you get, for example, 45°N. So you go to the chart and draw a line from that point in the opposite direction, to 225°. You see? Then you take another reference, one separated by a clear angle from the first: another cape, a mountain, whatever. If that gives you, for example, 315°, you draw your line on the chart toward 135°. Your ship is where the lines cross. If the land references are clear, the method is reliable. And if you complete it with a third bearing, better still."

Tánger's lips had tightened with concentration. She was staring at the eraser as if it were actually a ship sailing along the coast printed on the paper. Coy picked up a pencil and followed the drawing on the chart.

"This coast has shoals and sandy beaches," he explained, "but most of all areas of craggy slopes with tall rocks. There are lots of references for visual charting. I imagine the pilot of the *Dei Gloria* could have done it easily. Maybe he did it during the night, if there was a moon and he could make out the coast.... Although that's more difficult. In those days they didn't have the lighthouses we have now. A tower with a lantern at most. But I doubt there was anything there."

I'm sure there wasn't, he said to himself, looking at the chart. I'm sure that on that night of the third and early morning of the fourth of February, 1767, there wasn't any light or other helpful reference, nothing except maybe the line of the coast standing out in the moonlight, off the port side. He could imagine the scene: full sail overhead, the ship running at her best speed, the wind whistling in the rigging and the deck of the brigantine heeling to starboard, the sound of the water close to the rail, and windward, glints of moonbeams on a choppy sea. A reliable man at the wheel, and on the aft deck a guard, tense and alert, staring back into the darkness. Not a single light on board, and the captain standing on the poop, his worried face turned up toward the ghostly pyramid of unfurled sail, listening to the creaking and wondering whether the yards and rigging damaged by the storm would hold out. Silent, so that none of the men who are counting on him will sense his uneasiness, but mentally calculating distance, course, set, and drift, with the anguish of someone who knows that the wrong decision will carry the ship and her crew to disaster. He clearly does not know his exact position, and this increases his apprehension. Coy imagines him casting glances toward the black line of the coast two or three miles distant, close but out of reach, as dangerous in the dark as the enemy's guns behind him; his crew too was looking into the night, where, sometimes invisible, sometimes hazily glimpsed as a vague shadow slicing through the waves, the xebec corsair was giving chase. And again the captain glances toward the coast, at the night ahead and the sea at the stern, and then again overhead, alert to the creak of the rigging or groan of the topmasts that freezes the heart of the men bunched windward of the shrouds, black, silent silhouettes in the darkness. Men who, like the captain himself—all except one—will be dead at this time tomorrow.

"How does it look?"

Coy blinked, as if he had just returned from the deck of the brigantine. Tánger was observing him closely, awaiting a reply. It was obvious that she had gone over everything forward and backward, but she wanted to hear it from his mouth. He shrugged.

"Our first problem is that the crew of the *Dei Gloria* set their position on this chart, not on a modern one. And we have to chart ours on modern ones, even though we use this one as a point of departure. What we need to do is calculate the differences between Urrutia's chart and contemporary ones. Measure the exact degrees, and all that. We already know that Cabo de Palos is a couple of minutes too far south on the Urrutia." He indicated the spot with the pencil. "As you can see, this line of coast from Cabo de Agua was drawn as if it were nearly horizontal, when in fact it rises a little obliquely to the northeast. Look where La Hormiga bay is on the Urrutia, and where it is on the modern chart."

He took the compass, measured the distance from Cape Palos to the nearest parallel, and then placed the compass on the vertical scale at the left of the chart to get the number in miles. Tánger followed his every move, her hand motionless on the table, very close to Coy's arm.

"Let's calculate exactly. . . ." Coy noted the figures in pencil on a page of the notebook. "You see? We convert Urrutia's 37°35′. . . . Yes. 37°38′ true latitude. In fact, 37°37′ and thirty or forty seconds, which, expressed in figures on a modern nautical chart, where seconds are represented as decimal fractions added to the minutes, gives us 37°37′.5. Which makes a two-and-a-half-mile error here at the tip of Cabo de Palos. Maybe even a mile at Cabo Tiñoso. That difference is essential when we're dealing with a wreck. . . . With a sunken ship. That could place it near the coast, at sixty or seventy feet, where it would be easy to reach, or it could be too far, with soundings that keep going up past three hundred, five hundred feet, or more, making it impossible to dive, or even locate it. He paused, turning to her. Still bent over the chart, she was studying the numbers of the soundings marked on the chart. It was obvious that she knew all that very well. Maybe she needs someone to confirm it aloud, Coy thought. Maybe she wants someone to tell her that it's possible. The question remains: why me?

"Do you think you could dive to one hundred sixty-five feet?" she asked.

"I suppose so. I've gone a little lower than two hundred, although the safe limit is one hundred thirty. But I was twenty years younger then. . . . The problem is that at that depth you have very little time below, at least with normal compressed-air equipment. You don't dive?"

"No. It terrifies me. And yet . . ."

Coy continued to fit pieces together. Sailor. Diver. Knowledge of navigation under sail. It was clear, he told himself, that she didn't have him here because she was fascinated by his conversation. So don't get any ideas, kid. She's not interested in your pretty face. Supposing your face had ever been pretty.

"How far down do you think you could go?" Tánger wanted to know.

"You're going to let me go down alone, without watching what I do?"

"I have faith in you."

"That's what bothers me. That you have too much faith in me."

When he said that, she finally turned toward him. Damn, he thought. You would guess she spends her nights planning every gesture. His eyes were on the silver chain that disappeared into the neck of the white T-shirt, headed in the direction of suggestive curves molded beneath the open shirt. Not without effort, he repressed the impulse to pull out the chain and look at it.

"Unless you use special equipment, the deepest a diver can go without problems is two hundred sixty feet," he explained. "And that's very deep. Besides, if you're working you get tired and use up more air, and that complicates things. You have to use mixtures and detailed decompression tables."

"It isn't very deep. At least that's what I believe."

"You've already calculated it?"

"Within a range of possibilities."

"But you seem very sure."

Coy smiled. Only half a smile, but she didn't seem to like it.

"If I were very sure I wouldn't need you."

He leaned back in his chair. The movement disturbed Zas, who got up and gave him a couple of affectionate licks on the arm.

"In that case," he hazarded, "I may be able to go down. This matter of positions is always relative, though, even using modern charts and GPS. It isn't easy to locate a ship, or what remains of one. Much less a ship that sank two and a half centuries ago. It depends on the nature of the bottom and many other things. The wood will have rotted to hell, and the whole wreck may be covered with mud. And then there are the currents, poor visibility. . . ."

Tánger had picked up the cigarettes, but all she did was turn the box over and over. She contemplated Hero's picture.

"Do you have much experience as a diver?"

"I have some. I took a course at the naval diving center, and a couple of summers I worked cleaning ships' hulls with a wire brush, blind to anything farther away than my nose. During vacations, I also dived for Roman amphoras with Pedro el Piloto."

"And who is Pedro el Piloto?"

"The owner of the *Carpanta*. A friend."

"That's prohibited now."

"Having friends?"

"Bringing up amphoras."

She had set the cigarettes down and was watching Coy. He thought he saw a spark of interest in her eyes.

"I knew that at the time," he admitted, "but the secrecy made it exciting. Besides, in a port where you're known, none of the *guardias* check your seabag when you come back from a dive. You say Hi, he says Hi, you smile, and that's it. Those days, just off Cartagena, the coast was a huge field of archaeological artifacts. I was especially looking for necks of amphoras, which are very beautiful, and other vessels. I used a Ping-Pong paddle to fan away the sand that covered them. And I found dozens."

"What did you do with them?"

"Gave them to my girlfriends."

That wasn't true, at least not completely. Once back on land, with the amphoras discreetly spirited past the police, El Piloto and Coy had sold them to tourists and antiquarians, splitting the proceeds. As for the girlfriends, Tánger didn't ask whether there had been a lot or a few. In truth, Coy remembered only one with special affection from those days. Her name was Eve, and she was North American, the daughter of a technician at the Escombreras refinery. A healthy, blonde, tan girl with very white teeth and the shoulders of a windsurfer, with whom he spent a summer while he was still an apprentice. She laughed happily at the least thing, had beautiful hips, and was passive and tender when they made love in hidden coves tucked among steep black rocks, with the sea licking their legs and their skin coated with brine and sand. For a while, Coy carried the taste of her flesh and her sex on his fingers and lips. For a few years he had also kept a photograph of Eve by the sea, with bare breasts, wet hair, and her head tilted back drinking from a wineskin that left dribbles like blood between her small, insolent, girlish breasts. Like any good young *gringa,* her historical memory, only two or three centuries old, made it difficult for her to accept that the clay fragment Coy had given her from a wreck, the neck and handles of an elegant oil amphora from the first century, had for two thousand years lain at the bottom of the sea on whose shore they made love that summer.

"You know those waters well, then," said Tánger.

It wasn't a question but a reflection. She seemed satisfied, and he made a vague gesture toward the chart.

"In some places I do. Especially between Cabo Tiñoso and Cabo de Palos. I even dived on a couple of shipwrecks.... But I never heard of the *Dei Gloria.*"

"No one has, for several reasons. First of all, there was some mystery on board, which was proved by the limited information they got from the ship's boy, along with his strange disappearance. As well as the position he gave the authorities...."

"Assuming it was authentic."

"Let's assume that, since we don't have anything else."

"And if it isn't?"

Tánger raised her eyebrows and lay back in her chair with a sigh.

"Then you and I will have wasted our time."

Suddenly she seemed exhausted, as if Coy's appraisal had made her consider the possibility of failure. She was leaning back, frowning at the chart for only a moment. Then she set a firm hand on the table, stuck out her chin, and said there were other reasons no one had searched for the ship. The position the ship's boy gave was in an area difficult to get to in 1767. Later, technical developments made that kind of dive easy, but the *Dei Gloria* was already buried in files and dust, and no one remembered her.

"Until you came along," Coy pointed out.

"That's right. It could have been anyone, but it was me. I found the document and I got to work on it. What else was I going to do?" With her fingertips, she stroked, almost affectionately, the Hero on her cigarette box. "It was one of those things you dream about when you're a girl. The sea, a treasure..."

"You said there aren't any treasures to be found."

"That's true. There aren't. At least in silver ingots, doubloons, or pieces of eight. But the enchantment is still there.... I'm going to show you something."

She seemed different, younger, as she got up and went to the bookshelf. She moved with a vigor and decisiveness that set the tails of the open military shirt flying behind her. Her eyes were a deeper blue than ever and seemed to be smiling when she came back to the table carrying two of Tintin's adventure books in her hands: *The Secret of the Unicorn* and *Red Rackham's Treasure.*

"The other day you told me you aren't a Tintin fan. Is that right?"

Coy nodded in response to the strange question, and said, "Not at all, definitely not." His favorites had been *Treasure Island, Jerry on the Island,* and other books about the sea by Stevenson, Verne, Defoe, Marryat, and London, before he moved on lock, stock, and barrel to *Moby-Dick.* Conrad came later, quite naturally, with *Heart of Darkness* and with time.

"Is it really true you read only books about the sea?"

"Yes."

"Honest?"

"Honest. I've read all of them. Or nearly all of them."

"Which is your favorite?"

"I don't have a favorite. None is separate from the others. All books that involve the sea, from the *Odyssey* to the latest novel by Patrick O'Brian, are interconnected, like a library."

"Like Borges's library..."

She smiled and Coy shrugged, a simple gesture.

"I don't know. I never read anything by Borges. But it is true that the sea is like a library."

"Books describing things that happen on dry land are interesting too."

"If you say so...."

At that, clutching the two books to her chest, she began to laugh. She seemed like a different woman, laughing openly, happily, and then she said, "Thundering typhoons!" She deepened her voice and spoke like a one-eyed, peg-leg pirate with a parrot on his shoulder. Then, as the sun turned the asymmetrical tips of her hair even brighter gold, she sat down next to Coy and again opened the brightly colored books and began to turn the pages. "The sea is here too," she said. "Look. And adventure is still possible. You can get drunk a thousand times with Captain Haddock—Loch Lomond whiskey, in case you didn't know, holds no secrets for me. I also parachuted over a mysterious island with the green flag of the EFSR in my arms, crossed the border between Syldavia and Borduria more times than you can count, swore by the mustache of Kurvi Tasch, sailed on the *Karaboudjan,* the *Ramona,* the *Speedol Star,* the *Aurora,* and the *Sirius*—more ships than you, I'm sure. I searched for Red Rackham's treasure, westward, farther westward, and walked on the moon while Thompson and Thomson, with their green hair, performed as clowns in the Hiparco Circus. And when I'm lonely, Coy, when I'm very, very, very lonely, then I light one of your friend Hero's cigarettes, make love with Sam Spade, and dream of Maltese falcons while through the smoke I summon my old friends Abdullah, Alcázar, Jolyon Wagg, Chester, Zorrino,

Skut, Oliveira de Figueira, and listen to the CD of the jewel song from *Faust* on an old Bianca Castafiore recording."

As she spoke she set the two books on the table. They were old editions, one with a blue binding and the other green. The frontispiece of the first showed Tintin, Snowy, and Captain Haddock in a plumed hat, and a galleon under full sail. In the second, Tintin and Snowy were skimming along the bottom of the sea in a submarine shaped like a shark.

"That's Professor Calculus's submarine," said Tánger. "When I was a girl, I saved my money from birthdays, saint's days, and Christmas gifts to buy these books, pinching pennies as hard as Scrooge himself. You know who Ebenezer Scrooge is?"

"A sailor?"

"No, a miser. Bob Cratchit's boss."

"Never heard of him."

"It doesn't matter," she continued. "I saved every cent so I could go to the bookstore and come out with one of these in my hands, holding my breath, loving the feel of the hard covers, the colors of the splendid illustrations. And then, all by myself, I would open the pages and smell the paper and the ink before I dived into the story. So I collected all twenty-three, one by one. A lot of time has gone by since then, but to this day, when I open a Tintin I can smell the smell that I have associated with adventure and life ever since. Along with the movies of John Ford and John Huston, Richmal Compton's *Adventures of William,* and a few other books, these shaped my childhood."

She had opened *Red Rackham's Treasure* to page 40. In a large illustration in the middle of the page, Tintin, dressed in a diving suit, was walking along the bottom of the sea toward the impressive wreck of the sunken *Unicorn.*

"Look carefully," she said in a solemn voice. "That one picture marked my life."

With extreme delicacy she touched the page with her fingertips, as if she feared she might alter the colors. Coy was looking at her, not the book; she was still smiling absently, with an expression that made her seem as young as the girl in the framed snapshot, leaning back in her father's arms. A happy expression, he thought. From a time when the counter is still at zero. Later would come the dented silver cup with the missing handle. Junior swimming championship. First prize.

"I imagine," she said after a while, without looking up from the book, "that you had a dream too."

"Of course."

He could understand her. Not the books or the silver cup or the photo, not anything connected with things in her memory, but there was a point of contact, a territory where it was easy for him to recognize her. Maybe Tánger wasn't all that different after all. Maybe, he thought, in some way she's one of ours, even though by definition every one of ours sails, hunts, fights, and sinks alone. Ships that pass in the night. Lights in the distance, visible for a brief while, often going in the opposite direction. Sometimes a distant sound, the throb of engines. Then silence again when it passes, and darkness, and the glow extinguished in the empty blackness of the sea.

"Sure," he repeated.

That was all he said. His image, the vignette in his memory album, was of a Mediterranean port with three thousand years of history in its ancient stones, surrounded by mountains and castles with embrasures where once guns were mounted. Names like Navidad fort, de Curra jetty, San Pedro lighthouse. The smell of still water, of damp hawsers, and the *lebeche,* that south-southwest wind fluttering the flags of moored ships and the pennants on the trawl lines of the fishing boats. Idle men, men with nothing to do in retirement, facing the sea, sitting on dirty iron bollards. Nets in the sun, the rusting sides of merchant ships nestling against the docks, and that unique odor of salt, tar, and the age-old sea, of ports that have seen many ships and many lives come and go. In Coy's memory there was a boy moving through all that, a thin, dark-skinned boy with his schoolbag on his back, who had played hooky to gaze at the sea, to walk past the ships and watch the blond, tattooed men come ashore speaking incomprehensible languages. To see them cast off mooring lines that fell with a splash and were hauled on board before the iron hull moved away from the dock and the ship steered toward the harbor entrance, between the lighthouses, soon nothing but a strip of foamy wake, moving out toward the open sea in search of those unmarked highways to a place the boy was certain that he was going to go too. That had been his dream, the image that marked his life forever; early, before-the-fact nostalgia for a sea reached through old and wise ports peopled with ghosts that rested among the cranes huddled in the shade of the sheds. Iron worn away by the friction of cables. Men who sat quietly, motionless for hours, and for whom the fishing rod or the rum or the cigarette was only an excuse, who seemed not to care for anything in the world but to stare at the sea. Grandfathers who led their grandsons by the hand and, while the young ones asked questions or pointed to gulls, they, the old ones, turned their eyes toward the moored ships and the line of the horizon beyond the lighthouses, as if searching for some lost memory; a recollection, a word, an explanation of something that happened too long ago, or something that may never have happened at all.

"PEOPLE are so stupid," Tánger was saying. "Their dreams are limited to things they see on TV."

She had returned the Tintins to the shelf and was standing, hands in the pockets of her jeans, looking at him. Now everything about her was softer, from the expression in her eyes to the smile on her lips. Coy nodded, not knowing why. Maybe to encourage her to keep talking, or to indicate that he understood.

"What do you want to find on the *Dei Gloria,* really?"

She came toward him, slowly, and for a moment, caught off guard, he thought that she was going to touch his face.

"I don't know. I swear to you, I don't know." Now she was standing, right beside him, studying the nautical chart on the table. "But when I read the boy's testimony, transcribed in the dry language of a clerk, I felt . . . That ship fleeing under full sail, and the corsair giving chase . . . Why didn't they take refuge in Águilas? The atlases of the time showed a castle there, and a tower with two guns on Cabo Cope, where they could have sought protection."

Coy glanced at the chart. Águilas was beyond its boundaries, southwest of Cope.

"You made that point yesterday, when you told me the story," he said. "Maybe the corsair was between them and Águilas, and the *Dei Gloria* had to keep sailing east. The wind could have veered. Or maybe the captain feared the risk of a leeward tack at night. There's a stack of explanations for that. The fact is that she ended up sinking in the cove at Mazarrón. Maybe he wanted to take shelter under the tower at La Azohía. That tower is still standing."

Tánger shook her head. She didn't seem convinced.

"Maybe. In any case, she was a merchant brigantine, and yet when she saw all was lost, she engaged in combat. Why didn't she strike her colors? Was the captain a stubborn man, or was there something on board that was too important to hand over without a fight? Something worth the lives of all the crew, something not even the sole survivor said one word about?"

"Maybe he didn't know about it."

"Maybe. But who were those two passengers the manifest identified only with the initials N.E. and J.L.T?"

Coy rubbed his neck, amazed. "You have the manifest from the *Dei Gloria*?"

"Not the original, no. But I have a copy. I got it from the naval archives at Viso del Marqués. I have a good friend, a woman, who works there."

She gave no more details, but it was obvious that something was going through her head. Her lip twisted, and her expression was no longer soft. Tintin had exited the scene.

"Besides, there's something else."

She said that and again stopped, as if that "something else" was information he was never going to hear. Quiet, silence, for a long while.

"The ship," she said finally, "belonged to the Jesuits, remember? To Fornet Palau, a shipowner from Valencia who was their straw man. And another thing. Valencia was the destination. All this happens on February 4, 1767, two months before the royal decree of Charles III ordering 'the banishment of the Jesuits from Spanish domains and the appropriation of their temporalities. . . .' Do you have any idea what that meant?"

Coy said he didn't, that eighteenth-century history and Charles III were not his forte. So she elaborated. She did so very well, with few words, quoting key dates and facts without getting mired in superfluous details. The popular uprising of 1766 in Madrid against minister Esquilache, which shook the security of the monarchy and was said to have been instigated by the Society of Jesus. The Ignatian order's resistance to enlightened ideas spreading through Europe. The enmity of the monarch and his desire to rid himself of them. The creation of a secret counsel presided over by the Conde de Aranda, which prepared the decree of expulsion, and the unexpected coup of April 2, 1767, the immediate expulsion of the Jesuits, the seizure of their wealth, and the subsequent dissolution of the Order by Pope Clement XIV. That was the historical context in which the voyage and tragedy of the *Dei Gloria* had taken place. Of course, there was no proof of a direct connection between one thing and the other. But Tánger was a historian, she was trained to evaluate events and to find relationships among them, to formulate hypotheses and develop them. There could be a connection, or perhaps not. In any case, the *Dei Gloria* had gone to the bottom. At the very least, to sum it up, a sunken ship was a sunken ship—*stat rosa pristina nomine,* she recited cryptically. And she knew where.

"That," she concluded, "is justification enough to look for it."

Her expression had hardened as she spoke, as if at the hour of dealing with facts the ghost of the girl that had emerged as she looked at the pages of Tintin had faded away. Now the smile had disappeared from her lips and her eyes were shining resolutely, not provocatively. She was no longer the girl in the snapshot. She was becoming distant again, and Coy was annoyed.

"Tell me about the others."

"What others?"

"The Dalmatian with the gray ponytail. And the melancholy dwarf who was watching your house last night. They didn't look like historians, not by a long shot. I don't think the expulsion of old Charles III and the Jesuits would ever raise their limp pricks."

She seemed to be taken aback by his vulgarity. Or maybe she was just searching for an adequate response.

"That has nothing to do with you," she said slowly.

"You're wrong."

"Listen, I'm paying you for this job."

For the love of God, he said to himself. That's a serious mistake, beautiful. That is a really serious mistake, one that's unworthy of you—coming out with shit like that at this point in the game.

"Pay? What the fuck are you talking about?"

He saw clearly that Tánger was flustered. She lifted a hand. Take it easy, cool down, I was wrong. Come on, let's talk. But he was furious.

"Do you really believe I'm sitting here because you intend to pay me?"

He immediately felt ridiculous, because in fact he was. He stood up, overturning his chair so abruptly that Zas retreated, unsettled. "You misunderstood," she said. "Really. I'm only saying that those men have nothing to do with it."

"*Nothing* to do with it," she repeated.

She seemed frightened, as if all of a sudden she was afraid she would see him jerk open the door and stalk out, as if until that moment she had never considered the possibility. That gave Coy a twisted kind of satisfaction. After all, even if it was just self-interest, she was afraid she might lose him. That made him enjoy the situation. A crumb is a crumb.

"They have enough to do with it that I want you to clarify it for me or you'll have to look for someone else."

It was like a nightmare, but a nightmare that was strengthening his self-esteem. All very bitter, treading on the verge of rupture, of an end to it all, but he couldn't turn back.

"You aren't serious," she said.

"You bet I'm serious."

He heard himself as if he were a stranger speaking, an enemy willing to toss everything overboard and say good-bye to Tánger forever. His problem was that the only way he could go along was by being towed. As when the Torpedoman began to break things, and Coy had no choice but to gulp air, grab the neck of a broken bottle, and prepare for a battle royal.

"Look," he added. "I can understand that I seem a little simple-minded to you. . . . You may even take me for an imbecile. I'm not much on land, it's true. Clumsy as a duck. But you think I'm mentally retarded."

"You're here . . ."

"You know perfectly well why I'm here. But that isn't the question, and we can talk about that calmly another day if you want. In fact, I *hope* to be able to talk about it calmly another day. For the moment though, I'll limit myself to demanding that you tell me what I'm getting myself into."

"Demand?" She looked at him with sudden contempt. "Don't tell me what I should or shouldn't do. Every man I ever met wants to tell me what I must or I mustn't do."

She laughed quietly, humorlessly, as if exhausted, and Coy decided that she laughed with a European ennui. Something indefinable that had a lot to do with old whitewashed walls, churches with cracked frescoes, and black-clad women staring at the sea past grapevines and olive trees. Few North American women, he thought suddenly, could laugh like that.

"I'm not telling you what to do. I just want to know what you expect of me."

"I've offered you a job. . . ."

"Oh, shit. A job."

Saddened, he rocked on his toes as if he were on the deck of a ship and about to leap to land. Then he picked up his jacket and took a few steps toward the door, with Zas happily trotting at his heels. His soul turned to ice.

"A job," he repeated sarcastically.

She was standing between him and the window. He thought he saw another flash of fear in her eyes. Difficult to tell against the light.

"Maybe they think," she said, and she seemed to be choosing her words with care, "that it's about treasure and things like that. But it isn't a treasure, it's a secret. A secret that may not have any importance today, but that fascinates me. That's why I got into this."

"Who are *they*?"

"I don't know."

Coy took the last steps toward the door. His eyes paused for an instant on the small dented cup.

"It's been a pleasure knowing you."

"Wait."

He had her complete attention. She reminded him, he concluded, of a gambler with mediocre cards, trying to calculate what the other player held.

"Don't go," she said after a moment. "You're bluffing."

Coy put on his jacket.

"Maybe. Try me."

"I need you."

"There are sailors on every corner. And divers. Many as stupid as me."

"I need *you.*"

"Well, you know where I live. So it's up to you."

He opened the door slowly, with death in his heart. All the while, until he closed it behind him, he was hoping she would come take his arm, force him to look her in the eye, tell him anything to keep him from going. Hoping she would take his face in her hands and press her lips to his with a long, sincere kiss, after which, damn the Dalmatian and the melancholy dwarf! He would be willing to dive with her and her Captain Haddock and the devil himself to look for the *Unicorn* or the *Dei Gloria,* or the impossible dream. But she stood there with the golden light behind her, and did nothing and said nothing. Coy found himself going down the stairs, hearing the whimpering of Zas, who missed him. He went with a frightening void in his breast and his stomach, with his throat dry and an irritating tickle in his groin. With nausea that made him stop on the first landing, lean against the wall, and cover his mouth with trembling hands.

TERRA firma, he concluded after long deliberation, was nothing more than a vast conspiracy determined to harass the sailor. It had underwater peaks that didn't show on the charts, and reefs, sandbars, and capes with treacherous shoals; and besides, it was peopled by a multitude of officials, customs officers, shipowners, port captains, police, judges, and women with freckles. Sunk in such gloomy thoughts, Coy wandered around Madrid all afternoon. Wandered like the wounded heroes of films and books, like Orson Welles in *Lady from Shanghai,* like Gary Cooper in *The Wreck of the Mary Deere,* like Jim pursued from port to port by the ghost of the *Patna.* The difference lay in the fact that no Rita Hayworth or

Marlow spoke to him, and he wandered unnoticed and silent among the crowd, hands in the pockets of his blue jacket, stopping at red lights and crossing on green, as insipid and gray as everyone else. He felt insecure, displaced, miserable. He walked on, desperately searching for the docks, for the port, where at least in the smell of the sea and splashing of water beneath iron hulls he would find the consolation of the familiar, and it took a while—when he stopped indecisively on the Plaza de las Cibeles without knowing what direction to take—to get it through his head that this huge and noisy city didn't have a port. That reality hit him with all the force of an unpleasant revelation, and he slowed, almost stumbled, so weak in the knees that he sat down on a bench across from the gate of a garden by which two Army men with aiguillettes, red berets, rifles, and bandoleers, observed him with suspicion. Later, when he resumed his walk and the sky in the west was beginning to grow red at the far end of the avenues, and then somber and gray on the opposite side of the city, silhouetting the buildings where the first lights were being turned on, his desolation gave way to a growing exasperation, a contained fury composed of contempt for the image pursuing him in the reflection of the shop windows, and of anger toward all the people brushing against him as they passed, crowding and pushing when he stopped at crosswalks, waving their arms idiotically as they babbled into their cell phones, blocking his way with their huge shopping bags, ambling erratically in front of him, and stopping to engage in conversation. Once or twice he returned the shoves, rabid with rage, and once the indignant expression of a pedestrian turned to confusion and surprise when he glimpsed Coy's rock-hard expression, the malicious, menacing look in eyes dark as death. Never in his life, not even the morning the investigating commission sentenced him to two years without a ship, had he felt such empathy with the pain of the Flying Dutchman.

An hour later he was drunk, without any insistence on Sapphire blue or any other color. He had gone into a bar near the Plaza de Santa Ana, and after pointing toward an old bottle of Centenario Terry that must have been sleeping the sleep of the just on that shelf for at least half a century, retired to a corner supplied with it and a glass. Having a cognac hangover is exactly like being poleaxed, the Torpedoman had said one time when he had dropped to his knees and vomited up his guts after having put away enough to speak knowingly on the subject. Prognosis: terminal. Once, in Puerto Limón, the Torpedoman had got soused on Duque de Alba and passed out on top of a tiny little whore who'd had to yell for help to move the two hundred pounds that were about to squeeze the life out of her. And later, when he awoke in his berth—they'd had to find a van to take him back to the ship—he spent three days lightening ballast in the form of bile, in between bouts of the cold sweats and begging at the top of his lungs for some friend to put him out of his misery. Coy didn't have anyone to pass out on top of that night, or a ship to go back to, or even friends to carry him—the Torpedoman was God knows where, and Gallego Neira had ruptured his liver and his spleen when he fell from the Jacob's ladder of a tanker a month after earning a pilot's spot in Santander. But Coy did the honors to his cognac, letting it slide down his throat again and again, until everything began to fade into the distance, and his tongue and hands and heart and groin stopped hurting, and Tánger Soto was just one more among the thousands of women who every day are born, live, and die in this wide, wide world, and he observed that the hand going and coming between the glass and the bottle was beginning to move in slow motion.

The bottle was half empty, just a little below the Plimsoll line, when Coy, calling on one last scintilla of good sense, stopped drinking and took a look around. Everything seemed to be listing badly, until he realized that his head was resting on the table and he was the one off plumb. Nothing more grotesque, he thought, than some jerk all alone getting smashed in public. Slowly, he got up and went outside. Trying to disguise his condition, he proceeded very carefully, shoulder touching the walls of buildings to help keep to a straight line and parallel to the curb. When he crossed the plaza, the air did him good. He stopped and sat down on a bench beneath the statue of Calderón de la Barca. From there, with the palms of his hands on his knees, Coy observed the people passing before his unfocused eyes. He saw the beggars who'd shared the wine bottle, the three men and a woman who had been sitting on the ground drinking with their little mutt the other day, watched by RoboCop from the door of the Hotel Victoria. He shook his head when a Moroccan from the Magreb offered him some hashish—a joint's about the last thing I want, man—and finally, a little clearer of head, he started toward his lodging. Now that the Centenario Terry had been sufficiently diluted in his lungs, his urine, or wherever it might have made its way, things were a little less hazy. And as a consequence, he saw that the Dalmatian, that is, the guy from Barcelona with the gray ponytail and the one green and one brown eye, was sitting at a table in the bar, by the door, a glass of whiskey in his hands, legs crossed, waiting for him.

"TAKE my word for it," the man concluded. "They want us to take them to bed. That is, they want us to want to take them to bed. But most of all they want us to pay for it. With our money, our freedom, our mind . . . In their world, believe me, there's no such word as *gratis.*"

He was sitting there, whiskey in hand, as if he owned the place, and Coy was sitting across from him, listening. He had stopped being surprised a long time ago, and was taking it in with interest now, an untouched glass of tonic, ice, and lemon in front of him.

The cognac was still slipping smoothly through his blood. From time to time the Dalmatian rattled the ice in his glass, regarded the contents pensively, then lifted it to his lips and took a sip before continuing his monologue. Coy had confirmed that the man's Spanish did have a touch of a foreign accent—say Andalusian overlaid with British.

"And let me tell you something. When one of them decides to bully her way forward, there's no one . . . I'm here to tell you. When they finally come to a decision, whatever it is, they're hard as steel. I swear to you. I've seen them lie. . . . God almighty. I swear I've seen them lie . . . right there on my own pillow, talk to their husband on the phone . . . lie in cold blood. Incredible."

Next door there was a store that sold mannequins, and occasionally Coy glanced toward the window. Naked bodies in assorted postures—sitting, standing, men and women with no genital identity, some with wigs, others whose craniums were bare, synthetic flesh gleaming in the strong lights. Several severed heads smiled on a shelf. The female dummies had breasts with jutting nipples. A window dresser with a sense of humor, affecting prudery, an accidental or conscious classical reference, had positioned the arm of one of the mannequins modestly across its breasts and placed the other hand to cover its supposed sex. Venus rising directly from her shell, the transvestite Pris Nexus 6 in *Blade Runner.*

"Has she been on your pillow, then?"

The Dalmatian looked at Coy almost reproachfully. His hair was clean and combed straight back, fastened with a black elastic. His shirt was white, with a button-down collar he was wearing open, without a tie. Tan, but not excessively so. Impeccable shoes, comfortable, good leather. The expensive, heavy gold watch on the left wrist. Gold rings. Very carefully manicured fingernails. Another ring on the little finger of the right hand, wide, also gold. Gold chains visible at the neck, with medallions and an antique

Spanish doubloon. Gold cuff links flashing at the wrist. This guy, thought Coy, looks like a Cartier display case. You could cast a couple of ingots with what he had on.

"No. . . . Of course not!" The Dalmatian seemed sincerely scandalized. "I don't know why you say that. My relationship with her . . ."

He stopped as if the connection, whatever it might be, was obvious. A second later he must have realized that it wasn't, because he rattled the ice in his glass and, this time without taking a sip, brought Coy up to date on the story. At least, he brought him up to date on his version of the story. He was, after all, Nino Palermo, and that gave his tale only relative value. But this individual was the one person who seemed willing to tell Coy anything. He had no source for another, more authentic version, and he doubted very much that he ever would. So he sat very still, attentive, turning his eyes toward the window with the mannequins only when his tablemate fixed first the green, and then the brown, eye on him for too long a time—an uncomfortable ocular duality to sit across from. So he learned that Nino Palermo was the owner of Deadman's Chest, an enterprise devoted to recovering sunken ships and maritime salvage with a home base in Gibraltar. Maybe Coy, since Palermo understood that he was a sailor, had heard of Deadman's Chest when they were working on refloating the *Punta Europa,* a ferry that had sunk the year before in the bay of Algeciras with fifty passengers on board? Or—he added after a brief pause—at the time of the recovery of the *San Esteban,* a galleon carrying a cargo of Mexican silver salvaged five years ago in the Florida Keys? Or perhaps the most recent case, a Roman shipload of statues and pottery off Ifach rock, at Calpe?

At that point, Coy spoke aloud the words "treasure hunter," and the other man smiled broadly enough to show a tooth or two at the side of his mouth before saying, yes, in a way. Though this matter of treasure was a relative concept, according to, and how. . . . Besides, my friend, all that glitters is not gold. And sometimes, what doesn't glitter *is.* Then, between more unfinished sentences, Palermo crossed and uncrossed his legs, rattled the ice in his glass again, and took a long swallow that left the ice cubes beached on the bottom of the glass.

"It isn't adventure, it's work," he said slowly, as if he wanted to offer Coy every opportunity to understand. "It's one thing to go to the movies, or to live as if you're sitting in row fourteen eating popcorn with your sweetheart, and it's quite another to invest money, do your research, and do your prospecting with professionalism. I work for myself and for my partners; I raise the necessary capital, I obtain results, and I portion out the dividends, rendering to Caesar.... You know. The state, with its laws and taxes. I also make gifts to museums, institutions.... Things like that."

"Something must end up in your pocket."

"Of course. I try to make it be... God almighty. I have money. Listen. I try to risk my partners' money, naturally, but I also risk mine. I have lawyers, researchers, and experienced divers working for me. I'm a professional."

Having said all that, he sat a moment without speaking, his bicolor gaze fixed on Coy, weighing the effect. But Coy, whose expression hadn't changed, must not have seemed very impressed.

"The difficulty," he continued, "is that this work of mine calls for.... A person can't go around telling the story of his life. That's why you have to move with caution. I'm not talking about anything illegal, although sometimes... Oh, well. You take my word for it. The key word is *caution.*"

"And where does she fit into all this?"

As Palermo spoke his amiable air had turned hard, and anger suddenly showed in his eyes and mouth. Coy saw him clench a fist, the one with the wide gold ring on the little finger, and he would have burst out laughing at that fit of choler if he hadn't been so interested in the story his interlocutor was telling in a bitter, surly tone that at times was close to raw aggression. He had stumbled across a lead. The search for ancient shipwrecks always began with some simple, sometimes almost stupid lead, and he had. . . . God almighty. Chance, in the guise of a man named Corso, a man who liked to dig through libraries, a guy who fed him material having to do with the sea, ancient nautical charts, atlases, things like that—a sort of unscrupulous guy, if he might say so in passing, who charged him an arm and a leg—had placed in his hands a book on the maritime activities of the Society of Jesus, published in 1803. It was titled *The Black Fleet: The Jesuits in the East and West Indies,* and had been written by a Francisco José González, a librarian at the San Fernando naval observatory, and it was in this book that Palermo had found the *Dei Gloria.*

"Right there it was. . . . God almighty. I knew immediately. You *know* when something is there waiting for you." He rubbed his nose with his thumb. "I feel it here."

"I guess you're referring to treasure."

"I'm referring to a ship. To a good, old, and beautiful sunken ship. The business of any treasure comes later, if it comes at all. But don't think that. . . . Imperative isn't the word. No, it isn't."

He lowered his head, staring at his large ring. In that moment Coy took a really good look. Apparently another ancient, authentic coin. Arabic maybe, or Turkish.

"The ocean covers two-thirds of the planet," Palermo said unexpectedly. "Can you imagine all the stuff that has ended up on the bottom in the last three or four thousand years? Five percent of all the ships that ever sailed . . . I'm telling you. At least five percent is under water. The most extraordinary museum in the world. Ambition, tragedy, memory, riches, death. . . . Objects that are worth lots of money if we can bring them to the surface, but also . . . Understand? Solitude. Silence. Only a person who's felt a shiver of terror when he sees the dark silhouette of a sunken hull . . . I'm talking about that green murkiness below, if you know what I mean.... You know what I mean?"

The green eye and the brown one were fixed on Coy, lit by a sudden gleam that seemed feverish, or dangerous, and maybe both at once.

"I know what you mean."

Nino Palermo favored Coy with a vague smile of appreciation. He had spent his life, he said, getting into the water, first for others and then for himself. He had inspected coral-encrusted wrecks in the Red Sea, he'd discovered a cargo of Byzantine glass off Rhodes, he'd searched for gold sovereigns on the *Carnatic,* and off Ireland brought up two hundred doubloons, three gold chains, and a crucifix of precious stones from the galleon *Gerona*. He had worked with the salvage team that recovered mercury from the *Guadalupe* and the *Tolosa,* and with Mel Fisher on the *Atocha*. But he had also dived amid the ghostly ships of a sunken fleet at two hundred sixty feet in Martinique, near Mount Pelée, dived to the hull of the *Yongala* in the Sea of the Serpents, and of the *Andrea Doria* in the watery tomb of the Atlantic. He had seen the *Royal Oak* belly up at the bottom of Scapa Flow and the propeller of the corsair *Emden* on Los Cocos atoll. And at sixty-five feet, in a phantasmal gold and blue light, the collapsed skeleton of a German pilot in the cabin of his Focke-Wulf, downed over Nice.

"You won't deny," he said, "that's some résumé."

He paused and, signaling the waiter, ordered another whiskey for himself and a new tonic for Coy, who still hadn't touched the first. Lukewarm by now, Palermo said. Underwater searches were his life and his passion, he continued, staring at Coy as if he defied him to prove the contrary. But not all wrecks were important, he explained. Greek divers were already recovering treasure in ancient times. Which was why the best shipwrecks were ones with no survivors, because for lack of information about where they went down, they remained hidden and intact. Now Palermo had found a new lead. A good and beautiful and virgin lead in an old book. A new mystery, or challenge, and the possibility of looking for an answer.

"Then"—he raised his glass as if he were looking for someone whose face he could dash it in—"I made the mistake of... You know what I mean? The mistake of going to that bitch."

Fifteen minutes later the second tonic was untouched, as lukewarm as the first. As for Coy, the vapors of the Centenario Terry had dissipated a little more and he was getting the drift of the other side of the drama. Or at least the version held by Nino Palermo, a British subject residing on Gibraltar, owner of Deadman's Chest: Undersea Exploration and Maritime Salvage.

Six months earlier, Palermo had gone to the Museo Naval in Madrid, as he had other times, looking for information. He hoped to confirm that a brigantine that had sailed from Havana and disappeared before reaching its destination had sunk somewhere near the Spanish coast. The ship was not carrying cargo known to be valuable, but there were interesting hints: the name, *Dei Gloria,* for example, was in one of the letters seized when the Society was broken up during the reign of Charles III, which Palermo had found mentioned in the San Fernando librarian's book on the ships and maritime activity of the Jesuits. The quote, "but the justice of God did not allow the *Dei Gloria* to reach her destination with the people and secret she was carrying," was cross-checked by him with catalogues of documents in the Archives of the New World in Seville, in Viso del Marqués, and the Museo Naval in Madrid.... Bingo! In the catalogue of the museum's library he found a report dated February, 1767, in Cartagena, "on the loss of the brigantine *Dei Gloria* in an encounter with the xebec corsair presumed to be the *Serguí.*" That had led him to get in touch with the Museo Naval, and with Tánger Soto, who—curse the day and curse her and hers—was in charge of that department. After a first exploratory meeting, they had gone to have dinner at Al-Mounia, an Arab restaurant on calle Recoletos. There, over lamb couscous and vegetables, he had set out his case in a convincing manner. Not opening his heart to her, of course. He was a wise old dog and he knew the risks. He had mentioned the *Dei Gloria* among other matters, just the slightest offhand allusion. And she, polite, efficient, a pleasant goddamn witch, had promised to help him. That's what she had said, help him. Look up a copy of the documents for him if they were still in the papers entrusted to the institution, et cetera, et cetera. I'll call you, the bitch had promised. Without blinking an eye, by God. Not one blink. That had been months ago, and not only had she not called, she had used the influence of the Navy to block any access to the museum's archives. Even to documents pertinent to the cargo manifest of the brigantine in Havana, which he finally had located in the catalogue of the naval archives in Viso del Marqués. He had not been able to consult them, however, because they were—he was told—under official examination by the Ministry of Defense. Palermo had kept moving ahead, of course. He knew the drill and he had money to spend. His parallel inquiry was progressing well, and now he was reasonably sure that the brigantine had sunk near Cartagena, and that it was carrying something—objects or people—of major importance. Perhaps the attack by the corsair *Serguí*—an English *Chergui* with Algerian registry that had been lost in the same waters and same time frame—was not entirely coincidental. Palermo had tried many times to talk with Tánger Soto, to ask for explanations. To no avail. Total silence. She was very clever about ducking the issue, or she had luck, as she had in Barcelona when Coy walked up to them. By God, she had luck. In the end, Palermo had realized, idiot that he was, that she had not only played him along, but had been moving her own pieces on the sly. Suspicion became certainty when he saw her at the auction, bidding for the Urrutia.

"Little Miss Innocence," Palermo concluded, "had decided... God almighty. You get it? The *Dei Gloria* was hers."

Coy shook his head, although in truth he was digesting what he had just heard.

"As far as I know," he interjected, "she works for the Museo Naval."

Palermo's laugh was a snort.

"That's what I thought. But now... She's one of those women who can take a big chunk out of you without ever opening her mouth."

Coy touched his nose, still confused.

"In that case," he said, "get in touch with her superiors and blow the lid off her operation."

Palermo rattled the ice in his new whiskey.

"That would blow the lid off mine as well.... I'm not that stupid."

Again he smiled that quick smile that exposed a couple of teeth. This guy, Coy thought, smiles like a shark sighting a tasty squid.

"It's like a cross-country race, you know?" added Palermo. "I have better... God almighty. She gained the advantage because of my carelessness. But that kind of effort... I've gained ground. I'll gain more."

"Well, I wish you luck," Coy said.

"Some of that luck depends on you. I just have to look a man in the eye once to know...." Palermo winked the brown eye. "You get what I mean, no?"

"Wrong. I don't get what you mean."

"To know what it takes to buy him."

Coy didn't like the look he was getting. Or maybe he was annoyed by the intimate, complicitous tone of Palermo's last words.

"I'm out of it," he said coldly.

"You don't say."

The bantering tone did not improve matters. Coy felt his antipathy revive.

"Well, that's how it is. You'll have to deal with her." Coy tried to twist his lips into the most insolent sneer possible. "You two haven't tried to join forces? Apparently you're from the same litter."

Palermo did not seem the least offended. Instead, he was considering the idea with total calm.

"That's a possibility," he replied. "Though I doubt that she . . . She thinks she holds all the aces."

"She just lost a couple. Well, at least one joker."

Again, the shark smile. Now flavored with hope, which did not make it any more pleasant.

"Are you serious?" Palermo reflected, interested. "I mean about not working for her anymore."

"Of course I'm serious."

"Would it be indiscreet to ask why?"

"You said it a minute ago; she doesn't play fair. More or less like you. . . ." Suddenly he remembered something. "And you can tell your melancholy dwarf he can relax. Now I won't have to beat him to a pulp if I run into him."

Palermo, about to take a sip of his drink, stopped, looking at Coy over the rim of the glass.

"What dwarf?"

"Don't you be clever, too. You know who I'm talking about."

The glass was still poised; the bicolor eyes narrowed, astute.

"Don't get the wrong . . ." Palermo started to say something, but thought better of it and stopped, using the pretext of taking a sip. As he put the drink on the table, he changed the subject.

"I can't believe you're leaving her, just like that."

Now it was Coy's turn to smile. Of course I couldn't smile like this prick even if I tried, he thought. He felt swindled by everyone, including himself.

"I don't completely believe it myself," he said.

"Are you going back to Barcelona? What about your problem?"

"How about that." Coy shook his head, annoyed. "I see that now you're interested in my résumé, too."

Palermo raised his left hand, as if he'd been struck by an idea. He took a calling card from a thick billfold stuffed with credit cards, and wrote something on it. Lights from the window with the mannequins glinted off his rings. Coy glanced at the card before slipping it into his pocket: "Nino Palermo. Deadman's Chest, Ltd. 42b Main Street. Gibraltar." Palermo had written the telephone number of a hotel in Madrid on the bottom.

"Maybe I can compensate you in some way." Palermo paused, cleared his throat, took another swallow, and looked at Coy. "I need someone close to this Señorita Soto."

He left that sentence in the air. Coy sat quietly for a minute, observing Palermo. Then he leaned forward, placing his palms on the table.

"Shove it up your ass."

"I beg your pardon?"

Palermo had blinked, having expected something different. Coy started to get up, and with secret pleasure saw that the other man sat back a little in his chair.

"Just what I said. Up your ass. Up your bunghole. Shove it where the sun don't shine. You want me to draw you a picture?" Now the hands on the table had closed into fists. "That is, screw you, the dwarf, *and* the *Dei Gloria*. And don't forget her."

Palermo kept staring. The green eye seemed colder and more attentive than the brown one, wider, as if half his body was expressing fear and the other half was on guard, calculating.

"Think it over," said Palermo, and grasped Coy's arm at the cuff, as if attempting to convince him, or keep him from leaving. It was the hand with the gold coin ring, and to his displeasure Coy could feel it pressing on the tense muscles of his forearm.

"Get your hand off me," he said, "or I'll rip your head off."

V

Zero Meridian

With the first meridian established, situate all principal places by latitudes and longitudes.
—Mendoza y Ríos, TRATADO DE NAVEGACIÓN

He slept all night and part of the morning. He slept as if his life were draining away in sleep, or as if he wanted to hold life at a distance, as long as possible, and once he waked he stubbornly burrowed back toward sleep. He twisted and turned in his bed, covering his eyes, trying not to see the rectangle of light on the wall. Barely awake, he had observed that rectangle with desolation; the pattern of light appeared to be stable and varied in position almost imperceptibly as the minutes dragged by. To the uncritical eye it seemed as fixed as things tend to be on terra firma, and even before he remembered that he was in the room of a boardinghouse two hundred and fifty miles from the nearest coast, he knew, or felt, that he was not waking that day on board ship, there where light that comes through the portholes moves, gently oscillates up and down and side to side, while the gentle throb of the engines is transmitted through the metal hull, and the ship rocks in the circular sway of the swell.

He took a quick, torturous shower—after ten in the morning the taps provided only cold water—and went out without shaving, wearing jeans and a clean shirt, his jacket thrown over his shoulders, to look for an agency where he could buy a return ticket to Barcelona. He drank a cup of coffee and bought a newspaper, which he threw into a trash bin nearly unread, and walked through the city center with no fixed goal until he ended up sitting in a small plaza of old Madrid, one of those places where the trees of age-old convents line the far side of an adobe wall, and the houses have balconies with flowerpots and large entries with a cat and a maid at the gate. The sun was mild and lent itself to a pleasant sloth. He stretched out his legs, and pulled from his pocket the dog-eared paperback edition of Traven's *The Death Ship* that he finally had bought on Moyano hill. For a while he tried to concentrate on reading, but when he got to the place where the ingenuous sailor Pip-Pip, sitting on the dock, imagines the *Tuscaloosa* on the open seas and making her way back to home port, Coy closed the book and put it back in his pocket. His mind was too far from those pages. It was filled with humiliation and shame.

After a while he got up and, not in any hurry, started back toward the Plaza de Santa Ana, his gloomy expression accentuated by a chin darkened with a day and a half's growth of beard. Suddenly he was aware of discomfort in his stomach, and remembered that he hadn't eaten anything in twenty-four hours. He went to a bar and ordered a potato-and-egg omelette and a glass of rum. It was after two o'clock when he reached the inn. The Talgo was leaving an hour and a half later, and Atocha station was nearby. He could walk there and take the train to the Chamartín station, so he took his time packing his few effects—the Traven book, a clean shirt and a dirty one he slipped into a plastic bag, also some underwear and a blue wool jersey; his shaving gear was rolled up in a pair of khaki work pants. All of it went in his canvas seabag. He put on his sneakers and packed the old deck shoes. Each of these movements was carried out with the same methodical precision he would have used to chart a course, although damn his eyes if he had any course in mind. He was focusing all his concentration on not thinking. He paid the bill downstairs, and went out with his bag slung over his shoulder. His eyes squinted in the sun beating straight down on the plaza as he rubbed his queasy stomach. The omelet had settled like lead. After looking to the right and left he started walking. A quick trip, he thought. By an ironic association of ideas, the rhythms of "*Noche de samba en Puerto España*" came to mind. First a song, the words said. Then getting drunk, and in the end only the sob of a guitar. He had whistled half a chorus before he realized it, and stopped short. Remember, he told himself, never to whistle that again in all your fucking life. He stared at the ground, and the shadow that stretched out before him seemed to shake with laughter. Of all the fools in the world—and there had to be quite a few—she had chosen him. Although that was not exactly the case. After all, he was the one who had approached her, first in Barcelona and then in Madrid. No one forces the mouse, he'd read once somewhere. No one forces a dumb rodent to go nosing around, acting like hot shit and poking into mousetraps. Especially knowing full well that in this world there's more often a head wind than a following one.

He hadn't reached the corner yet when the clerk from the inn came running down the street after him, shouting his name. "Señor Coy. Señor Coy. You have a phone call."

"SONS of bitches," said Tánger Soto.

She was a reserved woman, and he could barely discern the slight tremor in her voice, a note of insecurity she tried to conceal as she spoke the appropriate words. She was dressed for going out, in a skirt and jacket, and was leaning against the wall of the small sitting room, arms crossed, her head tilted a little, staring at the corpse of Zas. On the stairs Coy had passed two uniformed policemen, and he found a third putting the equipment used to dust for fingerprints into a small case. His cap was on the table, and the radio transmitter clipped to his belt was emitting a quiet hum. The detective moved gingerly among scattered objects, though the disarray was not excessive—an open drawer here and there, books and papers scattered on the floor, and the computer with its screen detached and cords and connections exposed.

"They took advantage of my being at the museum," Tánger murmured.

Except for that slight tremble in her voice, she seemed more somber than fragile. Her skin had turned pale, her eyes were dry and her expression hard; her fingers were gripping her arms so tightly that her knuckles were white. She never took her eyes from the dog. The Labrador was lying on his side on the rug, his eyes glassy; a thread of whitish foam trickled from his half-open mouth. According to the police, the door had been forced, and before entering the intruders had tossed the dog a piece of meat laced with a rapidly acting poison, maybe ethyleneglycol. Whoever they were, they knew what they were looking for and what they were going to find. They hadn't done any serious damage, limiting themselves to stealing a few documents, and taking all the diskettes and the computer hard drive. They were undoubtedly people who knew the ropes. Professionals.

"They didn't have to kill Zas," she said. "He wasn't a watchdog. . . . He played with anyone who came in." Her voice cracked with a note of emotion she immediately repressed.

The policeman with the case had finished his work, so he put on his cap, saluted, and as he was leaving mumbled something about city employees coming by to pick up the dog. Coy closed the door—the lock still worked—but after another quick glance at Zas, he opened it again and left it ajar, as if closing the door with a dead dog inside the house was somehow wrong. Tánger, still leaning against the wall, hadn't moved a hair. He went into the bathroom and came back with a large towel. Then he bent over the Labrador looking with affection into the dead animal's eyes, remembering the friendly licks the day before, the tail happily wagging in anticipation of being petted, the intelligent, loyal gaze. He felt a deep sadness, a compassion that made him shudder: the distressing, almost childish feelings that every man believes he has forgotten. It felt as though he had lost a silent new friend, the kind you don't seek out because they choose you. Perhaps such sadness was uncalled for, he thought; after all, he had seen the dog only a couple of times, and had done nothing to earn his loyalty or mourn his death. Yet he found himself feeling an unwarranted grief, as if the forsakenness, the desolation, the paralysis of the unfortunate animal were his own. Maybe Zas had greeted his murderers with a happy bark, asking for a friendly word or pat.

"Poor dog," he murmured.

For a moment he stroked the Labrador's golden head, then covered him with the towel. As he stood up he saw that Tánger was watching him, somber and motionless.

"He died alone," said Coy.

"We all die alone."

HE stayed all that afternoon and part of the night. First, sitting on the sofa, after the city employees took away the dog, watching her restore order, stacking papers, putting books back on their shelves, closing drawers, standing in front of the gutted computer, hands on her hips as she evaluated the destruction, pensive. Nothing that can't be repaired, she'd said in answer to one of the few questions he had asked. She kept busy until everything was back in place. The last thing she did was kneel down where Zas had lain and, with a brush and water, clean up the remains of the foam that had dried on the carpet. She did it all with a disciplined, gloomy obstinacy, as if each task might help her control her emotions, hold at bay the darkness that was threatening to spill across her face. The tips of her golden hair swung at her chin, offering glimpses of her nose and cheeks. Finally she stood and looked around to see if everything was as it should be. Then she went to the table, picked up the Players and lit one.

"I saw Nino Palermo last night," Coy said.

She did not seem the least surprised. She stood by the table, cigarette between her fingers, hand slightly raised, elbow resting in the other hand.

"He told me you deceived him," Coy continued. "And that you will try to deceive me."

He was hoping for apologies, insolence, scorn. All he got was silence. The smoke from the cigarette rose straight to the ceiling. Not even a spiral, he observed. Not a twitch, not a shiver.

"You are not working for the museum," he added, leaving a deliberate pause between each word. "You're working for yourself."

It occurred to him suddenly that she resembled those women who look out from certain paintings: impassive gazes that sow uneasiness in the heart of any man who looks at them. The certainty that they know things they're not telling, things that you can gather from their unwavering pupils if you stand before them long enough. Hard, wise arrogance. Ancient lucidity. Some young girls looked like that, without having had the years to justify it, he thought, without having lived enough to learn it. Penelope must have had that look when Ulysses reappeared after twenty years, claiming his bow.

"I didn't ask you to come to Madrid," she said. "Or to complicate my life and yours in Barcelona."

Coy observed her a second or two, his half-open mouth giving him a somewhat stupid expression.

"That's true," he admitted.

"You're the one who wanted to play the game. All I did was establish a few rules. Whether they suit you or not is up to you."

Finally she had moved the hand that held the cigarette, and the tip glowed as she brought it to her lips. Then again she was motionless, and the smoke rose in a fine and perfect vertical line.

"Why did you lie to me?" Coy asked.

Tánger sighed softly. Barely a breath of annoyance.

"I haven't lied to you," she said. "I told you the version it suited me to tell. Remember that you butted in, and that this is my adventure. You can't demand anything of me."

"Those men are dangerous."

The perfect line of smoke broke into small spirals. Her laugh was quiet and restrained.

"You don't have to be very intelligent to deduce that, do you?"

She laughed again, but stopped abruptly, her eyes on the damp spot on the carpet. The deep blue of her eyes had become more somber.

"What are you going to do now?"

She did not answer immediately. She had walked over to put out the cigarette in the ashtray. She did it deliberately, not smashing it, but tamping it gradually until it was extinguished. Only then did she make a movement with her head and shoulders. She did not look at Coy.

"I'm going to keep doing what I was doing: looking for the *Dei Gloria.*"

She walked around the room slowly, checking to see that everything had been returned to its original order. She lined up a Tintin with others on the shelf, and adjusted the position of the framed snapshot Coy had studied—the blond teenager beside the tan, smiling military man in his shirtsleeves. She was behaving, he thought, as if she had ice water in her veins. But as he watched, she stopped, drew a deep breath and exhaled, less a moan than a rumble of fury. Then she slapped the table with the palm of her hand, brusque, quick, with an unexpected violence that must have surprised her, or even hurt, because she froze and again filled her lungs, staring with puzzlement at her hand.

"Damn them," she said.

She had regained control, and Coy could see the effort it cost to achieve. The muscles at her jawline were tense, her lips pressed tightly together as she breathed deeply through her nose and looked for something else to set in order, as if what had occurred ten seconds earlier hadn't happened.

"What did they take?"

"Nothing that can't be replaced." She kept looking around. "I took the Urrutia back to the museum this morning, and I have two good reproductions of the nautical chart to work with. They left all the contemporary charts except for the one with notes penciled in the margins. There was also some information on the hard drive, but it wasn't important."

Coy stirred, uncomfortable. He would have been more at ease were there a few tears, some indignant complaints. In those cases, he thought, a man knows what to do. Or at least he thinks he does. Everyone plays his role, the way they do in the movies.

"You need to forget this happened."

She turned, almost in slow motion, as if he had become one of the objects she needed to move to a different place.

"Look, Coy. I didn't ask you to get involved in my affairs. And I haven't asked you to give me advice now. Is that clear?"

She's dangerous, he thought. Maybe even more dangerous than whoever cased her house and killed the dog. More than the melancholy dwarf and the Dalmatian treasure hunter. All this is happening because she is dangerous, and they know it, and she knows that they know. Dangerous for me, too.

"Yes, it's clear."

He shook his head, half evasive, half resigned. That woman had an awesome talent for making him feel responsible, and at the same time reminding him that his presence there was superfluous. Even so, Tánger did not seem satisfied with Coy's unadorned answer. She kept observing him like a boxer who ignores the bell, and the referee's warning.

"When I was a girl I loved cowboy movies," she said unexpectedly.

Her tone was far from reminiscent, or tender. It almost seemed to contain a gentle mockery of herself. But she was dead serious.

"Did you like those movies, Coy?"

He looked at her, not knowing what to say. To answer that question would have required a brief period of transition, and she didn't give him time to come up with an answer. Nor did it seem to matter to her.

"Watching them," she continued, "I decided that there are two kinds of women: the kind who start screaming as the Apaches attack, and the kind who pick up a rifle and start firing out the window."

Her tone wasn't aggressive, just firm, and yet Coy felt that her firmness was aggressive as hell. She had finished, and it seemed she was not going to add anything.

But after a moment, she stopped before the framed snapshot and narrowed her eyes. Now her voice was hoarse and low: "I wanted to be a soldier and carry a rifle."

Coy touched his nose. Then he rubbed the nape of his neck and, one after the other, executed a routine of movements that in him tended to characterize confusion. I wonder, he asked himself, if this woman knows my thoughts or if in fact she's the one who puts them in my mind and then shuffles them and spreads them on the table as if this were a game of cards.

"This Palermo," he said finally, "offered me a job."

He held his breath. He had taken the calling card with the telephone number of the man from Gibraltar from his pocket. He held it between his second and third fingers, waggling it slightly. She didn't focus on the card, but on him. And she did it with enough concentration to have burned a hole in his brain.

"And what did you tell him?"

"That I'd think about it."

He saw a hint of a smile. A second of calculation and two seconds of disbelief.

"You're lying," she declared. "If that were true you wouldn't be sitting here now, looking at me." Her voice seemed to grow softer. "You're not that kind."

Coy turned his eyes toward the window, glancing outside, into the distance. You're not that kind. In some dusty corner of his memory Brutus was asking Popeye if he was a man or a mouse, and Popeye replied, "I'm a sailor man." A train was slowly approaching the long roof that covered the platforms of Atocha station, its elongated, articulated form following a route mysteriously traced through the labyrinth of tracks and signals. He felt a rancor sharp as a knife blade. You, he thought, don't have any idea what kind of man I am. He looked at his wristwatch. The Talgo, for which he was carrying a second-class ticket in the inside pocket of his jacket, had for some time now been rolling toward Barcelona. And here he was again, as if nothing had changed. He stared at the carpet where Zas had lain. Or maybe, he reflected, maybe he was there again precisely because some things had changed. Or because . . . Damn if he had a clue about anything! Suddenly his stomach turned over and something crossed his mind like a powder flash. He knew, as clear as could be, that he was there because someday he was going to teach this woman something. The thought so agitated him that it showed on his face, and she looked at him questioningly, surprised by the change in his expression. Coy almost stammered it out in his own silence. He was going to teach her something she thought she knew but didn't, something she could not control as easily as she did her expressions, her words, the situations around her, and, apparently, Coy himself. But he would have to wait before that moment came. That was why he was there; all he had was the wait. That was why they both knew that this time he wouldn't leave. That was why he was trapped, nibbling at the cheese until he sprang the trap. Snap. Man *or* mouse. At least, he consoled himself, it didn't hurt. Maybe at the end, when it's my turn, it will hurt. But not yet. He uncrossed his legs, crossed them again, and leaned back a little in the sofa, his hands at his sides. He felt his pulse beating, slow and strong, in his groin. I suppose, he told himself, the precise word is fear. You know there are rocks ahead, and that's that. Navigate, eyes on the sea, feel the breeze in your face and salt on your lips, but don't be fooled. Know.

I have to say something, he thought. Something that has nothing to do with what I'm feeling. Something that will let her take over the helm again, or, rather, that will let me see her there again. After all, she's the one giving the orders, and we're still a long way from my watch.

He tore the card in two and put the pieces on the table. There were no comments. Matter closed.

"I still don't see it clearly," said Coy. "If there's no treasure, why is Nino Palermo interested in a ship that sank in 1767?"

"People who search for sunken ships aren't only after treasure." Now Tánger was close, sitting in a chair opposite Coy, leaning forward to narrow the distance between them. "A ship that sank two and a half centuries ago can be of great interest if it's well preserved. The State pays the costs.... They organize traveling exhibitions.... There's more than gold in the galleons. Consider the collection of Oriental porcelain on board the *San Diego,* for example. Its value is incalculable...." She paused, lips parted, before continuing. "Besides, there's something more. The challenge. You understand? A sunken ship is an enigma that fascinates a lot of people."

"Yes. Palermo talked about that. The 'green murkiness below,' he called it. And all the rest."

Tánger nodded, serious, grave, as if she knew the meaning of those words. And yet it was Coy who had been on sunken ships, as well as on ships afloat . . . and on grounded ships. Not her.

"Besides," Tánger reminded him, "no one knows what was on the *Dei Gloria*."

Coy let a sigh escape.

"So maybe there is a treasure after all."

She imitated Coy's sigh, although maybe not with the same motivation. She arched her eyebrows mysteriously, like someone exhibiting the wrapping that hides a surprise.

"Who knows?"

She was leaning toward him, close to him, and her expression lighted her freckled face, lending it the complicitous air of a determined little boy, an elemental, sharply physical attractiveness composed of flesh and young, vibrant cells, and golden tones and soft colors that imperiously demanded proximity and touching and brushing of skin against skin. Again blood throbbed in Coy's groin, and this time it wasn't fear. Again that flash of light. Again that certainty. So he let himself drift with the current, without concessions or regrets. At sea all roads are long. After all—and this was his advantage—he had no crew whose ears he had to stop with wax, no one to lash him to the mast to enable him to withstand the voices singing on the reefs, no gods to affect him unduly with their hatred or their favor. He was, he calculated in a quick summing up, fucked, fascinated, and alone. Under those conditions, this woman was as good a course to follow as any.

THE afternoon was fading, and the yellow light that first illuminated the low clouds and then snaked across Atocha station, covering the intricate reflections in the labyrinth of track with elongated horizontal shadows, now filled the room, outlining Tánger's profile as she bent over the table, casting her dark silhouette beside

Coy's on the paper of the Naval Hydrographic Institute's nautical chart number 463A.

"Yesterday," he recapitulated, "we identified a latitude: 37°32′ N. . . . That allows us to draw an approximate line, knowing that the moment she went down the *Dei Gloria* was somewhere on that imaginary line between Punta Calnegre and Cabo Tiñoso, between one and three miles off the coast. . . . Maybe more. That can give us soundings of one to three hundred feet."

"In fact it's less than that," Tánger put in.

She was following Coy's statements about the chart with close attention. Everything was as professional as if they were in the chartroom of a ship. With pencil and parallel rulers they had drawn a horizontal line that started at the coast, a mile and a half above Punta Calnegre, and ran to Cabo Tiñoso below the great sandy arc formed by the gulf of Mazarrón. The depth, which was gentle and sloping on the west side, increased as the line neared the rocky coast farther east.

"In any case," Coy emphasized, "if the ship is too far down, we won't be able to locate her with our means. Much less dive down to what's left of her."

"I told you yesterday that I figure it at a maximum of two hundred feet. . . ."

Cold and silence, Coy remembered. And that greenish murk Nino Palermo had referred to. He could feel on his skin the sensation of his first deep dive twenty years before, the silvery light of the surface seen from below, the bluish and then green sphere, the gradual loss of color, the pressure gauge on his wrist, with the needle indicating the increasing internal and external pressure on his lungs, and the sound of his own breathing in his chest and eardrums, inhaling and exhaling air through the regulator. Cold and silence, naturally. And also fear.

"Even one hundred sixty-five feet is too much," he said. "That dive will take equipment we don't have, or brief dives with long decompression periods, something both uncomfortable and dangerous. Let's say that the reasonably safe limit, in our case, is one hundred thirty. Not a foot more."

She was still bent over the chart, thoughtful. He watched her chew a thumbnail. Her eyes were following the depths marked along the pencil line drawn by Coy, which ran almost twenty miles. Some of the numbers indicating depths were accompanied by a letter: S, M, R. Sand and mud bottoms, with occasional rock. Too sandy and too muddy, he thought. In two and a half centuries that kind of bottom could cover a lot of things.

"I think it will be enough," she said. "It will do for forty."'

I'd like to know where she gets that kind of certainty, he thought. The only sure thing about the sea—Coy, like many sailors referring to its physical attributes, sometimes thought of it as feminine, *la mar,* though he had never thought of giving it a female personality—was that nothing about it was sure. If you managed to do things right, if you stowed the cargo properly, set the correct heading for bad weather, and moderated the engines, and if you didn't steam through raging waves and a wind that was force 9 on the Beaufort scale, the bad-humored old bastard—*el mar*—might tolerate intruders.... But challenge him? Never. When it came to a showdown, he always won.

"I don't believe it's any more than that." Tánger again.

She seemed to have forgotten about Zas and her apartment, Coy noted with amazement. She was focused on the legends of degrees, minutes, and tenths of a minute that bordered the charts, and once again he admired that apparent willpower. He heard her speaking the appropriate words, with no boasting or unnecessary verbiage. If this is normal, I'll eat my left ball, he said to himself. No woman can be as much in control of herself as she seems to be. She's harassed, she has just been given a sinister warning, and she's high as a kite, scribbling notes on a nautical chart. She's either a schizophrenic or, to put it another way, an extraordinary woman. In either case, it's obvious that she can hold her own, that she's capable, after everything she's been through, of standing here and wielding that pencil and compass as cold-bloodedly as a surgeon wields a scalpel. Maybe she's the one doing the harassing after all, and Nino Palermo, the melancholy dwarf, the Berber chauffeur, and the secretary—and me, for that matter—are just members of her chorus, or her victims. All of us.

He tried to concentrate on the chart. Having correlated the latitude with the corresponding parallel, they now needed to situate the longitude: the point where that parallel intersected the meridian. The trick was to determine *which* meridian it was. Conventionally, in the same way the line of the Equator constitutes zero parallel for calculating latitude north or south, the Greenwich meridian is universally considered 0°. Nautical longitude is also measured in degrees, minutes, and seconds, or tenths of minutes, counting 180° degrees to the left of Greenwich for longitude west and 180° to the right for longitude east. The problem was that Greenwich hadn't always been the universal reference.

"The longitude seems to be clear," Tánger answered: "4°51′E."

"I don't see that it's clear. In 1767 the Spanish didn't use Greenwich as the prime meridian. . . ."

"Of course they didn't. First it was Hierro island, but then every country ended up using their own. Greenwich didn't become the universal reference until 1884. That's why Urrutia's chart, printed in 1751, has scales for four different longitudes: Paris, Tenerife, Cádiz, and Cartagena."

"Well"—Coy looked at her with respect—"you know a lot about this. Almost as much as I do."

"I've tried to study it. It's my job. If you look carefully, you can find everything in books."

Coy silently questioned that. He had read about the sea all his life, and he had never found anything there about a porpoise's scream of anguish as it leaps through the water with one flank ripped away by an orca's teeth. Or about the shortest night in his life, as the light of dawn blended into dusk on the reddish horizon of the Oulu inlet a few miles from the Arctic circle. Or the song of the Kroomen, black stevedores on the aft superstructure one moonlit night near Pointe-Noire, in the Congo, with holds and deck stacked with trunks of okoume and akaju wood. Or the terrifying clamor of a sudden storm on the Bay of Biscay, when sky and water were indistinguishable beneath a curtain of gray spume, fifty-foot seas, and an eighty-knot wind, with the waves crumpling the containers on deck as if they were paper before tearing them loose and sweeping them overboard, the sailors with watch duty clinging somewhere on the bridge, terrified, and the rest of the crew in their cabins, tossed across the deck into the bulkheads, vomiting like pigs. It was like jazz, really, the improvisations of Duke Ellington, the tenor sax of John Coltrane, or the percussion of Elvin Jones. You couldn't read that in a book either.

Tánger had unfolded a map with less detail, much more general than the others, and was referring to imaginary vertical lines on it.

"It can't be Paris," she said. "That meridian passes through the Balearic Isles, and in that case the ship would have gone down halfway between Spain and Italy. Or Tenerife, because that would put it in the middle of the Atlantic. That leaves Cádiz and Cartagena. . . ."

"It isn't Cartagena," Coy said.

He could see that at a glance. If the *Dei Gloria* had sunk almost five degrees east of that meridian, she would have been too far out to sea, almost two hundred and fifty miles farther, in depths—he leaned a little closer to the chart—of 9,850 feet.

"Then it has to be Cádiz," she stated. "They found the ship's boy the next day, some six miles south of Cartagena. Calculating the longitude from there, it all comes together. The chase. The distance."

Coy looked at the chart, trying to estimate the drift of the survivor in his skiff. He calculated distance, wind, and currents. Then nodded. Six miles was a logical distance.

"If that's so," he concluded, "The wind would have shifted to the northwest."

"It's possible. In his statement, the boy said that the wind veered at dawn. . . . Is that normal in that area?"

"Yes, the southwesterlies, which we call *lebeches* here, often blow in the afternoon, and sometimes through the night, which was, according to you, what happened during the chase of the *Dei Gloria*. In the winter the wind tends to veer to the northwest and blow offshore in the mornings. A west wind or a mistral could push it to the southeast."

He watched her out of the corner of his eye. Again she was chewing a thumbnail, her eyes fixed on the chart. Coy tossed down his pencil and it rolled across the paper.

"Besides," he said, "we should throw out anything that doesn't fit your hypothesis. . . . Right?"

"It isn't a question of my hypothesis. The normal thing would be for them to calculate the longitude from the Cádiz meridian. Look."

She unfolded another of the reproductions of the Urrutia chart she had brought from the Museo Naval that morning. With a blunt-tipped index finger, she followed the different meridians as she explained to Coy that Cádiz, first in that city's observatory and then in the observatory of San Fernando, had been the prime meridian Spanish sailors used in the second half of the eighteenth century and a good part of the nineteenth. The San Fernando meridian, however, was not used until 1811, so that a reference in 1767 was still the line from pole to pole that passed through the observatory located in the Guardiamarinas castle in Cádiz.

"So it was natural for the captain of the *Dei Gloria* to use Cádiz as a meridian to measure longitude. Look. That way all the figures fit, especially that 4°51′ the ship's boy gave as the last known position of the *Dei Gloria*. If we count east from the Cádiz meridian, the point where the ship went down would be here. You see? Right here, east of Punta Calnegre and south of Mazarrón."

Coy studied the chart. It was relatively sheltered and near the coast, not the worst area.

"That's on the Urrutia chart," he said. "What about the modern ones?"

"That's where things get complicated, because when Urrutia put together his *Atlas Marítimo* longitude was established with less precision than latitude. They still hadn't perfected the marine chronometer that allowed an exact calculation. So errors of longitude tend to be greater.... Cabo de Palos, where you immediately noticed an error of a couple of minutes latitude, is at longitude 0°41.3′ to the west of the Greenwich meridian. To situate it with regard to the Cádiz meridian on modern charts you have to subtract the difference in longitude between Cádiz and Greenwich. Isn't that right?"

Coy agreed, amused and expectant. Not only had Tánger learned her lesson well, she could calculate degrees and minutes with the ease of a sailor. He himself would not have been able to keep all that information in his head. He realized that she needed him for the practical aspects of the project more than anything else, and for confirming her own calculations. Navigating on paper in a fifth-floor apartment across from Atocha station wasn't the same as being at sea on the heaving deck of a ship. He focused on the penciled annotations she had written on a notepad.

"That gives us," Tánger explained, "a position of 5°50′ from Palos with respect to the Cádiz meridian on modern charts. But on Urrutia's, the position is 5°34′, you see.... So we have a margin of error of two minutes in the latitude and sixteen in longitude. I've used the correction tables given in Néstor Perona's *Aplicaciones de Cartografía Histórica*. If you apply them along the coast from Cádiz to Palos, it allows us to situate each of Urrutia's positions with respect to Cádiz at contemporary positions relative to Greenwich."

The twilight had by now retreated to the walls and ceiling of the room, covering the table with angular shadows, and Tánger interrupted what she was doing to turn on a lamp, illuminating the center of the chart. Then she crossed her arms and stood looking at what she'd drawn.

"Applying the corrections, the position to the east of the Cádiz meridian that the ship's boy reported for the *Dei Gloria* would be 1°21′ west of Greenwich on modern charts. Of course, this isn't absolutely correct, and the margins of reasonable error would leave a rectangle a mile long and two wide. That is our search area."

"You don't think that's too small?"

"As you said the other day, they undoubtedly took their position from land bearings. Using the same chart and a compass, that allows us to refine the location."

"It isn't that simple. Their ship's compass may have been off; we don't know whether the magnetic declination was significant in those days, and they may have had to rush the reading. Lots of things could throw off the calculations. There's no assurance that yours are going to coincide with theirs."

"We have to try it, don't we?"

Coy studied the area on the chart, trying to translate it into seas. He was considering a search zone of three to five square miles, a difficult task if the waters were murky or time had deposited too much mud and sand over the wreck. Sweeping the area could take a month at least. He used the pair of compasses to calculate longitude east with respect to Cádiz on the Urrutia, then turned to the modern chart 463A and transposed that figure to longitude west from Greenwich, then transferred the estimate back to the Urrutia. He consulted the correction tables Tánger had drawn up. Everything was within acceptable margins.

"Maybe it can be done," he said.

Tánger hadn't missed a single detail of his movements. She took up a pencil to draw a rectangle on chart 463A.

"The idea is that the *Dei Gloria* is somewhere in this band. At a depth that varies from sixty-five to one hundred thirty feet."

"What's the bottom like? I suppose you've checked that."

She smiled before unfolding a large-scale chart, number 4631, corresponding to the Gulf of Mazarrón from Punta Calnegre to Punta Negra. Coy observed that it was a recent edition, with corrections of warnings to sailors dated that same year. The scale was very large and detailed, and every sounding was accompanied by the corresponding nature of the sea floor. It was the most precise reading available for the zone.

"Sandy mud and some rock. According to the references, relatively clear."

Coy set the compasses on the scale at the side, calculating the area again. One mile by two, off Punta Negra and the Cueva de los Lobos. Considering that a minute of longitude was equal to 0.8 miles in that location, the sector was defined between 1°19.5′ and 1°22′W, and between 37°31.5′ and 37°32.5′N. He observed with pleasure the familiar ocher-colored coast, the water growing bluer over the sandbanks as they descended from the coast. He compared those drawings with his own recollections, mentally situating references of inland mountains on the circles of topographical levels that clustered closer together on the peaks of Las Víboras and Los Pájaros, and on Morro Blanco.

"This is all very relative," he said after a moment. "We can't be sure of anything until we're on the water, setting our position with the charts and the bearings we take on land. It's pointless to define the area of search from here. All we have now is an imaginary rectangle drawn on paper."

"How long would it take us to sweep that?"

"Us?"

"Of course." She held the pause. "You and me."

Coy smiled, barely, and shook his head.

"We'll need someone else," he said. "We'll need El Piloto."

"Your friend?"

"Him. More water has dripped off his T-shirts than I've sailed on in a lifetime."

Tánger asked him to tell her about his friend, and Coy did so, very superficially, with that slight hint of a smile as the memories returned. He talked briefly about his own boyhood, about the graveyard of ships with no name, about his first cigarette and the thin, tan, prematurely gray sailor, about their dives looking for amphoras, their fishing trips, about waiting at dawn for squid that came to the Punta de la Podadera to sleep. El Piloto, his wineskin, his black tobacco, and his boat rocking on the ocean swell. Or maybe he didn't say as much as he thought he did, maybe he only briefly recounted some unconnected episodes and his memories did the rest, crowding together in the line of that smile. And Tánger, who was listening attentively without missing a gesture or a word, realized what that name meant to Coy.

"You said he has a boat."

"The *Carpanta:* a forty-six-foot sailboat with a midship cockpit, a stern deck, a sixty-horsepower engine, and an air compressor."

"Would he rent it?"

"He does that sometimes. He has to live."

"I mean to us. To you and me."

"Of course. He'd scuttle the boat if I asked him." Coy thought for a moment. "Well, maybe not scuttle it. But anything else I asked."

"I hope that won't be much," Tánger seemed uneasy. "In this first phase we'll have limited resources. We'll be using my savings."

"We'll manage," Coy soothed her. "In any case, if the ship is lying at the depth you say, the equipment we'll need to look for her will be minimal. We can get along with a good fishing sounding device and an aquaplane tow; you do that with a sheet of plywood and one hundred sixty-five feet of line."

"Perfect."

She didn't ask if his friend was trustworthy. She just looked at Coy as if his word were a guarantee.

"Besides," Coy said, "El Piloto was a professional diver. If you guarantee him enough salary to cover his costs, and a reasonable percentage if there are profits, we can count on him."

"Of course I'll guarantee it. As for you. . . ."

He looked into her eyes, expecting her to continue, but though she held his gaze she said nothing. There is the spark of a smile hiding inside there, he told himself. She can smile because now she has two sailors and a ship and a rectangle of one mile by two drawn on a nautical chart. Or maybe . . .

"We already talked about my share," said Coy. "For the present you're covering my expenses, right?"

She stood motionless, looking at him with the same expression and the little spark that seemed to dance in the depths of her navy-blue irises. It's just an effect of the light, he thought. Maybe the twilight, or the reflection of the lamp.

"Of course," she said.

HE decided to sleep there, and did so without either of them saying much about it. They worked till very late, and finally she thrust back her elbows and rolled her head as if her neck pained her. She smiled a little at Coy, exhausted and distant, as if everything on the table beneath the cone of lamplight—the navigational charts, the notes, the calculations—had ceased to interest her. Then she said, I'm tired, I can't do any more, and got up, looking around her oddly, as if she had forgotten where she was. Her eyes came to a stop, however, and darkened when she came to the spot where the corpse of Zas had lain. She seemed to remember then, and unexpectedly, in the same way someone carelessly half-opens a door, Coy saw her stumble forward, and he captured the shiver that traveled across her skin as if a current of cold air had blown through the window, the supporting hand on a corner of the table, the helpless look that darted from object to object, seeking someplace to shelter until she composed herself, just before her eyes reached Coy. By then she seemed master of herself again, but he had already opened his mouth to suggest, I can stay if you want, or, Maybe it would be better not to leave you alone tonight, or something like that. He froze, mouth open, because at that moment she moved her shoulders in an almost questioning way, searching his eyes. Still he said nothing, and she repeated the gesture, the deliberate way she had of shrugging her shoulders that she seemed to reserve for questions whose answers were unimportant. Then he did say, "Maybe I should stay," and she said, "Yes, of course," in a low voice, with her usual coldness, and nodded her head as if she thought the suggestion appropriate, before going to her bedroom and returning with a military sleeping bag—an authentic green military sleeping bag that she unrolled on the sofa, placing a cushion beneath it for a pillow. With a minimum of words, she explained where he would find a clean towel, before going to her room and closing the door.

Below, in the distance, through darkness that stretched beyond the station, the long chains of train lights moved with deceptive slowness. Coy went to the window and stood there quietly, watching the muted glow from the farthest suburbs, the streetlights below him, the headlights of a few cars traveling along the deserted street. The sign on the gas station was still illuminated, but he saw no one except the attendant, who was stepping out of his little cubicle to serve a customer. Neither the melancholy dwarf nor the treasure hunter was in sight.

Tánger had left the tape playing. It was a sad, slow melody Coy had never heard. He went to the player and checked the title: "*Après la pluie.*" He didn't know anything about this E. Satie—maybe some friend of Justine's—but the title seemed appropriate. Yes, after the rain. The music made him think of the wet deck of a ship becalmed on a gray sea where concentric circles of the last drops of rain lingered on the water, small undulations resembling the movement of medusas on the surface, or minute waves of radar, and of someone watching all that whose hands rested on a wet gunnel as somber clouds, low and black, receded on the line of the horizon.

He felt nostalgic as he looked up, vainly hoping to see a star. The glow of the city veiled the sky. He made a shield of one hand, which he lined up beneath his eyes, and when they adjusted he could see one or two tiny, weak points glinting in the distance. Above cities, when you could see anything at all, the stars always seemed dull, different, stripped of their brilliance and meaning. Above the sea, however, they were useful references, highways, companions. Coy had spent long hours of his watch on the flying bridge watching Sirius disappear in the springtime, and the seven Pleiades drop from the evening sky in the west and reappear on the other end of the night in the east in the early-morning summer sky. He even owed his life to the stars and, during a brief and intense period in his youth, they had helped him avoid imprisonment in Haifa. Before dawn one dreary morning, about to enter Lebanese waters on board the *Otago,* a small cargo ship navigating without lights between Larnaca and Saida in order to run the Israeli blockade, and before reaching the lighthouse at Ziri—one flash every three seconds, visible at six miles—Coy, as he awaited the appearance of Castor and Pollux on the eastern horizon, had sighted the black silhouette of a patrol boat lurking in the shadow of the dark line of the coast toward which they were sailing. Their three-thousand-ton ship—registered in Monrovia, with a Spanish owner, a Norwegian captain, and a Greek and Spanish crew—which officially transported salt between Torrevieja, Trieste, and Piraeus, cut her engines and lay to while Captain Raufoss, with night binoculars at his eyes and Viking curses on his lips, confirmed that it was indeed a patrol boat. Slowly he changed course, hard to starboard and easing forward, with not so much as a cigarette lighted on board in order to slip away discreetly in the darkness, an anonymous echo on the Israeli radar, and head back toward Cape Greco. The visual acuteness of the young second officer with the ink not yet dry on his license had been rewarded by Raufoss with a bottle of Balvenie malt and a clap on the back that Coy felt for a week. Sigur Raufoss, stocky, sanguine, redheaded, and an excellent sailor, had been his first captain as an officer. Like most men of his nationality, he lacked the arrogance of English captains and surpassed them in professional competence. He didn't trust pilots unless they had gray in their hair, was capable of threading his ship through the eye of a needle, and was never sober when docked or drunk when sailing. Coy served with him in the Mediterranean for three hundred and seven days, and then he changed ship just in time, two voyages before Captain Raufoss's luck ran out. Carrying loose scrap from Valencia to Marseilles, the *Otago*'s cargo shifted during a force 10 winter mistral in the gulf of Léon. The ship capsized, going to the bottom with fifteen men aboard, leaving no trace other than an SOS picked up by the shore radio at Mont Saint-Loup over channel 16 VHF: *Otago* at 42°25′N and 3°53.5′E. Lying to at sea, listing badly. Mayday. Mayday. Afterward, not a scrap floating, not a life jacket, not a marker buoy. Nothing. Only silence, and the impassive sea that hides its secrets for centuries.

He looked at his watch: not yet midnight. The door of Tánger's room was closed and the music had stopped. Coy felt the silence that followed rain. He ambled aimlessly around the room, appraising the Tintins on their shelf, the carefully aligned books, the postcard of Hamburg, the silver cup, the framed snapshot. That Coy was not a brilliant fellow, and that he knew it, is clear. Nevertheless, he had a unique sense of humor, a natural ability to make fun of himself and his clumsiness. He had a Mediterranean fatalism that permitted him to cut a deal and warm himself at any fire. That awareness, or certainty, may have made him less stupid than another man would have been in the identical situation. That, added to his training in observing the sky and the sea and the radar screen for signals to interpret, had sharpened a certain kind of instinct or intuition. In that context, every single thing in that house seemed filled with meaning. They were, he decided, revealing milestones in a biography that was apparently straightforward, solid, free of fissures. And yet, some of those objects, or the fragile aspect of their owner they revealed like the tip of an iceberg, could also inspire tenderness. Unlike the attitudes, words, and maneuvers she flourished to achieve her goals, in the small signs spread about the apartment, in her equivocal irrelevance, in all the circumstances that involved Coy as witness, actor, and victim, the absence of calculation was evident. Those clues were not exhibited in any deliberate manner. They were part of a real life, and had a lot to do with a past, with memories that were not explicit but that undoubtedly sustained all the rest—the little girl, the soldier, the dreams, memory. In the frame, the blonde girl was smiling within the protective tanned arm of the man in the white shirt. The smile had an obvious relationship with others Coy knew, including the dangerous ones, but it also registered a marked freshness that made it different. Something luminous and radiant. Life filled with unrevealed possibilities, highways to travel, perhaps even happiness. It was as if in that photo she was smiling for the first time, in the same way the first man awakened on the first day and saw around him the newly created world, when everything was still to be lived, starting with a unique zero meridian, and there were no cell phones or black seas or AIDS virus or Japanese tourists or police.

Basically, that was the question. Once I smiled like that, too, he thought. And those modest objects scattered around—the dented cup, the photograph of the girl with the freckles—were the remains of the shipwreck of her smile. To sense that was to feel something turn inside him, as if the music no longer playing had slowly seeped through his gut to suffuse his heart. Then he saw himself, forsaken, as if it were he and not Tánger who smiled in the snapshot with the man in the white shirt. No one can ever protect another person. He recognized himself in that image, and that made him feel as if he were orphaned, loyal, and furious. First came a feeling of personal desolation, of extreme loneliness that rose from his chest to his throat and eyes, and then a clear, intense anger. He looked at the place where Zas had lain, and then his eyes fell on Nino Palermo's card, ripped in two and left on the table. He stood stock-still. Then he consulted his watch again, matched the two pieces, and picked up the telephone. He dialed the number, taking his time, and after a while heard the voice of the seeker of sunken ships. He was in the bar of his hotel, and of course he would be happy to meet Coy in fifteen minutes.

As the uniformed doorman saw Coy come through the glass double doors and enter the vestibule of the Palace Hotel, he stared with suspicion at his sneakers and the frayed jeans below the uniform jacket. Coy had never been there before, so he went up the steps, walked across the rugs and white marble floor, then stopped, indecisive. To the right was a large antique tapestry and to the left the door to the bar. He walked toward the center rotunda and paused beneath the columns that encircled the area. In the rear, an invisible pianist was playing *"Cambalache,"* and the music was muffled by the quiet hum of conversation. It was late, but there were people at nearly all the tables and sofas, well-dressed people; men in jacket and tie, bejeweled, attractive women, impeccable waiters gliding soundlessly by. A small cart displayed several bottles of champagne chilling on ice. All very elegant and correct, he could appreciate. Like a movie.

He walked a few steps into the rotunda, ignoring a waiter who asked if he would like a table, and steered a direct course toward Nino Palermo, whom he had glimpsed sitting on a sofa beneath the large central chandelier suspended from the glass cupola. Palermo was accompanied by the secretary Coy had seen at the auction in Barcelona, now dressed in a short dark skirt, legs revealed to mid-thigh, knees modestly together and inclined to one side, high-heeled shoes. The model of the perfect secretary on a night out with the boss, page five, dress code section. She was sitting between Palermo and two Nordic types. The seeker of sunken ships did not see Coy until he was very close. Then he stood, buttoning his double-breasted jacket. His ponytail was tied with a black ribbon, and he was wearing a dark-gray suit, silk tie against a pale-blue shirt, and black shoes; the gold chains and watch glittered more brightly than his smile. The ring with the ancient coin also gleamed when he reached out to shake Coy's hand. Coy ignored it.

"It's good that you've come to your senses..." Palermo said.

The friendly tone froze on his lips in mid-sentence, his outstretched hand disregarded. He looked at it, amazed to see it untouched, and slowly pulled it back, confused, inquisitively studying Coy with his bicolored eyes.

"You've gone too far," said Coy.

The other's confused grimace intensified to arrogance.

"So you're sticking with her?" he asked coldly.

"That's beside the point."

Palermo seemed to reflect. He made a show of looking sideways at the two men waiting on the sofa.

"You said yesterday that you were . . . Didn't you? Out of it. And when you telephoned a while ago . . . God almighty. I thought you were agreeing to work for me."

Coy drew a deep breath. Palermo was more than a head taller than he. Coy stood looking up at him, his large hands hanging threateningly at his sides. He rocked a little on his toes.

"You've gone too far," he repeated.

The greenish pupil was more dilated than the brown one, but both seemed icy. Palermo again looked toward his companions. His mouth twisted scornfully.

"I never dreamed you were coming to make a scene," he said. "You're . . . an ass. That's it. You're making an ass of yourself."

Coy nodded slowly. Twice. His hands were a little farther now from his sides, and he felt the muscles of his shoulders, arms, and stomach tense as tight as a fisherman's knotty knuckles. Palermo had begun to turn away, as if to end the conversation.

"I can see," he said, "that the bitch has her hooks in you good."

With those last words, he made a move toward the sofa, but that's all it was, a move, because Coy had already made a quick calculation. He knew that Palermo was taller, and that he wasn't weak, or alone, and that it was best to hit a man while he's still talking because his reflexes are slower then. So again Coy rocked on his toes, composed a quick smile to give Palermo a sense of confidence, and in the same instant kneed him in the testicles, so brutally that a second later, when Palermo was bent over with the breath knocked out of him and his face congested, Coy was able without much trouble to deliver a second blow, a head butt to Palermo's nose, which crunched beneath his forehead as if someone had broken a piece of furniture. Coy had learned that move with choreographic precision during a dustup in the port of Hamburg. The third move, in the improbable case that the adversary was still in the game, consisted of another knee to the face; and as a finale, all your tricks and a few of the pipe-fitters' thrown in. But he saw that it wasn't necessary: Palermo had dropped to his knees, white and loose as a sack of potatoes, his face against Coy's thigh, staining his jeans with the shockingly red blood streaming from his nose.

In the next five seconds, all hell broke loose. The secretary began to scream and scooted back in the sofa, so unnerved in her scrambling that she showed her panties, which were black. The two foreigners, at first stupefied, jumped up to help the downed man. As for Coy, he could see out of the corner of his eye that all the waiters in the room, and a few of the customers, were running toward him, and he found himself tackled, pinned by strong hands that lifted him off the ground and hustled him toward the door as if they intended to lynch him before the indignant and astonished eyes of employees and clients. The glass doors opened, someone shouted something about calling the police, and at that moment Coy saw, in succession, the illuminated façade of the building of the Cortes, the green lights of the taxis parked at the door, and to their mutual surprise, the melancholy dwarf, staring at him from the nearest traffic light. Coy was unable to see more, because someone had a tight grip on his hair, but even so he caught a glimpse of the Berber chauffeur's tough face—everyone in the cast seemed to be at the Palace that night—before he felt a furious tug that snapped his head back and then came one, two, three, four, professional punches to the solar plexus that took his breath away. He fell to the pavement, gasping for air and his mouth working like a fish out of water. LNA: the Law of No Air, or... you're never there when I need you. At that point he heard a police siren and said to himself: You've torn it now, sailor. You'll get six years and a day for this, and the girl will have to dive by herself. Then after several fruitless attempts to catch his breath he was able to get some air, although when he did it hurt as it rasped in and out of his lungs. His lower ribs seemed to move of their own accord, and he thought one was broken. Sonofabitch. He was still on the ground, face down, when someone handcuffed his wrists—click-click—behind his back. He was consoled by the thought that for the next few days, Nino Palermo, every time he looked in the mirror, would remember Tánger Soto, him, and poor Zas. He was pulled to his feet as a whirling blue light hit him full in the face. He missed Gallego Neira, the Tucumán Torpedoman, and the rest of Crew Sanders. But these were different times, and different ports.

VI

Of Knights and Knaves

There is a wide variety of puzzles about an island in which certain inhabitants . . . always tell the truth and others . . . always lie.

—Raymond M. Smullyan, WHAT IS THE NAME OF THIS BOOK?

The gypsy went away after insisting a little longer, and Coy thought as he watched her go that perhaps he should have let her read his palm and tell his fortune. She was a woman of middle age, her dark-skinned face furrowed with an infinity of wrinkles, her hair pulled back with a silver comb. Big-boned, fat, the hem of her skirt whirled as she swung her hips gracefully, stopping to offer sprigs of rosemary to the travelers returning along the palm-shaded avenue that spilled down behind the castle of Santa Catalina in Cádiz. Before she left, peeved by Coy's refusal to take the rosemary in exchange for a few coins, or to allow her to tell his fortune, the gypsy murmured a curse, half joking, half serious, that he was now mulling over: "You will have only one journey without cost." Coy was not a superstitious sailor—in this day of the Meteosat and the GPS, few of his calling were—but he maintained certain apprehensions appropriate to life at sea. Maybe for that reason, when the gypsy disappeared beneath the palms on Avenida Duque de Nájera, Coy contemplated his left palm uneasily, before sneaking a look at Tánger, who was sitting at the same table on the terrace talking with Lucio Gamboa, the director of the San Fernando observatory, where the three of them had spent part of the day. Gamboa was a captain in the Navy, but he was in civilian clothes—checked shirt, khaki pants, and very old and faded canvas espadrilles. Cordial but unkempt, nothing about him betrayed his military affiliation. He was chunky, bald, and loquacious, with a scruffy, graying beard and the light eyes of a Norman. He had been talking for hours, showing no signs of fatigue, as Tánger asked questions, nodded, or took notes.

Only one journey without cost. Coy again regarded the lines in his hand, telling himself once more that maybe he should have let the gypsy read his palm. If he didn't like the prediction, he thought, he could change the lines with a razor blade, any way he wanted, like that comic pen-and-paper sailor, Corto Maltés, tall, handsome, gold earring in one ear, whom he wouldn't have minded in the least looking like every time he noticed Tánger's eyes fixed on him. Eyes that at times stopped paying attention to Gamboa's explanations to fall on Coy for a moment, expressionless, serene—confirming that he was still there and that everything was under control.

Coy felt a stab in the lower ribs of his left side, still painful from the Berber chauffeur's punches. The incident had been resolved with thirty-two hours in the jail of the de Retiro police station and charges of disturbing the peace and assault and battery, which would come to trial in a few months' time. Nothing stood in the way, therefore, of his traveling to Cádiz with Tánger. As for Nino Palermo, after leaving the clinic where he was given emergency treatment for his nose, which the doctor on call diagnosed as badly bruised but not broken, he had made the interesting decision not to go to his lawyers to file legal proceedings. That was far from reassuring though, because, as Tánger had said when Coy left the police station and found her waiting at the door, Palermo was the kind of man who didn't need police or courts to settle his affairs.

Again he studied his hand. Unlike Tánger, who had a long, clean line crossing her palm, his life, death, and love lines, and whatever the hell the others were, crisscrossed in a wild tangle like the halyards of a sailing vessel after a difficult maneuver in strong winds and high seas, as if someone had shaken them in a dice cup and thrown them out every which way. This made him smile inside. Not even the sharpest gypsy in the world could have made any sense out of those lines. The keys to the voyage, whether without cost or with prompt payment, were hidden not in those lines, but in the eyes that fell on him from time to time. That, he concluded with resignation, was the real journey Athena had arranged for him.

He looked under the table. Tánger's legs were crossed beneath her full blue skirt, and she was slowly swinging a leather-sandaled foot. He observed her freckled ankles, and then her profile, which at that moment was bent over the little notebook in which she was jotting notes with her silver pencil. Behind her, so golden it turned the tips of her hair almost white, the sun was an hour and a half from falling below the line of the Atlantic horizon beyond La Caleta beach, precisely between the castles that stood at either end. Coy contemplated the ancient walls, their empty embrasures, the turrets with rounded cupolas set into the corners, the black track of water that at high tide was licking at rocks worn by centuries of waves. Maintaining a prudent distance from the San Sebastián shoals, a sailboat was moving slowly in the distance, heading north, pushed by a fresh southwester. Force 5, he calculated, as he noted the whitecaps that rippled the sea and dashed small sprays of spindrift onto the isthmus that joined the land with the castle, its enormous lighthouse rising tall behind the merloned walls of ancient batteries. Sky and water were impeccably blue, so luminous they hurt the eyes, though soon they would begin to be streaked with the reddish tones that were the prelude to sunset.

"A couple of things," said Gamboa, "are most unusual about our story."

Coy stopped looking at the sea and paid attention to the conversation. Because of their professions, Tánger and the director of the observatory had previously exchanged a number of calls. They had gone to see him at San Fernando as soon as they arrived from Madrid—a train to Seville and then a rented car to Cádiz—so he could provide some documentation on the *Dei Gloria* and the corsair *Chergui,* and clear up a few obscure points. Afterward, Gamboa had taken them to the old city and treated them to shrimp omelettes at Ca Felipe, on calle La Palma, where fresh fish were displayed to customers under the sign "Nearly all these fish were extras in the films of Captain Cousteau." They had ended up by the ocean, on the terrace at La Caleta.

"I wish it were only a couple of things," sighed Tánger.

Gamboa, smoking a cigarette, laughed, and his Nordic eyes made his bearded face seem boyish. His teeth were crooked and stained by nicotine, with a gap between the incisors. He had an easy laugh for the least thing and nodded his head as he did, as if every pretext were welcome. Despite his Merchant Marine prejudices regarding the Navy, Coy liked Gamboa. Even his pleasant, open way of flirting with Tánger—a gesture, a look, a way of offering her the cigarettes she refused—was inoffensive and likable. When they had called on him late that morning at his office, Gamboa had been happy to discover, as he said with no beating around the bush, how pretty his colleague from Madrid was, and how it was his misfortune that until now he had known her only by telephone and letter. Then he looked Coy over closely before shaking hands, retaining the hand in his grasp, as if touch might allow him to calculate the nature of the relationship between his colleague from the Museo Naval and this unexpected, quiet, short, broad-shouldered individual with large hands and a clumsy gait who was escorting her. She had simply introduced him as a friend who was helping her with the technical aspects of her problem. A sailor with a lot of free time.

"That brigantine," Gamboa continued, "came from America

without protection. . . . And that's strange, considering that because of the English, the corsairs, and the pirates, it was mandated that every merchant ship cross the Atlantic in convoy."

As he spoke, he nearly always addressed Tánger, although at times he turned to Coy, perhaps to avoid making him feel replaced. I gather you don't mind, the gesture said. I don't know your role in this story, friend, but I suppose it won't bother you if I talk to her and smile at her. Get this straight: you two are here for only a short while, and she's attractive. A sailor with free time, or complete dedication, or whatever you are . . . I don't know what there is between you, but I just want to enjoy her a while. A couple of beers and a laugh or two, you know, to charge my batteries. That's what I plan to collect for my services. Before long, she'll be yours again, or whatever part you get, and you can go on testing your luck. After all, life is short, and it isn't often that a woman like this comes along. At least I don't run into them.

"They weren't at war with England at that moment," Tánger pointed out. "Maybe the escort wasn't necessary."

Gamboa, who had just lighted his umpteenth cigarette, exhaled smoke between his front teeth and nodded in agreement. In addition to his military appointment, he was a naval historian. Before being assigned to the observatory, he had been in charge of the historic patrimony of the Navy in Cádiz.

"That could be one explanation," he conceded. "But it still seems strange. . . . In 1767, Cádiz had a monopoly on commerce with America. It wasn't until eleven years later that Charles III issued a decree liberalizing the trade policy, changing the dictate that designated Cádiz as the obligatory port of call for a ship returning directly from America. So the voyage of that brigantine from Havana was slightly illegal, if we read the royal orders strictly. Or at least it was irregular." Reflecting, he took long drags on his cigarette. "The normal thing would have been to call in here before continuing on to Valencia, or whatever the final destination was." Another drag. "And apparently that didn't happen."

Tánger had an answer. In fact, Coy had realized, she seemed to have answers for almost everything. It was as if more than researching new information, she was trying to confirm what she already had.

"The *Dei Gloria,*" she explained, "had the benefit of special status. Don't forget she belonged to the Jesuits, and they had certain privileges. Their ships had specific exemptions; they sailed to America and the Philippines using the Society's captains, pilots, navigation routes, and nautical charts, and they were surrounded by what today we would call fiscal opacity.... That was one of the matters brought against them in the trial for expulsion that was being prepared in secret."

Gamboa was listening attentively.

"So it was the Jesuits, eh?"

"Exactly."

"That would explain several inexplicable things."

She has spent hours, Coy said to himself, in that house I know across from Atocha station, going over and over all this. She has spent days and months lying on that bed I glimpsed once, sitting at the table covered with books and documents, tying up loose ends in that cool head of hers, the way someone plays a game of chess having planned all the moves in advance. Setting courses for all of us. I'm convinced that this conversation, this bearded, smiling man, the landscape here at La Caleta, and maybe even the hours of high tide and low tide, were calculated ahead of time. All she's doing now is outfitting her ship carefully, nailing down every last detail before setting out to sea. Because she is one of those women who don't forget anything on shore. She may never have sailed, but I'm sure that in her imagination she has already dived dozens of times to the wreck of the *Dei Gloria.*

"At any rate," said Gamboa, "it's a pity we don't have more documentation." He turned a little toward Coy. "The archive here in Cádiz is the only one that wasn't sent to the marine archives at Viso del Marqués, where they centralized nearly all the important documents in El Ferrol and Cartagena, postdating what was conserved in the Archivo de Indias in Seville. Here, a pigheaded admiral refused to let go of them. As a result the complete collection was destroyed in a fire, all the papers from the eighteenth and nineteenth centuries, including some original cartography plates of Tofiño."

Gamboa took another drag and chortled jovially.

"Bound to happen, no?" he said to Tánger. "The obligatory fire. But I suppose that lends the charm of adventure to your job."

"Not everything was lost," she replied.

"Not everything, that's true. Some of it had been misplaced. No one knows what we have lying around here. The plans of the *Dei Gloria,* for example, were forgotten, and in a totally illogical place—under mountains of dusty papers in the storeroom for nautical instruments in the shipyards at La Carraca. . . . Thrown in with stuff from scrapped ships, logbooks, charts, and a thousand things that have never been catalogued. I saw them by chance about a year ago, when I was looking for something else. And when I got your telephone call, I remembered. . . . It was pure luck that the ship was constructed here."

In fact, Gamboa clarified to Coy, it wasn't the plans for the *Dei Gloria* herself, but the *Loyola,* her twin, because both were built in Cádiz between 1760 and 1762, within a short period of time. But Lady Luck didn't favor either of them. The *Loyola* was lost in 1763 in a violent storm near Sancti Petri, before her sister ship went down. Funny how things turn out. Very close to the place where she'd been launched only a year before. Some ships are just bad-luck ships, as Coy undoubtedly knew from professional experience. And those two brigantines had a bad star.

Gamboa had provided Tánger with a copy of the plans after he had showed the two of them around the observatory—white facade with columns and cupola shimmering in the sunlight, whitewashed corridors with showcases of antique instruments and nautical and astronomy books, a line on the floor indicating the exact delineation of the Cádiz meridian, and the magnificent library of dark woods and overflowing shelves. There, on a vitrine table that contained works by Kepler, Newton, and Galileo, the *Viaje a la América Meridional* and the *Observaciones* of Jorge Juan and Antonio de Ulloa, as well as other books on eighteenth-century expeditions for measuring a degree of meridian, Gamboa had unfolded various plans and documents. Some copies were meant for Tánger, and the rest, originals difficult to reproduce, she photographed one by one with a small camera she had in her leather purse. She had taken two rolls of thirty-six exposures, her flash reflecting in the paintings on the wall and in the glass of the showcases, while Coy, out of professional curiosity, took a look at the ancient tables of nautical ephemerides and precision instruments scattered around the room, vestiges of a time when the San Fernando observatory was the essential reference in the Europe of the Illustration: a Spencer octant, a Berthoud clock, a Jensen chronometer, a Dollond telescope. As for the *Dei Gloria,* Coy was presented to her when Gamboa, after a deliberate and theatrical pause, pulled out four plans on a scale of 1:55 that he'd had photocopied for Tánger. A slim brigantine one hundred feet in length and with a twenty-five foot beam, she had two masts, square sails, a fore-and-aft sail on the mainmast, and was armed with ten iron four-pounders. Those copies were there before them now, spread on a table on the terrace.

"She was a good ship," said Gamboa, contemplating a distant sail that had passed the beach and was disappearing beyond the castle of Santa Catalina. "As you can appreciate on the plans, she had clean lines and was very seaworthy. A modern ship for her time, constructed of the heart of oak and teak, with the usual flush deck and guns mounted on the deck; five gunports on each side. Swift and trustworthy. If a xebec could catch her, she must have suffered a lot of damage during the Atlantic crossing. Otherwise . . ." Now the observatory director was looking at Tánger with smiling intensity. "That's another point of the mystery. Why she didn't put into Cádiz for repairs?"

Tánger didn't answer. She was playing with her silver pencil, focused on the white cupolas of the resort to their left, built on pilings in the sand.

"And the *Chergui*?" Coy asked.

Gamboa, who was watching the woman, turned slowly. Oh, the matter of the corsair was clear, he answered. And they were in luck, because among the new documents was valuable material. For instance, a copy of the description of the *Chergui,* the original of which had been located in the Privateering and Prizes section in Viso del Marqués. Unfortunately, there were no plans for that ship, but he had found one for a xebec of similar characteristics, the *Halconero,* which was very close in length, armament, and rigging.

"We don't know the place or year of construction," Gamboa explained, taking a folded piece of paper from his shirt pocket, "but we do know that she operated using Algiers and Gibraltar as bases. There are also detailed descriptions of what she looked like, given by her victims or by people who saw her in ports when she was flying British colors—which she changed as the occasion demanded, since she was fitted out by an Algerian businessman and by a Maltese located on Gibraltar. We have evidence that documents the *Chergui*'s fortunes between 1759 and 1766. The most meticulous, however," the observatory director consulted his notes, "was that of don Josef Mazarrasa, captain of a small coastal boat, the *Podenco,* which succeeded in escaping a xebec he identified as the *Chergui* in September 1766, after a skirmish near Fuengirola. Since they were on the point of being boarded, he was able to observe her, much to his displeasure, at close quarters. There was a European on her quarterdeck, whose description may coincide with that of an Englishman known as Slyne, or Captain Mizen, and the rather numerous crew seems to have been composed of Moors and Europeans—the latter undoubtedly English." Again Gamboa consulted his notes. "The *Chergui* was a three-masted xebec with a jib boom and classic poop, paired main and mizzen masts, and a foremast rigged with a lateen sail; she was relatively swift among ships of her class, some one hundred and ten feet in length and with a thirty foot beam. According to this Captain Mazarrasa, who sustained five dead and eight wounded in the encounter, she was carrying four long six-pounders, eight four-pounders, and at least four *pedreros,* devices for throwing rock and scrap iron. It seems she had been fitted out in Algiers with good bronze pieces, old but efficient, off a captured French corvette, the *Flamme.* That armament made her fearsome against ships of lesser tonnage and more fragile lines, like the *Podenco* and the *Dei Gloria.* . . . Supposing, that is, she did in fact meet up with your ship."

"Of that much I'm sure," said Tánger. "They met."

She had stopped gazing at the domes of the resort and was frowning slightly, with a stubborn set to her jaw. Gamboa folded the paper and gave it to her. Then he raised a hand, as if he was not contesting her conviction.

"In that case, the captain of the *Dei Gloria* had to be a pretty cool customer. Not just anyone would have stood up under the pursuit, chosen not to take shelter in Cartagena, and engaged the *Chergui* in almost gunnel-to-gunnel combat. And that voyage from Havana without port calls . . ." Gamboa studied Coy and then the woman, smiling knowingly. "I guess that's what it's all about. No?"

Coy leaned back in the chair over which he had draped his jacket. Why are you asking me, his gesture said. She's the one in charge.

"There are things I want to clear up," said Tánger after a brief silence. "That's all."

Very carefully she put the paper with Gamboa's notes into her handbag. Gamboa sent her a penetrating look. For a moment the observatory director's placid expression seemed to lose its innocence.

"A pretty piece of work, anyway," he said, cautious. "Besides, maybe there was something on board.... I don't know."

He reached for the pack of cigarettes in his pocket. Coy observed that he took more time than necessary, as if he had something in mind he wanted to say.

"Although the truth is," he said finally, "that neither the ship, nor the route, nor the period are good indicators if you're looking for treasure."

"No one's talking about treasure," Tánger said very slowly.

"Of course not. Nino Palermo wasn't talking about that either."

Dead silence. They heard the voices of the fisherman below, working on boats in dry dock, or rowing among the small craft anchored bow to the wind. A dog was racing along the beach, barking at a gull that planed undisturbed before winging off in the direction of the open sea.

"Nino Palermo was here?"

Tánger watched the gull grow smaller in the distance, and she voiced her question only when the bird was nearly out of sight. Gamboa bent his head to light a new cigarette, protecting the flame of the match in both hands. The breeze filtered smoke between his fingers as his pale eyes sparkled with amusement.

"Of course he was here. To pick my brain, like you two."

THE southwester had freshened a couple of knots, Coy calculated. Enough to splash seafoam on the breakwater that ran along the ancient south wall of the city. Gamboa told his story slowly, enjoying the telling. It was obvious he liked the company and was in no hurry. He smoked as he walked between his two companions, pausing from time to time to gaze at the sea, the houses in the barrio of La Viña, the fishermen sitting like statues beside fishing poles lodged among the rocks, contemplating the Atlantic.

"He came to see me about a month ago.... He came, as they all come, everything very ambiguous, lots of smoke and mirrors. Asking about this ship and that document, various things that prevent you from getting a good idea of what they're really looking for." At times Gamboa smiled at Tánger, and the gap in his teeth accentuated the smile. "He brought a very long shopping list, and on it, in eighth or ninth place, camouflaged among other things, was the *Dei Gloria.* I already knew you were on that trail, because we'd talked several times by phone. It was obvious that this Palermo was panting after a fresh clue."

He fell silent, watching a fish struggle at the end of a line. A mojarra. The fisherman, a skinny type with bushy sideburns and wearing a white shirt and suspenders, delicately removed it from the hook and tossed it into a pail, where it lay weakly flicking its tail among other silvery reflections.

"So as soon as Palermo mentioned the *Dei Gloria,* I put it together." Gamboa started walking again. "Then I let him invite me to eat at El Faro, where I listened attentively, nodded, made four or five general comments, gave him information about what I thought were the least important things on his list, and got rid of him."

"What did you tell him about the *Dei Gloria*?" Tánger asked.

The wind pasted the light cloth of her skirt to her thighs and whipped the open neck of her blouse. She was very well favored, but she didn't play the part of the beautiful girl. Or act helpless. Coy liked that. She seemed cool, competent. Talking like old friends with Gamboa: being colleagues, why should we hide anything from each other? Let's talk friend-to-friend. We're civil servants in a hostile world, et cetera, et cetera, and what can I tell you that you don't know? Life is hard and everyone navigates through it as best he can. Of course I'll keep you informed. I owe you that.

She's clever, Coy decided. She's very clever, or maybe so intuitive that it's almost sick, with a sharp sense of ways to manipulate men. He remembered the frigate captain in the Museo Naval in Madrid, his expression as he talked with Tánger in the hallway outside her office. She's obviously one of ours, Admiral. And it came to mind that things were going the same way with the observatory director. One of ours.

Now Gamboa was smiling again, as if her question was unnecessary.

"I told him what I should," he said. "That is, nothing. Whether he believed me, now that I don't know. . . . At any rate, he was very guarded." He turned toward Coy, as if he expected confirmation of his words. "I suppose you know Nino Palermo."

"He knows him well," she said.

Too quick to point that out, Coy thought. He looked at Tánger, and she was aware he did, because she turned with exaggerated attention toward the ocean. I may know Palermo, he said to himself, but not all that well. You said that a little too fast though, darling. You said that probably a second too soon. And that's not good. Not in a clever girl like you. Too bad that at this point you're still making that kind of mistake. That or you take me for a fool.

"Not that well," Coy answered Gamboa. "In fact, I don't know the guy as well as I'd like to."

"Well, you must be the only one in this business."

"He isn't in this business," said Tánger.

The observatory director stood looking at them. Again he seemed to reflect upon the relationship between them. Finally he spoke to Coy.

"Gibraltarian, with a Maltese father and an English mother . . . that is, one hundred percent pirate genes. I've known Palermo for a long time, since the time I worked classifying archives in the museum in Cádiz. He made one of the attempts to salvage the *Santísima Trinidad,* maybe the most serious. In its time the *Trinidad* was the largest warship in the world, a ship of the line with four bridges and a hundred and forty guns; she sank during the battle of Trafalgar as the English were trying to tow her into Gibraltar." He pointed somewhere out to sea, toward the south. "She's out there still, a little off Punta Camarinal. He tried to do what the Swedes did with the *Wasa,* or the English with the *Mary Rose,* but the attempt, like most of these things, foundered because of the Spanish administration's lack of enthusiasm, that is. . . ."

"Like the dog in the manger," Tánger interjected.

"Exactly. Neither eat nor let eat."

Gamboa threw his cigarette butt into the foam breaking on the rocks of the jetty, and kept talking. Palermo was quite well known in that area. He had that Mafioso look; Coy would understand what he was talking about, very Mediterranean. Morocco was only a few miles away; from Gibraltar and Tarifa you can see it on clear days. That was the frontier of Europe. Palermo had started Deadman's Chest six or eight years before, and was known for being unscrupulous. He had interests in Ceuta, Marbella, and Sotogrande, and he worked with dangerous people on both sides of the Strait, advised by a legal firm specializing in contraband and shell companies that pulled his chestnuts from the fire when things got too hot.

"No one has been able to prove it, but, among other dirty tricks, he's credited with the clandestine sacking of the wreck of the *Nuestra Señora de Cillas,* a galleon out of Veracruz that sank in 1675 in the cove of Sanlúcar with a cargo of silver ingots." Gamboa grimaced. "It wasn't a huge fortune, but during the sacking the divers destroyed the ship, leaving it useless for any serious archaeological research. He's suspected of more than one despicable act like that."

"Is he efficient?" Coy wanted to know.

"Palermo? Extremely efficient." Gamboa looked at Tánger as if he expected her to confirm what he said, but she said nothing. "Maybe the best of the guys we see operating around here. He's worked on wrecks around the world, and made money by combining that with salvaging and scrapping sunken ships. . . . Some time ago he tried to link up with one of the attempts by Fisher, whom he'd worked for as diver on the *Atocha*. They intended to make an all-out effort at the mouth of the Guadalquivir, where they calculated some eighty ships had gone down on their way to unload in Seville with more gold aboard than the Banco de España has. But this isn't Florida; they couldn't get official authorization. There were other problems, too. Palermo is one of those guys who defend the classic doctrine of treasure hunters—since they do all the work and the State merely issues the permits, four-fifths of the proceeds should go to the rescuer. But in Madrid they said no way, and he had the same luck with the council of Andalusia."

Gamboa was enjoying the conversation. He was talkative and this was his terrain, and he gave Coy a long lecture on the role of Cádiz in the history of shipwrecks. Between 1500 and 1820, two to three hundred ships carrying ten percent of all the precious metals brought from America had sunk there. The problem was the murky water, the sand and mud covering the wrecks, and also suspicion on the part of the Spanish state. Even the Navy, he added with a twist of his lips, had a good number of wrecks pinpointed. But some old admirals thought of the sunken ships as tombs that shouldn't be violated.

"How did the interview with Palermo go?" Coy asked.

"It was cordial and cautious on both sides." The observatory director studied Tánger an instant before turning back to Coy. "So you know him, then?"

Coy, who was walking with his hands in his pockets, shrugged.

"She exaggerates a little. The truth is we had, uh . . . superficial contact."

Gamboa looked at him closely, interested.

"Contact, you say?"

"Yes."

"How do you mean, superficial?"

"Just that." Again Coy shrugged. "Limited to the surface."

"He head-butted his nose," Tánger said.

Coy glimpsed a smile through the golden hair the sea breeze was blowing across her face. Gamboa had stopped and looked at them in turn.

"His nose? Go on, you're joking." Now he spoke to Coy with renewed respect. "You have to tell me about that, my friend. I'm dying to know."

Coy told him in a few words, with no adornments. Dog, hotel, nose, police station. When he was through, Gamboa studied him, pensive, amused, scratching his beard.

"Hey! And yet, even for someone who doesn't know his story, Palermo is a dangerous man.... Besides, he has that disturbing way of looking at you; you don't know which eye to focus on." He hadn't taken his own eyes from Coy, as if evaluating his capacity for punching people in the nose. "Superficial contact, you say. Is that right? Superficial."

He laughed. Coy studied Tánger and she held his gaze, the smile still playing on her lips.

"I'm glad someone gave that arrogant bastard a lesson," Gamboa said finally, after they had started walking again. "I already told you that he came by here the way everyone does. Smoke and mirrors, false trails: the Florida Keys, Zahara de los Atunes, Sancti Petri, the Chapitel and Diamante reefs. Even the Vigo estuary and its famous galleons..."

They had left the sea behind and were walking into town along old streets bordering the cathedral, near the brick tower and walls of Santa Cruz. The plaza sloped downhill, with its Christ in a vaulted niche, and lanterns and geraniums and shutters on the balconies of old houses where whitewashed walls, like most in the city, were pocked by wind and dampness from the nearby sea. Almost everything was in shadows, and the light from the setting sun was fading from the tile roofs. The paving of that plaza, Gamboa told Coy, was cobbled with American stones, ballast from ships that plied the route to the Indies.

"As I said," he continued, "going back to Nino Palermo. I had been warned. So I let him wander around without offering any worthwhile clues."

"I appreciate that," said Tánger.

"It wasn't just for you. That sly fox played me a bad turn a while back, when he was on the trail of the four hundred gold and silver bars—though others were talking about a half-million pieces of eight—taken from the *San Francisco Javier*. . . . But in those cases, instead of creating an uproar that doesn't do anyone any good, it's best not to say anything about it, and just keep it to yourself. Our paths will cross again."

They threaded between parked cars blocking the street, passing some rough-looking men along the way. The area was packed with dark little bars filled with unemployed fishermen, scroungers, and beggars. A young boy in sneakers, and with the look of someone who could win the 100-yard dash, followed them for a while, his eye on Tánger's purse, until Coy turned, set his feet in the middle of the street and scowled, at which the boy decided to test the air elsewhere. Prudent, Tánger shifted her purse. Now she carried it tucked against her ribs.

"What is it exactly that Palermo asked you?"

Gamboa stopped to light a cigarette. Again smoke escaped through the incense burner of his fingers.

"Same as you. He was looking for plans." He put away the lighter and turned toward Coy. "In any research involving shipwrecks, plans are of vital importance. If you have them, you can study the structure of the ship, estimate measurements, and all the rest. It isn't easy to get your orientation under water, because what you find, unlike what you see in the movies, tends to be a pile of rotted wood, often buried under sand. Knowing where the bow is, or the length of the waist, or where the hold was, is a big step forward. With plans and a metric tape you can make a reasonable assessment of life down there." He gave Tánger a meaningful look. "Of course, it depends on what you expect to find."

"It isn't a matter of looking for anything, at first," she said. "This is just research. The operative phase will come later, if it comes at all."

A thread of smoke filtered from between Gamboa's nicotine-stained incisors.

"Right. The operative phase." He narrowed his eyes maliciously. "What was the *Dei Gloria*'s cargo?"

Tánger also laughed softly, placing a hand on his arm.

"Cotton, tobacco, and sugar from Havana. You know that perfectly well."

"Sure." Gamboa scratched his beard. "At any rate, if someone locates the ship and goes on to—what did you call it?—the operative phase, everything will also depend on what you're looking for. If it's documents or perishable goods, there is nothing you can do."

"Of course," she said, as imperturbable as if this were a game of poker.

"Paper dissolves, and, poof! *Arrividérci.*"

"Naturally."

Gamboa scratched his whiskers again before taking another drag on his cigarette.

"So . . . Cotton, tobacco, and sugar from Havana, you say?"

His tone was teasing. She raised both hands, like an innocent little girl.

"That's what the cargo manifest says. It isn't great, but it gives you a pretty good idea."

"You were lucky to find it."

"Very much so. It came to Spain among the papers concerning the evacuation from Cuba in 1898. Not to Cádiz, where it would have been lost in the fire, but to El Ferrol. From there it was sent to

Viso del Marqués, where I was able to see it in the Navegación Mercantil section—you know, matters of commerce."

"You were lucky," Gamboa repeated

"I went to see if I could find anything, and suddenly there it was before my eyes. Ship, date, port, cargo, passengers . . . Everything."

Gamboa studied her intently.

"Or almost everything," he said in a bantering tone.

"What makes you think there's something more?" Coy asked.

Gamboa smiled calmly. He shook his head.

"I don't think, friend. I just observe this young woman. . . . And then I weigh Nino Palermo's interest in the same matter. And my own sense of it, because I wasn't born yesterday and I've been at this for years. This voyage from Havana to Valencia without a call at Cádiz—never mind the squeaky-clean Havana manifest you found in Viso del Marqués—smells of an undercover operation. And if we consider the date and who chartered her, the conclusion is obvious: there was something fishy about the *Dei Gloria*. What that corsair sank was anything but an innocent ship."

Having said that, the director of the observatory winked and again laughed as cigarette smoke seeped from between uneven teeth.

"Like her," he added.

He looked at Tánger. Then Coy saw her laugh in turn, the way she had before, with the same ease—intelligent, mysterious, complicitous. Gamboa did not seem the least bit bothered, only amused, like someone tolerant of a naughty little girl who for some reason has your sympathy. And Coy observed that, as in so many other things, she knew how to laugh the right way. So again he felt that vague despair, that sense of being left out of everything, supplanted and uncomfortable. I wish we were already at sea, he thought, far away from all the others, on board ship where she has no choice but to look in my eyes all the time. Her and me. Looking for bars of gold, silver ingots, or whatever the fuck she wants.

Gamboa seemed to sense Coy's discomfort, for he shot him a friendly grin.

"I don't know what she's looking for," he said. "I don't even know whether you know. But in any case, very few things survive for two and a half centuries under water. Shipworm goes after the wood, iron corrodes and gets crusted with scale . . ."

"And what happens to gold and silver?"

Gamboa looked at him with sarcasm.

"She says she isn't looking for that."

Tánger listened in silence. For an instant, Coy caught her serene gaze; she seemed indifferent to their conversation.

"What happens to them?" he persisted.

"The advantage of gold and silver," Gamboa explained, "is that the sea affects them scarcely at all. Silver gets dark, and gold . . . Well. Gold is much appreciated in wrecks. It doesn't oxidize, or turn green, or lose its brilliance or color. You bring it up just as it was when it went to the bottom." He winked, interrupting himself, and then turned to Tánger. "But we're talking about treasures, and that's a big word, don't you think?"

"No one has said anything about treasure," she said.

"Of course not. No one. Not even Palermo. But a buzzard like him isn't motivated by love of art."

"That's Palermo's business, not mine."

"Sure." Now Gamboa addressed Coy, jovial. "Sure."

Callejón de los Piratas, Coy suddenly saw on the front of a building. That narrow street with flaking white walls was called Pirates' Alley. Again he read the name in the ornamental tiles, incredulous, confirming there was no mistake. He'd been in Cádiz before; he knew the area around the port, especially the now-vanished bars on calle Plocia, often frequented in the days of Crew Sanders, but he didn't know this part of the city. And certainly not this alleyway, whose picturesque name nearly made him burst out laughing. Maybe not so picturesque after all. Nothing more appropriate, he reasoned, for a place like this and a pair like them—a sailor without a ship and a woman looking for sunken ships, the two of them roaming about the Phoenicians' Gades, the millenary city from which so many ships and so many men had sailed year after year, century after century, never to return. When you thought about it, it made sense. If the footsteps of pirates and corsairs still sounded off these dark round stones, the ancient ballast of the ships that brought gold from America, then the ghost of the *Dei Gloria* and her crew lost at the bottom of the sea, and Tánger and he, might waken appropriate echoes. Maybe what seemed relegated to certain pages and images, the territory of childhood, the exclusive ambit of dreams, might somehow be possible. Or maybe it was because a certain kind of dream lay waiting among whispers of stone and paper, on tombstones and walls eaten by time, in books that were like doors opened to adventure, in yellowed files that could signify the beginnings of passionate, dangerous days at sea that could multiply one life into a thousand lives, with its Stevenson and Melville phases, and its inevitable Conrad phase. "I have swum through libraries and sailed through oceans," he had read once, a long time ago, somewhere. It could also simply be that all those things were accessible in one form and not another, because there was a woman who gave them meaning. And because beginning from a certain moment, when you cleared a point of land and a part of a man's life lay ahead with wide-open seas, a woman, *the* woman, might be the one reason to look back. The one possible temptation.

He watched Tánger walking on the other side of Gamboa, her purse secured beneath her elbow, eyes lowered, contemplating the ground before her leather sandals, oblivious to street names because she didn't need them—she trod her own streets—her hair still tousled by the sea breeze. The problem, Coy told himself, is that nautical science is completely useless the moment you need to navigate on dry land, or anywhere near a woman. No land or nautical charts give their soundings. Then he asked himself whether Tánger was looking for the magical gold of dreams or the more concrete yellow metal that survived time and shipwrecks unaltered.

"At any rate," Gamboa was saying, focused on Coy, "all recovery of objects from the sea is illegal without an administrative permit."

Legislation in regard to sunken ships, he explained, involved a variety of factors: ownership of the boat and its cargo, historical rights, territorial and international waters, cultural patrimony, and other details. Great Britain and the United States tended to be receptive to private initiative, leaning more toward the business than the cultural end. The Anglo-Saxon principle, he summarized, was search, find, and collect. But in Spain, as in France, Greece, and Portugal, the State was very strict, with constraints that went back to Roman law and the Code of the Siete Partidas.

"Technically," he concluded, "to take even a piece of an amphora is a crime. Simply looking for it is."

They had now come out onto the plaza in front of the cathedral, with its two white towers and neoclassic façade dominating the esplanade. Older couples and mothers with baby carriages strolled beneath the palm trees, and children raced among the tables on the nearby terraces. As the last light was fading, doves flocked to the eaves, where they would spend the night nested among Ionic pilasters. One of them swept very close to Coy's face.

"There's no problem as far as this phase is concerned," said Tánger. "Research doesn't jeopardize anything."

Gamboa's stained teeth showed in another of his placid smiles. It was obvious he was having a good time. You, his expression said, are really laying it on thick. At my age, and with my experience as a ship's captain.

"Of course not," he said.

"Absolutely not!"

"That's what I said."

Tánger walked on a few steps, unperturbed, her eyes still on the ground before her. Coy gazed at the line of her bent head, the nape of her neck. It was deceptively fragile. When he turned toward Gamboa, he realized that the observatory director had been studying him with interest.

"Maybe a little farther along," Tánger said without looking up, "if we find anything, we can propose a plan for a serious search. . . ."

Coy heard Gamboa's low laugh. He was still looking at him.

"That is, if Palermo doesn't get there first."

"He won't."

They walked past a large old house with a faded exterior and a rusted iron balcony above the main door. Coy read the marble plate screwed onto the wall. "In this house died D. Federico Gravina y Nápoli, Admiral of the Fleet, as a result of a wound received on board the *Príncipe de Asturias* in the memorable battle of Trafalgar."

"I just love self-confident girls," Gamboa was saying.

Coy glanced at him. He was speaking to Coy, not to Tánger, and Coy didn't like the friendly sarcasm gleaming in those Norman eyes. You must know what you're getting into, they said. In any case, know or not know, if I were in your shoes I'd keep my eyes open, friend. That is, proceed slowly, and keep dropping your sounding line. There aren't many fathoms beneath the keel, and rocks everywhere. It is obvious that this woman knows what she's looking for, but I doubt you're as clear about it as she is. You only have to compare her words to your silences. You only have to look at your face, and then look at hers.

THEY had said good-bye to Gamboa and were walking through the old shell of the city, looking for a place to eat. The sun had gone down some time ago, leaving a strip of light in the west beyond the roof tiles that stepped down toward the Atlantic.

"This was the place," said Tánger.

Since they'd been alone again, her attitude had changed. More relaxed and natural, as if she'd let down an imaginary guard. Now she paused from time to time as she talked, full blue skirt swinging from the cadence of her steps, as they wound through narrow streets. When he turned to look at her, he saw the pale light of the street lamps reflected in her blue irises.

"Here is where the Guardiamarinas castle stood," she told him.

They had stopped in a street ascending to the Roman theater and the old city wall, beside ruins topped with stone columns and two ogival arches that once had supported a roof. There was a third, semicircular arch a little farther ahead that marked the entrance to an alleyway. The air bore the salt tang of the ocean, which could be heard pounding against the walls beyond, and the smell of ancient stone, urine, and filth. It had the stench, Coy thought, of dark corners in decaying ports that had never seen batteries of halogen lights atop cement towers, places technology and plastic seemed to have passed over, trapping them in dead time like the foul water below the docks, and strewing them with cats and garbage pails, red lights, glowing tips of cigarettes in the shadow, broken bottles on the ground, cheap cocaine, women for so much a quarter-hour, bed not included. Not even the port of Cádiz—on the other side of the city—had any connection with this area now, where former brothels and boardinghouses had been replaced by bars and respectable inns. There were no stalks of bananas piled beside sheds and cranes, no drunken crewmen looking for their ships at dawn, no patrols of shore police or wounded Yankee sailors. Such scenes existed elsewhere in the world, but even there things were different. There were still a few places like Buenaventura, with its narrow streets and fruit stands, its Bamboo bar, its whorehouses and copper-skinned girls in clothes so tight and thin they seemed painted on their bodies. Or Guayaquil, with its lobster cocktails and iguanas running up the trees in the city center to the peal of the bells in the four cathedral clocks, and the tedious night watchmen with lantern and SOS pistol at the waist to warn of pirate attacks. But those were exceptions. Now, for the most part, ports were at some distance from the heart of cities and had been converted into large lots for parking trucks. Ships docked at precise hours to offload their containers, and Filipino and Ukrainian sailors stayed on board watching TV in order to save money.

"The Cádiz prime meridian ran right through where we're standing now," Tánger explained. "It was official for only the twenty years after 1776, before it was moved to San Fernando, but from the middle of the century, on Spanish navigation charts it officially replaced the traditional meridian of Hierro island, which the French had already changed to Paris and the English to Greenwich. That means that if the longitude they established that morning aboard the *Dei Gloria* referred to this line, the brigantine must have sunk at four degrees and fifty-one minutes from where we are now. If we use the corrections in the Perona tables, that is exactly five degrees and twelve minutes east longitude."

"Two hundred and fifty miles," said Coy.

"Exactly."

They took a few steps, passing beneath the arch. One street lamp with a broken glass pane threw yellow light on a window with an iron grill. On the other side, under the open sky, Coy could distinguish broken columns and more ruins. Everything gave the sensation of desolation and abandonment.

"It was Jorge Juan who built the first astronomy observatory here," she said. "In a tower that was on that corner, where the school is now."

She had spoken in a low voice, as if she felt intimidated by the place. Or maybe it was the darkness, only slightly diminished by the damaged street lamp.

"This arch," she continued, "is all that remains of the old castle. It was constructed on the site of an ancient Roman amphitheater, and it housed a company of Guardiamarinas. The professors and men in charge of the observatory were famous sailors and men of science. Jorge Juan and Antonio de Ulloa had published works on the measurement of a degree of meridian at the Equator, Mazarredo was an excellent naval tactician, Malaspina was about to undertake his famous voyage, Tofiño was preparing the definitive hydrographic atlas of the Spanish coastline. . . ." She turned in a circle, taking in her surroundings, and her voice was sad. "It all ended at Trafalgar."

They walked a little farther into the alley. White bedding hung overhead between balconies, like motionless winding sheets in the night.

"But in 1767," Tánger continued, "this place meant something. About then they closed the navigation school run by the Jesuits, and the nautical library of the observatory was enriched by those books and by others bought in Paris and London."

"The books we saw this morning," said Coy.

"Yes, those. You saw them in their glass cases. Treatises on navigation, astronomy, voyages. Magnificent books that hold secrets even today."

Their shadows touched the wall, naked brick and old stone. A drop of water from a sheet fell on Coy's face. He looked up and saw a solitary star blazing in the blue-black rectangle of the sky. By the hour and position, he calculated it might be Regulus, the foremost claws of the constellation Leo, which at that time of the year should already have crossed the north-south axis.

"The castle," Tánger continued to recount, "was occupied by Guardiamarinas until they were transferred to a different site, and then to the island of León, which today is San Fernando. But the observatory was maintained a few years more, until 1798. Then they moved the Cádiz meridian twelve and a half miles to the east."

Coy touched a wall. The plaster crumbled in his fingers.

"What happened to the castle?"

"It was turned into a barracks, then into a prison. Finally they demolished it, and all that's left is a couple of old walls and an arch. This arch."

She turned back and again contemplated the dark, low vault.

"What is it you're looking for?" he asked.

He heard her soft laugh, very quiet, in the shadows that veiled her face.

"You already know that. The *Dei Gloria*."

"I don't mean that. Or treasures or any of that . . . I'm asking what *you're* looking for."

He waited for an answer but none was forthcoming. She was silent, immobile. On the other side of the arch the headlamps of an automobile lit a stretch of the street before driving on. For a moment, the brightness outlined her face against the dark wall.

"You know what I'm looking for," she said finally.

"I don't know anything." He sighed.

"You know. I've seen you look at my building. I've seen you look at me."

"You don't play fair."

"Who does?"

She moved as if she was going to walk away, but instead she stopped still. She was one step away from him, and he could almost feel the warmth of her skin.

"There's an old riddle," she added after a silence. "Are you good at solving riddles, Coy?"

"Not very."

"Well, I am. And this is one of my favorites. There's an island. A place inhabited by only two kinds of people—knights and knaves. The knaves always lie and deceive, the knights never do. . . . You get the situation?"

"Of course. Knights and knaves. I understand."

"All right. Well, one inhabitant of that island says to another: 'I will lie to you and I will deceive you.' Understand? I will lie to you and I will deceive you. And the question is, who is speaking? The knight or the knave? Which do you think?"

Coy was puzzled.

"I don't know. I'd have to think about it."

"Fine." She stared at him hard. "Think about it."

She was still very close. Coy felt a tingling in his fingertips. His voice sounded hoarse.

"What do you want of me?"

"I want you to answer the riddle."

"That isn't what I'm talking about."

Tánger tilted her head to one side.

"I need help." She looked away. "I can't do it alone."

"There are other men in the world."

"Maybe." There was a long pause. "But you have certain virtues."

"Virtues?" The word confused him. He tried to answer, but found that his mind was blank. "I think . . ."

He stood there, mouth half open, frowning in the darkness.

Then Tánger spoke again. "You're no worse than most men I know."

After a brief pause, she added, "And you're better than some."

This isn't the conversation, he thought, irritated. This wasn't what he wanted to hear at the moment, nor was it what he wanted to talk about. In fact, he decided, he didn't want to have a conversation at all. Better just to be standing beside her, sensing the warmth of her freckled flesh. Better to stand in the shelter of their silence, though silence was a language Tánger controlled much better than he did. A language she had spoken for thousands of years.

He turned, making sure she was watching him. He glimpsed navy-blue glints beneath the pale splash of hair.

"And what is it that you want, Coy?"

"Maybe I want you."

A long silence this time, as he discovered it was much easier to say this in the penumbra that covered their faces and muted their voices. It was so easy that he'd heard his words before he'd thought of speaking them, and all he felt afterward was faint surprise.

"You are too transparent," she whispered.

She said it without moving back, standing firm even when she saw him inch forward and slowly lift a hand toward her face. She spoke his name as you would a warning; like a small cross or blue dot on the white of a nautical chart. Coy, she said. And then she repeated: Coy. He moved his head, to one side then the other, very slowly and very sadly.

"I'll go with you to the end," he said.

"I know."

Just as he was about to touch her hair, he looked over her shoulder and froze. He saw a small, vaguely familiar silhouette beneath the arch at the end of the alley. It stood there waiting, tranquil. Then the headlights of another automobile flashed down the street, the shadow slid from wall to wall beneath the arch, and Coy easily recognized the melancholy dwarf.

VII
Ahab's Doubloon

And so they'll say in the resurrection, when they come to fish up this old mast, and find a doubloon lodged in it. . . .
—Herman Melville, MOBY-DICK

When the waiter at the Terraza set his beer on the table, Horacio Kiskoros raised it to his lips and took a prudent sip, watching Coy out of the corner of his eye. Foam whitened his mustache.

"I was thirsty," he said.

Then he surveyed the plaza with satisfaction. The cathedral was lighted now, and the white towers and the large cupola over the transept stood out against the dark sky. People were strolling under the palm trees and sitting on tables on nearby terraces. Some young people were drinking beer on the steps beneath the statue of Friar Domingo de Silos. One was playing a guitar, and the music seemed to attract Kiskoros, who from time to time observed the group and moved his head in time, his air nostalgic.

"A magnificent night," he added.

Coy had learned his name only fifteen minutes before, and it was difficult to believe that the three of them were sitting there drinking like old friends. In that brief span of time the melancholy dwarf had acquired a name, an origin, and a character of his own. Argentine by nationality, he was called Horacio Kiskoros, and he had, as he said as soon as it was possible to do so, an urgent matter to present to the lady and gentleman. All the details did not surface immediately, for his unexpected appearance under the Guardiamarinas arch had preceded a reaction by Coy even the most favorable witness would have qualified as violent. To be exact, when the sliding shadow in the headlights had allowed Coy to recognize who it was, he had marched straight toward him without missing a beat, not even when he heard Tánger, at his back, call his name.

"Coy, please. Wait."

He hadn't waited. In truth, he didn't want to wait, or know any reason why the hell he should wait, why he should do anything other than exactly what he did do: walk eight or ten steps, adrenaline pumping, take several deep breaths along the way, grab the little man by the lapels and shove him against the nearest wall, under the yellow light of a street lamp. He needed desperately to do that, and to smash the man's face before he got away from him as he had at the service station in Madrid. Which is why, ignoring Tánger, he lifted the dwarf onto his tiptoes and, pinning him to the wall with one hand, he raised the other, making a fist. Between the gleam of brilliantined hair and the thick black mustache, a pair of dark protruding eyes stared at him intently. He didn't resemble a pleasant little frog now. There was surprise in those eyes, Coy thought. Even pained reproach.

"Coy!" Tánger called again.

Hearing the click of a switchblade, low and to his left, he glanced down, and saw the reflection of naked steel close to his side. An uncomfortable thrill shot through his groin; a knife-thrust upward, at such close quarters, was the worst way to end this. In such a situation the definitive argument would normally be Anchors aweigh! with a no-return ticket. But others had tried to knife Coy before, so before reflecting on this turn of events, he had instinctively jumped back and chopped down on the other's arm, as if a cobra had leaped from his pocket.

"Come and get it, asshole," he said.

Naked fists against a knife; that had a good sound. Of course he was bluffing, but he was angry enough to see it through. He had whipped off his jacket the way Tucumán Torpedoman had taught him once in Puerto Príncipe, wrapping it a couple of times around his left arm, waiting for his adversary, crouched, the arm with the jacket held out to protect his belly and the other poised to deliver a knockout punch. He was furious, and he felt the muscles of his shoulders and back knot, tense and hard, with his blood pounding rhythmically through his veins. Just like the old days.

"Come and get it," he repeated. "So I can bust your balls."

The dwarf was holding the switchblade aloft, his eyes glued on Coy, but he seemed uncertain. With his short stature, his hair and clothing disheveled, his skin pale in the yellow light, he was somewhere between sinister and grotesque. Without the knife, Coy decided, he wouldn't have a chance. He watched as this nameless so-and-so straightened his jacket and ran a hand over his hair, smoothing it back. He put his weight on one foot, then the other, rose up to his full height, and lowered the hand with the knife.

"Let us negotiate," he said.

Coy measured the distance. If he could get close enough to kick him in the groin, the dwarf wouldn't feel like negotiating with his own whore of a mother. He moved a little to the side and his opponent stepped back, prudent. The blade shone in his hand.

"Coy," said Tánger.

She had come up behind him, and now was at his side. Her voice was serene.

"I know him," she added.

Coy gave a quick nod, without taking his eyes from the little man, and in the same instant kicked with all his strength; the man with the knife escaped the worst because he had anticipated Coy's move and scooted backward to get out of range. Even so, he took a vicious hit on the knee, stumbled, and spun around, catching himself against the wall. Coy seized the opportunity to go on the attack, first with the arm wrapped in the jacket, then with a punch that struck his adversary at the base of the neck, dropping him to his knees.

"Coy!"

The cry increased his rage. Tánger tried to grab his arm, but he shook her off roughly. Go to hell. Someone had to pay, and this guy was the right person. Later she could say whatever she wanted, explanations he wasn't sure he wanted to hear. As long as he was fighting, there was no opportunity for words, so he kicked the so-and-so a second time, but he slithered round in an impossibly small space, and Coy felt the knife slice like lightning against the jacket-wrapped arm. He had underestimated the dwarf, he realized suddenly. He was quick, the little bastard. And very dangerous. So he retreated two steps and caught his breath, sizing up the situation. Easy does it, sailor. Calm down or not even a can of spinach will get you out of this one. Forget that he's small; any man, no matter how short, is tall enough to sever an artery. And besides, on one occasion he'd seen a real dwarf, an authentic Scots dwarf, sink his teeth into the ear of an enormous stevedore and hang on like a leech as his victim ran screaming down the dock in Aberdeen, unable to shake him off. So caution is the watchword, he told himself. There's no enemy, short though he may be, and no knife that can't fuck you for good. He was panting for breath, and between inhaling and exhaling he could hear the other man breathing hard. Then he saw him hold up the knife, as if to show it to him, and slowly raise his left hand, palm open, in a conciliatory gesture.

"I bring a message," the dwarf said.

"Well, you can stick it up your ass."

The dwarf's head moved slightly. You don't seem to hear what I'm saying, the gesture said.

"A message from Señor Palermo."

So that was it. A meeting of old acquaintances. The social club of seekers of lost ships was complete. That explained a few things, but muddied others. He breathed once, twice, and took a step toward his adversary, fist cocked again, ready to strike.

"Coy."

Suddenly Tánger stepped in front of him, blocking his way, and stared straight into his eyes. She was dead serious, hard as he'd never seen her. He opened his mouth to protest, but then just stood there with a stupid expression. A man in a fog. Indecisive, because she was touching his face the way someone tries to calm a raging animal, or a child that is beside itself. And over her shoulder, through the gold tips of her hair, he saw the melancholy dwarf closing the knife blade.

Coy didn't touch his beer. With his jacket over his shoulders, his hands in his pockets, and leaning back in his chair, he watched the man seated across from him drink.

"I was thirsty," the man repeated.

They were on the way from the alley to the plaza, after Tánger had restrained Coy and he had finally yielded, mechanically, with the sensation of moving through a surreal mist. The melancholy dwarf had again smoothed his hair and straightened his clothing. Except for a slight rip in the upper pocket of his jacket, which he had discovered with pained eyes and an accusing look, he appeared respectable again, if a little eccentric, his own southern European and bizarrely English composite.

"I have a proposal from Señor Palermo. A reasonable proposal."

His Argentine accent was so strong it seemed affected. Horacio Kiskoros, he had said once the streams were back within their banks. Horacio Kiskoros, at your service. He'd said that with a nod of the head, and in a courteous tone completely free of irony, as he and Coy were getting their breath back. He expressed himself in the scrupulous and slightly anachronistic Spanish spoken by some Latin Americans, using words that on the eastern side of the Atlantic sounded old-fashioned. He had said "at your service" as he was checking his disordered clothes and adjusting the bow tie that had twisted to one side in his contortions. Beneath his jacket he was wearing strange suspenders with stripes that were white down the middle and blue on each side.

"Señor Palermo wishes to reach an accord."

Coy turned to Tánger. She had walked with them without saying a word. He was aware that she was avoiding looking at him, at the face she had touched for the first time only a few minutes before, perhaps to escape giving the inevitable explanations.

"An accord," Kiskoros reiterated, "with terms that are reasonable for everyone." He studied Coy and pointed toward his nose with his thumb to remind Coy of the scene at the Palace. "With no hard feelings."

"No reason to have an agreement with anyone about anything."

Tánger had spoken at last, as if her voice were filtered through ice cubes, Coy observed. She was looking directly into Kiskoros's sad, protruding eyes, her right hand resting on the table. The stainless-steel watch lent an unexpectedly masculine flavor to the long fingers with the short, rough nails.

"That is not what he believes," the Argentine replied. "He has access to resources you lack: technical equipment, experience.... Money."

A waiter brought a platter of squid *à la romana* and fried roe, and the melancholy dwarf said thank you with impeccable good manners.

"A lot of money," he repeated, examining the contents of the platter with interest.

"And what does he expect in return?"

Kiskoros had taken a fork and was delicately spearing a circle of squid.

"You have done a lot of research." He chewed the mouthful with delight, but didn't speak until his mouth was empty. "You have valuable facts. Is that not true? Details that Señor Palermo has not as yet acquired. That has led him to believe that a partnership would be advantageous for both parties."

"I don't trust him," said Tánger.

"Nor does he trust you. You can work together."

"I don't even know what I'm looking for."

Kiskoros seemed to be hungry. He had tried the roe, and now returned to the squid between sips of beer. For an instant he half-turned, listening to the guitar music from the steps of the cathedral, then smiled, pleased.

"Perhaps you know more than you think you do," he said. "But those are details you should discuss with him. I am merely a messenger, as you are aware."

Coy, who until that point had not opened his mouth, spoke to Tánger.

"How long have you known this jerk?"

She took exactly three seconds to turn toward him. The hand on the table had closed into a fist. She lifted it slowly from the table and put it in her lap.

"For some time," she said calmly. "The first time Palermo threatened me, Kiskoros was with him."

"That is true," Kiskoros confirmed.

"He has been using him to pressure me."

"That too is true."

Coy ignored the Argentine. He was hanging on her words.

"Why didn't you tell me?"

Tánger's sigh was audible.

"You agreed to play by my rules."

"What else haven't you told me?"

She stared at the table, and then at the plaza. Finally she turned toward Kiskoros again.

"What does Palermo propose?"

"A meeting." The Argentine looked at Coy before going on, and Coy thought he detected a gleam of irony in the frog eyes. "To negotiate. On terms you consider suitable. He is currently in his office in Gibraltar." He took a card from his pocket and pushed it across the table. "You can find him there."

Coy got to his feet. He left his jacket on the back of his chair and, without looking at either of them, walked across the plaza in the direction of the cathedral steps. His brain was buzzing, and in a rage he squeezed his fists in his pockets. Without planning it, he ended up near the group of young people with the guitar. There were two girls and four boys, almost surely students. The one with the guitar was thin, with gypsy good looks and a cigarette smoldering at the corner of his mouth. One of the girls was following the beat of the music, swaying in place, her hand on his shoulder. The other focused on Coy, smiling, and handed him a bottle of beer. He took a drink, thanked her, and stood there, wiping his lips with the back of his hand. He then sat down on the steps. The guitarist was not accomplished, but the melody sounded fine at that hour of the night in the half-empty plaza, with the palm trees and the lights of the cathedral overhead. Coy stared at the ground. Tánger and Kiskoros had left the table in the bar and were approaching the plaza. She had Coy's jacket doubled over her arm. Sweet Jesus, he thought. I'm up to my neck in goddamn shit.

"A beautiful city," said Kiskoros, smiling at the young people. "It reminds me of Buenos Aires."

Tánger was silent, standing beside Coy. He did not get up.

"I believe you are a sailor, is that not correct?" the melancholy dwarf asked. "I, too, was a sailor. The Argentine Navy. Retired CPO Horacio Kiskoros." His brow furrowed with nostalgia, as if listening to a distant, familiar sound he could not recapture. "I was also in the Malvinas, with the amphibious commandos."

"So what the hell are you doing so far from home?"

The melancholy in the protruding eyes intensified. He had slipped his hand into a pocket, exposing his suspenders, and suddenly Coy understood the significance of those blue and white stripes—the Argentine flag. The sonofabitch was wearing suspenders with the colors of the Argentine flag.

"Things changed in my beloved country."

He sat down beside Coy, but first he pulled up the legs of his trousers at the knee, carefully, to keep the crease sharp.

"Have you heard about the dirty war?"

Coy's lips twisted with sarcasm.

"Of course. The *tupamaro* terrorists and all that."

"The *montoneros,*" Kiskoros lectured, wagging a finger. "The *tupamaros* were in Uruguay."

Coy heard him sigh with emotion. Impossible to know if he lamented the whole thing or missed it.

"The fact is," he added after a moment, "that there was a war in Argentina, even though it wasn't official. Do you understand? I fulfilled my obligation. Some do not accept that."

"So why are you telling me?" Coy asked.

Kiskoros did not seem discouraged by Coy's hostility.

"I found it necessary to travel," he continued. "And I told you that I have experience as a diver. I met Señor Palermo during the recovery efforts on the *Agamemnon,* Nelson's ship that went down in the River Plate."

Coy turned away rudely.

"I don't give a fart about your life."

The frog eyes blinked, injured.

"Very well, señor. Just a little while ago, back in that alley, I was on the verge of killing you. I thought . . ."

"So kill me, and blow it out your ass."

Kiskoros said nothing, mulling over the insult. Coy stood up. Tánger was watching him.

"He killed Zas," she said.

There was a long silence as Coy remembered the Labrador's warm breath on his arm. He could see—it had been only a week—his moist muzzle and loyal gaze. Then, darkly, came the image of the motionless dog on the rug, his glassy, half-open eyes. Something turned over inside him; he felt a strange anguish and he scanned the plaza uneasily, the lights of the cathedral and the street lamps. Beside him, the notes of the guitar seemed to be sliding down the steps. The girl who had smiled at him was kissing one of the boys. One of the young men set the beer bottle on the ground.

"Well, that's true." Kiskoros also got to his feet, brushing off his trousers. "And believe me, I regret that, señor. I am fond . . . Let me assure you. I am fond of domestic animals. Why I have a Doberman of my own."

Thicker silence. The Argentinean assumed a circumspect expression.

"In my own way," he insisted, "I am still a military man. Do you understand? I had orders. And that included the señora's home."

He set his face in a sad rictus: accept responsibility, and all that. "Mendieta," he said suddenly. "My dog is named Mendieta." In the meantime, Coy's eyes went to the bottle, which was at his feet on the steps. For a second, he calculated the possibilities of shattering it over the other man's head. When he looked up he met the melancholy eyes of the Argentine.

"You seem to be a very impulsive man," said Kiskoros in an amiable tone. "That has its problems. The señora, on the other hand, seems to have a more gentle character. Whatever the case, it is not a good thing for a lady to be wandering around this shady part of town. I recall an instance in Buenos Aires. A *montonera* killed two of my fellows when we went to look for her. That woman defended herself like a lioness, and we could only subdue her by throwing grenades. Then it turned out that she had a baby hidden under the bed. . . ."

He paused and clicked his tongue thoughtfully. Beneath his mustache was a mouth that may have been smiling.

"There are women who are very macho, I assure you," he continued. "Although later, things went soft in ESMA. You know what I'm referring to." He analyzed Coy carefully. "No, I don't think you do. *Regio.* Cool. It may be better that way."

Coy's eyes met Tánger's, but she wasn't seeing him, as if she had just contemplated distant horrors. Within seconds, coming back to herself, her eyes seemed to focus on reality, though a vacant darkness remained. She pressed Coy's jacket to her breast, as if suddenly she felt cold.

"ESMA," she said, "was the Escuela de Mecánica de la Armada.... The Navy's torture center during the military dictatorship."

"True," Kiskoros conceded, gazing around with a distracted air. "I fear some ill-informed fools refer to it in that manner."

SHELLY Manne on the brushes had softly introduced "Man in Love," and Eddie Heywood was launching into the first solo at the piano. Standing bare-chested at the open window of his room in the Hotel de Francia y París, in his mind Coy leaped ahead to another phrase of the melody. He was wearing headphones, and when he heard the expected passage, he nodded in time to the music. Three floors below, the small plaza was in shadow. The two large central street lamps had been turned off, the foliage of the orange trees was dark, and the awning of the Café Parisien was rolled up. Everything seemed deserted, but Coy wondered if Horacio Kiskoros was still hanging around. In real life the bad guys take a rest too, he thought. In real life things don't happen the way they do in novels and films. Maybe now the Argentine was snoring like a buzz saw in some hotel or boardinghouse close by, with those suspenders carefully draped over a clothes rack. Dreaming of happy times of sausage, 348 Corrientes, and 1,500-volt currents in the cellars of ESMA.

Pum-pum, pum. The second solo was ending, and Coy expectantly awaited the entrance of the third: the tenor sax of Coleman Hawkins, which was the best thing on that cut, with its half time and quick time and strong-light, and corresponding rhythmic surprises when that cadence was broken with the expected unexpectedness. "Man in Love." He had just thought about the title, and that made him smile into the shadows of the plaza before he glanced up to the ceiling. Tánger was there, on the fourth floor, in the room right above his. Maybe she was sleeping, maybe not. Perhaps she was awake at the window like him, or sitting at the table with her notes, reviewing the information she'd been given by Lucio Gamboa. Going over the pros and cons of Nino Palermo's proposal.

They'd talked earlier. A long discussion after Horacio Kiskoros said good-bye and "*hasta la vista*" in a way that would have sounded friendly to someone who didn't know of his past what Coy now knew. As the two of them departed, Kiskoros watched them from those deceptive, sad little frog eyes, and when they left the plaza he was still in the same place, standing in front of the cathedral like a harmless nocturnal tourist. Coy looked back, and then up to read the name of the street they were on—calle de la Compañía. In this city, he told himself, everything was signs and symbols and markers, exactly like those on a nautical chart. The difference was that the ones having to do with the sea were much more precise, with their colored shoals and scales for miles in the margins as opposed to timeless stone, supposedly accidental meetings, and plaques with unique street names. He didn't doubt that signs and dangers were visible to the eye in the city's streets and alleys, just as on printed charts, but here there were no codes to interpret them.

"Calle de la Compañía, a street named after the Society of Jesus," she'd said when she saw the name. "This is where the Jesuits' school of navigation stood."

She never said anything casually, so Coy scanned the area, the old building on the left, the decaying de Gravina house on the right. He suspected that later, for some reason or other, he would need to remember something about this place. They walked for a while, slowly climbing toward the Plaza de las Flores. Twice he turned toward Tánger, but she kept walking, expressionless, eyes straight ahead, purse tight to her ribs, tips of hair brushing the stubborn chin and mouth rhythmically, until he took her arm and made her stop. To his surprise, she didn't protest, and there she was, so close, after she'd whirled to face him, almost as if she had been waiting for an excuse.

"Kiskoros, at Nino Palermo's instigation, has been watching me for quite a while," she volunteered. "He is an evil and dangerous man."

She paused, as if wondering whether there was something more she should say.

"Earlier, at the Guardiamarinas arch," she added, "I was afraid for you."

She said it straight out, with no emotion. And afterward was again silent, looking over Coy's shoulder in the direction of the plaza, the closed flower kiosks and post office, the outdoor tables of the corner cafés where the last customers of the long day lingered.

"Ever since he came with Palermo to see me," she concluded, "that man has been my nightmare."

She wasn't asking for sympathy, and maybe Coy couldn't help feeling sorry for her for that very reason. There was something childlike, he decided, in that obstinate adultness, in the poise with which she faced the consequences of her adventure. Again the silver cup. Again the framed snapshot. The girl within the protective arm of the man no longer around, the vulnerability of the eyes laughing from the threshold of a time when all dreams were possible. He recognized her in spite of everything. Or, to be more exact, the more time he spent with her, the more of her he recognized.

He suppressed the caress vibrating on his fingertips, and pointed with that hand to the bar behind her. Los Gallegos Chico, it was called. Domestic wines, good coffee, outside food allowed—all that was advertised on placards on the door and in the window. The word "liquors" was enough for Coy, and he realized that she needed a drink as much as he. So they went in. Elbows on the zinc counter, he ordered a gin and tonic for himself—he saw no shade of blue anywhere—and, without asking, a second for her. Gin gleamed moistly on her lips when she looked at him and recounted in minute detail Palermo's first visit, relaxed and friendly, and later a second visit, this time with the cards face up, the pressures and threats seasoned by the sinister presence of Kiskoros. Palermo had wanted to be sure she would recognize the Argentine, that she would know his story and not forget his face, so that when he was standing under her window, walking down the street, or in her bad dreams, she would always think hard about the intrigue she was getting herself into. So she would learn, the treasure hunter had said, that bad little girls cannot walk through the forest with impunity, without exposing themselves to dangerous encounters.

"That's what he said." A vague, somewhat bitter smile hardened her expression. "Dangerous encounters."

At that moment, Coy, who was listening and drinking in silence, interrupted to ask why she hadn't gone to the police. She laughed quietly, a muted laugh, slightly hoarse, as filled with disdain as it was devoid of humor. "The fact is," she said, "I am a bad little girl. I tried to put one over on Palermo, and as for the museum, I'm working on my own. If you haven't picked that up by now you're more naive than I thought."

"I'm not naive," he'd said, uncomfortable, twirling the cold glass.

"I agree." She gazed into his eyes, her lips not smiling but less hard. "You aren't."

She barely tasted her drink. It's late, she'd said, after looking at her watch. Coy tossed down his gin, signaled a waiter, and left a bill on the table. One of his last, he confirmed disconsolately.

"They'll pay for what they've done," he said.

He didn't have the remotest idea of how he could execute that statement, or what he could do to help, but he thought it was the right thing to say. Such sayings exist, he thought. Soothing phrases, consoling words, clichés that you hear in films and read in novels, and that have their value in real life. He glanced at her, afraid she might be scoffing at him, but she was holding her head to one side, absorbed in her own thoughts.

"I don't care whether they pay or not. This is a horse race, you understand. The only thing that matters to me is to get there before they do."

It was almost time for the sax. Tánger was like jazz, Coy decided. A melody line with unexpected variations. She evolved constantly around an apparently fixed concept, like a thematic structure of AABA, but closely following those evolutions required a consistent attention that definitely did not exclude surprise. Suddenly he would hear AABACBA, and a secondary theme would emerge that no one had imagined was there. The only way to follow was to improvise, wherever it might lead. Follow without a score. Courageously. Blindly.

A nearby clock on the plaza struck three. Coy heard it, muffled by the headphones and the music, and finally came the sax of Hawkins, the third solo that tied together all the lines of the tune. He listened with half-closed eyes, calmed by the cadence of familiar notes, soothed by the repetition of the expected. Now Tánger was in the melody, altering its delicate structure. He lost the thread, and an instant later he clicked off the Walkman and held the headphones in his hand, frustrated. For a moment he thought he heard footsteps overhead, just as the crew of the *Pequod* heard the sound of the bone leg as their captain played over his obsessions alone at night on deck. He stood there alert, waiting, then he threw the Walkman onto the unmade bed with irritation. That didn't follow; it brazenly mixed genres. His Melville phase, like the preceding one, the Stevenson phase, had been left behind long ago. Theoretically, Coy was very clearly in his Conrad phase, and all heroes authorized to move through that terrain were weary heroes, more or less lucid, aware of the danger of dreaming when at the helm. Men stranded in resignation and boredom, from whose restless dreams had vanished the endless processions of whales swimming two by two, escorting in their midst a ghost hooded like a snow-capped mountain.

And yet the conditional *yes* at the gate of the oracle of Delphos, whom Coy knew as Melville, but which that author had taken in turn from books Coy hadn't read, still echoed in the air, a storm playing the harp in the rigging, even after the sea closes over the pinioned albatross and the signal flag, and the *Rachel* rescues another orphan. All at once, to his great surprise, Coy discovered that literary or life phases, call them what you will, are never neatly closed, and that although the heroes have lost their innocence and are too exhausted to believe in ghost ships and sunken treasure, the sea is unchanging, filled with its own memory. It's all the same to the sea if men lose their faith in adventure, in the hunt, in sunken ships and treasure. The enigmas and the stories the sea holds have a life of their own, they are sufficient unto themselves, and will be there forever. And that is why, until the very last instant, there will always be men and women who question the cachalot as it turns its head toward the sun and dies.

So, despite all the lucidity he could muster, there he was again, calling himself Ishmael after having been shipwrecked as Jim; again, at his age, preparing the harpoon with his own blood and the ancient obligatory cry: let drink or the devil take him to the end, and get on with the disabled boat and the disabled body, et cetera, et cetera. Watching—fascinated by the certainty of an inevitable fate because he had read it a hundred times—the woman with the freckled skin affix her doubloon of Spanish gold to the wooden mast. But that sound wasn't only in his imagination. He had gone to the window, hoping for a breeze from the ocean, and when he heard it again he had looked toward the ceiling. Now he did think he could hear restless footsteps overhead, on the deck. Tap tap tap. Apparently, like him, she couldn't rest, and was hunting her own white ghosts, funeral carriages with elaborate wrought iron. And he had never dreamed, in any of his ships or books or ports or previous, innocent lives, of such a seductive Ahab enticing him to sail over his tomb.

He lay down on the bed. Until the last port, he remembered before falling asleep, we all live tangled in the line of a whale harpoon.

"THERE is a direct connection," said Tánger, "between the voyage of the *Dei Gloria* and the expulsion of the Jesuits from Spain."

It was Sunday, and they were having a breakfast of hot bread, cocoa, coffee, and orange juice beneath the awning of the Café Parisien, across from the hotel. There was a gentle breeze, bright light, and pigeons strutting across the sunny rectangle of the plaza among the feet of people coming from mass. Coy was eating half a roll, and between bites he stared at the white and ocher facade and the bell tower of the church of San Francisco.

"In 1767 Charles III, who earlier had been king of Naples, was ruling Spain. From the very beginning of his reign the Jesuits were opposed to him, because, among other reasons, at that moment the battle of new ideas was being unleashed across Europe, and the Society of Jesus was the most influential of all the religious orders. That had created enemies for it everywhere. In 1759 the Jesuits had been expelled from Portugal, and in 1764 from France."

She was drinking chocolate milk from a tall glass, and every time she lifted it to her lips a line of foam was left on her upper lip.

She had come outside straight from her shower, her still-wet hair dripping on the red-and-blue-checked shirt she was wearing outside her jeans, sleeves rolled above her wrists, her hair drying into soft waves, making her skin look fresh and young. From time to time Coy stared at the line of cocoa on her mouth and shivered inside. Sweet, he thought. Sweet lips, and she had made the drink sweeter by adding a packet of sugar. He wondered how those lips would taste to his tongue.

"In Spain," she continued, "tensions between the Ignatians and Charles's enlightened ministers were growing. The fourth vow of obedience to the Pope placed the Society in the center of the polemic between religious power and the authority of the kings. It was also accused of controlling a lot of money and of excessively influencing university teaching and administration. Besides, there was the recent conflict between the missions in Paraguay and the Guaraní war." She leaned across the table toward Coy, glass in hand. "Did you see that Roland Joffe film, *The Mission*? The Jesuits taking the part of the natives?"

Coy vaguely remembered the film—a video on board ship, one you end up seeing three or four times, in bits and pieces, during a long voyage. Robert De Niro, he seemed to remember. And maybe Jeremy Irons. He hadn't even remembered they were Jesuits.

"All that," Tánger added, "meant that the Spanish Jesuits were sitting on a powder keg, and the only thing missing was the match."

No sign of Horacio Kiskoros, Coy noted as he looked around. A young married couple was sitting at the next table, tourists with two blond little boys, an unfolded map, and a camera. The kids were playing with plastic slingshots similar to the ones from his childhood, when he'd played hooky to wander the docks. He'd made his sling himself from a V-shaped piece of wood, strips of old inner tubes, a scrap of leather, and a few inches of wire. Now, he thought nostalgically, such things were sold in stores and cost an arm and a leg.

"The match," Tánger continued her story, "was Esquilache's uprising. Although the direct intervention of the Jesuits in the disorder hasn't been proved, it is true that about that same time they were trying to boycott Charles's enlightened ministers.... Esquilache, who was Italian, proposed, among other things, that the broad-brimmed hats and capes the Spanish cloaked themselves in be banned, and that was the source of serious disturbances. Calm was restored, the minister was dismissed, but the Jesuits were thought to be the instigators. The king decided to expel the Society and to seize their wealth."

Coy nodded mechanically. Tánger was talking more than usual, as if she had prepared her comments during the night. It was only logical, he told himself. With the appearance of Kiskoros on the scene and the meeting suggested by Nino Palermo, she had no choice but to compensate by giving him more information. The closer they came to the objective, the more she realized that Coy was not going to be satisfied with crumbs. Basically stingy with her information, however, she kept doling out her supply with an eyedropper. That may have been why, to Coy's disappointment, he didn't feel the same interest he had at other times. He too had had a long night to reflect. Too many facts, he was thinking now. Too many words, but very few were concrete. Everything you tell me, beautiful, I studied more than twenty years ago in school. You hope to string me along with historical swill, without ever getting to the meat of the matter. You are pretending to show with one hand what you're hiding in the other fist.

He was fed up, and he thought less of himself for staying. And yet... That line of foam on her upper lip, the reflection of the bright morning light in the navy-blue irises, the damp tips of the blond hair framing her freckles—taken together, it worked a singular, nearly seductive magic. Every time he looked at this puzzling girl, Coy was sure he was in too deep, he was sailing so far into the dark area on the nautical chart of his life that it was impossible to turn back now. Knights and knaves: I will lie to you and deceive you. The truth was that he didn't give a damn about the mystery of the lost ship. It was the girl—her doggedness, her quest, all that she was prepared to undertake for a dream—that kept him on this course despite the unmistakable sound of the sea perilously breaking on rocks nearby. He wanted to get as close to her as he could, to see her face as she slept, sense her waking and looking at him, touch that warm skin and know, in the depths of the skin and flesh that contained her, the smiling girl of the photograph in the silver frame.

She had stopped talking and was studying him suspiciously, silently asking whether he was paying attention to what she was saying. Not without effort, Coy pushed his thoughts aside, fearful that she could read them, and looked back at the pigeons. Among them, one male, very sure of himself and very much the gallant, puffed out his chest amid a bevy of feathered beauties running in circles and casting sidelong glances at him, kiss-kissing and cooing. And at that moment, the boys at the next table swooped toward the peaceful birds, shouting war whoops. Coy checked out the father, very calmly occupied with his newspaper. Then the mother, making sure that occasionally she cast a lazy eye over the plaza. Finally, he turned to Tánger. With her back to the scene, she picked up the story.

"Everything was prepared in the greatest secrecy in Madrid. By direct order of the king, a small group was formed that excluded anyone who was a partisan of the Society, or even impartial. The objective was to gather evidence and prepare the decree of expulsion. The result of what came to be called the *Pesquisa Secreta,* the secret inquiry, was a prosecutorial document that accused the Ignatians of conspiracy, defense of the doctrine of assassination, loose morals, an appetite for wealth and power, and illegal activities in America."

The business of the secret inquiry sounded good, and Coy felt a stir of interest as he observed the boys again. They had caught the male unaware, and with one stone had interrupted both the idyll and the digestion of crumbs pecked beneath the tables. Emboldened by their success, the children fired at the pigeons with the lethal precision of Serbian snipers.

"In January of 1767," Tánger went on, "meeting in deepest secrecy, the Council of Castile approved the expulsion. Between the night of March 31 and the morning of April 2, in an efficient military operation, the one hundred and forty-six houses in Spain belonging to Jesuits were surrounded. The priests were loaded onto ships; Rome had to take responsibility for them, and six years later Clement XIV dissolved the Society."

There was a pause while Tánger finished her chocolate, and wiped her mouth with a hand. She had shifted in her chair to survey, indifferently, the romping boys and the pigeons, but soon turned back to Coy. I can't imagine her with children, he thought. And I know that, whatever happens, I won't be growing old beside her. He could imagine her in later years, amid books and papers, slim and elegant despite the gnawed fingernails. A single woman with class, and wrinkles fanning from her eyes, drawing on memories of a long red glove, an antique nautical chart, a broken fan, a jet necklace, a record of Italian songs from the fifties, the photo of an old lover. My photo, he fantasized. Oh God, if only it could be my photo.

He snapped to attention because she was talking. What happened after the expulsion of the Jesuits from the dominions of the Spanish wasn't of much interest to them, she said. The important period was the year between Palm Sunday of 1766, the first day of Esquilache's uprising, and the night of March 31, 1767, when the decree of expulsion was served on the Spanish Jesuits. During that interval, in a way that recalled what had happened to the Knights Templar in the fourteenth century, the Society ceased to be a respected, feared, and powerful force. Instead, the Jesuits found themselves exiled and imprisoned.

"Don't you think that's interesting?"

"Oh, very."

She studied him appraisingly, as if she had caught the irony in his response. Coy kept a straight face. One of these times, he thought, she's going to end up telling me something that's actually worth listening to. He looked over her shoulder. The children were running back, sweaty, victorious; as trophies they were carrying tail feathers from the male, who at this moment, Coy calculated, must be winging toward Ciudad El Cabo at about one hundred and twenty miles an hour. Maybe, he thought, Herod's massacre dispatched more than innocence.

Tánger had fallen silent again, as if considering whether it was worth the effort to continue. Her head was tipped to one side and her fingers were drumming on the edge of the table with a rhythm that may have betrayed impatience.

"Are you at all interested in what I'm telling you?"

"Of course I'm interested."

For some reason, her irritation made him feel better about himself. He settled into a more comfortable position and adopted an expression of keen attention.

After a slight hesitation, Tánger went on. "When Charles III decided to create the cabinet for the *Pesquisa Secreta,* he appointed Pedro Pablo Abarca de Bolea, Conde de Aranda, as head. He was from Huesca in Aragon, twice a grandee of Spain, and had been a military man and a diplomat. He was captain general of Valencia when, right in the middle of Esquilache's mutiny, the king summoned him to Madrid to entrust him with a governorship, the presidency of the Council of Castile, and the position of captain general of New Castile. Intelligent, cultivated, and enlightened, he went into the history books as a Mason, although it was never proved that he belonged to any lodge, and modern historians refute that affiliation. To the contrary, there was evidence that he was an eclectic, and, of all the members of the secret cabinet, he may have been the one who best knew the Ignatians, by whom he had been educated and with whom he had many ties, including a brother who was a Jesuit. Compared to rabid anti-Jesuits like the treasurer, Campomanes, the minister of justice, Roda, and José Moñino, the future count of Floridablanca, Aranda could be considered moderate in his feelings toward the Society. Even so, he agreed to head the cabinet and countersign its conclusions. The inquiry began in Madrid on June 8, 1766, with Aranda presiding. He was accompanied by Roda, Moñino, and other confirmed anti-Jesuits, or, as they were called then, Thomists, to contrast them with the pro-Ignatians or 'friends of the fourth vow.' And the investigation was carried out so discreetly that even the confessor to the king was not apprised.

"Nevertheless," Tánger continued, "there was an important connection between one man in the secret cabinet and a renowned Ignatian.... Paradoxically, one of the best friends of the Conde de Aranda was a Jesuit from Murcia, Padre Nicolás Escobar. Their relations had cooled slightly, but we know absolutely that until Aranda left his post as captain general of Valencia, bidden by the king, they were close friends. Although Aranda later destroyed his correspondence with Escobar, a few letters survive that corroborate their friendship."

"Have you seen those letters?"

"Yes. There are three, and they're in the library of the Universidad de Murcia, signed in Aranda's own hand. I obtained copies through a professor of cartography there, Néstor Perona, when I consulted him by telephone about the corrections we needed to apply to Urrutia's chart."

Another conquest, Coy thought. He imagined Tánger's effect, even by telephone, on any professor. Devastating.

"I have to admit that you've done your homework."

"You'll never know how hard I've worked. Which is why I'm not eager to let anyone snatch it out of my hands."

Now, Coy conceded, things were getting interesting. The story was moving away from handbooks and getting down to the fine print. Letters from this fellow Aranda. Maybe after all her ho-hum stories of secret cabinets and uncompromising kings, she was actually getting somewhere.

"Nicolás Escobar," Tánger continued, "was an important Jesuit, well-connected in the circles of power and with the nobles' seminary, which rotated among Rome, Madrid, Valencia, and Salamanca. Two decades earlier he had been director of the Ignatian college in Salamanca, the stronghold of the Society, whose presses—and this is just one of the coincidences—printed..."

She stopped. Now guess... et cetera, et cetera. Coy couldn't help but smile. She had made it too easy and it was impossible to disappoint her. You and I are a team. You tell and I believe.

"The Urrutia," he said.

She nodded, pleased.

"Exactly. Urrutia's *Atlas Marítimo,* printed in the Jesuit college of Salamanca in 1751 under the protection of another minister friend, the Marqués de la Ensenada, the driving force behind the Navy and nautical studies in Spain. And when the secret cabinet was being formed, Padre Escobar, a friend of famous mariners like Jorge Juan and Antonio de Ulloa, was in Valencia. Can you guess where?"

"No. I'm afraid this time I don't have a clue."

"In the house of an old acquaintance of yours and mine. Mine especially: Luis Fornet Palau, 'friend of the fourth vote,' straw man for the Jesuits' fleet and owner of the *Dei Gloria.*"

She stopped, pleased by Coy's expression, and leaned across the table, looking deep into his eyes. He glimpsed in hers an ambition glittering hard and pure as dark polished stone. The dream had ceased to be a dream some time ago, he realized. Now there was obsession, solid and concrete. As she reached out and placed her hand over his, he was desperately searching for the right word to describe her. He felt the weight of that warm hand, the fingers laced with his. Soft, warm, strong, so sure of herself that the gesture seemed the most natural thing in the world. That hand was not meant to console him, or fire him up, or pretend. In that instant it was sincere; it shared. And the word for her obsession, which finally came to him, was "implacable."

"The *Dei Gloria,* Coy," she said in a low voice, her hand still in his. "We are talking about the brigantine that leaves Valencia for America on November 2, when the secret cabinet had been meeting for five months, and returns to the coast of Spain a few weeks before they deliver the final blow to the Jesuits." The pressure of her fingers increased. "Are you tying the loose threads? The rest—that is, the *what* or *who* could have been on board, and the *why*—I will tell you on the way to Gibraltar. Or, as they said in the old newspaper serials, in the next installment."

VIII
The Reckoning Point

The location at which the ship finds itself as a result of prudent judgment only, or of data about which there is considerable uncertainty, is called the reckoning point.

—Gabriel de Ciscar,

Curso de estudios elementales de marina

The small polished guns in the plaza were gleaming. The terrace of the Hungry Friar was full, and groups of Anglo-Saxon tourists were photographing the changing of the guard at the convent, visibly enchanted that Britannia still had colonies from which to rule the waves. Beneath the lazily waving flag in a Gothic arch, a sentinel stood at attention with his Enfield rifle, rigid as a statue, faithful to the scene and the setting. The sergeant in charge barked orders in the compulsory military jargon, shouting at the top of his lungs, inches from the guard's face. England is counting on you to do your duty to the last drop of blood, Coy thought as he watched them. He stretched his legs beneath the table, leaned back to drain the last of his beer, and squinted at the sky. The sun was reaching its zenith; it was blazing hot, and above the Rock a plume of clouds was beginning to disperse; the wind had shifted from east to west and in a couple of hours the temperature would be more bearable. He paid for his beer, got up, and made his way through the crowds in the plaza.

The focus of dozens of camera lenses, the sweating sergeant was still shouting martial commands at the unflinching sentinel. As he walked away, Coy made a mocking face. This morning, he told himself, he had been tapped for guard duty.

He walked through the main street of Gibraltar, mingling with the crowd as he ambled past store after store—Chinese pajamas, T-shirts with silk screens of the Rock and its apes, mantillas, radios, liquor, cameras, perfumes, Lladró and Capodimonte porcelain, Bossom porcelain miniatures. Coy had docked at Gibraltar before, when the British colony was still a conventional port in the old sense, a base for dealers who ran black-market tobacco and Moroccan hashish through the Strait, before Gibraltar had become a tourist beehive and financial haven for drug traffickers and the thousands of English who had retired to the Costa del Sol. In truth, any place near the Mediterranean was a tourist trap by now. But in Gibraltar, along with hamburger joints and fast-food restaurants and drinks in plastic cups, businesses owned by Hindus and Jews alternated with the facades of banks and houses with discreet signs beside the door—lawyer's offices, real estate companies, import-export companies, Spanish S.A. companies, English Ltd. companies, shell companies. More than ten thousand businesses were registered here, where Spanish and English money was laundered and every kind of business transacted. The flag of the European Union flew at the border, and tourism and the flimflam of fiscal paradise had superseded contraband as the principal source of income. Slick young lawyers who spoke perfect English with a Spanish accent were replacing local Mafia godfathers and the once ubiquitous lowlife. Old sea dogs with gold rings in their ears and tattoo-covered arms, the last pirate scum of the western Mediterranean, were languishing in Spanish or Moroccan jails, serving hamburgers at McDonald's, or loafing around the port, gazing longingly at the fifteen miles that separated Europe from Africa, a distance that a decade earlier they had crossed on moonless nights, skimming over the waves between Punta Carnero and Punta Cires at forty knots, with ninety-horse outboards powering their black Phantoms.

Coy walked along the sidewalk that offered the most shade, his sweat-soaked shirt stuck to his back, checking the numbers of the houses. Tánger had kept her word, at least in part. Between Cádiz and Gibraltar, as he had maneuvered the rented Renault around the S turns of the highway that snaked along the hills of Tarifa and the cliffs overlooking the Strait, she finished the story of the Jesuits and the *Dei Gloria*. Or at least the portion she thought it convenient for him to know—that is, why the brigantine had traveled to America and why it had returned from Havana.

"They wanted to abort the coup," she summarized.

With her eyes fixed on the road, she expounded her theory for Coy. The cabinet of the *Pesquisa Secreta* was not so secret after all. There was a leak, a hint of what was being plotted. Maybe the Jesuits had an informer there, or intuitively suspected what was being schemed.

"Of all the members of that cabinet," Tánger explained, "only one was not a pure Thomist. The Conde de Aranda could be considered, if not a 'friend of the fourth vow,' at least more favorable to the Ignatians than the radical Roda, Campomanes, and others. Maybe he was the one who dropped a few timely words to his former social intimate, Padre Nicolás Escobar. It wouldn't have had to be a confidence, not even words. Among people so schooled in nuances and diplomacy, silence itself could be read as a message."

Then Tánger had fallen silent, leaving Coy to imagine the era and the cast. Her left hand was resting on her knee, on the blue cotton skirt an inch from the gearshift. Occasionally, Coy brushed against it when he shifted from fourth to fifth on the straightaway or shifted down before a curve.

"And then," she said, "the Jesuit leadership formulated a plan."

Another silence, with that thought in the air. She should write novels, Coy thought admiringly. She handles the unfinished story better than anyone I know. And though I don't know which of her assertions are true, I never saw anyone state them with such aplomb. That's not even considering the way she gradually lets out line—just enough slack that the fish doesn't get away, just enough tension that it doesn't throw the hook before she sinks a gaff into its gills.

"A risky plan," she said, taking up the story, "with no guarantee of success. But it was based on knowledge of the human condition and the Spanish political situation. As well, of course, as familiarity with Pedro Pablo Abarca, Conde de Aranda."

In a few words, in the objective tone of someone reading off data, never taking her eyes from the asphalt ribbon that undulated before them in the searing heat, Tánger described Charles's minister: an aristocrat with all the privileges of breeding, brilliant military and diplomatic careers, French intellectual and social influences; pragmatic, enlightened, energetic, impetuous, a bit insolent. A fine choice to head the Council of Castile and the cabinet for the secret inquiry. Also given to luxury, to expensive carriages with splendid horses and liveried servants, and theater and bullfights in an open coach, he was popular, ambitious, a free-spender and good friend to his friends. Wealthy, and yet always in need of more funds to maintain a lifestyle that at times verged on excess.

"The words," Tánger continued, "were money and power. Aranda was vulnerable in those areas, and the Jesuits knew that. It wasn't for nothing he had been their student, or was well known to the Society's directors.

"The plan was conceived with meticulous audacity. The best of their ships, the fastest and safest, with the best captain, secretly set sail for America. Padre Escobar was a passenger. There was no official record of his leaving Valencia, because the shipping documents for that stage of the *Dei Gloria*'s voyage were not preserved, but the Jesuit was definitely on board the return voyage. His initials, along with those of his companion, Padre José Luis Tolosa, were on the manifest of the brigantine when it left Havana on January 1, 1767. And they had certain documents and objects with them. Keys to influencing the will of the Conde de Aranda."

With his hands on the wheel, Coy laughed quietly. "In short, they wanted to buy him."

"Or blackmail him," she replied. "In one way or another, the fact is that the mission of the *Dei Gloria,* of Captain Elezcano and the two Jesuits, was to bring back something that would change the course of events."

"From Havana?"

"Precisely."

"And what did Cuba have to do with all this?"

"I don't know. But in Havana they brought something on board that could convince Aranda to manipulate the secret inquiry. Something that would nullify the storm that was going to be unleashed upon the Society."

"It could have been money," Coy suggested. "The famous treasure."

He tried to underplay the importance of his words, but he felt a shiver as he spoke the word "treasure."

Tánger, eyes straight ahead, was stony as a Sphinx. "It could have, it's true," she said after a bit. "But that doesn't mean money is always involved."

"And that is what you intend to find out."

He stole a glance at her from time to time. Her eyes never left the blacktop.

"I intend to locate the *Dei Gloria* first of all. And then find out what she was carrying... Whatever it was, whether by chance or by the cold calculations of the Society's enemies, it never reached its destination."

Coy slowed as they came to a tight curve. On the other side of a fence were real bulls, grazing beneath an enormous one-dimensional black bull advertising a well-known sherry.

"Do you think it was a coincidence that the corsair xebec was where it was?"

"Anything is possible. Maybe the other side knew what was going on and wanted to get a head start. Maybe Aranda himself was dealing from two decks.... Or if the *Dei Gloria* was carrying something that could be used against him, he might have wanted to neutralize it."

"Well, depending on what it was, it's also possible that it hasn't withstood two and a half centuries at the bottom of the sea. Lucio Gamboa said..."

"I remember perfectly well what he said."

"Well, so you know. Treasure, maybe. Anything else, forget it."

Now the highway wound downhill through brilliant green meadows before again ascending. One of Andalusia's famous white villages lay up to the right, hanging from the peak of a mountain. Vejer de la Frontera, Coy read on a road sign. Another arrow pointed toward the sea: Cape Trafalgar, 16 kilometers.

"I hope it's treasure," Coy said. "Spanish gold. Bars of silver. Maybe our Aranda could be bribed." After a pensive moment, biting his lower lip, he asked, "How could we bring it up without anyone knowing?"

He was amused at the idea. Jesuit treasure. Bars of gold piled up in a hold. Unloading by night on a beach amid the rattle of stones dragged by the undertow. Doubloons, Deadman's Chest... yo, ho, ho, and a bottle of rum. He ended up laughing aloud. Tánger did not join in, and he turned to look at her.

"I know for sure you have a plan," he added. "You're the kind of person who always has a plan."

He had accidentally brushed her hand as he shifted, and this time she drew it back. She seemed annoyed.

"You don't know what kind of person I am."

Again he laughed. The idea of the treasure, the pure absurdity of it, had put him in a good mood. He felt years younger: Jim Hawkins was making faces at him from a book-filled shelf in the Admiral Benbow Inn.

"Sometimes I think I know," he said sincerely, "and sometimes I don't. In any case, I'm not taking my eye off you. With a treasure or without it. And I hope you've thought about my share, partner."

"We're not partners. You're working for me."

"Oh shit, I'd forgotten."

Coy whistled a few bars of "Body and Soul." Everything was in order. She had orchestrated the song of the sirens, the doubloon of Spanish gold was gleaming from the mast before the eyes of the sailor without a ship, and meanwhile the rented Renault was leaving Tarifa behind, with its constant wind and ghostly blades whirling on wind-energy towers. The engine was getting too hot on the hills, so they stopped at a scenic overlook above the Strait. The day was clear, and on the other side of the strip of blue they could see the coast of Morocco. More distant and to the left were Mount Acho and the city of Ceuta. Coy watched the slow progress of an oil tanker sailing toward the Atlantic. It was a little outside its lane, crowding the markers separating the two-way traffic, and would obviously have to alter its course to make way for a cargo ship approaching its bow. He imagined the watch officer on the bridge—at that hour it would be the third in command—eyes glued to the radar, waiting till the last minute to see if he was lucky and the other ship would alter course first.

"Besides, you're going too fast, Coy. I never said anything about treasure."

She hadn't spoken for at least five minutes. Now she was out of the car, beside him, staring at the sea and the coast of Africa.

"That's true," he conceded. "But you're running out of time.

You're going to have to tell me the rest of the story when we get there."

The white wake of the tanker traced a slight curve toward the European shore in the Strait below. The watch officer had thought it prudent to give sea room to the closing merchant ship. Ten degrees to starboard, Coy calculated. No officer touched the controls unless the captain authorized it, but correcting by ten degrees and then returning to course was reasonable.

"We're not," she said in a low voice, "there yet."

THE offices of Deadman's Chest, Ltd., were at 42b Main Street, on the lower floor of what looked like a colonial building with white walls and window frames painted blue. Coy looked at the plaque screwed to the door, and after a brief hesitation rang the bell. Tánger had refused to meet with Nino Palermo in his office, so he had been charged with the exploratory mission, and, if the signs were favorable, with setting up a meeting for later that day. Tánger had given him precise instructions, detailed enough for a military operation.

"And what if they beat me to a pulp?" he'd asked, remembering the rotunda of the Palace.

"Palermo puts business before personal matters," was her answer. "I don't think he'll try to settle accounts. Not yet."

So there he was, staring at his stubble-covered face in the brass plaque, breathing as if preparing for a death-defying dive.

"Señor Palermo is expecting me."

The Berber standing inside the open door looked even more menacing in the daylight, his funereally black eyes dissecting Coy, recognizing him before he stood aside to let him pass. The vestibule was small and paneled with precious woods, with a few nautical touches. There was an enormous ship's wheel, a diving suit, and the model of a Roman trireme in a large glass jar. Also a desk of modern design, and behind it the secretary Coy remembered from the auction in Barcelona and the Palace rotunda. A comfortable chair was positioned beside a coffee table with copies of *Yachting* and *Bateaux,* and there was a straight chair in one corner. On that chair sat Horacio Kiskoros.

This wasn't a gathering in which you smiled and said "Hello," so Coy did neither; in fact, he did nothing but stand quietly in the entryway, expectant, while the Berber closed the door behind him. The three pairs of eyes focused on him were not exuding excessive human warmth. The Berber, stolid and unthreatening, mechanically and efficiently patted Coy down, starting at his ankles.

"He never carries a weapon," Kiskoros offered from his chair, in an almost amiable tone.

Now is when they begin to push me around, Coy thought, with the memory of the Berber's solid efficiency. Now they begin to give me mine back, with a few extras thrown in, until I'm tender enough for the grill, and then they'll drag me out of here—if in fact I *get* out of here—with my teeth in a little cone of folded newspaper. LWGACA: Law of What Goes Around Comes Around.

"Well, look what we have here," said a voice.

Nino Palermo was at a just-opened door on the opposite side of the room. Dark brown trousers, blue-striped shirt with the cuffs turned back, no necktie. Expensive moccasins.

"I'll give you this much," he said, surprised to see Coy. "God almighty, you've got balls."

"Were you expecting her?"

"Of course I was expecting her."

The bicolor eyes of the seeker of sunken ships were hard, hypnotic as a snake's. His nose was still slightly swollen and he had the remnants of two black eyes. Behind his back Coy heard the soft footsteps of the Berber, saw the look that Palermo directed over his shoulder, and involuntarily tensed his muscles. Nape of my neck, he thought. That SOB is going to chop me on the neck.

"Come in," said Palermo.

Coy stepped inside and his host closed the door, walked across the room, and leaned against the edge of a mahogany table covered with books, papers, and nautical charts filled with penciled notes, which Palermo covered discreetly with a copy of the *Gibraltar Chronicle.* An antique bar of silver weighing a couple of pounds acted as paperweight. In order to look at anything other than Palermo's face, Coy studied an oil painting on the wall. It depicted a naval battle between a North American and an English ship, two frigates battering each other, their rigging nearly destroyed. The plate on the lower edge of the frame read "Combat of the *Java* and the *Constitution.*" Smoke from the cannonade was blowing in the right direction, as dictated by the clouds, waves, and set of the sails. It was a good painting.

"Why did she send you alone? She should be here."

The green eye and the brown eye were observing Coy with more curiosity than rancor. He didn't know where to direct his gaze, but finally decided on the brown eye. It seemed less unnerving.

"She doesn't trust you. Which is why I am here. Before she sees you, she wants to know what you have in mind."

"Is she in Gibraltar?"

"She's where she should be."

Palermo slowly shook his head. He had picked up a small rubber ball from the table and was squeezing it.

"I don't trust her either."

"Nobody trusts anybody here."

"You're a . . . God almighty." As the left hand squeezed, ballasted with rings and the enormous gold watch, the muscles in Palermo's forearm contracted. "An idiot. That's what you are. You're a puppet and she's pulling your strings."

Coy concentrated on the brown eye.

"Mind your own business," Coy said.

"This is my business. It was mine alone until that bitch stuck her nose in. My good will . . ."

"Cut the shit with that stuff about 'my good will.'" Coy decided to try the green eye for a change. "I saw what your dwarf did to her dog."

The hand squeezing the ball froze, and Palermo shifted his position against the edge of the table. Suddenly he seemed uncomfortable.

"I want to tell you, I never . . . God almighty. Horacio went too far. He's used to measures . . . There in Argentina . . . Well . . ." He stared at the ball as if suddenly it was objectionable, and set it back on the table beside an ivory letter opener with a handle in the shape of a naked woman. "I think that in his country he went over the edge. . . . And then there was the business of the Malvinas. Horacio came out on the cover of *Time* with his English prisoners. He's very proud of that cover, and always carries a copy. . . . When democracy came in, he had to . . . You can imagine. Too many people had recognized him, thanks to that blessed photo, as the one who attached the electrodes to their genitals."

He paused and shrugged lightly, implying that he wasn't responsible for Kiskoros in that period. Coy nodded. Palermo hadn't offered him a chair, so he was still on his feet.

"And you gave him a job."

"He was a good diver," Palermo admitted. "So here you have him, tiny as he is, an efficient bastard for a certain kind of . . . Well . . ." Again he shifted position, gold chains and medallions clinking. "I'm not telling you anything you don't know. Besides, I've always preferred efficient employees to enthusiastic volunteers. A well-paid mercenary doesn't leave you twisting. . . ."

"It depends on who pays the most."

"I pay the most."

Palermo inspected the gold coin he wore on the finger of his right hand. Then automatically he polished it on his shirt.

"Horacio is a complex little sonofabitch," he continued. "Former Argentine military with a Greek father and an Italian mother, who speaks Spanish and thinks he's English. But he's a well-mannered sonofabitch. And I like well-mannered people. He even supports his elderly mother in Río Gallegos, sends her money every month. Just like the tango ballads, you know? How about that."

His hand rose slightly, as if he were going to touch his face, but he immediately interrupted the gesture.

"As for you . . ."

Now the brown eye expressed rancor, and the green one menace. But only for an instant.

"Listen," he said. "This has ballooned into something absurd. We're all overreacting, aren't we? All of us. Her. Me too, maybe. Horacio is even killing dogs, which is . . God almighty. Over the top. And you, of course. You . . ."

The seeker of sunken ships stumbled to a stop, hunting for a term that would define Coy's role in the intrigue.

"Look!" He picked up a key and opened a drawer, then took out a shiny silver coin and threw it on the table. "You know what that is? It's what we call a columnar in my trade—an eight reales silver coin minted in Potosí in 1739 by order of King Philip V. You're looking at. . . . Take a good look. That is one of the famous 'pieces of eight' that figure in all the stories of pirates and treasures."

He took out a larger coin and tossed it beside the first. This was a commemorative medal with three figures, one kneeling, and an inscription. Coy picked it up and read "The pride of Spain humbled by Vernon." On the reverse side were a number of ships and a second inscription: "The capture of Carthagena April 1741." He set the medal on the table beside the piece of eight.

"It was an empty boast, because they didn't ever take Cartagena," Palermo explained. "Admiral Vernon withdrew, defeated, without ever sacking the city. The person supposedly kneeling on the medallion is the Spaniard Blas de Lezo, who never knelt—among other reasons because he had only one arm and was lame. But he defended the city with tooth and claw, and the English lost six ships and nine thousand men. Vernon had brought medallions already struck for the triumph, but now he had to get rid of them. And he did, except for the ones that went to the bottom of the bay. Hard to find."

He put his hand in the drawer and pulled out a handful of different coins, which he hefted before dropping them with a metallic clatter. Gold and silver glittered as it spilled through his ring-laden fingers.

"I got that one from a sunken English ship," said the treasure hunter. "That one, these, and many others: silver coins of four and eight reales, the columnars, pre-1850 coins, gold doubloons, ingots, jewels. . . . I'm a professional, you understand? I know the miles of shelves in the Archivo de Indias, and the archives in the English Admiralty as well. I know the palace of the Inquisition in Cartagena de Indias, Simancas, Viso del Marqués, Medina-Sidonia. . . . And I'm not about to let a couple of amateurs . . . God almighty. Blow a lifetime of work."

He picked up the piece of eight and the Vernon medallion and returned them to the drawer. His smile made him look like a white shark who had just been told a joke about shipwreck victims.

"So I'm going to be in this to the end," he stated. "With no mercy and no misgivings. I'm going to. . . . I swear to you. And when I'm done, that woman . . . she'll see. And as for you, you must be mad." He locked the drawer and put the key in his pocket. "You don't have the faintest idea of the consequences."

Coy scratched his unshaven face.

"So did you send that asshole dwarf to Cádiz to make us come and listen to this?"

"No. I asked you to come in order to propose a final deal. Last chance. But you . . ."

He left the sentence unfinished, although the meaning was

clear. He didn't consider Coy qualified to carry out the negotiations. Neither did Coy, and they both knew that.

"I only came to check the lay of the land," he said. "She's agreeable to meeting you."

Palermo's eyes were slits, but a gleam of interest shone through.

"When and where?"

"She thinks Gibraltar is fine. But she won't come to the office. She prefers neutral ground."

The smile now revealed teeth that were strong and white. The shark was swimming in his own waters, thought Coy. Catching a scent.

"And what does that woman consider neutral ground?"

"The turnoff on the Rock that looks down on the airport would be fine."

Palermo reflected.

"Old Willis overlook? Why not? What time?"

"Tonight, at nine."

Palermo glanced at his watch and thought a second. The cruel smile began to take shape again.

"Tell her I'll be there.... Will you come, too?"

"You'll know when you show up."

The less than friendly eyes studied Coy from head to toe, and the treasure hunter laughed a disagreeable laugh. He didn't seem even slightly impressed.

"You think you're a tough kid, don't you?" Suddenly his tone was more intimate, but much less pleasant. "God almighty. You're a puppet, like all the others. That's what you are. They use us like... Use us and throw us away. Oh yes. That's what they do. And you... I know your situation. I have my ways.... Well... You know what I'm saying. I know your problem. After Madrid I made it my job to find out. That ship in the Indian Ocean. Two years' suspension is a long time, isn't it? I, however... What I mean is that I have friends with ships who need officers. I could help you."

Coy frowned. Palermo's words made him feel intruders were going through all his drawers. The sense of turning to a window and finding someone there, spying.

"I don't need help."

"Sure. I see. . . ." Palermo looked him over again. "But you're not fooling anyone, you know? You must think you're different, but. . . . God almighty. I've seen a hundred like you. Wise up. You think you're the only one who reads books and goes to movies? But these aren't Asian ports, and you're not . . . Your story wouldn't make a good B movie. Peter O'Toole had a lot more class. And when she . . . Well. She'll set you adrift, like those plundered ghost ships whose crews have vanished. . . . In this novel there aren't any second chances. Let's see if you can get that straight. In the mystery of this lost ship the captain loses his license permanently. And the girl. Shit. The bitch spits in his face. . . . No, don't look at me like that. I don't have any power to see into the future. But your problem is so elementary it makes me laugh."

He didn't laugh, however. He was somber, still leaning against the table, gripping it. The green and the brown eyes were focused somewhere beyond Coy, absorbed.

"I know them inside out," he said. "Bitches."

He shook his head. For a while he seemed to be in a trance, then he looked around, as if recognizing where he was. His own office.

"They play," he added, "with weapons we don't even know exist. And they're much cleverer than we are. While we were spending centuries talking in loud voices and drinking beer, going off to Crusades or football games with our pals, they were right there, sewing and cooking and watching. . . ."

Gold clicked as he went to a small cabinet and took out a bottle of Cutty Sark and two short, wide glasses of heavy crystal. He took ice from a bucket, poured a generous shot of whiskey into each glass, and returned with them.

"I know what you're feeling," he said.

He kept one glass and set the other on the table in front of Coy.

"They have been, and still are, our hostages, you know? He took a drink, and then another, his eyes never leaving Coy. "That means that their morals and ours are . . . I don't know. Different. You and I can be cruel because of ambition, lust, stupidity, or ignorance. For them, though . . . Call it calculation, if you want. Or necessity . . . A defensive weapon, if you get my meaning. They're bad because they gamble everything, and because they need to survive. That's why they fight to the death when they fight. The damned whores have no fallback position."

The shark's smile was back. He pointed to his wrist.

"Imagine a watch . . . a watch that has to be stopped. You and I would stop it like any other man—smash it with a hammer. Not a woman. No. When she has the opportunity, she takes it apart piece by piece. Lays out every single part, so no one can ever put it back together. So it will never tell time again. Ever. God almighty. I've seen them. . . . Yes. They take even the most *manly* man's works apart, with a gesture, or a look, or a simple word."

Again he drank, and his lips twisted. A rancorous shark. Thirsty.

"They kill you and you keep walking, not even knowing you're dead."

Coy resisted the impulse to reach out for the untouched glass on the table. Not just for the drink, which was the least of it, but to be drinking with the man there before him. Crew Sanders was too far away; he was tempted by the ancient male ritual, and after all, he reflected, it was only logical he would be. He was now desperately nostalgic for bars filled with guys spouting incoherent words with alcohol-thickened tongues, bottles turned upside down in ice buckets, and women who didn't dream of sunken ships or had stopped believing in them. Blondes who weren't young but were bold, like the ones in the song of the Sailor and the Captain, dancing alone, not caring that lots were being cast for them. Refuge and oblivion at so much an hour. Women who didn't have silver-framed photos of themselves as little girls, times when dry land was habitable for a brief while, a kind of stopover before returning past cranes and sheds gray in the pale morning light to any ship about to cast anchor, while cats and rats played hide and seek on the dock. I went ashore, the Tucumán Torpedoman had said once in Veracruz. I went ashore, but I only got as far as the first bar.

"Nine o'clock at the overlook," said Coy.

He was filled with a uneasy, desolate self-loathing. He gritted his teeth, feeling the muscles of his jaw tighten. Then he turned on his heel and walked to the door.

"You think I'm lying?" Palermo asked to his back. "God almighty. You'll find out before long. . . . Damn it to hell, man. You should be at sea. This is no place for you. And you'll pay for it, of course." Now his voice was exasperated. "We all pay sooner or later, and your turn is coming. You'll pay for what happened at the Palace, and you'll pay for not wanting to listen to me. You'll pay for believing that lying bitch. And then it won't be a question of finding a ship, but of finding a hole to crawl into. . . . When she, whatever she has in mind, and I, have both finished with you."

Coy opened the door. Only one voyage will you make without cost, he remembered. The Berber was there, quiet and threatening, blocking his way. The secretary peered with curiosity from her desk, and in the background, on his chair, Kiskoros was cleaning his fingernails as if none of it had anything to do with him. After consulting his boss, questioning and silent, the Berber stepped aside. As Coy walked out the door, the treasure hunter's last words echoed in his ears.

"You still don't believe me, do you? Well, ask her about the emeralds on the *Dei Gloria*. Asshole."

ACCORDING to navigation manuals, the reckoning point was when all the instruments on board failed, and there was no sextant, moon, or stars, and you had to find the ship's position by using the last known position along with the compass, speed, and miles sailed. Dick Sand, the fifteen-year-old captain created by Jules Verne, had used that method to steer the schooner *Pilgrim* during the course of its troubled voyage from Auckland to Valparaiso. But the traitor Negoro had put a sliver of iron in the compass, throwing off the needle, and so young Dick, in the midst of furious storms, had sailed past Cape Horn without seeing it and had mistaken Tristan da Cunha for Easter Island, finally running aground on the coast of Angola when he thought he was in Bolivia. An error of that magnitude had no equal in the annals of the sea, and Jules Verne, Coy had decided when he read the book as a young seaman, didn't know the first thing about navigation. But the distant memory of that story came to mind now with all the force of a warning. Sailing blind, basing everything on reckoning, did not present grave problems if a pilot was able to fix a position from distance traveled, drift, and deviation, and apply that information to the chart to establish the supposed position. The problem only became serious as you approached landfall. Sometimes ships were lost at sea, but much more often ships and men were lost on land. You touched pencil to chart, said I am here, and in fact you were *there,* on a shoal, on reefs, on a leeward coast, and suddenly you heard the crunch of the hull splitting open beneath your feet. And that was the end of it.

Of course, there was a traitor on board. She had put a bit of iron in the compass, and once again he found he had badly processed the information available to him. But what once had been less important, and even lent emotion to the game, now, in the uncertainty of approaching land, seemed disturbing. All the alarms in Coy's maritime instincts were blinking red as he walked along the wood quay of Marina Bay. There was a breeze blowing across the isthmus, ringing the halyards of the sailboats against the masts, a background to Tánger's calm voice. She was talking with incredible serenity about emeralds, as cool as if it were something they'd alluded to many times. She had listened to Coy's recriminations in silence, not responding to the sarcastic remarks he had prepared during the walk from Nino Palermo's office to the marina where she was awaiting his report. Later, after he had exhausted his arguments and was standing looking at her, furious, barely able to contain himself, demanding an explanation that would keep him from tying up his bedroll and cutting out that minute, Tánger had begun talking about emeralds as if that were the most natural thing in the world to do, as if for days she had only been waiting for Coy's question to tell him everything. He wondered whether *everything* was everything this time.

"Emeralds," she had said by way of introduction, thoughtfully, as if the word reminded her of something. She had fallen silent, contemplating the waters of that very color that filled the semicircle of Algeciras Bay. Then, before Coy started cursing for the third time, she began her disquisition on the most precious and most delicate of stones. The most fragile, and the one in which it was most difficult to find the desired attributes combined—color, clarity, brilliance, and size. She'd even had time to explain that, along with the diamond, sapphire, and ruby, the emerald was one of the basic precious stones, and that like the others it was crystallized mineral. But while the diamond was white, the sapphire blue, and the ruby red, the color of the emerald was a green so extraordinary and unique that in order to describe it you had to fall back on its own name.

Coy stopped walking after this peroration, and that was when he blasphemed the third time. A sailor's curse, short and direct, that took the name of the Lord in vain.

"And you," he added, "are a fucking liar."

Tánger stared at him, unblinking. She seemed to weigh those six words one by one. Her eyes were hard again, not like the fragile stone she had just described with such sangfroid, but like the dark stone, sharp as a dagger, that lies hidden beneath the breakers.

Then she turned toward the end of the quay where the mast of the *Carpanta* rose among others, the mainsail carefully furled on the boom. When she turned back to Coy, her eyes were different. The breeze blew tendrils of hair across her face.

"The brigantine was carrying emeralds from mines the Jesuits controlled in the Colombian beds at Muzo and Coscuez. . . . They were sent from Cartagena de Indias to Havana, and then taken on board with all secrecy."

Coy stared at his feet, then the wood planks of the quay, and paced nervously. He stopped and stared at the sea. The bows of the boats anchored in the bay swung slowly into the breeze from the Atlantic. He shook his head, as if denying something. He was so dumbfounded that he kept refusing to admit his own stupidity.

"The emerald," Tánger continued, "has two weaknesses: its softness, which makes it vulnerable as it's cut, and inclusions—opaque areas, spots of uncrystallized carbon sometimes trapped in the stone, spoiling its beauty. That means, for example, that a one-carat stone is more valuable than a two-carat one if the first has better attributes."

Now she was talking smoothly, almost sweetly. The way you explain something complicated to a slow child. A military plane took off from the nearby airport, the sound of its engines thundering in the air. For a few seconds the noise drowned out Tánger's words.

". . . for the faceted cut made by specialized jewelers. That way, a twenty-carat emerald with no inclusions is one of the most valuable and sought-after gems." She paused, then added, "It can be worth a quarter of a million dollars."

Coy's eyes were still focused on the sea, above which the airplane was gaining altitude. At the other end of the bay rose the smoke of the Algeciras refinery.

"The *Dei Gloria*," said Tánger, "was transporting two hundred perfect emeralds, from twenty to thirty carats each."

A new pause. She moved to stand facing Coy and looked him straight in the eye.

"Uncut emeralds," she insisted. "Big as walnuts."

Coy could have sworn that her voice trembled slightly this once. Big as walnuts. It was only a fleeting impression, because when he focused on her, he found her as self-controlled as ever. She was indifferent to his accusations, free of the need to utter a single word of apology. It was her game and she made the rules. It had been that way from the beginning, and she knew that Coy knew. I will lie to you and deceive you. On that island of knights and knaves, no one had promised the game would be clean.

"That cargo"—she was emphatic—"was worth a king's ransom. Or, to be more exact, the ransom of the Spanish Jesuits. Padre Escobar wanted to buy the Conde de Aranda. Maybe the cabinet of the *Pesquisa Secreta* as well. Perhaps the king himself."

Almost despite himself, Coy realized that curiosity was replacing his anger. He blurted out the question.

"And they're down there? On the bottom?"

"They may be."

"How do you know?"

"I don't know. We have to dive to the brigantine to find out."

We have to. That plural felt like salve on a wound, and Coy was aware of that.

"I was going to tell you once we were there.... Can't you understand?"

"No. I don't understand."

"Listen. You know the risks. With all those people around, I didn't know how you might react. I still don't know. You can't blame me."

"Nino Palermo knows. Every bloody soul seems to know."

"You're exaggerating."

"Bullshit I'm exaggerating. I'm the last to know, like a husband."

"Palermo thinks there are emeralds, but he doesn't know how

many. And he doesn't have any description of them or know why they were on the brigantine. He's only heard rumors."

"Well, to me he sounded very well informed."

"Look. I have spent years with that ship on my mind, even before I confirmed that it existed. Nobody, not even Palermo, knows what I know about the *Dei Gloria*. Do you want me to tell you my story?"

I don't want you to tell me another string of lies, Coy was about to say. But he didn't say it, because he wanted to hear. He needed more pieces, new notes that would score with greater precision the strange melody she was humming in silence. And so, standing there on the quay with the breeze blowing at his back, he prepared to listen to Tánger Soto's story.

THERE was a letter, she said. A simple yellowed sheet with writing on both sides. It had been sent from one Jesuit to another, and then, forgotten by everyone, had lain in a pile of papers seized at the time the Society of Jesus was dissolved. The letter was written in code, and came with a transcription, done by an anonymous hand, possibly a functionary charged with examining the confiscated documents. Along with many other letters on various subjects and with similar transcriptions, it had spent two centuries at the bottom of an archive catalogued as "Clergy/Jesuits/Varia n° 356." She had come across it by accident doing research at the national historical archive while writing a thesis on the Machinada of Guipúzcoa in 1766. The letter was signed by Padre Nicolás Escobar, a name that at the time meant nothing to her, and was addressed to another Jesuit, Padre Isidro López.

Esteemed Padre:

Divested of support, defamed before the King and the Holy Father, and object of the odium of fanatical persons whom you, Esteemed Padre, know but too well, we are come very close to the conscientiously intrigued

Catastrophe being elaborated with such stealth. The Ecclesiastics themselves, who feel enmity toward the Society, have no aversion to acting as couriers and procurers of the calumnies that circulate with such impunity. As a result we are being forced to fall back upon our own resources by those who believe any act is licit in achieving their ends and in capturing the will not only of Our Sovereign, who is suspicious of us by reason of bad advice, but also our former friends.

Everything, Esteemed Padre, presages a coup against our Order, to be effected in the ominous manner of the crime in France and in the Portugal of the impious Pombal. By safe and most direct conduct Abbot G. has confirmed the list known to your most esteemed person, that of the individuals who are plotting the maneuver and the manner in which they are working to execute it. But in that vast enterprise cloaked as a Secret Inquiry, there remains a tiny glimmer of hope. I write you the present missive, which will reach you by safe-conduct along our habitual route, for the purpose of urging you to endure as we carry out the undertaking that may influence in our favor the will of the most powerful.

*In previous consultation with our superiors, and with regard to the proposition of which you are already apprised, I am preparing to voyage with the hope that—*Ad Maiorem Dei Gloriam *(with that name and that refuge I prepare to embark)—the wind will blow from an auspicious quarter. Two hundred arguments in the form of untouched flames of green fire, perfect and large as walnuts (the Devil's irises, the good abbot calls them), await in Cartagena de Indias in the care of Padre José Luis Tolosa, who is a dependable young man and well to be trusted. I shall be in Havana, be it God's will, toward the end of the month; and in the same manner expect to return to Our Port as quickly as possible, and with as much stealth, and as directly, as the privileges of the Society afford, avoiding dangerous intermediary calls in port. Our admired don P.P. has promised the abbot to wait, and despite all that has happened, and even in the face of his new dispositions and ambitions, we may still consider him sympathetic, for what he may find of benefit in this enterprise is very great.*

I shall add, E.P., the happy news that yesterday I learned through our esteemed abbot that some close friends privy to the circle of the deeply mourned Queen Mother have remained amicable toward us, as is the worthy V. and also H.—although this latter cannot be entirely trusted because of his bent for intrigue. As for the abbot, he continues in the favor of royal persons and is plying to our benefit the threads of the enterprise, and he tells us that don P.P. remains very receptive to what occupies our concern. Until my return, therefore, nothing but Tacere et Fidere. *And trust that Divine Providence will prevail.*

Accept, Esteemed Padre, respectful greetings from your brother in Christ

Nicolás Escobar Marchamalo, S.J.
In the port of Valencia,
November 1 A.D. 1766

Over time, Tánger had identified all the people mentioned in the letter. Queen Mother Isabel Farnesio, very favorable to the Society of Jesus, had died six months before. The recipient of the letter was Padre Isidro López, the most influential of the Spanish Jesuits, who enjoyed an excellent position in the court of Charles III and would die in Bologna eighteen years after the dissolution of the Society, without being allowed to return from exile. As for the initials, they presented no difficulty for someone accustomed to working with historical sources: P.P. was Pedro Pablo Abarca, Conde de Aranda. Behind the initial H. was a thinly veiled Lorenzo Hermoso, born in the New World but now located in Spain, an intriguer and conspirator who was involved in Esquilache's uprising, and who after the fall of the Jesuits was taken prisoner and exiled, although the prosecutor asked for *tanquam in cadavere,* severe corporal punishment. The person designated as V. was Luis Velázquez de Velasco, Marqués de Valdeflores, a man of learning and intimate of the Society, who would pay for that friendship with ten years in the prisons of Alicante and Alhucemas. And the initial G.

alluded to Abbot Gándara, known in the court of Charles III as the Jesuits' principal supporter within the circle of the king, whom he accompanied as gun bearer in his hunting parties. His real name was Miguel de la Gándara, and his misfortune may have inspired *The Count of Monte Cristo* or *The Iron Mask.* Taken prisoner shortly before the fall of the Order, he lived in prison the remaining eighteen years of his life, and died in the dungeon of Pamplona without anyone ever having established a clear cause for his incarceration.

The story of Abbot Gándara had fascinated Tánger, to the point that she ended up writing her thesis on him. That led her to examine all the papers relating to his trials and imprisonment, which were kept in the Grace and Justice section of the national archive in Simancas. She even determined the name of the Jesuit ship referred to only in veiled fashion in the letter—the *Dei Gloria.* Through her research she had ascertained that Padre Nicolás Escobar's farewell to Padre López, in which he mentioned Gándara, was written one day before the latter's arrest, effected on November 2, 1766, the same day Escobar sailed for America aboard the brigantine on which, during the return voyage, he would disappear at sea. Tánger's thesis was titled "Abbot Gándara, Conspirator and Victim," and earned high marks for her master's degree in history. It was filled with facts about the abbot's long years in prison, his interrogations and judicial trials, and his imprisonment in Batres and then Pamplona, where he was secluded until his death. No one ever provided a reason for the zealous cruelty Aranda and others of Charles's ministers reserved for him—except perhaps his friendship with the Society of Jesus, whose members, among them the recipient of the letter, were arrested five months after the abbot and exiled to Italy, their Order disbanded. As for Padre Escobar's voyage to Havana, and those two hundred flames of green fire to which he cryptically alluded, he never received an answer from Gándara, although some of the interrogations referred to the subject. The secret of the *Dei Gloria* died with him.

Afterward life followed its course, and Tánger had other matters to occupy her. The competitive examinations for the Museo Naval and her work consumed her attention, and new interests took the forefront in her life. Until Nino Palermo appeared one day. In searching through books and catalogues, the treasure hunter had happened upon a reference to a report in the maritime section in Cartagena, dated 8 February 1767, regarding the loss of the *Dei Gloria* in battle with a corsair. The index referred to documents that had been sent to the Museo Naval in Madrid, so Palermo had gone there seeking information, and chance had set Tánger in his path. She was the person assigned to respond to the Gibraltarian's inquiries. He had approached the subject in the way of his trade, camouflaged with false scents and a studied lack of interest in his real purpose. But in the middle of their conversation, she had heard the name *Dei Gloria.* A brigantine lost, said Palermo, en route from Havana to Cádiz. That triggered Tánger's recollections, forming specific connections among what had until then been loose ends. She had hidden her excitement, dissembling as much as she was able. Later, after getting rid of the treasure hunter with vague promises, she verified that the document that interested him had been sent some time earlier to the general maritime archive in Viso del Marqués. The next day she was there, and in the section on Privateering and Prizes she found the name of the ship: "Account of the loss of the brigantine *Dei Gloria,* 4 February, 1767, in combat with the xebec corsair presumed to be the *Sergui...*" There was everything officially known about the sinking, along with the statement of the only survivor. It was the answer to the mystery, the dénouement of the adventure whose beginnings she had glimpsed years before in the Jesuit's letter. There was the reason the brigantine never reached port, and why the abbot Gándara was interrogated until his death in prison. There was clarified the fate of the two hundred flames of green fire that were intended to convince the members of the cabinet of the *Pesquisa Secreta,* and maybe the king himself, not to annul the Ignatian order.

She was dazed and fascinated, but also furious. She had all this right before her eyes years ago, and hadn't seen it. She hadn't been ready. But unexpectedly, as when you find the key piece to a complex jigsaw puzzle, everything fell into place. She went back to her notebooks and her old research notes, adding the new information. Now the tragedy of Abbot Gándara—which not even the nuncio of Rome could explain to the Pope in correspondence—was clear. The abbot knew what the *Dei Gloria* was transporting. His proximity to the king, his presence at court, made him the appropriate intermediary for the ambitious bribery scheme the Jesuits were weaving; he was the person charged with negotiating with the Conde de Aranda. But someone had wanted to forestall the maneuver, or to make off with the booty for himself, and Gándara was arrested and interrogated. Then the corsair *Chergui* sailed onto the scene, either by accident or by plan, and everything ended badly for everyone concerned. The Jesuits were expelled, the ship was sunk under hazy circumstances, and Gándara was the key to the entire affair. Which was why authorities had kept him under lock and key for eighteen years. Now the clues scattered among the records of the various trials took on meaning. Until his death they were trying to get him to reveal what he knew about the brigantine. But he had kept silent, carrying the secret to the tomb. He lifted a corner of the veil only once, in an intercepted letter written by him in 1778, eleven years after the events, to the missionary Jesuit Sebastián de Mendiburu, who was exiled in Italy: "They ask about the large and perfect Devil's irises, orbs clear as my conscience. But I say nothing, and though I am the tortured one, it is that which in their ambition tortures them."

With all that material Tánger had been able to construct, almost step by step, the history of the emeralds and the voyage of the *Dei Gloria.* Padre Escobar had sailed from Valencia on November 2, unaware, paradoxically, that Abbot Gándara had been arrested in Madrid that very day. The brigantine, commanded by Captain Elezcano—brother of one of the superiors of the Society—crossed the Atlantic, arriving in Havana on December 16. There he met with Padre Tolosa, the "young, dependable, and well to be trusted" Jesuit who had been sent ahead with the mission of secretly gathering two hundred emeralds from mines the Society controlled in Colombia. These were uncut stones, the largest and best in color and purity. Tolosa had fulfilled his mission and then sailed from Cartagena de Indias aboard a different ship. His crossing was delayed by unfavorable winds between Grand Cayman and the Isle of Pines, and when finally they rounded Cape San Antonio and passed beneath the guns at El Morro castle, the *Dei Gloria* was already waiting in Havana Bay, at a discreet anchorage between Barrero cove and Cruz key. The transfer of the cargo was undoubtedly made at night, or camouflaged amid the declared merchandise on the ship's manifest. Padres Escobar and Tolosa were listed as passengers, along with a crew of twenty-nine men that included the captain, don Juan Bautista Elezcano, the pilot, don Carmelo Valcells, the fifteen-year-old ship's boy, don Miguel Palau, an apprentice seaman and the nephew of the Valencian shipowner Fornet Palau, and twenty-six sailors. The *Dei Gloria* set sail from Havana on January 1. It traveled along the coast of Florida to the thirtieth parallel, continued five degrees north and followed a line between just south of Bermuda and the Azores, and on that course suffered the storm that damaged the rigging and made it necessary to man the pumps. The brigantine continued east, avoiding the port at Cádiz—spared that obligatory call by the still-effective privileges of the Society—and passed Gibraltar on the first or second of February. The next day, after they had sailed around Cabo de Gata and were heading northeast toward Cabo de Palos and Valencia, the *Chergui* gave chase.

The part played by the corsair xebec remains an enigma that

may never be clarified. Its ambush from some hidden inlet on the coast of Andalusia, or perhaps its departure from Gibraltar itself, may have been coincidental . . . or perhaps not. It was documented that the *Chergui* sailed with English or Algerian letters of marque—depending on the circumstance—and that Gibraltar was one of its usual bases, although at that time a precarious peace between Spain and England was still in effect. The corsair may have targeted the *Dei Gloria* by chance, but the tenacity of the pursuit, and her presence at that precise time and place, appear too opportune to be coincidental. It was not difficult to imagine a part for the corsair in the complex game of self-interests and complicities of that era. The Conde de Aranda himself, or any of the members of the cabinet of the *Pesquisa Secreta* that had ordered the arrest of Abbot Gándara—who was a political adversary of Aranda—could have had information about the plan and had designs on the treasure of the Jesuits even before it was offered to him, killing two birds with one stone.

Whatever the fact, the pursuers had not counted on the tenacity of Captain Elezcano, which must have been reinforced by the presence of the two resolute Jesuits on board. He chose to fight, both ships were sunk, and the emeralds went to the bottom of the sea. The information provided by the surviving ship's boy was satisfactory, and the naval authorities charged with the initial investigation had no reason to dig deeper, a ship sunk by a corsair being routine in those days. By the time the order came from Madrid to make a more detailed inquiry, the witness had flown—a mysterious and timely disappearance, organized by the Jesuits, who had not as yet lost the cooperation of local authorities. Undoubtedly the Society studied the possibility of a clandestine recovery of the brigantine, but it was too late. The blow fell: imprisonment and diaspora. Everything was lost in the morass that followed the fall of the Order and its subsequent dissolution. The silence of Abbot Gándara, and the exile of those who knew the secret, cast an even heavier veil over the mystery. There was evidence of two official attempts by naval authorities to find the wreckage during the time the Conde de Aranda was still in power, but neither was successful. Later, as new dramas shook Spain and Europe, the *Dei Gloria* was forgotten. Apart from a passing mention in a book entitled *La flota negra,* The Black Fleet, written by the librarian of San Fernando in 1803, there was one last and curious proposal, made later to Manuel Godoy, first minister to King Charles IV, requesting a search for "a certain ship said to have sunk coming with emeralds from Cuba," this according to Godoy's own account in his memoirs. But the plan did not flower, and in handwritten annotations in the margin of the proposal, the original of which Tánger had located in the national historical archive, Godoy's skepticism was evident: ". . . because of the illogic of the idea and because, as is well known, Cuba never produced emeralds." So, for nearly two centuries, the *Dei Gloria* had sunk back into oblivion and silence.

TÁNGER and Coy had stopped near the bow of a small schooner. She was looking across the bay, where the skyline of Algeciras was sharp and clear. The water was calm, a blue-green barely rippled by the breeze. There were more clouds in the sky now, moving slowly toward the Mediterranean. Opposite the port, at the foot of the massive Rock, boats at anchor dotted the water. Maybe the *Chergui* had sailed from this very spot on its last voyage, after lying to in the shelter of the English batteries on Gibraltar. A lookout in the crow's nest with a spyglass, a sail glimpsed on the horizon, moving west to east, an anchor quickly and stealthily hoisted. And the chase.

"Nino Palermo knows there were emeralds," Tánger concluded. "Not how many or their size and quality, but he knows. He's seen some of the documents I've seen. He's intelligent, he knows his business, and he knows how to draw conclusions. But he doesn't know everything I know."

"At least he knows you deceived him."

"Don't be ridiculous. You don't deceive men like him. You fight them with their own weapons."

She turned toward the far end of the quay, where the *Carpanta* was tied up. Through the masts and rigging of neighboring boats, Coy could see El Piloto, who was completing some chores topside. He had arrived that morning, sleepy and unshaven, with dark skin cracked by sun, rugged hands, rough when you shook them, and eyes that always recalled a winter sea. Three days' sail from Cartagena. Steamers, he had said—El Piloto always called merchant ships steamers—had not let him get a wink of sleep the whole trip. He was getting too old to be sailing by himself. Too old.

"I worked it all out, you know," Tánger continued. "All Palermo did was accidentally provide the mental click that fit everything into place. Set things in order that had been there, waiting... The kinds of things that for some reason you sense will have meaning someday, and that you store in a corner of your memory till that time."

Now she was being sincere, and Coy realized that. Now she had told the real story, and was still talking about it; at least with regard to concrete facts, she had nothing left to hide. Now he had the keys, the account of events. He knew what was at the bottom of the ocean and about the mystery. Even so, he was not exactly tranquil, or relieved. I will lie to you and deceive you. Some unknown, unidentifiable note was vibrating somewhere, like an almost imperceptible change in the rhythm of a diesel or the melodic insinuation of an instrument whose appropriateness is not possible to establish immediately, a deliberate or improvised line that seems mysterious until the end, when it can be properly assessed. He was remembering a piece by the Thelonious Monk Quartet, a blues classic that was called precisely that—"Misterioso."

"Intuition, Coy," she said. "That's the word. Dreams you are sure will materialize someday." She kept gazing at the sea as if replaying that dream, her skirt blowing in the breeze, hair blowing in her face. "I worked on that even before I knew where it was leading me, with a persistence you cannot imagine. I burned the midnight oil. And suddenly, one day, click! Everything was clear."

She turned, a smile on her lips. A reflective smile, almost expectant when she looked at him, squinting slightly because of the light. This was a smile that extended to the freckled skin around her mouth and cheeks, so warm he could sense the flush spreading down her neck and shoulders and arms beneath her clothing.

"Like a painter," she added, "who's carrying around a world inside, and suddenly a person, a phrase, a fleeting image, creates a painting in his head."

She smiled in that way beautiful and wise females have, serenely self-aware. There was flesh behind that smile, he thought, uneasy. There was a curve that blended into other perfect lines, a miracle of complicated genetic combinations. A waist. Warm thighs that hid the greatest of true mysteries.

"That's my story," Tánger concluded. "It was destined for me, and all my life, my studies, my work at the Museo Naval were leading me to it before I realized it. . . . That's why Palermo is nothing more than an interloper. For him it's only a ship, one among many possible treasures." She turned her eyes from Coy to gaze again at the sea. "For me, it's the dream of a lifetime."

Awkward, he scratched his unshaven chin. Then the back of his neck, and finally he touched his nose. He was looking for words. Something ordinary, everyday, that would wash the impression of that smile from his flesh.

"Even if you find it," he pointed out, "you won't be able to keep the treasure. You can't just go out and salvage a ship."

Tánger was focused on the bay. The clouds were gradually turning the water gray. A splotch of sunlight slipped past them before striking the water lapping the quay, flashing emerald.

"The *Dei Gloria* belongs to me," she said. "And no one is going to take it away. It's my Maltese falcon."

IX
Forecastle Women

There is nothing I love as much as I hate this game.
—John McPhee, LOOKING FOR A SHIP

"It's time," said Tánger.

He opened his eyes and saw her across from him, waiting. She was sitting on a teak bench in the cockpit of the *Carpanta,* looking at him intently. Coy was lying on the other bench with his jacket as cover, his head toward the bow and feet close to the tiller and compass. There was no wind, and the only sound was the gentle slapping of the swell against the sides of boats tied up at the quay in Marina Bay. Overhead, beyond the slightly swaying mast, the highest cumulus clouds were touched with soft pink.

"Right," he answered hoarsely.

Coy had the habit of waking up alert, fully lucid. An ability acquired from many early shifts on watch. Setting his jacket aside, he stretched a bit to loosen his stiff neck and went below to splash water on his face and hair. He returned and combed it back with his fingers after shaking his head like a wet dog. His beard rasped as he felt his chin; he had neglected to shave because of his long nap, which was necessary since they planned to sail at night. Tánger hadn't moved, and now she was studying the heights of the Rock with the preoccupied air of a mountain climber preparing to make an assault. She had changed from the long blue cotton skirt to jeans and a T-shirt, with a black sweater knotted around her waist. They were surrounded by the screams of gulls in the fading light. El Piloto was polishing the brightwork with a rag, his hands black. Take care of your boat, he always said, and she will take care of you. The *Carpanta* was a classic sailboat with a center cockpit and single mast, built in La Rochelle before plastic replaced iroko, teak, and copper.

"Piloto," he said.

The gray eyes, circled with dark wrinkles, glanced up from beneath thick eyebrows and gave Coy a friendly, tranquil wink. According to his own words, although he wasn't much given to words, El Piloto had sailed for sixty years with the wind at his back. He had given orders on the cruise ship *Canarias* when one still gave orders with a cornet, and had also worked as a fisherman, sailor, smuggler, and diver. His hair was the same lead gray as his eyes, curly, and very short, his skin tanned like old leather, his skillful hands rough. Fewer than ten years ago he was still good-looking enough to have played a heartthrob in an action film—say a sponge diver or a pirate—with Gilbert Roland or Alan Ladd. Now he had put on a little weight, but his shoulders were as broad as ever, his waist reasonably trim, and his arms still powerful. As a young man he'd been an excellent dancer, and in those days women in the bars of Molinete had fought over a bolero or paso doble with him. Still today, mature women who rented the *Carpanta* to fish or swim or just sightsee in the vicinity of Cartagena, felt their legs tremble when he held his arms in a little circle and invited them to take the helm.

"Everything OK?"

"Everything's OK."

They had known each other since Coy was a boy playing hooky to fool around the docks, where there were ships with foreign flags and sailors who spoke languages he could not understand. El Piloto, son and grandson of sailors who had also been called Piloto, could be found mornings outside some bar in the port, an honest man for hire, waiting for clients for his aging sailboat. Besides taking out women tourists, whose behinds he cupped to help them aboard, in those days El Piloto would dive to clear line from propellers, scrape barnacled hulls, and salvage outboard motors that had fallen into the water. In his free time he devoted himself, like everyone in those days, to small-time smuggling. Nowadays his bones were a little old to soak for too long, and he earned a living taking families out for Sunday outings, as well as crews from the tankers anchored at Escombreras, pilots on stormy days, and staggering-drunk Ukrainian sailors who tossed their cookies leeward after having drunk themselves blind in the bars. The *Carpanta* and El Piloto had seen it all. A vertical sun, without a breath of air, focusing laser heat on the mooring stones in the port. The sea really wild: God jumping and skipping. A westerly zinging in the rigging like harp strings. And those long red Mediterranean sunsets when the water looks like a mirror and the peace of that world is peace itself, and you understand that you are only a tiny drop in three thousand years of eternal ocean.

"We'll be back in a couple of hours," Coy said, shooting a glance up at the Rock, "and then shove off straightaway."

El Piloto nodded, continuing to polish a brass cleat. By his side an adolescent Coy had learned a few things about men, the sea, and life. Together they dived for Roman amphoras and quietly sold them, fished for squid at sunset on the Punta de la Podadera, caught swordfish, *marrajo,* and sharks on trotlines off Cope, and twenty-pound sea bass with a harpoon among the black rocks of Cabo de Palos—when there were still sea bass to fish for. In the Graveyard of Ships With No Name, to which old tubs made their last voyage, to be cut up and sold as scrap, El Piloto had taught Coy to identify each of the parts that composed a ship as they squeezed lemon juice on raw clams and sea urchins, long before Coy went off to be a seaman. And in that desolate landscape of rusted iron, superstructures beached on the sand, funnels that would never smoke again, and hulls like dead whales beneath the sun, El Piloto had pulled out a packet of unfiltered Celtas—the first cigarette in Coy's life—and lit one with a metal pocket lighter that had an acrid, burnt-wick smell.

Coy picked up his jacket and jumped to the quay. Tánger followed, the strap of her shoulder bag secure across her chest.

"What will the weather be like tonight?" she asked.

Coy took a look at the sea and the sky. A few isolated clouds were beginning to break apart, streaking the sky in several directions.

"Good weather. Not much wind. Maybe a mild sea when we round Punta Europa."

Surprise, enjoyment, a flash of vexation when she heard the word "sea." It would be funny, he thought, if she got seasick. Until that moment he had never considered the possibility of seeing her glassy-eyed like a tuna, skin yellowed, clinging weakly to the gunnel.

"You have any Dramamine? Maybe you'd better take one before we shove off."

"That's none of your business."

"You're wrong. If you get seasick, you'll be in the way. That is my business."

There was no answer, and Coy shrugged. They walked down the quay toward the Renault parked in the marina's parking lot. The setting sun, visible over Algeciras, shone red on the vertical face of the Rock, picking out the dark hollows of the former artillery gunports drilled into the rock. Two battered smugglers' launches, retired from sea duty and with blue and black paint dribbled down their sides in gobs, were rotting on sawhorses amid rusted engines and empty steel drums. The sounds of the city intensified as they got closer to the parking lot. A bored customs officer was watching television in his guardhouse. A long queue of automobiles was lined up to cross the border in the direction of La Línea de la Concepción.

It was Tánger who took the wheel. She drove carefully, handbag in her lap, confident and without haste, down the street that ran behind the border barriers to the bay, then left, toward the rotunda of Trafalgar cemetery.

"What's the plan?" Coy asked.

There wasn't any plan, she replied. They were going to drive up to Old Willis overlook to hear what Nino Palermo had to say. They would do exactly that, and then go back to the port, leave the car in the parking lot and the keys in the Avis mailbox, and shove off as planned.

"And if there are complications?"

Coy was thinking of Horacio Kiskoros and the Berber. Palermo wasn't the type who would be satisfied with offering a proposal and having them say, Well, we'll see, and See you later. With that in mind, before he left the boat he had picked up a Wichard bosun's knife, very sharp, with a four-inch blade and marlinspike, which El Piloto kept to sever halyards in an emergency. He could feel it in the back pocket of his jeans, between his right buttock and the seat. It wasn't a big deal, but it was better than making a social call empty-handed.

"I don't think there will be any complications," she answered.

At the cemetery, Tánger stood for a long time in front of the tombstones for Captain Thomas Norman, RM, who died December 6, 1805, of wounds received aboard the *Mars,* at Trafalgar. Then they went to the lookout to study the place they were to meet Palermo at nightfall. Coy watched as she walked over the old concrete mounts, now empty of guns. She studied everything carefully: the access road and the one that climbed toward the tunnels of the Great Siege, the empty whitewashed military barracks, the British flag flying over Moorish Castle, the isthmus where the airport was located, and the broad Atunara beach that stretched northeast to Spanish territory. She brought to mind an officer studying the terrain before a battle, and Coy found himself doing the same—calculating possibilities, safe havens and dangers, the way you study charts of a treacherous coast you want to reach by night.

Back at the cemetery gate, Tánger said, "Whatever happens, I don't want you to interfere."

That's easy to say, Coy thought. So he said nothing. He'd thought about asking El Piloto to come with them. In such situations three was a better number than two. But he didn't want to involve his friend too deeply. Not yet.

Tánger consulted her watch, opened her purse, and took out a pack of Players. He hadn't seen her smoke since Madrid, and it may well have been the same pack because there were only four cigarettes left. She flicked the lighter and slowly drew on the Player, holding the smoke a long time before exhaling.

"Are you sure everything's all right?" He wanted to know.

She nodded. On her right wrist, the minute hand passed 8:45. The glowing tip of her cigarette had burned down to her short fingernails. She rolled down the window and threw the butt into the street.

"Let's go."

Just like those films she liked, Coy concluded admiringly. Henry Fonda leaning against the fence in a black-and-white sunrise, readying himself for his walk to the O.K. Corral. And yet there was something so damnably real in her attitude, so strong in the way she started the motor and drove up the hill, passing the Hotel Rock and dropping to half speed as the grade of the road became steeper, that it stripped the situation of any possible artifice. This was totally real, and Tánger was not playing a role for his sake. She wasn't trying to impress him. She was the one who was driving, who was concentrating on keeping the car away from the dangerous precipices, who took the tight curves with cold purpose, confident, one hand on the wheel and the other on the gearshift, glancing from time to time toward the top of the mountain with a frown of concentration. When they arrived at the small turnoff of the mirador, she maneuvered the car until it was headed toward the road, downhill. Ready to speed away, Coy thought uneasily, as she opened the car door and got out, her sweater knotted around her waist, and her bag in her hands.

A Rover was parked nearby, next to the wall of the old bulwark. That was the first thing Coy saw when he got out of the car, along with the Berber chauffeur leaning against the hood. Then his eyes followed a semicircle to the left, the road to the tunnels, the rise toward the rugged peak of the Rock, the abandoned casemates and the balcony overlooking the airport, with the isthmus and Spain in the background, dark mountains, dark sky, gray ocean to the west and black to the east, and the lights of La Línea coming on below in the twilight. A bad place for a talk, he told himself. He looked to the railing of the mirador, where Nino Palermo was waiting for them.

Tánger was already there. He followed her, breathing in the aromas of salt, thyme, and resin on the breeze that stirred the shrubs and treetops. Another look around but no sight of Horacio Kiskoros anywhere. Palermo stood leaning against the railing, hands in the pockets of a light, collarless hunting jacket, a garment that made him seem even more corpulent than he was.

"Good evening," he said.

Coy murmured an automatic "Good evening," and Tánger said nothing. She stood stone still before the treasure hunter.

"What is your proposition?" she asked.

As if she weren't there, Palermo spoke to Coy.

"Some women get right to the point, don't they?"

Coy didn't answer, refusing to accept the complicity Palermo was offering. He stood back a little, at a distance but alert, listening. She was the boss, and that night he was acting more as bodyguard than anything else. He felt the weight of the knife in his back pocket; the Berber wasn't all that efficient, after all, watching from so far away. He frisked you when you were clean and didn't frisk you when he should have. Maybe he was following orders from Palermo, who wanted to appear diplomatic.

The treasure hunter turned to Tánger. The fading light was beginning to obscure the features of her face.

"This hide-and-seek game is ridiculous," he said. "We're wasting powder in salvos, when in the end we're all going to end up at the same place."

"What place is that?" Tánger asked.

Her voice was absolutely serene, neither provocative nor insecure. Palermo laughed briefly.

"At the wreck, of course. And if I'm not there, the police will be. Current law . . ."

"I know the current law."

Palermo gestured as if to say, Well, if that's the case he had little to add.

"You have a proposition," said Tánger.

"I do. I have. . . . God almighty. Of course I have a proposition. We're starting with a clean slate, señorita. You have fucked me and I have fucked you." He paused. "Speaking metaphorically, of course. We're even."

"I don't know where you get the idea that we're even."

She had spoken in such a low voice that Palermo moved forward slightly, bowing his head to hear better. The gesture gave him an unexpectedly courtly air.

"I have resources you two will never have," he said. "Experience. Technology. The right contacts."

"But you don't know where the *Dei Gloria* is."

This time she had spoken loudly and clearly. Palermo snorted.

"I would if you hadn't put so much time and effort into throwing tacks in my path. Blocking access to that mafia of archivists and librarians . . . Damn it to hell. You took advantage of my good faith."

"You haven't had good faith since they took away your pacifier."

The treasure hunter turned to Coy.

"You hear her?" he asked. "I could get to like this woman, I swear. I . . . God almighty. Have you . . . ? Damn!" He was being sarcastic, panting like a bloodhound after a long run. "You'd better get yours, my friend, before she squeezes you like a lemon and tosses you aside too."

Stars were beginning to blink in the sky, as if someone were hitting a light switch. Shadows were closing in over the treasure hunter's face, and now it was the glow of the lights from La Línea, below and behind him, that made his silhouette darker against the railing.

"Emeralds, don't forget." Palermo was still addressing Coy. "The treasure of the Jesuits. I suppose she hasn't had any choice but to tell you about it by now. . . . A cargo of emeralds worth . . . God . . . a fortune anywhere, including the black market. That is, of course, if she can handle the job and get them out of Spanish waters before the State swoops in on her."

The same brightness that silhouetted Palermo's broad shoulders lighted Tánger's face. It hardened her features, sharpening her profile against the light curtain of her hair.

"If she can," Coy said arrogantly, "she has no reason to share anything with you."

"You forget that I set her on the trail," Palermo protested. "And that I have been working on this for a long time. You forget I have ways of setting up a cooperative arrangement that will benefit us all. . . . And you forget that ambition did in the wise little mouse."

Overhead, like a stage curtain perforated with luminous pinholes, the sky was now black. The sun had to be about fifteen degrees below the horizon, Coy calculated. He watched Ursa Minor take form above Palermo's head and Ursa Major over his right shoulder.

"Listen, both of you," the seeker of sunken ships was saying. "I want to propose something.... Something reasonable. Finding treasure isn't just a matter of getting there and opening the coffer. It took Mel Fisher twenty years to find the *Atocha*.... I contributed my resources and my contacts. That includes connections and bribes so no one interferes.... I even have a market for the emeralds. That means... Do you realize?" Now he was speaking only to Tánger. "A lot of money for us. For all of us."

"On what terms?"

"Fifty percent. Half for me and half for you."

She motioned with her head toward Coy.

"And him?"

"He's... Well. Your affair, isn't he? It isn't up to me to reward him for his time."

He was being sarcastic again, speaking in a low voice, again with the snuffling laugh of a huge, hard-run dog. He hadn't moved from the railing.

"All you have to do is give me two pieces of information: the latitude and longitude, so I can locate them on Urrutia's nautical charts.... And, of course, the cargo manifest and official report of the sinking."

Tánger took her time answering. She seemed to consider the proposition.

"You can find all that in the archives," she said.

Palermo swore without the least embarrassment.

"You know that.... goddamn you.... You have boxed me out of the archives, the same way you stole the Urrutia in Barcelona from under my nose. Even so, I was able to find a reproduction of the chart. I also went to check the goddamn archives and they told me. . . ." He took a deep breath and let it out noisily. "You know what they told me. Those documents aren't there. They've been requested for research. End of story."

"What a shame."

Palermo was far from appreciating her condolence.

"No," he said, irritated. "It's a dirty trick that you're responsible for."

"Is that what you were looking for in my house?"

"That's what Horacio was supposed to get." The treasure hunter hesitated a few seconds. "As for the dog, I swear to you. . . ."

"Forget the dog."

Every syllable was like ice. Coy saw Palermo shift uncomfortably. Now the light from below shone on a serious face. One push, Coy thought. One push and that so-and-so would take a walk straight down, one or two hundred yards onto the rocks below. Splat. Something you could call LOG: Law of Opportune Gravity. Then he remembered the Berber posted by the car and considered the possibility that they might be the ones doing the pushing. LDG: Law of Disquieting Gravity.

"If we add what you know to what I know," Palermo was saying, "and if we stop trying to give each other a hard time, I'll promise to put this wreck through a sieve in less than a month. . . . Deadman's Chest has a specially fitted boat—radar with a lateral sweep, fathometer, echo sounder, magnetometer, metal detectors, diving equipment . . . everything we need. Then, once we're down, we have to work with the plans, mark, measure, lay out a grid, suck off sand and mud. . . . You don't have a clue what's involved. Besides, emeralds are fragile. . . . Imagine. . . . centuries of crap to be removed, proper cleaning . . . You don't even know what an electrolytic bath for cleaning a simple silver coin is. I don't want to think what the damage might be. You two would muck it up. You're amateurs."

He laughed, without a trace of humor. Suddenly an unexpected flash of light blinded Coy, who was still absorbed in thoughts of pushers and pushees. The light startled him.

"Besides, you don't have the contacts." Palermo held the lighter to his cigarette. "I know the underground market where this kind of find has to be handled. And I control . . ." The cigarette between his lips blurred his words. "God almighty. Eighty percent of the world's emerald traffic is under the counter, overseen by the Jewish mafia of Belgium and Italy. You think I don't know why you went to Antwerp?"

Antwerp. Coy had been to that enormous port, with its miles of cranes and sheds and ships. That Tánger had been there was another surprise—although suddenly he remembered the postcard beside the silver cup in the apartment on Paseo Infanta Isabel. So he determined to listen carefully, but with a low level of expectation. When it came to this woman there was no news that turned out to be soothing, or pleasant.

"Don't tell me she didn't talk to you about Antwerp." The glowing ember shone like an ironic eye pointing at Coy from the treasure hunter's mouth. "Really . . . Well, hear this: before you two met in Barcelona, she made a discreet little trip. A few calls that . . ." He lowered his voice so the chauffeur couldn't hear. "Including a certain address on Rubenstraat—Sherr and Cohen. Specialists in cutting stones to change their appearance and obliterate distinguishing marks . . . I have people who tell me things, too."

Coy smelled the aroma of the tobacco. The light gray smoke spiraled against the light before it broke up and drifted away from Palermo's silhouette.

"So she didn't tell you that either. Incredible."

I have sold my soul, Coy thought. I have sold my soul to this Lorelei, and they're all going to work me over and leave me like a rag doll. Her. This guy. Even the Berber. This is like thinking you can swim with sharks at feeding time. If I were half clever, and at this point it's clear that I'm not, I would start running as fast as I can down this mountain, jump onto the *Carpanta,* tell El Piloto to cast off and get out of here posthaste.

The red eye was again pointing at Coy.

"She hasn't talked to you yet about emeralds? She hasn't told you that they're the most valuable of all precious stones? I've seen plenty. I brought up several when I was with Fisher. And I can tell you that in Antwerp they will pay anything for a bagful of those old, uncut stones. Your little friend here . . . she's well aware of that."

"And if I don't agree?"

Tánger pressed her handbag to her breast and the darkness snipped out a mannish profile. I wouldn't be a bit surprised, thought Coy, if she's carrying a pistol in that fucking purse.

"We'll be sticking to you two like your own shadows." The ember rose and fell as Palermo gave that information in an objective tone, as if he were reciting a manual of instructions. "The area between Cabo de Gata and Cabo de Palos . . . All right. That isn't too much ground to cover, and as soon as I identify your boat, I can use a helicopter. . . . Find you, you understand? Precisely as you locate the prize. And if we are unsuccessful, I'll see to it that you get a visit from a coast guard patrol boat."

Coy heard that canine snuffle for the third time. Shooting stars were streaking through the sky like fallen angels, or souls in pain, or spent missiles. That's me up there, Coy thought. Leave room for me.

"If you don't count me in," Palermo added, "you won't have a chance. Quite aside from certain physical risks."

A long silence, and then Tánger said, "You frighten me."

She didn't seem frightened in the least. On the contrary, her words sounded arrogant. They sounded cold as a sliver of ice, and also very dangerous. Palermo took the cigarette from his mouth and spoke to Coy.

"She has class, doesn't she? She's a bitch with a lot of class. I'm not surprised she has you by the balls."

He drew on his cigarette and the red grew more intense. This guy, Coy reflected, almost with gratitude, has the rare virtue of providing an escape valve just when you need one. He was feeling that wave of gratitude as he moved forward to deliver his first punch. To make sure it was a good one, because Palermo was considerably taller, Coy raised his elbow slightly and swung with all his might, upward, and slightly on the diagonal, smashing the tip of Palermo's cigarette into his lips. To his right, he heard a muted cry from Tánger, who tried to contain it, but in that same instant Coy had hit the Gibraltarian with a second punch that slammed him kidney-first against the railing. I don't need you to fall over, Coy thought with a thread of lucidity. I don't want to kill you, so don't do something fancy and lose your balance. Which was why he tried to grab Palermo's coat, to pull him toward him and to get in the third punch without having him fall over the railing and yell *aaaaaaah!* all the way down like the bad guys in the movies. But in the interval Palermo seemed to recover; he raised his fists and Coy felt something explode by his left ear. The stars overhead mixed with the ones his abused senses generated. He staggered back a few steps.

"Mover fucker!" Palermo grunted. "Mover fucker!"

The *v* indicated that the treasure hunter must have the cigarette ground into his gums. That was some small consolation for Coy, but while he was trying to keep his balance he heard the footsteps of the Berber racing toward him over the concrete paving, and realized that his chances were approaching zero, and that he'd be lucky ever to pronounce anything again. LSHF: Law of Shit Hits the Fan. So when all is lost. . . . He took a deep breath, ducked his head, and, being low and compact anyway, charged Palermo with the fury of a blinded bull. If I get there before your homo Moor, he thought, you'll be over the railing with me, as sure as there's a God in Heaven.

He didn't get there. He who gets in the first blow gets two; but what the old saying didn't make clear was that after those two you can get two hundred in return. The Berber caught him from behind. Coy heard his jacket tear down one seam, and by then Palermo already had his fist cocked, so that in a matter of seconds Coy found himself on the ground on his knees with the breath knocked out of him, his head buzzing, his eardrums vibrating, and one eye that wouldn't open. He was furious with himself, and wondered why his knees and his arms didn't obey his orders to get up and fight. He tried again and again but failed. Paraplegic, he thought. These sonsofbitches have left me paralyzed. His mouth had the taste of old iron. He spit, knowing it would be blood. They're beating the living shit out of me, he told himself.

He felt faint, and everything around him whirled. Then he heard Tánger's voice and he thought: Poor girl, it's her turn now. He tried to get to his feet, to give a hand to that brassy little witch. To see that they didn't touch a hair of her head as long as he had the strength to open and close a fist. But he was in no shape to close a fist, or close anything except the swollen eye—and then he hit the pavement like a prizefighter seeing birdies. Still, he couldn't leave her, not in the hands of Palermo and the Berber, even though in her way she was worse than the two of them put together. So with one last supreme effort, resigned, desperate, he choked back a moan and staggered to his feet. Only then did he remember El Piloto's knife. He felt for it in his back pocket as he cast a quick look around, like a pugilist whose bell had been rung. He saw his two challengers standing docilely side by side. Their eyes were on Tánger, who was still standing quietly by the railing; like her, they were not moving, as if mesmerized by some powerful attraction. Coy focused his good eye. What had captured their attention was something Tánger had in her hand, holding it out as if she was showing it to them. He told himself that he must be in worse shape than he thought, really punch-drunk, because the thing glinted like metal and looked very much like—he didn't want to confirm something so unthinkable—a huge, menacing handgun.

TÁNGER said little, or at least nothing meant expressly for Coy, in the few brief words she had spoken up there at the mirador before they hurried to their car, leaving the other two behind at the railing like little Christmas shepherds gloriously petrified by the vision of the hardware Tánger had exhibited as if against her will. "It's your fault," she informed him, less in a tone of reproach than as simple information, while she manipulated the wheel and gearshift, her handbag in her lap and the headlamps lighting the hairpin curves descending the Rock. He was coughing like a tubercular heroine in a film, like Marguerite Gautier, and a few drops of blood escaped the tissue and hit the windshield. A thug. He was a thug, and none of that had been necessary, she added later. Totally unnecessary; all he had done was complicate things. Coy frowned as much as his hematomas allowed, exasperated. As for the last lines of the dialogue conducted between Tánger and Nino Palermo under the somber nose of the silent Berber, they had been of the nature of "This man is a lunatic," from the treasure hunter, while she tried to lighten the highly charged atmosphere with "Coy is impulsive by nature and tends to solve things his own way.

"And you, Palermo, you're an imbecile."

The revolver, a heavy, snub-nosed 357 magnum that Coy had never seen in Tánger's possession, helped Palermo digest those words without making too bad a face. What about the deal, he'd said then. I have to think about it, was her response. At the moment, she added, she couldn't tell him yes or no.

Palermo, who seemed to have recovered the use of his *th*'s, told her that she and the mother who bore her could blow it out their ass. That was exactly what he said: she and the mother who bore her, and this time he seemed truly apoplectic. You're not going to lead me down the garden path, bitch, he spat at her from the railing, visibly regaining lost ground before the silent approval of his chauffeur. All that, vocalized several feet from a handbag cannon with six acorn-size bullets in the cylinder, placed Palermo at a creditable, almost admirable, level for brass. Though fuzzy-headed and with a face like a road map, Coy could appreciate the performance out of pure masculine solidarity. "I will send you my answer," she said, looking like a model of propriety with the black sweater tied around her waist. She would have given the impression that she had never broken so much as a plate if she hadn't had that threatening piece in her hand. He remembered that Palermo had said Tánger was the kind of woman who could sink her teeth in you without opening her mouth. Now she was holding that piece of metal without aiming, arm at her side, barrel to the ground, almost as if wishing she were elsewhere; and that, curiously, gave her more credibility than if she were adopting a stance from a detective flick. I will tell you whether or not we have a deal, she said. Just give me a few days. And Palermo, who still didn't believe her and maybe never would believe her, or maybe had caught her sarcasm, let fly with a string of extremely baroque and Mediterranean curses, no doubt related to his Maltese blood. The mildest among them was that he was going to trim the rigging of her lunatic sailor. All that was floating in the air behind Tánger as she walked to the Renault, after putting a hand on Coy's shoulder and getting a grunt in answer to her question of how he felt.

"Like shit," he said, when Tánger asked a second time, on the road down. Suddenly she burst out laughing. The laugh of a lighthearted, self-contained happy child that he heard with amazement as he examined her profile with his one good eye.

"You are truly incredible," she said. "You nearly blew everything, but you *are* incredible." She laughed again, and was still laughing, with admiration, when she turned and shot him a quick glance of sympathy. "Sometimes I think I love watching you fight."

The reflection of the headlights laid a lamina of steel in her eyes, but that steel shone as if in bright sunlight. She took her hand from the gearshift and rested the backs of her fingers on Coy's neck, touching the stubble of his unshaved chin, puffy now from the fists of Palermo and the Berber. And Coy, exhausted and surprised, leaned back against the headrest. He felt a warmth where her fingers lay, and also in the place where soap operas say the heart is. He would have smiled like a goofy kid, had his swollen lips permitted.

FREE of the last line, the *Carpanta* eased away from the quay. The deck vibrated softly as the sailboat sat motionless in the light reflected in the water. Then El Piloto revved the motor and the boat gradually moved forward. The pier lights marched slowly by, more quickly as the boat picked up speed, bow pointed toward the open sea. In the distance the lights of La Línea, the San Roque refinery, and the city of Algeciras marked the outline of the bay. Coy finished coiling the line in the bow, secured it, and moved back to the cockpit, holding onto the shrouds when—now they were outside the protection of the port—the ship began to pitch in the waves. The lights of Gibraltar still illuminated the *Carpanta,* silhouetting El Piloto at the wheel, the lower part of his face red in the glow of the compass, where the needle was turning gradually toward the south.

Coy breathed the air with pleasure, sniffing the proximity of open sea. From the first time he had stepped onto the deck of a ship, the moment of leaving port had produced in him a sensation of singular calm, something very like happiness. The land lay behind, and everything he could need was traveling with him, circumscribed by the tight limits of the ship. At sea, he thought, men traveled with their houses on their backs, like the knapsack of an explorer or the shell that moves with the snail. All you needed was a few gallons of gasoline, oil, or some sail and a favorable wind, for everything that dry land provided to become superfluous, disposable. Voices, noise, people, smells, the tyranny of the clock had no meaning here. To sail out until the coast fell far behind the stern—that was one goal met. Facing the menacing and magical presence of the omnipresent sea, sorrow, desire, sentimental attachments, hatreds, and hopes bubbled away in the wake, dwindling until they seemed far away, meaningless, because the ocean brought people back to themselves. There were things that were unbearable on shore—thoughts, absences, anguishes—but could be borne on the deck of a ship. There was no painkiller as powerful as that. He had seen men survive on ships who would have lost their reason and tranquillity forever anywhere else. Course, wind, waves, position, the day's run, survival; out there only those words had meaning. Because it was true that real freedom, the only possible freedom, the true peace of God, began five miles from the nearest coast.

"Everything OK, Piloto?"

"Everything's OK. In half an hour we'll clear Punta Europa."

Motionless at the stern, Tánger was watching the lights they were leaving behind. She had put on her sweater and was holding one of the backstays beside the lazily flapping pennant. She was looking up toward the top of the dark mass of the Rock, as if she couldn't leave behind things that were worrying her. The bow of the *Carpanta* was now pointing directly south, and behind them on the port side were the luminous garlands of the main port, the ships anchored at the docks, the black line of the breakwater, and the white flashes, one every two seconds, of the large beacon on the south dock.

El Piloto maneuvered to avoid a large anchored merchant ship and then set the engine at 2,500 rpms. The needle of the binnacle's electronic log established their speed as five knots, and the pitching became more pronounced. Coy went down to the cabin to activate the radio, Sailor VHF. He set channels 9 and 16 to transmit and receive. Then he went to the stern to join Tánger. The stern light suffused the straight line of the boat's wake with phosphorescence.

"Palermo's right," said Coy.

"Don't start," she replied.

And said nothing more. She was still focused on the heights of the huge dark rock, which looked like a threatening cloud hovering over the city.

"He can squash us if he puts his mind to it," Coy insisted. "And it's true that he has ways to locate the *Dei Gloria*. His offer . . ."

"Look. . . ." She was profiled in the light they were leaving behind, over the stern quarter. "I did all the work. Let's see if you can get that in your head. That ship is mine."

"Ours. That ship is ours. Yours and mine." Coy pointed to El Piloto. "And now it's his, too."

Tánger seemed to mull that over.

"All right," she said after a second. "He needs to do his thing, and you do yours. . . . But Palermo isn't your business."

"If there are problems, Palermo will be everyone's business."

"If anyone's causing problems, it's you. You and your macho fits." She laughed, but not pleasantly. "The only time you seem happy is when someone's bashing your face in."

Well now, he thought. LOE: Law of Opposing Enticements. One a carrot and the other a stick. Now you're not putting your hand against my neck, beautiful, or smiling. Not right this minute. Not when you're cool as you are now, and you start thinking that my blunders alter your plans.

All Coy said was, "You still think you can handle everyone, don't you?"

"I still think I know exactly what I'm doing."

Her eyes were back on something high on the dark rock. Coy took a look for himself. Farther down on the side, a tiny blue spark seemed to be climbing upward, while higher up something glowed red, like a bonfire. I hope, he thought, that the Berber has driven the car over the side and they're both sizzling like popcorn.

"Where did you get that gun?" As he said the word "gun" he felt a twinge of irritation. "You shouldn't be carrying something like that around."

"I can if I choose to."

Coy touched his injured eye and turned toward the luminous wake of the *Carpanta,* trying to think of an adequate answer. At the first opportunity, he decided, that bit of equipment is going overboard. He didn't like handguns, or guns in general. He didn't even like knives, though El Piloto's unused Wichard was still in the back pocket of his jeans. A person who carries that kind of utensil, he thought, does so with the clear intention of piercing, stabbing, or slashing. Which means that he's either very frightened or not a very nice guy.

"Weapons," he concluded aloud, "always create problems."

"They also get you out of them when you act like a fool."

He half-turned. Wounded.

"Hey. You said you like to see me fight."

"I said that?"

Now the glow of the distant city and the stern light in the wake revealed the angle of a smile forming beneath the shining tips of her windblown hair. Coy felt his irritation draining away into other feelings.

"Easy," she said, and laughed. "I'm not planning to use it against you."

THE meridional lighthouse was visible now off the port beam—five seconds of light and five seconds of darkness. Open water was making the *Carpanta* pitch more violently, and atop the mast, weakly sketched by the running lights, the wind vane and the blade of the anemometer were spinning intermittently, at the whim of the rocking boat and the absence of wind. By instinct Coy, back in the cockpit, calculated their distance from land, and glanced toward the starboard quarter, where a merchant ship that had been closing on them from the east was now in a free lane. With his hands on the helm—a classic six-spoke wooden wheel nearly three feet in diameter, located in the cockpit behind a small cabin with a windshield and canvas awning—El Piloto was gradually changing course, heading east and keeping the beacon light in his peripheral vision. Without needing to consult the lighted repeater of the GPS over the binnacle beside the automatic pilot, or the patent log or the echo sounder, Coy knew they were at 36°6′N and 5°20′W. He had drawn courses toward or away from that lighthouse too many times on nautical charts—four of the British Admiralty and two Spanish—to forget the latitude and longitude of Europa Point.

"What do you think of her?" he asked El Piloto.

He didn't look at Tánger. She was still clinging to the backstay and contemplating the black Rock behind them. El Piloto took a while to answer. Coy didn't know whether he was considering the question or consciously delaying the answer.

"I suppose," El Piloto said finally, "you know what you're doing."

Coy twisted his lips in the darkness.

"I'm not asking for my sake, Piloto. I'm asking for her."

"She's one of those people who's worth more when they stay ashore."

Coy was about to say the obvious: But she hasn't stayed ashore. He could also have added: She's the kind all sailors tell about or invent for their pals, in the cabin or in those old-time forecastles. The kind that all of them had met in some port somewhere. It was on the tip of his tongue, but he didn't say it. Instead, he stared at the black sky above the swaying mast. Most of the stars must be out, though the glow from the coast obscured them.

"We could run into problems, Piloto."

El Piloto didn't answer. He kept correcting the course, spoke by spoke, keeping a wide berth between them and the point. Only after several minutes did he tip his head a little, as if he were checking the echo sounder.

"There are always problems at sea," he said.

"This time it won't only be the sea."

El Piloto's silence communicated his concern.

"Any risk of losing the boat?"

"I don't think it will go that far," Coy reassured him. "I'm referring to problems in general."

El Piloto seemed to think it over.

"You said there might be some money," he said finally. "That would be welcome. There's not a lot of work around."

"We're going after treasure."

El Piloto didn't react to that revelation. He kept his focus on the helm and the lighthouse.

"Treasure," he repeated at last in a neutral tone.

"That's right. Emeralds from a long time ago. They're worth a bundle."

His friend nodded, implying that all old emeralds must be worth a bundle, but that he wasn't thinking about that. He released the wheel long enough to reach for the wineskin hanging from the binnacle, throw his head back, and take a long drink. Then he gripped the wheel again, wiping his mouth with the back of the other hand before passing the wineskin to Coy.

"Remind me some time," he said, "to tell you stories I've heard about treasures."

Coy repeated Piloto's motions, holding up the wineskin, gauging the rocking of the boat to prevent spilling wine on himself. He recognized it. An aromatic, fresh claret from near Cartagena.

"This story is pretty convincing," he said before taking his last swallow. "And I think we can locate the wreck."

"Wreck from when?"

"Two hundred and fifty years ago." Coy put the stopper in the skin and hung it up. "Mazarrón bay. Not down very far."

El Piloto shook his head, skeptical.

"She must have broken up. Fishermen spend their lives snagging their nets on old wrecks.... Sand will have covered everything. What there was to find has already been found, or is lost for all time."

"Ah, you're a man of little faith, Piloto. Like your soul mates at the Sea of Galilee. Until they saw the man walk on water they didn't take him seriously."

"I don't see you walking on water."

"No, I guess not. Or her either."

They both looked at Tánger, motionless at the stern, still outlined against light from the coast. El Piloto had taken a cigarette from his jacket and put it in his mouth.

"Besides," he said, seemingly on a tangent, "I'm getting old."

Or maybe it wasn't a tangent. El Piloto and the *Carpanta* were getting old in the same way that schooner in the port of Barcelona was rotting away, that in the Graveyard of Ships With No Name the superstructures of merchant ships cut up for scrap were rusting in the rain and sun, corroded by salt, licked by waves on the dirty sand. Just as Coy himself had been rotting as he wandered around the port, tossed up on the shore from a rock in the Indian Ocean that wasn't on any chart. Although, as El Piloto himself—though maybe he wasn't the same Piloto now—had told him more than twenty years ago, men and ships should always stay out to sea, and sink there with dignity.

"I don't know," Coy said, sincerely. "The truth is, I don't know. It may be that in the end we'll end up with a fistful of nothing. You and me, Piloto. Maybe even her."

El Piloto gave a slow affirmative nod, as if that conclusion seemed the most logical. Then he took his lighter from his pocket, struck the wheel on his open palm, blew on the wick, and held it to the tip of the cigarette in his mouth.

"But it isn't the money, is it?" he murmured. "At least you're not here for that."

Coy smelled tobacco mixed with the acrid scent of the wick, which the breeze, beginning to freshen from behind Europa Point, rapidly carried west.

"She needs . . ." He stopped suddenly, feeling ridiculous. "Well. Maybe 'help' isn't the word."

El Piloto took a long pull on his cigarette.

"You're the one who needs her, is more like it."

On the binnacle, the compass needle showed 070°. El Piloto touched the corresponding key on the repeater of the automatic pilot, transferring the course to it.

"I've known women like that," he added. "Um-hmmm. I've known a few."

"A woman like that . . . What do you mean, like that? You don't know anything about her, Piloto. There are still a lot of things I don't know myself."

El Piloto didn't answer. He had abandoned the wheel and was checking the automatic pilot. Beneath his feet he felt the hum of the direction system correcting the course degree by degree in the swell.

"She's bad, Piloto. Real bitching bad."

The master of the *Carpanta* shrugged and sat down on the teak bench to smoke, protected from the breeze blowing stronger from the prow. He turned toward the motionless figure at the stern.

"Well, she must be cold, with only that jersey."

"She'll put something on."

El Piloto sat smoking in silence. Coy was still standing, leaning against the binnacle, legs slightly spread and hands in his pockets. The night dew began to collect on the deck and seep through the ripped seams in the back of his jacket, the collar and lapels of which he had turned up. In spite of everything, he was relishing the familiar rocking of the boat, his only regret was that the headwind was preventing them from unfurling the sails. That would lessen the motion of the boat and eliminate the annoying sound of the engine.

"There aren't any bad women," El Piloto suddenly announced. "Just like there aren't any bad boats . . . It's the men on board who make them one way or the other."

Coy said nothing, and El Piloto fell silent again. A green light was swiftly slipping up between them and the land, approaching the starboard quarter. Against the light from the beacon Coy recognized the long, low silhouette of an HJ turbolaunch run by Spanish customs. Based in Algeciras, this was a routine patrol to interdict hashish from Morocco and smugglers from the Rock.

"What are you looking for in her?"

"I want to count her freckles, Piloto. Have you noticed? She has thousands, and I want to count all of them, one by one, trace them with my finger as if she was a nautical chart. I want to trace a course from cape to cape, drop anchor in the inlets, and sail every inch of her skin, hugging the coast the whole time. You understand?"

"I understand. You want to get her in bed."

From the customs launch a light exploded, casting for the name of the *Carpanta,* for the registration number and port of registry on her sides. From the stern, Tánger asked what they wanted. Coy told her.

"Jack-offs," El Piloto murmured, cupping his hands above his eyes, dazzled by the spot.

He never had anything bad to say, and Coy had rarely heard him swear. He had the old upbringing of humble, honorable people, but he couldn't abide customs officers. He had played cat and mouse with them too often back in the days when he would row his little lateen-rigged sailboat, the *Santa Lucía,* to round off the day's work by picking up boxes of blond tobacco thrown overboard from merchant ships to people signaling with a flashlight, hidden outside Escombreras island. One part for him, another for the Guardia Civil at the dock, and the main portion for the people who hired him and never ran the risks. Tobacco could have made El Piloto rich had he worked for himself, but he was always satisfied with enough for his wife to have a new dress on Palm Sunday, or to get her out of the kitchen and invite her to a fish fry in one of the cafés around the port. Sometimes, when friends pushed hard and there was too much blood boiling and too many devils to get rid of, the fruit of one whole night's risk and labor fighting a murderous sea would be shot in a few hours' time, on music, drinks, and commercial ass in the dives of Molinete.

"That isn't it, Piloto." Coy couldn't take his eyes off Tánger, lit now by the customs spotlight. "At least, it isn't just that."

"Of course it is. And until you go to bed with her you'll never clear the decks. . . . Supposing you ever get anywhere with her."

"This woman's got balls. I swear."

"They all do. Think of me. When I have a pain, it's my wife who takes me to the doctor's office. 'Sit right here, Pedro, the doctor's coming. . . .' You know her. But let me tell you, she would bust before she'd say a word. There are women who if they were cows would give birth to nothing but bulls for the ring."

"It isn't just that. I saw an old snapshot. And a dented silver cup. And a dog licked my hand, and now it's dead."

El Piloto took the cigarette from his mouth and clicked his tongue.

"Out here, anything you can't put in a logbook is useless," he said. "You have to leave all the rest on shore. If you don't, you lose ships and men."

Its inspection complete, the customs launch changed course. The green light on its side turned to white at the stern, and then red when it swerved and showed its port side before cutting all lights and getting on more discreetly with the night's hunt. Seconds later, it was nothing more than a shadow moving rapidly west in the direction of Punta Carnero.

The *Carpanta* gave a lurch, and Tánger appeared in the cockpit. In the pitching and rolling she was moving at the pace of a toddler, trying to get a careful grip and maintain her balance before taking each step. As she moved past them, she put her hand on Coy's shoulder, and he wondered if she was getting seasick. For some perverse reason, the thought amused the hell out of him.

"I'm cold," she said.

"There's a slicker below," El Piloto offered. "You can use it."

"Thank you."

They watched her disappear down into the well. El Piloto continued to smoke for a while in silence. When finally he spoke, it was as if he were renewing an interrupted conversation.

"You always read too many books.... That can't lead to any good."

X

The Coast of the Corsairs

You put your life within three or four fingers' width of death,
the thickness of the ship's wood hull.
—Diego García de Palacios,
INSTRUCCIÓN NAÚTICA PARA NAVEGAR

The east wind was blowing onshore, though as soon as the sun rose a little above the horizon they were again heading directly into it. It wasn't very strong, barely ten or twelve knots, but enough to change a gentle swell into rough, choppy waves. Pitching and propelled by the motor through a spray that sometimes left traces of salt on the cockpit windshield, the *Carpanta* passed to the south of Málaga, reached parallel 36°30′, and then set a course due east.

At first Tánger showed no sign of being seasick. Coy watched her sitting quietly on one of the wood seats affixed to the rail of the stern deck, wrapped in El Piloto's warm slicker with the lapels turned up to hide half her face in the darkness. A little after midnight, when the waves were growing stronger, he took her a self-inflating life jacket and a security harness and fastened the carabiner to the backstay himself. He asked her how she was; she replied fine, thank you, and he was amused remembering the box of Dramamine he'd just seen lying open on the bunk El Piloto had assigned her in a stern cabin when he went to get the jackets and harnesses. Sitting where she was, the night breeze in her face would make her feel less queasy. Even so, he told her she would be better off sitting on the port fin, farther away from the exhaust fumes. Tánger said that she was just fine where she was. He shrugged and returned to the cockpit. She held on another ten minutes before moving.

At four in the morning El Piloto took over, and Coy went below to rest. In the narrow cabin, which was a little larger than a ticket booth, he lay down on a sleeping bag and minutes later, rocked by the waves, fell into a deep, dreamless sleep in which blurred shadows like ships floated through a phantasmagorical green darkness. Finally he was wakened by a ray of sunlight beaming through the porthole, rising and falling with the waves. He sat up in his bunk and rubbed his neck and injured eye, feeling the rasp of his beard on the palm of his hand. A good shave wouldn't hurt, he thought. He went down the narrow passageway toward the head, peering into the other cabin on the way. The door and porthole were open to let in the air, and Tánger was sleeping on her stomach in the bunk, still wearing the life jacket and harness. He couldn't see her face because her hair had fallen across it. Her feet, still in her shoes, hung over the edge of the bunk. Leaning against the door frame, Coy listened to her breathing, punctuated by an occasional sharp intake or a moan. Then he went to shave. His swollen eye wasn't too bad, and his chin was painful only when he yawned. Considering everything, he mused, consoling himself, he'd come through the conversation at Old Willis reasonably well. Animated by that thought, he connected the water pump to wash up a little, then heated coffee in the microwave. Trying to keep from spilling, he drank one cup and carried another up to El Piloto. He found his friend sitting in the cockpit, a wool cap on his head, his beard gray against his coppery skin. The Andalusian coast was visible two miles off the port beam.

"You'd no more than gone down to sleep when she vomited over the side," El Piloto told him, taking the hot cup. "She lost everything. That was one sick girl."

Proud bitch, Coy thought. He regretted having missed the show—the queen of the seas and sunken ships, all flags flying, hanging onto the taffrail and tossing her cookies. Wonderful.

"I can't believe it."

It was obvious he did believe it. El Piloto looked at him thoughtfully.

"Seemed she was just waiting till you got out of sight."

"No doubt about that."

"But she never complained. Not once. When I went over to ask if she needed anything, she told me to go to hell. Then when she was a little calmer, she went down to bed like a sleepwalker."

El Piloto took several sips of coffee and clicked his tongue, the way he did every time he reached a conclusion.

"Don't know why you're smiling," he said. "That girl has class."

"Too much, Piloto." Coy's brief laugh was bitter. "Too much class."

"She even felt her way leeward before she heaved. . . . She didn't rush, just made her way calmly, never losing her cool. But as she went past me, I saw her face in the light from the cabin. She was bone white, but she found enough voice to tell me good evening."

Having said that, El Piloto was silent for a while. He seemed to be reflecting.

"Are you sure she knows what she's doing?"

He offered Coy the half-filled cup. Coy took a sip and handed it back.

"The only thing I'm sure about is you."

El Piloto scratched his head beneath the cap and nodded. He didn't seem convinced. Then he turned to study the vague outline of the coast, a long dark blotch to the north. It was difficult to see clearly through the mist.

THEY passed few sailboats. Tourist season on the Costa del Sol hadn't yet begun, and the only pleasure craft they sighted were a French single-master and later a Dutch ketch, sailing with a free wind toward the Strait. In the afternoon, nearing Motril, a black-hulled schooner headed in the opposite direction passed by a half-cable's length away, flying an English flag atop the spanker of the mainmast. There were also working fishing boats to which the *Carpanta* frequently had to give way. The rules of navigation demanded that all ships keep their distance from a fishing boat with lines in the water, so during his turns at watch—he and El Piloto relieved one another every four hours—Coy disconnected the automatic pilot and took the wheel to avoid the drift nets. He did not do so happily, because he had no sympathy for fishermen; they were the source of hours of uncertainty on the bridge of the merchant ships he'd sailed on, when their lights dotted the horizon at night, saturating the radar screens and complicating conditions of rain or fog. Besides, he found them surly and self-interested, remorselessly eager to drag every inch of the sea within reach. Bad humored from a life of danger and sacrifice, they lived for today, wiping out species with no thought of anything beyond immediate gains. The most pitiless among them were the Japanese. With the complicity of Spanish merchants and suspiciously passive marine and fishing authorities, they were fishing out the Mediterranean red tuna with ultramodern sonars and small planes. Fishermen were not the only guilty parties, however. In those same waters Coy had seen finbacks asphixiated after swallowing floating plastic bags, and whole schools of dolphins crazed by pollution beaching themselves to die while children and volunteers weeping with impotence tried to push them back into a sea they refused.

It was a long day of maneuvering among unpredictable fishing vessels, which might plow straight ahead one moment and then turn suddenly to port or starboard to lay out or pull in their nets. Coy steered among them, changing course with professional patience, thinking of how sailors acted with considerably less circumspection aboard merchant ships and in less carefully governed waters. Sailboats and working fishing vessels had theoretical right of way, but in practice they were well advised to keep a wide berth from merchant ships moving at top speed, with their Indian, Filipino or Ukrainian crews cut back to save money, commanded by mercenary officers and with a flag that best suited their operation, a course set as straight as possible to economize on time and fuel, and sometimes, at night, with a minimal watch on the bridge, unattended engines, and a sleepy officer relying almost completely on onboard instruments. And if by day the engines or wheel were seldom touched to alter speed or course, at night such a ship became a lethal threat to all small craft crossing its path, whether or not they had legal priority. At twenty knots, which is more than twenty miles an hour, a merchant ship beyond the horizon could be upon you in ten minutes. Once, en route from Dakar to Tenerife, the ship Coy was second officer on had run down a fishing boat. It was five minutes after four in the morning, and Coy had just ended his watch on the bridge of the *Hawaiian Pilot*, a seven-thousand-ton traditional cargo ship. As he was going down the companionway toward his cabin he thought he heard a muffled sound from the starboard side, as if something had scraped the ship from stem to stern. He went back on deck just in time to see a dark shadow capsizing in the wake, and a faint glimmer that looked like a low-wattage lightbulb dancing crazily before suddenly going out. He rushed back to the bridge, where the first officer was calmly checking the set of the gyroscope. I think we just sank a fishing boat, Coy sputtered. And the first officer, a phlegmatic, melancholy Hindu named Gujrat, stood there looking at him. On your watch or mine? he asked finally. Coy said that he'd heard the noise at 0405 and seen the light go out. The first officer stared at him a little longer, thoughtful, before stepping out on the wing bridge to take a quick look toward the stern and check the radar, where the echoes of the waves showed nothing special. Nothing new on my watch, he concluded, again giving his full attention to the gyroscope. Later, when the first officer reported Coy's suspicions to the captain—an arrogant Englishman who made lists of the crew separating British subjects from foreigners, including officers—he approved the fact that the incident had not been entered in the logbook. We're in open waters, he said. Why complicate life?

AT ten in the evening they reached 3° longitude west of Greenwich. Except for brief appearances on deck, always with the air of a somnambulist, Tánger spent almost every moment secluded in her cabin. When Coy went by and found her asleep, he noticed that the box of Dramamine was quickly being depleted. The rest of the time, when she was awake, she sat at the stern, quiet and silent, facing the coastline slowly passing on the port side. She barely tasted the food El Piloto prepared, although she agreed to eat a little more when he told her it would help settle her stomach. She went to sleep almost as soon as it was dark, and the two men stayed in the cockpit, watching the stars come out. They headed into the wind all night, forcing them to use the motor. That meant they had to go into port at Almerimar at six the next morning, to refuel, take a break, and restock provisions.

THEY cast off at two that afternoon, with a favorable wind: a fresh south-southeaster that allowed them to shut down the motor and set first the mainsail and then the Genoa almost as soon as they rounded the buoy at Punta Entinas, on the starboard tack with the wind on her quarter and at reasonable speed. The seas were calmer, and Tánger felt much better. In Almerimar, where they had docked next to an ancient Baltic fishing boat refitted by ecologists for following whales in the sea of Alborán, she had helped El Piloto hose down the deck. She seemed to hit it off with him, and he treated her with a mixture of attentiveness and respect. After lunch at the seamen's club, they had coffee in a fisherman's bar, and there Tánger described to El Piloto the journey of the *Dei Gloria,* which had been following, she said, a course similar to theirs. El Piloto was interested in details of the brigantine, and she answered all his questions with the aplomb of someone who had studied the matter down to the last particular. A clever girl, El Piloto commented as an aside, when the three of them were on their way back to the boat, loaded with food and bottles of water. Coy, who was watching her as she walked ahead of them along the dock—in jeans, T-shirt, and sneakers, her hair blown by the breeze, a supermarket bag in each hand—agreed. Maybe too clever, he was about to say. But he didn't.

She didn't get seasick again. The sun was beginning to sink toward the horizon behind them. The *Carpanta* was moving under full sail past the Gulf of Adra, showing four knots on the log and with the wind, now veering toward the south, abeam. Coy, whose swollen eye was considerably better, was watching the bow. In the cockpit, with hands expert at mending nets and sails, El Piloto was sewing up the jacket ripped during the incident at Old Willis, never missing a stitch despite the rolling of the boat. Tánger's head appeared in the companionway; she asked their position and Coy told her. After a moment she came and sat between them with a nautical chart in her hands. When she unfolded it in the protection of the small cabin, Coy saw that it was number 774 of the British Admiralty: Motril to Cartagena, including the island of Alborán. For long distances, the smaller-scale English charts, which were all the same size, were more manageable than the Spanish ones.

"It was here, and more or less this hour, when they sighted the corsair's sails from the *Dei Gloria,*" Tánger explained. "It was following in their wake, gradually gaining. It could have been any ship at all, but Captain Elezcano was a distrustful man, and it seemed strange to him that the other ship would begin to approach after leaving Almería behind, just when there was a long stretch of coast ahead that offered no refuge for the brigantine.... So he ordered them to put on more sail and keep a close watch."

She indicated the approximate position on the chart, eight or ten miles to the southwest of Cabo de Gata. Coy could easily imagine the scene—the men gathered at the elevated stern, anxiously straining to see, the captain on the poop, studying his pursuer through his spyglass, the worried faces of the two priests, Escobar and Tolosa, and the chest of emeralds locked in the cabin. Suddenly the yell, the order to lay on sail that sent sailors scurrying up the ratline to unfurl more canvas, the jibs fluttering above the bowsprit before filling with wind, and the ship heeling a couple of strackes more as she felt the additional sail. The straight wake of foam cutting the blue sea behind her, and there on the horizon, the white sails of the *Chergui* now openly giving chase.

"It was close to nightfall," Tánger continued, after glancing toward the sun, lower and lower off the stern. "More or less like right now. And the wind was blowing from the south, and then the southwest."

"Here's what's happening," said El Piloto. He had finished stitching the jacket and was observing the dancing waves and the look of the sky. "It's going to veer a couple of quarters astern before nightfall, and we'll meet a fresh *lebeche* when we round the cape."

"Fantastic," she said.

The navy-blue eyes moved from the chart to the sea and the sails, expectant. Her nostrils were dilated, and she was taking deep breaths through half-open lips, as if in that moment she were contemplating the rigging of the *Dei Gloria*.

"According to the report of the ship's boy," Tánger continued, "Captain Elezcano at first hesitated to hoist all the sails. The ship had suffered damage during the storm in the Azores, and its upper masts weren't to be trusted."

"You're referring to the topmasts," Coy informed her. "The upper masts are called topmasts. If you say they weren't in good shape, too much canvas could finish springing them. If the brigantine had a wind abeam the way we do, I suppose she'd be carrying her jibs, lower staysails, main course, and fore course, well braced to leeward, and reserving the upper sails, the topgallants, to avoid risk. At least for the moment."

Tánger nodded, and studied the sea behind them as if the corsair were there.

"She must have flown across the water. The *Dei Gloria* was a swift ship."

Coy, in turn, looked back. "Apparently the other ship was too."

Now he transported himself in his imagination to the deck of the corsair. According to the details of the ship Lucio Gamboa had described to them in Cádiz, the *Chergui*, a three-masted xebec, would have been under full sail, the enormous lateen on the foremast swollen with wind and hauled to the bowsprit, the sails on the mainmast unfurled, lateen and topsail on the mizzenmast, cutting through the waves with the slender lines of a ship constructed for the Mediterranean, her gunports closed but the battle-trained crew preparing the guns. And that Englishman, that Captain Slyne, or Misián, or whatever the SOB's name was, would have been standing on the high, slanting poop, never taking his eyes off his prey. The chase would be long, as the brigantine he was pursuing was also swift. The crew of the corsair would have been calm, aware that unless something went wrong they wouldn't close in on the prize until after dawn. Coy could imagine the crew of renegades, the dangerous scum of the ports. Maltese, Gibraltarians, Spaniards, and North Africans. The worst from every rooming house, whorehouse, and tavern, qualified pirates who sailed and fought under the technically legal cover of letters of marque, which in theory kept them from hanging if they were captured. Desperate, daring, and cruel rabble with nothing to lose and everything to gain, under the command of unscrupulous captains who operated as privateers commissioned by Moorish tribal kings or His Most Britannic Majesty, with accomplices in any port where complicity could be bought. Spain, too, had people like that—officers drummed out of the Armada, stripped of their title or fallen into disgrace, adventurers seeking their fortune or some way to find their way back onto a ship, who served at the orders of anyone who would have them, and the commercial alliances that armed ships and sold the booty calmly through normal channels. In another time, Coy reflected with deeply personal sarcasm, a dishonored officer like him without a berth might have ended up on a corsair himself. With the vagaries of the sea, he might just as well have found himself on board the prey as on the hunter, sailing those same waters under full sail, with the dark silhouette of Cabo de Gata visible on the horizon.

"We will never know whether it was a chance encounter," Tánger said.

She was gazing pensively at the sea. A chance raid by a corsair in search of booty, or a black hand reaching from Madrid to guide the *Chergui* to intercept the *Dei Gloria,* sabotage the Jesuits' maneuver and seize the shipment of emeralds? Someone could have been playing a double game in the cabinet of the *Pesquisa Secreta.* But that might be one mystery that could never be solved.

"Maybe they followed them from Gibraltar," said Coy, tracing a horizontal line across the chart with his finger.

"Or maybe they were hiding in some cove," she proposed. "For several centuries that coast was a hunting ground for pirates. They often hugged the coastline, sheltering on hidden beaches to protect themselves from the winds or replenish water supplies, and especially to lie in wait for prey. You see?" She pointed to a place on the chart between La Punta de los Frailes and La Punta de la

Polacra. "This cove here, the one that is called Los Escullos now, was still called the cove of Mahommed Arráez at the beginning of the nineteenth century, and that's what it's called on the charts and atlases of the day. An *arráez,* among other things, was the captain of a Moorish corsair ship. And look here, this place is still called Moro island. Moors again. That's why all the towns were built inland, or on a promontory, to guard against attacks by pirates."

"Moors on the coast," El Piloto said, referring to the old saying for danger.

"Yes. That's the origin of that phrase. The coast was lined with watchtowers, manned by lookouts charged with alerting the citizenry."

The sun, lower and lower at the stern, was beginning to tinge her freckled skin. The breeze whipped the nautical chart in her hands. She was observing the nearby coast with avid concentration, as if its geographic features held ancient secrets.

"That afternoon of February 3," she continued, "no one had to alert Captain Elezcano. He knew the dangers all too well, and he must have been forewarned. That's why the corsair couldn't surprise them, and why the pursuit took so long." Now Tánger traced the shoreline on the chart in an ascending line. "It lasted all night, with a following wind, and the corsair was only able to attack when, in setting more sail, the *Dei Gloria* sprang her foremast."

"Undoubtedly," Coy commented, "because at last he decided to set the topgallants. If he did that despite damage to the masts, it's because the corsair was upon him. A desperate measure, I'd guess." He consulted El Piloto. "Too much tophamper."

"He would have been trying to reach Cartagena," was El Piloto's opinion.

Coy observed his friend with curiosity. His habitual phlegm seemed to be giving way to an interest Coy had rarely witnessed. He too, Coy thought with amazement, was being infected by the atmosphere. Gradually, as fascination with the mystery intensified,

Tánger was enlisting a strange crew, seduced by the ghost of a ship enveloped in murky green shadows. Nailed to the stump of the rotten mast, Captain Ahab's gold doubloon beckoned them all.

"Right," Coy agreed. "But he didn't get anywhere."

"So why didn't he give up, instead of fight?"

As usual, Tánger had an explanation.

"If the corsairs were Berbers, the captured sailors would have been forced into slavery. And if they were English, the fact that Spain was at relative peace with England would have made things worse for the crew of the *Dei Gloria*. . . . That kind of action tended to end with the elimination of witnesses, in order not to leave evidence. And besides, there were the emeralds. So it isn't strange that Captain Elezcano and his men would fight to the end."

With wineskin in hand, El Piloto studied the chart. He took a drink and clicked his tongue.

"They don't make sailors like them anymore," he said.

Coy was of the same mind. Added to the relentless cruelty of the sea, and to the infamous conditions on board, the sailors of that era faced perils of war such as gun broadsides and boardings. It was terrible enough to face a storm at sea, but how much worse an enemy ship. He remembered his training on the *Estrella del Sur,* and shuddered just to imagine climbing the swaying rigging of a ship to furl a sail in the midst of grapeshot, cannonballs, severed halyards, and wood splinters flying everywhere.

"What they don't make anymore," Tánger murmured, "is men like them."

The *Carpanta*'s sails billowed in the wind, and as she gazed at the sea Tánger's voice throbbed with nostalgia for all she had never known, for the enigma contained in old books and nautical charts, alerting her, like the distant flash from a lighthouse across the waves, that there were still seas to be sailed, shipwrecks to be found, and emeralds and dreams to bring to the light of day. Framed by the hair slapping her face, her eyes appeared to see listing decks, dashing waves, the foaming wake, and the chase that seemed to come to dramatic life before her eyes and to drag the sailor without a ship and the sailor without dreams along with her. And suddenly Coy understood that on that distant evening of February 3, 1767, Tánger Soto would have wanted to be aboard one of those ships. What he wasn't sure of was whether she would have preferred being the hunted or the hunter. But maybe it was all the same.

As El Piloto had predicted, the wind shifted to stern when they rounded Cabo de Gata at dusk, with the sun below the horizon and the beam from the lighthouse periodically illuminating the rocky cliffs of the mountain. So they hauled down the mainsail and continued toward the northeast, the loose sheet of the jib hauled now to port. Before it was completely dark, the two sailors prepared the boat for night sailing—lifelines along both sides, self-inflating life jackets with safety harnesses, binoculars, lanterns, and white flares within easy reach. Then El Piloto fixed a quick supper, primarily fruit, turned on the radar, the red light over the chart table, and the running lights for sail, and went below to sleep a while, leaving Coy on watch in the cockpit.

Tánger stayed with him. Rocked by the rolling boat, with her hands in the pockets of Piloto's slicker and the collar turned up, she watched the lights dotting the craggy outline of the coast of Almería in the distance. After a while she mentioned that she was surprised to see so few lights, and Coy told her that from Cabo de Gata to Cabo de Palos was the one stretch of the Spanish Mediterranean shore still free of the cement leprosy of tourist development. Too many mountains, the rocky coast, and a scarcity of roads were miraculously keeping that coast nearly virgin. For the moment.

Farther out to sea, a few dots of light beyond the horizon betrayed the presence of merchant ships following courses parallel to the *Carpanta*'s. Their headings, more to open water than the sailboat's, kept them at a distance, but Coy tried not to lose sight of them, and took mental sightings of their respective positions at intervals. A constant bearing and closing range, according to the old marine principle, meant certain collision. He bent over the log to verify course and speed. The bow of the *Carpanta* was fixed at 40° on the compass, and she was making four knots. Propelled by a quiet *lebeche,* with the sound of the water against the hull, the boat was gliding easily across the water under a dark dome now filled with stars. The polestar was in place, the immutable sentinel of the north, vertical on the port beam. Tánger followed his upward gaze.

"How many stars do you know?" she asked.

Coy shrugged before answering that he knew thirty or forty. Those indispensible for his line of work. That was the master star Polaris, he said. To its left you could see Ursa Major, which looked like an upside-down comet, and a little above it Cepheus. That group in the form of a W was Cassiopeia. W for whiskey.

"And how can you tell them apart from the others?"

"At any given hour, and according to the season of the year, some are more visible than others. . . . If you take the polestar as a beginning point and trace imaginary lines and triangles, you can identify the principal ones."

Tánger looked up, interested, her face barely illuminated in the reddish light from the companionway. The stars were reflected in her eyes, and Coy remembered a song from his childhood:

There was a girl
I taught to sing. . . .

He smiled in the darkness. Who would have thought, some twenty years later.

"If you form a triangle of the polestar and the two lowest stars in Ursa Major," he said, "there in the third corner . . . see? . . . you find Capella. There, above the horizon. At this hour it's still very low, but it will climb in the sky because those stars rotate west around the polestar."

"And that glowing little cluster? It looks like a bunch of grapes."

"Those are the Pleiades. They'll shine brighter once they're higher."

She repeated "the Pleiades" in a low voice, gazing at them for a long time. The light in her pupils, Coy thought, makes her look surprisingly young. Again the snapshot and the dented cup floated through his memory, enfolded in the old song:

I'd like to know
the names of the stars.

"The one that's shining so bright is Andromeda." He pointed. "It's there beside the Great Square of Pegasus, which the ancient astronomers pictured as a winged horse seen in reverse. . . . And up there, a little to the right, is the Great Nebula. See it?"

"Yes . . . I see it."

There was soft excitement in her voice, the discovery of something new. Something impractical, unexpected, and beautiful.

What a night that was,
when I gave a thousand names
to every star.

Coy sang very quietly. The rocking of the boat and the night growing ever darker, along with Tánger's nearness, put him in a state very close to happiness. You go to sea, he thought, to live moments like this. He had handed the 7x50 binoculars to Tánger, and she was observing the sky—the Pleiades, the Great Nebula, looking for the luminous points he was naming.

"You still can't see Orion, which is my favorite. . . . Orion is the

Hunter, with his shield, his belt, and the sheath for his sword. His shoulder stars are called Betelgeuse and Bellatrix, and his left foot is called Rigel."

"Why is he your favorite?"

"He's the most impressive constellation in the sky. More spectacular than the Milky Way. And once he saved my life."

"Really? Tell me."

"There isn't much to tell. I must have been about thirteen or fourteen. I had gone out fishing in a little sailboat, and some bad weather blew up. It was very cloudy, and night fell before I got home. I didn't have a compass and couldn't get oriented.... Suddenly the clouds opened for a moment and I recognized Orion. I set a course and got back to port."

Tánger didn't say anything. Maybe she's thinking about me, Coy hazarded. A little boy lost at sea, looking for a star.

"The Hunter, and Pegasus." She was again searching the sky. "Do you really see all those figures up there?"

"Sure. It's easy when you've been looking for years and years. At any rate, it won't be long before stars shine above the ocean for nothing, because men won't need them anymore to find their way."

"That's bad?"

"I don't know whether it's bad. I do know it's sad."

There was a light in the distance, off the bow on the starboard side, that appeared and disappeared beneath the dark shadow of the sail. Coy gave it a close look. Maybe it was a fishing boat, or a merchant ship navigating close to the coast. Tánger was watching the sky and Coy thought a moment about lights—white, red, green, blue, or any other color. Someone who didn't know the sea could never suspect what they meant to a sailor. The intensity of their language of danger, warning, and hope. What it meant to look and identify them on difficult nights amid high seas or even during calm approaches to port, the binoculars pressed to your eyes, trying to distinguish the flash from a lighthouse or a buoy from thousands of hateful, stupid, absurd lights on land. There were friendly lights, murderous lights, and even lights tied to remorse, like that time when Coy, the second officer aboard a tanker en route from Singapore to the Persian Gulf, had thought that he saw two red flares in the distance at three in the morning. Even though he wasn't completely sure they were distress signals, he had wakened the captain, who came up to the bridge half-dressed and sleepy-eyed to take a look. But there had been no further flares, and the captain, a dry and efficient man from Guipúzcoa named Etxegárate, had not thought it expedient to alter course. They had already lost too much time passing the Raffles lighthouse and fiendishly busy Malacca Strait, he said. Coy spent the rest of his watch that night with one ear tuned to channel 16 of the ship's radio, to see if he could capture the call of a craft in distress. There was nothing, but he had never been able to forget the two red flares. Perhaps it was the emergency signal some desperate sailor shot off in the darkness, his last hope.

"Tell me," said Tánger, "what that last night aboard the *Dei Gloria* was like."

"I thought you knew everything there was to know."

"There are things I can't know."

The tone of her voice was different from any he'd heard before. To his surprise, it sounded very near, and almost sweet. That made him shift uncomfortably on the teak bench, and at first he didn't know what to say. She was waiting.

"Well," he said at last. "If the wind was anything like what we have now, almost steady astern, the logical thing is that captain . . ."

"Captain Elezcano," she prompted.

"Yes, that's it. That Captain Elezcano would douse the jibs and stow the staysails, if he was carrying them. He would surely have left the mainmast without canvas, so that the large driver staysail didn't tug the rudder or steal the wind from the fore-topsail and foresail; or maybe he just struck the staysail and left the main topsail. He might also have set his foretopmast studdingsails, although I doubt he would have done that at night. The one sure thing is that, knowing his ship, he got her ready to make the best possible time without putting on canvas that would spring a mast."

The wind freshened slightly, always astern, kicking up a slight swell. Coy glanced at the anemometer and then studied the enormous shadow of the sail. He put the crank in the slot of the starboard winch, hauled in the sheet a couple of turns, and the *Carpanta* heeled a few degrees, picking up a half knot.

"According to what you told me," he continued after returning the crank to its place and coiling the tail of the sheet, "the wind must have been a little stronger than what we're experiencing. There's sixteen knots of true wind. Possibly they had twenty or so, which would be force 5 or 6. Enough to move them along, for sure. They'd be traveling faster than we are, heeling slightly to starboard, with a steady wind astern."

"What were the men doing?"

"They weren't getting much sleep, especially your two priests. Everyone must have had the pursuing ship on their minds, which they would barely have been able to make out at night. If there was a moon, they may have sighted the shadow of her sail astern from time to time.... Both of them would have been running without lights, in order not to betray their position. The men on watch would be gathered at the foot of the masts, dozing a little or standing at the gunnels with worried faces, waiting for the order to scramble up again and adjust the canvas. The others would be close to the guns, warned to be at the ready if the corsair suddenly overtook them. The captain would never have left the poop, his attention on the drama behind him and the creaking of the rigging and flapping of sail overhead. A helmsman at the tiller, maintaining course... No question that the best of them would have been at the helm that night."

"And the ship's boy?"

"Near the captain and the pilot, awaiting their orders. Copying down in the logbook the orders, times, maneuvers . . . He was young, wasn't he?"

"Fifteen."

Coy noted a tone of commiseration in Tánger's voice. Just a boy, it meant. At least, Coy thought, he had lived to tell the tale.

"In those days they went to sea at ten or twelve to learn the trade. . . . I suppose he would have been excited by the adventure. At that age you're not easily frightened. And that boy was already a veteran. At the very least he had crossed the Atlantic in both directions."

"His report was very precise. He was a clever boy. We can reconstruct approximately what happened thanks to him. And you."

Coy grimaced.

"I can only imagine how what you tell me happened."

The reddish light from the companionway still glowed on Tánger's face. She was avidly listening to Coy's words, with an attentiveness she had never paid him on land.

"And the corsair?" she asked.

Coy tried to evoke the situation on board the xebec. Professional hunters hot on the chase.

"With this course and this wind," he ventured, "they may have had the advantage of the large lateen sail on the foremast. On a ship designed to sail the Mediterranean, adapting to shifts in the wind or no wind at all . . . That night, that sail at the bow undoubtedly carried them very fast. Besides, having three masts allowed them to set a maintopsail, and maybe the main topgallant staysail. I think she would have set a course that put her between the *Dei Gloria* and the coast, in order to cut off any possibility of the brigantine's running for Águilas when the wind veered at dawn."

"It had to be heart-stopping."

"You bet it was."

Coy looked at the slightly darker line of the coast, which by now obscured the beam of the Gata lighthouse. The shadowy shape of a point of land began to announce the luminous bay of San José. With those two references Coy made a couple of mental calculations, placing them upon an imaginary chart. He thought about the crew of the brigantine climbing blindly up the masts. Making or shortening sail according to the wind and the needs of the maneuver, the rough canvas in their stiff fingers, stomachs pressed against the yards, feet dancing in empty space, their only support the footropes.

"I think that was more or less what happened," he concluded. "And Captain Elezcano hoped all through the night that they would leave the xebec behind. Maybe he tried some evasive maneuver, like changing course and trying to lose them in the darkness, but that fellow Misián must have known every trick in the book. As day dawned, the crew of the *Dei Gloria* must have lost heart when they saw the *Chergui* still there, between them and land, closing in. . . . Maybe then, while the pilot was calculating their position, the captain of the brigantine made a desperate decision: more sail, unfurl the topgallants. That was when the mast sprung, and the corsair was upon them."

And speaking of "upon them," Coy noted, the light off the bow that the Genoa jib hid from time to time seemed to be closer, in the same position as before. So he picked up the Steiner binoculars and walked along the windward side, holding onto the shrouds, up to the bow foredeck, next to where the anchor was secured on its capstan. The light was too much for a simple fishing boat, but he couldn't clearly identify its shape. If it was a ship coming toward them, maybe a merchant ship judging by the quantity and size of the lights, he should be able to see the port red or starboard green lights, or both if the other craft's bow was aimed straight for them. But he couldn't see those. And yet, he decided uneasily, it seemed much too close.

Sailing at night was a goddam crock of shit, he told himself with irritation, returning to the cockpit. Tánger was watching him with curiosity.

"Put on your life jacket," he told her.

Something wasn't right, and his sailor's instinct began to click into place. He went below to the midship cabin and flipped on the waiting radar: a black echo appeared on the green screen. Coy took note of distance and bearing, calculating that it was two miles away and headed directly for them. A large, threatening echo.

"Piloto!" he yelled.

He didn't know what the hell it was, but very soon it was going to be on top of them. As he ran up the companionway he made rapid calculations. In the immediate area of Cabo de Gata, the pattern for separation of traffic required merchant ships heading south to maintain a course five miles offshore. The *Carpanta* was sailing close to that limit, so it had to be a boat navigating closer to land than usual. Its speed would be about fifteen knots; added to the *Carpanta*'s five, that meant she would cover twenty nautical miles in sixty minutes. Two miles in six minutes—that was the amount of time one or the other of them had to make some maneuver if a collision was to be averted. Six minutes. Maybe fewer.

"What's going on?" Tánger asked.

"Problems."

Coy made sure she had put on her self-inflating life jacket, which had a strobe light that was activated on contact with the water. He shrugged into his, picked up the lantern, and went back to the bow, illumined as he went by the red portside light located in the shrouds. The lights of the other vessel, threatening now, were coming closer and closer, with no alteration in course. He turned on the lantern and beamed intermittent signals in their direction, and then aimed the light onto the *Carpanta*'s large unfurled sail. Any sailor on the bridge of a merchant ship should see that. For an instant he turned the light on his watch. Eleven fifty-five. That was the worst possible hour. On board the oncoming ship they would be about to change the watch. The officer, trusting the radar, would be sitting at the chart table, entering orders in the logbook before being relieved, and the man scheduled for the next watch would not yet be on the bridge. Maybe there was a drowsy Filipino, Ukrainian, or Indian helmsman lazing about somewhere. Bastards.

Coy hurried back to the cockpit. El Piloto was already there, asking what was going on. Coy pointed to the lights at their bow.

"Jesus," El Piloto murmured.

Alarmed, Tánger watched them, the wide red band of the life jacket fastened tightly over the slicker.

"Is it a boat?"

"It's a sonofabitching boat, and it's coming straight at us."

She had the carabiner of the safety harness in her hand, and looked from one of them to the other as if she didn't know what to do. To Coy she seemed unbearably vulnerable.

"Don't hook that onto anything," he counseled. "Just in case."

It wasn't a good idea to be attached to a boat that might be split in two. He went back down to the cabin and glued himself to the radar screen. They were navigating under sail, and theoretically had right-of-way, but right-of-way was moot at this point. It was already too late to maneuver and get out of the way of the larger ship. There was no doubt that this was a big ship. Much too big. Coy cursed himself for being careless, for not having foreseen the danger sooner. There still were no red or green lights visible, and yet the vessel was there, traveling toward them in a straight line, barely a mile away. He felt the shudder of the *Carpanta*'s engine. El Piloto had started it up. Coy went back on deck.

"They don't see us," he said.

Yet the *Carpanta* had her running lights on, he had signaled with the lantern, and the sailboat also had a good radar reflector atop the mast. Coy fastened his life jacket. He was furious and confused. Furious with himself for having been distracted by the stars and the conversation and not having foreseen the danger. Confused because he still hadn't sighted the red and green lights of whatever was coming at them.

"Can't you advise them by radio?" asked Tánger.

"There isn't time."

El Piloto had disconnected the automatic pilot and was steering manually, but Coy recognized the problem. The most logical evasive maneuver was to starboard, because if the merchant vessel sighted them at the last moment, it too would change course to starboard. The dilemma was that since the other ship was navigating so close to the coast, starboard might take her too close to land, and it was possible therefore that the officer on the bridge would perform the opposite maneuver, veering to port and the open sea. LWPC: Law of the Worst Possible Consequence. If that happened, in trying to vacate the merchant's route, the *Carpanta* would end up directly in the middle of it.

They had to make themselves seen. Coy grabbed one of the white flares from the cockpit and ran back to the bow. The lights now looked like a carnival, a luminous mass that was less than half a mile away by now. From the water came a dull roar, constant and sinister—the sound of the merchant ship's engines. Coy hung onto the bow rail and took one last look, trying at least to understand what was happening before the oncomer swamped them. And then, only two cables' length away, looming like a dark ghost against the blaze of her own lights, he distinguished a black mass, tall and terrible—the bow of the merchant vessel. Now he could make out several containers stacked on deck, and suddenly, finally, Coy realized what had happened. From a distance, the port and starboard lights had been obscured by other, brighter ones. From the much lower perspective of the sailboat, it was the ship's bow and broad hull themselves that had blocked them out.

Now there was less than a minute. Clamping his knees onto the rail, thrusting his body in front of the Genoa stay, Coy removed the top of the flare, turned the base, held it away from his body by extending his arm as far leeward as possible, and struck the trigger with the palm of his other hand. Come on, he begged, don't be dead. There was a loud hiss, a cloud of smoke, and a blinding glare illuminated Coy, the sail, and a good portion of the sea around the *Carpanta*. Clinging to the stay with one hand and blinded by the intense radiance, he watched as the bow of the merchant vessel held course a few instants and then began to veer to starboard, less than a hundred yards away. The agonizing light of the flare revealed the enormous wave cut by the prow, a white crest hurling itself toward the sailboat. Coy threw the flare into the sea and hung on with both hands as El Piloto turned the *Carpanta*'s wheel hard to starboard. The black coast, illuminated from overhead as if during a fiesta, moved past very close amid the roar of the engines, and the sailboat, struck by the wave, bobbed crazily. Then the enormous jib, catching wind from the far rail, quartered brusquely and struck Coy, who felt himself swept over the rail and into the sea.

It was cold. It was too cold, he thought, stunned, as black water closed over his head. He felt the turbulence of the sailboat's propellers when the hull passed near him, and then a more violent motion that made the dark liquid sphere he was bouncing in boil around him—the great propellers of the merchant vessel. The water was filled with the deafening sound of the engines, and in that instant he realized he was going to drown, because the turbulence was pulling his pants and jacket downward and at some moment or other he was going to have to open his mouth to breathe, to fill his lungs with air, and what was going to rush in was not going to be air but murderous gallons of saltwater. It wasn't his life that flashed through his head in quick images, but a blind fury at ending things in this absurd way, along with a desire to stroke upward, to survive at all cost. The problem was that the turbulence had turned him over and over in his accursed black sphere, and up and down were relative concepts—supposing that he was in any condition to swim. Water was beginning to fill his nose with irritating needles of sensation, and he told himself: This is it, I'm drowning. I'm checking out. So he opened his mouth to curse with his last breath, and to his surprise met pure air, and stars in the sky. The strobe light on his self-inflating life jacket flashed beside his ear, blinding his right eye. With the left, less bedazzled, he saw the glare of the retreating merchant ship, and on the other side, a half cable away, its green starboard light appearing and disappearing behind the enormous shadow of the Genoa jib shivering in the wind, the dark silhouette of the *Carpanta*.

He tried to swim toward her, but the life jacket hobbled him. He was painfully aware that at night a boat can pass a man in the water a hundred times and not see him. He felt for the emergency whistle that should have been next to the strobe light. It wasn't there. Shouting from that distance was pointless. The swell was frustrating, with choppy waves that made him rise and fall, and his view of the *Carpanta* come and go. And also hiding him from the two on board, he thought despondently. Slowly he began to breaststroke, trying not to exhaust himself, with the goal of shortening the distance between them. He was wearing his sneakers, but they weren't too great a handicap and he decided to leave them on. He didn't know how long he would be in the water, and they would protect him a little. The Mediterranean's waters weren't frigid, and at that time of year someone who went overboard dressed and in good health could last several hours.

He kept seeing the lights of the *Carpanta*, and it seemed to him they were taking in the jib. From his position relative to her and to the merchant ship, Coy realized that as soon as El Piloto saw him go overboard, he had dropped the sails, slowing the ship, and now was preparing to backtrack and try to reach the point Coy had gone over. Undoubtedly he was on one rail and Tánger on the other, searching for him in the tossing sea. Maybe they'd launched the emergency life raft with the luminous buoy attached by a short line, and were heading there now to see if Coy had found it. As for his own light, the one on his life jacket, he was sure the swell hid it from them.

The green starboard light went by close in front of him, and Coy yelled, futilely waving an arm. The movement plunged him beneath a breaking crest, and when he reemerged, snorting the saltwater that smarted in nostrils, eyes, and mouth, the green light had become the white light at the stern. The *Carpanta* was moving away from him.

This is really stupid, he thought. He was beginning to feel the cold, and the light sparkling at his shoulder seemed invisible to everyone but him. The jacket inflated around his neck kept his head above water most of the time, but now he couldn't see any of the *Carpanta*'s lights, only the glow of the merchant ship in the distance. There is a good possibility, he told himself, that they won't find me. And that this damned light will wear out the batteries and go dead, and I'll be out here in the dark. LLOOOW: Law of Lights Out and On Our Way. Once, playing cards, an old engineman had said, "There's always one fool who loses. And if you look around and don't see him, it's because you're the fool." He looked around him. Dark water splashed against the inflated collar. No one. Sometimes someone dies, he added to himself. And if you don't see another person, the one who may die is you. He looked up at the stars. With their help he could establish the direction of the coast, but it wouldn't do any good, he was too far to reach it swimming. If El Piloto, who would have pinpointed where he went overboard, radioed a Mayday, man overboard, the search wouldn't get underway before dawn, and by that time he would have been in the drink five or six hours, with serious hypothermia. There was nothing he could do except husband his strength and try to slow the loss of body heat. Position HELP, Heat Escape Lessening Posture, as the manuals called it. Or something like that. So he tried to adopt a fetal position, pressing his bent legs to his belly and folding his arms across his chest. This is ridiculous, he thought. Tucked up like a baby, at my age. But as long as the strobe light kept flashing, there was hope.

LIGHTS. Drifting, jostled by the waves, eyes closed, and moving as little as possible, to conserve warmth and energy, with the white flashes rhythmically blinding him, Coy kept thinking about lights, to the point of obsession. Friendly lights, enemy lights, stern, anchor, port and starboard, green beacons, blue beacons, white beacons, buoys, stars. The difference between life and death. A new crest whirled him around like a buoy in the water, once again dunking him. He emerged shaking his head, blinking to clear the salt from his burning eyes. Another crest and again he whirled, and then, right before him, at less than forty feet, he saw two lights, one red and one white. The red was the portside of the *Carpanta*, and the white was the beam from the lantern Tánger was holding at the bow as El Piloto slowly maneuvered to place Coy to windward.

LYING in his berth, Coy listened to the sound of water against the hull. The *Carpanta* was sailing northeast again, with a favorable wind. And the castaway was rocked to sleep and cozy in a sleeping bag and warm layer of blankets. They had pulled him on board at the stern—after tossing him a line spliced to loop beneath his arms—exhausted and clumsy in his dripping clothes and life jacket, and with the light that kept flashing at his shoulder until once on deck he himself yanked off the jacket and threw it into the water. His legs gave way by the time he reached the cockpit. He had begun to shake violently, and between them, after throwing a blanket around him, El Piloto and Tánger got him to his cabin. Dazed and docile as a baby, devoid of will and strength, he let them undress him and towel him down. El Piloto tried not to rub too hard, to prevent the cold that had numbed Coy's arms and legs from rising toward his heart and brain. They had stripped off his last clothing as he lay on the bunk, lost in the mist of a strange day-dream. He had felt the rough touch of El Piloto's hands, and also Tánger's smoother ones on his naked skin. He felt her fingers taking his pulse—which beat slow and steady. She had held his torso as El Piloto pulled off his T-shirt, his feet as they took off his socks, and finally his waist and upper legs when they eased off his soaked undershorts. At one moment, the palm of Tánger's hand had held his buttock, just where it joined the leg, resting there, light and warm, a few seconds. Then they zipped up the sleeping bag and pulled blankets over the top, turned out the light, and left him alone.

He wandered through the green darkness that called from below, and stood interminable watch through a daze of snows and fog and echoes on the radar. With his wax pencil he traced straight routes on the radar screen while up on deck horses ate wooden containers marked "Horses" and silent captains strode back and forth without a word for him. The calm gray water looked like undulating lead. It was raining on seas and ports and cranes and cargo ships. Seated on mooring stones, motionless men and women, soaked by the rain, were absorbed in oceanic dreams. And deep below, beside a bronze bell silenced in the center of a blue sphere, sperm whales slept peacefully, their mouths curving in something like a smile, heads down, tails up, suspended in the weightless dreams of broody cetaceans.

The *Carpanta* pitched slightly and heeled a bit more. Coy half-opened his eyes in the darkness of the cabin, cuddled in the comforting warmth that was gradually restoring life to his stiff body, rolled tight against the hull by the list of the ship. He was safe. He had escaped the maws of the sea, as merciless in its whims as it was unpredictable in its clemency. He was on a good ship steered by friendly hands, and he could sleep whenever he wanted without worrying, because other eyes and other hands were watching over his sleep, helping him follow the ghost of the lost ship that waited in the shadows into which he had nearly sunk forever. The woman's hands that had touched him as they removed his clothes returned to turn back some of the blankets and then feel his forehead and take his pulse. Now, at the recollection of that touch, that palm against his naked buttock, a slow, warm erection swelled in the haven of warming thighs. That made him smile, quiet and drowsy, almost with surprise. It was good to be alive. Later he went back to sleep, frowning because the world wasn't as wide as it had been, and because the ocean was shrinking. He dreamed of forbidden seas and barbarous coasts, and islands where arrest warrants, and plastic bags, and empty tin cans never washed ashore. And he wandered at night through ports without ships among women accompanied by other men. Women who looked at him because they weren't happy, as if they wanted to pass their unhappiness on to him.

He wept silently behind closed eyes. To console himself he rested his head against the wooden hull of the ship, listening to the sea on the other side of the thin planking separating him from Eternity.

XI

The Sargasso Sea

". . . the sun-resorts of Sargasso where the bones come up to lie and bleach and mock the passing ships."
—Thomas Pynchon, GRAVITY'S RAINBOW

When he went up on deck, the *Carpanta* was becalmed in the windless dawn, with the sheer coastline very near and a cloudless sky shading from blackish gray to blue in the west. The sun's rays shone horizontally on the rock face, the sea to the east, and the *Carpanta*'s mast, painting them red.

"It was here," said Tánger.

She had a nautical chart unfolded on her knees, and beside her El Piloto was smoking a cigarette and holding a cup of coffee. Coy went back to the stern. He had put on dry pants and a T-shirt but his lips and tangled hair still had traces of salt from the nocturnal dip. He looked around him at the circling gulls that cawed and planed before alighting on the waves. The coast stretched not much more than a mile to the west, and then opened in the form of a cove. He recognized Punta Percheles, Punta Negra, and the island of Mazarrón in the distance. Some eight miles to the east rose the dark mass of Cabo Tiñoso.

He went back to the cockpit. El Piloto had gone below to get a cup of warm coffee for him, and Coy gulped it down, his face screwing up as he tasted the last drops of the bitter brew. On the chart Tánger pointed to the landscape that lay before her eyes. She was wearing the black sweater and was barefoot. Blond strands of hair escaped from beneath Piloto's wool cap.

"This is the place," she said, "where the *Dei Gloria*'s mast broke and she had to fight."

Coy nodded, eyes fixed on the nearby coast as Tánger described the details of the drama. Everything she had researched, all the information gathered from yellowed files, manuscripts, and Urrutia's old nautical charts, was woven together in her calm voice, as if she had been there herself. Coy had never listened to anyone with so much conviction. Listening to her as his eyes searched the semicircle of dark coast stretching to the northeast, he tried to reconstruct his own version of the facts. This is how it was, or more precisely, how it could have been. To do that, he called on the books he'd read, his experience as a sailor, and the days and nights of his youth, when he was borne by silent sails across this sea she had brought him back to. That was why it was easy to imagine it, and when Tánger paused and looked at him, and El Piloto's blue eyes also turned to him, Coy bunched his shoulders a little, touched his nose, and filled in the holes in the narrative. He gave details, ventured situations, and described maneuvers, placing them all in that dawn of February 4, 1767, when the *lebeche* veered to north as the sun rose, making hunter and prey alike sail close to the wind. In those circumstances, he said, the apparent wind was added to the true wind, and the brigantine and the xebec would have been sailing close-hauled, making seven or eight knots—driver, mainsail, jibs, topsails, and the yards braced well to leeward on the *Dei Gloria*: lateens on the fore- and mizzenmast sharp as knife blades on the corsair, and sailing closer to the wind than square-rigged ones. Both heeling to starboard, with water pouring through the lee scuppers, helmsmen alert at the tiller, captains focused on wind and canvas, knowing that the first to commit an error would lose the race.

Errors. At sea—as in fencing, Coy had heard somewhere—everything turned on keeping your adversary at a distance and anticipating his moves. The black cloud forming flat and low in the distance, the slightly dark area of rippled water, the almost imperceptible foam breaking on the surface—all augured deadly thrusts that only constant vigil could parry. That made the sea the perfect metaphor for life. The moment to take in a reef, went the sensible seafaring saying, was precisely when you asked yourself if it wasn't time to take in a reef. The sea hid a dangerous and stubborn old scoundrel, who lay waiting in apparent camaraderie for the chance to bare his claws at the first sign of inattention. With ease but no pity, he killed the careless and the stupid, and the best good sailors could wish for was to be tolerated and not harassed. To pass unnoticed. Because the sea had no sense of remorse and, like the God of the Old Testament, never forgave, unless by chance or by whim. The words "charity" and "compassion," among many others, were left behind when you cast off. And in a certain way, Coy believed, it was fair.

The error, he decided, had in the end been committed by Captain Elezcano. Or maybe it wasn't an error, and it just so happened that the law of the sea tilted in favor of the corsair. With the enemy drawing nearer, preventing her from reaching safe haven beneath the guns of the Mazarrón tower, the brigantine had set her canvas despite the damage to the masts. It wasn't difficult to picture the rest: Captain Elezcano staring upward, apprehensive, while sailors, swaying on the footropes and overhanging the sea to starboard, untie the gaskets securing the upper sails, which snap free with a brief flap, straining to lift them to the yards and haul the sheets. The ship's boy approaching the poop with the latitude and longitude obtained by the pilot, and the distracted order to enter them in the logbook from the captain, who never shifts his gaze from on high. Then the boy by his side, gazing upward as he tucks the paper with the penciled coordinates into his pocket. Suddenly the sinister creaking of the wood as it splits, and halyards and canvas dropping to leeward, tangled by the wind, and the suicidal lurch of the ship and all men aboard with their heart in their mouth, knowing at that instant their fate is sealed.

There must have been sailors aloft, cutting the useless rigging and throwing the wreckage of the topmast and sail into the sea, while on deck Captain Elezcano gave the order to open fire. The gun ports would have been open since first light, loaded and ready, gunners waiting. Maybe the captain decided suddenly to swing and surprise the approaching pursuer, undoubtedly giving him the starboard broadside, with men bent behind the guns, waiting for the hull and sails of the xebec to bear across before them. Battle waged almost yardarm to yardarm, said the report written by the maritime authorities from the ship's boy's testimony. That meant that the two ships would have been extremely close, the men on the corsair ready to fire and board, when the *Dei Gloria* showed her starboard beam with open gun ports spouting smoke from lit fuses, letting fly a cannonade at point-blank range—five guns spitting four-pound balls. It had to have caused some damage, but at that moment the corsair must have come around to starboard, unless the lateen sails allowed her to maintain her course, sailing close to the wind, and cut the wake of the brigantine, in turn loosing a mortal broadside in retaliation, sweeping the *Dei Gloria*'s deck from stern to stem. Two long six-pounders and four four-pounders; some twenty-eight pounds of ball and shot shattering line, wood, and body parts. Then, as the gunners aboard the corsair yelled jubilantly, seeing the wounded and dying enemy drag themselves across decks slick with blood, the two ships would have approached each other, more slowly each time, until they were nearly motionless, firing ferociously at each other.

Captain Elezcano was a tenacious Basque. Resolved not to surrender, he must have run through the brigantine, urging on his desperate gunners. There would have been guns blown from their trucks, wood splinters, roundshot and musket balls flying in every direction, pieces of line, masts, and sails dropping from overhead. By that time the two Jesuits would have been dead, or maybe they had gone below to the captain's cabin to defend to the last breath the coffer of emeralds—or to throw it into the ocean. The last broadsides from the corsair were undoubtedly devastating. The *Dei Gloria*'s foremast, its sails ripped like winding sheets, would have split before falling onto the bloody slaughterhouse of the brigantine's deck. Perhaps by then Captain Elezcano, too, was dead. The ship was adrift, crippled and without direction. Maybe the terrified fifteen-year-old ship's boy awaited the end huddled among coils of rope, boarding sword in his trembling hand, watching the masts of the *Chergui* approach through the smoke, preparing for boarding. But then he saw fire aboard the corsair. The point-blank gunfire from the brigantine, or that from the xebec herself, had set alight one of the lower sails, which had not been taken in because of the unexpectedness of the maneuver. Now that sail was blazing and falling onto the deck of the corsair, it may have been near a charge of gunpowder, or the open hatchway of the magazine. Hazards of the sea. Suddenly there was a flash, and a brilliant explosion struck the dying brigantine with a fist of air, toppling the second mast and filling the sky with black smoke and pieces of wood and embers and human flesh that rained down everywhere. Standing on the rail of the blood-covered deck, deafened by the explosion, eyes bulging with horror, the ship's boy could see that the nothing remained of the corsair but smoking wood sputtering as it sank into the sea. At that moment the *Dei Gloria* heeled over in her turn, water pouring into the belly of her shattered hull, and the ship's boy found himself floating through pieces of wood and cordage.

He was alone, but near him floated the skiff Captain Elezcano had ordered jettisoned to clear the deck minutes before the battle began.

"IT must have happened more or less like that," said Tánger.

The three of them were silent, regarding a sea as still as a tombstone. Somewhere below, half-hidden in the sand of the ocean floor, were the bones of nearly a hundred dead men, what was left of two ships, and a fortune in emeralds.

"The most logical conclusion," she continued, "is that the *Chergui* disintegrated in the explosion, and that the remnants of it are scattered. The brigantine, however, went down intact, except for the masts. Since it isn't too deep here, you'd expect to find her on her keel, or on one side."

Coy was studying the chart, calculating distances and depths. The sun was beginning to warm his back.

"The bottom is mud and sand," he said. "With some rocks. It's possible she's so deeply buried that we can't dig."

"It's possible." Tánger bent over the chart, so close her hair brushed the paper. "But we won't know until we go down. The part that's covered will be in better shape than what has been exposed to the waves and currents. Shipworms will have done their work, boring into the planking. What hasn't been protected by sand will be gone. The iron rusted. It also depends on how cool the water is. A ship can remain intact at low temperatures, or disappear in short order in warm waters."

"It isn't very cold here," El Piloto put in. "Except for an occasional current."

He was showing interest but staying a little apart, his face showing no expression. His calloused fingers were mechanically tying and untying knots in a section of halyard, his fingernails as short and ragged as Tánger's. His eyes, tranquil and faded by years of Mediterranean light, moved back and forth between them. It was a stoic gaze that Coy knew well—that of a fisherman or sailor who expects nothing more than to fill his nets with a reasonable catch and return to port with just enough to go on living. He wasn't a man of illusions. Everyday life on the sea watered down chimeras, and deep down the word "emeralds" was as nebulous as the place where the rainbow meets the sea.

Tánger had pulled off the wool cap. Now one hand rested carelessly on Coy's shoulder.

"Until we've located the hull with the help of the plans, and we know where each part of the ship lies, we won't be sure of anything. The important thing is whether the area of the poop is accessible. That's where the captain's cabin will be, and the emeralds."

More and more her attitude was different from her mood on dry land. Natural, and less arrogant. Coy felt the light pressure of her hand on his shoulder, and the nearness of her body. She smelled of the sea, and of skin warmed by the slowly rising sun. You need me now, he thought. Now you need me more, and it shows.

"Maybe they threw the emeralds overboard," he said.

She shook her head. Her shadow on the 463A chart was gradually shortening. For a while she was silent, but finally she said, "Well, maybe." That was impossible to know just yet. At any rate, they had a perfect description of the coffer, a wood, iron, and bronze chest twenty inches long. The iron wouldn't have aged well under water, and by now it would be a blackish, unrecognizable mass. The bronze would have fared better, but the wood would be gone. Inside, the emeralds would be crusted together. They would look more or less like a block of dark stone, a little reddish, with greenish veins of the bronze. They would have to search for it among all the wreckage, and it wasn't going to be easy

Of course not. Coy yearned for it to be difficult. A needle in a haystack, as Lucio Gamboa, between laughs and cigarettes, had suggested in Cádiz. If the wreck was buried, they would need hoses to suction off the mud and sand. No way to be discreet.

"Well, now it doesn't matter," Tánger concluded. "First we have to find it."

"What about the depth finder?" Coy asked.

El Piloto finished a double bowline knot.

"No problem," he said. "We'll get that hooked up this afternoon in Cartagena, and also a GPS repeater for the cockpit." He observed Tánger with suspicious gravity. "But all that will have to be paid for."

"Of course," she said.

"It's the best fish-sounding equipment I could find." El Piloto was talking to Coy. "A Pathfinder Optic with three beams, like you asked. The transducer can be installed on the stern without much trouble."

Tánger looked at Coy, inquisitive. He explained that with that sound they could cover a 90-degree fan beneath the *Carpanta*'s hull. The machine was generally used to locate schools of fish, but it also gave a clear and very detailed profile of the bottom. Most important, thanks to the use of different colors on the screen, the Pathfinder differentiated bottoms according to density, hardness, and composition, detecting any irregularity. An isolated rock, a submersed object, even changes of temperature, showed up quite clearly. And metal, say the iron or bronze of the guns if they projected above the sand, would be seen in intense, darker color. The fishing sounder wasn't as precise as the professional systems Nino Palermo had at his disposal, but it would do in a depth of sixty-five to one hundred seventy feet. Navigating slowly until they had combed the search area and assigned coordinates for each submersed object that caught their attention, they could trace a map of the zone, determining possible sites for the wreck. In a second phase they would explore each location with the aquaplane, a towed wooden sled that would keep a diver within view of the bottom.

"Strange," said El Piloto.

He had taken the wineskin from the log and drank head tilted back, eyes to the sky. Coy knew what he was thinking. With a wreck no deeper than that, fishermen would have snagged their nets on it. Someone would know about it. And by now someone would have taken a look, out of curiosity. Any amateur diver could do it.

"Yes. I'm wondering why some fisherman hasn't said anything about a wreck out here. They tend to know the bottom better than the hallway in their homes."

Tánger showed them the chart: S, M, R. The small letters dotted the area beside the numbers that gave the depths.

"It says rocks too, see? That might be protecting the wreck."

"Protect it from fishermen, maybe," Coy offered. "But a wooden ship deposited among rock doesn't last long. In shallow seas the waves and currents destroy the hull. There won't be anything left like your illustration in *Red Rackham's Treasure.*"

"Maybe," she said.

She was staring at the sea with a stubborn expression. El Piloto's eyes met Coy's. Suddenly, once again, the whole thing seemed crazy. We're not going to find anything, the sailor's expression said as he handed the wineskin to Coy. I'm here because I'm your friend, and besides, you're paying me, or she is, which is the same thing in the end. But this woman has your needle spinning. And the real kicker is that you haven't even got her in bed.

THEY were in Cartagena. They had sailed close to the coast, beneath the escarpment of Cabo Tiñoso, and now the *Carpanta* was entering the inlet of a port used by Greeks and Phoenicians. Quart–Hadast: the Carthago Nova of the feats of Hannibal. Comfortable in a teak chair on the sailboat's stern, Coy was observing

Escombreras island. There, below the slash in the south face, he had dived as a boy for Roman amphoras, wine and oil vessels with elegant necks, long curving handles, and the marks of their makers in Latin, some sealed just as they had sunk into the sea. Twenty years before, that zone had been an enormous field of debris from shipwrecks, and also, it was said, from navigators who threw offerings into the sea within view of the temple dedicated to Mercury. Coy had dived there many times, and come up, never faster than his own bubbles, toward the dark silhouette of the *Carpanta* waiting on the glossy surface, her anchor line curving downward into the depths. Once, the first time he went to two hundred—two hundred seven, the depth gauge on his wrist recorded—Coy had gone down slowly, with pauses to adapt to the change in pressure on his eardrums, letting himself fall deeper into that sphere where colors were disappearing, shading into a ghostly, diffuse light where only tones of green remained. He had eventually lost sight of the surface and then fallen slowly onto his knees on the clean sand bottom, with the cold of the deep rising up his thighs and groin beneath his neoprene suit. Seven point two atmospheres, he thought, amazed at his own audacity. But he was eighteen. All around him, to the edge of the green circle of visibility, scattered every which way on the smooth sand, half buried in it or grouped in small mounds, he saw dozens of broken and intact amphoras, necks, and pointed bases—millenary clay that no one had touched or seen for twenty centuries. Dark fish flashed among narrow amphora mouths in which evil-looking morays had taken up residence. Intoxicated by the feel of the sea on his skin, fascinated by the darkness and the vast field of vessels motionless as sleeping dolphins, Coy had pulled the mask from his face, keeping the air hose between his teeth, to feel on his face all the shadowy grandeur surrounding him. Then, suddenly alarmed, he put the mask back on, clearing it of water with air expelled through his nose. At that moment, El Piloto, made taller by his rubber fins, turned into another dark green silhouette descending at the end of a long plume of bubbles, had swum toward him, moving at the slow pace of men in the depths, signaling with a harsh gesture to the depth gauge on his wrist, and then touching his temple with a finger to ask, silently, whether Coy had lost his mind. They ascended together very slowly, following the bubbles that preceded them, each carrying an amphora. And when they were almost at the surface, and the sun's rays began to filter through the smooth turquoise above their heads, Coy had turned his amphora upside down and a shower of fine sand, shining in the watery light, spilled from inside and enveloped him in a cloud of gold dust.

He loved the sea that was as old and skeptical and wise as the endless women in the genetic memory of Tánger Soto. Its shores bore the imprint of the centuries, he thought, contemplating the city Virgil and Cervantes had written about, clustered at the back of the natural port among high rocky walls that for three thousand years had made it nearly impregnable against the assault of enemies and winds. Despite the decay of its crumbling, filthy facades and the empty lots where houses had tumbled down and not been rebuilt, the city looked beautiful from the sea, and its narrow alleyways were resonant with the echoes of men who had fought like Trojans, thought like Greeks, and died like Romans. Now he could make out the ancient castle on a hillock above the wall, on the other side of the breakwater that protected the inlet and entrance to the arsenal. The old abandoned forts of Santa Ana and Navidad passed by slowly to starboard and port of the *Carpanta*, still with empty gun embrasures that continued to stare toward the sea like blinded eyes.

Here I was born, thought Coy. And from this port I first dipped into books and oceans. Here I was tormented by the challenge of faraway things and the before-the-fact nostalgia for all that I didn't know. Here I dreamed of rowing toward a whale with a knife between my teeth and the harpooner poised in the bow. Here I sensed, before I could speak English, the existence of what the *Mariners Weather Log* calls the ESW: Extreme Storm Wave. I learned that every man, whether he encounters it or not, has an ESW waiting somewhere. Here I saw the gravestones of dead sailors on empty tombs and realized that the world is a ship on a one-way voyage. Here I discovered, before I needed it, the substitute for Cato's sword, for Socrates's hemlock: the pistol and the bullet.

As the *Carpanta* motored into port, Coy watched Tánger, sitting ramrod straight beside the anchor, with one hand holding onto the Genoa jib rolled on its stay, and smiled at himself. In the cockpit, El Piloto was steering manually through waters he could have sailed blind. A gray Navy corvette, making out to sea from the San Pedro dock, passed on the starboard side, its young sailors hanging over the rail to get a look at the motionless woman in the bow of the sailboat—a gilded figurehead. The offshore breeze carried the scent of the nearby hills. They were bare and dry, baked by the sun, with thyme, rosemary, palmetto, and prickly pear sprouting from dark crags, dry gullies spotted with fig trees, and orderly rows of almond trees in rock-walled terraces. Despite the cement and glass and steel and steam shovels, and the interminable succession of bastard lights blemishing its shores, the Mediterranean was still there, enduring amid the quiet murmur of memory. Oil and red wine, Islam and Talmud, crosses, pines, cypresses, tombs, churches, sunsets crimson as blood, white sails in the distance, rocks carved by man and time, that unique hour in the evening when everything was still and silent except for the song of the cicada, and nights in the light of a driftwood bonfire and a slow moon rising above the sea. Sardines on the spit and bay and olives, watermelon rinds washing back and forth in quiet waves at dusk, the sound of rolling pebbles in the dawn undertow, boats painted blue, white, or red beached on shores with ruined windmills and gray olive trees, and grapes yellowing in the arbors. And in the shadows, eyes lost in the intense blue stretching eastward, men staring at the sea, swarthy, bearded heroes who knew about shipwrecks in coves designed by cruel gods in the guise of mutilated statues sleeping, open-eyed, through the silence of centuries.

"What's that?" asked Tánger.

She had come to the stern deck and was pointing past the Navidad dock and the large twin concrete tunnels that formerly berthed submarines, to where the black El Espalmador beach was littered with the junk of boats cut up for scrap.

"That's the Graveyard of Ships With No Name."

El Piloto had turned toward Coy. He had a half smoked cigarette between his lips and was looking at him with eyes flooded with memories, on the verge of some emotion that he refrained from showing. On the shore, beyond rusted hulls partly sunk among superstructures, bridges, decks, and funnels, lay boats gutted like great hapless whales, their metal ribs and naked bulkheads exposed, their steel plates cut and stacked on the beach at the foot of the cranes. That was where boats sentenced to death, stripped of name, registration, and flag, made their last voyage before ending up under the blowtorch. City planners had fingered that graveyard for extinction, but it was taking months to finish scrapping and clearing away the junk that lay scattered on the beach. Coy saw an ancient bulkcarrier of which only the deckhouse, half sunk in the sea, remained, now nearly indistinguishable among the chaos of metal on the beach. There were dismantled parts everywhere—a dozen large anchors dripping rust onto the dark sand, three funnels absurdly saved and lined up in a row, with traces of paint and the flags of their owners still visible, and a little farther away, by a watchtower, the nearly hundred-year-old superstructure of the *Korzeniowski*, a Russian or Polish packet that had been there as long as Coy could remember. It had a rusted iron bridge, once white, rotted decks, and a nearly intact wheelhouse, where as a boy he had dreamed of feeling the movement of a ship beneath his feet and seeing open water before his eyes.

For many years that had been his favorite place, the site of ocean-going dreams as he walked along the breakwater with a fishing pole or harpoon and fins, or later when he was helping El Piloto scrape the hull of the *Carpanta,* tied up at El Espalmador in shallow water. There, in the endless dusks when the sun was starting to hide behind the inert skeletons of the junked ships, El Piloto and he had talked, with words or with silence, about their belief that ships and men should always end their days at sea, with dignity, and not as scrap ashore. And later, very far from there, on an island, south of Cape Horn and the Drake Passage, Coy had experienced an identical state of mind when he stepped onto a sandy beach that was as black as this one, among thousands of bleaching whale bones as far as the eye could see. The sperm oil of those mammals had been burned in lamps long before Coy was born, but the bones were still there, like a mockery, in that strange Antarctic Sargasso. Among the remains was an ancient harpoon of rusted iron, and Coy found himself staring at it with repugnance. Deception Island was a good name for that place, after all. Whales cut up for scrap, ships cut up for scrap. Men cut up for scrap. The harpoon was embedded in one flesh, because the story was always the same.

THEY tied up with other pleasure craft and walked along the dock, feeling, as one always does when first stepping onto land, that it was rocking slightly beneath their feet. At the commercial dock on the other side of the yacht club was a standard cargo ship, the *Felix von Luckner,* which belonged to Zeeland. Coy knew the ship because of his familiarity with the Cartagena-Antwerp route. Just seeing her evoked long hours of waiting in the rain, wind, and yellow light of winter, with the phantasmagorical silhouettes of the cranes rising from the flat land, the Escalda River, and the interminable waiting to enter the locks. Even though he had known much more pleasant corners of the world, Coy couldn't help feeling a stab of nostalgia.

The three of them went to the terrace of the Valencia bar, which was near the hundred-year-old tile featuring the verses Miguel de Cervantes had dedicated to the city in his *Viaje del Parnaso.* The tile was mounted at the foot of a wall constructed by Charles III when the *Dei Gloria* had been at the bottom of the sea only three years. There they drank big pitchers of cold beer, enjoying the view of the clock in the town hall, palm trees rustling in the freshening *lebeche,* and the monument to sailors killed in Cuba and Cavite. Dozens of names were engraved on its marble plaques, along with the names of ships that like the sailors had been in the silence of the deep for a hundred years. Afterward, El Piloto went to see about the sounding equipment, and Tánger walked with Coy through the narrow, deserted streets of the old city, beneath balconies with pots of geraniums and sweet basil and past porches where occasionally a woman with her embroidery in her hands watched them with curiosity. Most of the balconies were closed and the sunporches stripped of curtains. There were whole houses with condemned windows and doors growing grimy with disuse. Coy searched vainly for a familiar face, a familiar tune filtering through green shutters, a child playing on the corner or in the next plaza, where he might recognize someone or be recognized himself.

"I was happy here," he said suddenly.

They had stopped on a dark street before the rubble of a house wedged between two others that remained standing. Strips of wallpaper dangled from the walls. Rusty nails that once held picture frames, a shattered table leg, and frayed electric cords told the story. Coy's eyes took it all in, trying to recapture what he remembered—bookshelves, mahogany and walnut furniture, tiled hallways, rooms with ovals of glass in the transoms, yellowed photographs encircled by a whitish aura that intensified their ghostly air. The clock repair shop was gone from the ground floor, as were the coal merchants and the grocers at the end of the street, and even the tavern with the marble fountain in the center and ads for Anís del Mono and bullfight posters on the walls. Now there were only memories of the sharp tang of wine as he walked past the door and saw the backs of taciturn men at the counter, bent over glasses filled with red light, whiling away the hours. The boy in short pants who had walked down that same street with a siphon bottle in each hand, and pressed his nose, enchanted, to the lighted shop windows filled with toys for Christmas, had long ago been borne away by the sea.

"Why did you leave?" Tánger asked.

Her voice sounded extremely sweet. Coy kept staring at the walls of the ruined house. He nodded over his shoulder, in the direction of the port at the other side of the city.

"There was a road there." He turned slowly. "I wanted to do what others only dream of."

She bowed her head in a sign of understanding. She was studying him in the unique way she sometimes had, as if seeing him for the first time.

"You went a long way," she whispered.

She seemed to envy him as she said that. Coy shrugged, with a smile that held time and shipwrecks. A deliberate, self-conscious grimace.

"There's something I read," he said, and then again looked at that shell of a house. "A page I read upstairs in that house."

He recited it, remembering without difficulty.

"Come hither, brokenhearted; here is another life without the guilt of intermediate death; here are wonders supernatural, without dying for them. Come hither! Bury thyself in a life which . . . is more oblivious than death. Come hither! Put up thy gravestone, too, within the churchyard, and come hither, till we marry thee! Hearkening to these voices, East and West, by early sunrise, and by fall of eve, the blacksmith's soul responded, Aye, I come! And so Perth went a-whaling."

He shrugged again when he finished, and she kept looking at him the same way. The navy-blue eyes were focused on his lips.

"You were what you wanted to be," she said.

Her voice was still a pensive whisper. Coy turned up the palms of his hands.

"I was Jim Hawkins, then I was Ishmael, and for a while I even thought I was Lord Jim. . . . Later I learned that I was never any of them. That relieved me in a certain way. Like being freed of some annoying friends. Or witnesses."

He gave one last look at the bare walls. Dark shadows waved to him from upstairs—women in mourning talking in the waning light of late afternoon, an oil lamp before the figure of the Virgin, the soothing click of bobbins making lace, a black leather trunk with silver initials, and the aroma of tobacco on a white mustache. Engravings of ships under full sail among the crisp pages of a book. I fled, he thought, to a place that no longer existed from a place that no longer exists today. Again he smiled, at emptiness.

"As El Piloto is known to say, never dream with a hand on the wheel."

Tánger had said nothing after hearing that, and said nothing now. She had taken out the pack bearing the likeness of Hero and slowly lit a cigarette, holding the box in her hands, as if that bit of colored cardboard consoled her for her own ghosts.

THEY ate *michirones* and fried eggs and potatoes in the Posada de Jamaica, on the far side of the old calle Canales tunnel. El Piloto joined them there, his hands stained with grease, and said that the sounding equipment was installed and was working well. There was a hum of conversation, tobacco smoke collecting in gray strata beneath the ceiling, and in the background, on the radio, Rocío Jurado was singing, *"La Lola se va a los puertos."* The old eating house had been refurbished, and instead of the oilcloth table coverings

Coy remembered from a lifetime ago, there was now new linen and cutlery, as well as tiles, decorations, and even paintings on the walls. The clientele was the same, especially at noon—people from the neighborhood, stonemasons, mechanics from a nearby repair shop, and retirees drawn by the family-style, reasonably priced meals. At any rate, as he told Tánger, serving her more sangria, the name of the place alone made it worth coming.

As El Piloto peeled a mandarin orange for dessert, they worked out the search plan. They would cast off early the next morning so they could begin to comb the zone by mid-morning. The initial search sector would be established between 1°20′ and 1°22′W and 37°31.5′ and 37°32.5′N. They would start on the outside of that one-mile-long, two-mile-wide rectangle, working from deepest to shallowest in decreasing soundings, beginning with one hundred sixty-five feet. As Coy pointed out, starting farther off the coast meant it would take longer, as they gradually came closer to land, for the *Carpanta*'s movements to be noticed. At a speed of two or three knots, the Pathfinder would allow them to make detailed soundings of parallel tracks some one hundred sixty-five to two hundred feet in width. The area of exploration would be divided into seventy-four of those tracks, so that, counting the time lost in maneuvering, it would take an hour to run each one, and eighty to cover the complete area. That placed the hours of real work time at about a hundred or a hundred and twenty, and they would need ten or twelve days to cover the search area. If and as weather allowed.

"The forecast looks good," said El Piloto. "But I figure we'll lose a few days."

"Two weeks," Coy calculated. "At a minimum."

"Maybe three."

"Maybe."

Tánger was listening attentively, elbows on the table and fingers under her chin.

"You said we would attract attention from land. . . . Would that raise suspicions?"

"At first, I don't think so. But as we work our way closer, maybe. This time of year people are already coming to the beach."

"There are also fishing boats," El Piloto pointed out, with a slice of orange in his mouth. "And Mazarrón's pretty close."

Tánger looked at Coy. She had picked up a piece of peel from El Piloto's plate and was tearing it into little pieces. The aroma perfumed the table. "Is there some way we can justify what we're doing?"

"I suppose so. We can be fishing, or looking for something we've lost."

"A motor," El Piloto suggested.

"That's it. An outboard motor that dropped off. It's to our advantage that El Piloto and the *Carpanta* are well known in the area, and don't attract much attention. . . . As for what happens ashore, that won't present any problems. We can tie up one night in Mazarrón, another in Águilas, sometimes in Cartagena, and the rest of the time drop anchor outside the area. There's nothing strange about a couple renting a boat for two weeks of vacation."

He was joking when he said that, but Tánger didn't seem to find it amusing. Or maybe it was the word "couple." She tilted her head, the orange peel still in her hands, considering the situation.

"Are there patrol boats?" she asked without emotion.

"Two," El Piloto answered. "Customs and the Guardia Civil."

Coy explained that the Customs HJ generally operated at night, and concentrated on contraband. They didn't need to worry about them. As for the Guardia, their assignment was to watch the coast and enforce the laws regarding fishing. The *Carpanta* wasn't their affair in principle, but there was always the possibility that when they saw them there day after day, they'd come and nose around.

"The good thing is that El Piloto knows everyone, including the Guardias. Things have changed now, but when he was young he worked with some of them a little. You can imagine—blond tobacco, liquor, a percentage of the profits." He looked at El Piloto with affection. "He always found a way to make a living."

El Piloto made a fatalistic and wise gesture, ancient as the sea he sailed, the heritage of countless generations of adverse winds.

"Live and let live," he said simply.

Coy had accompanied him once or twice in those days, taking on the role of cabin boy in clandestine nocturnal outings near Cabo Tiñoso or over toward Cabo de Palos, and he remembered the episodes with the excitement appropriate to his youth. In the dark, waiting for lights from a slowing merchant ship that stopped just long enough to lower a couple of bales to the deck of the *Carpanta*. Boxes of American tobacco, bottles of whiskey, Japanese electronics. Then the return trip in the black of night, maybe unloading the smuggled goods in a quiet cove, transferring it to the hands of shadows that waded out in water up to the chest. For the boy Coy was then, there was no difference between that and what he'd read, which was enough to justify the adventure. From his point of view, those pages of *Moonfleet* and *David Balfour* and *The Golden Arrow* and all the others—waiting for a burst of gunfire in the dark remained for a long time his deepest yearning—were pretext enough. The fact was that later, when they got back to port and threw an innocent line to be tied to the bollard, there was always a Guardia Civil or minor coast guard official waiting to collect the lion's share. After paying the bribe, what was left for El Piloto, after risking his boat and his freedom, was barely enough to get him to the end of the month. Live and let live. But there's always someone who's living better than you are. Or at the cost of others. Once, in the Taibilla bar, as they were eating *bocadillos,* someone took El Piloto aside and proposed a more involved venture, going out on a moonless night to meet a fishing boat coming from Morocco. Pure

Ketama, he said. One hundred pounds. And that, the guy explained in a low voice, would earn a thousand times what El Piloto got from his little night excursions. From their table, sandwich in hand, Coy watched El Piloto listen carefully. Then he finished his beer and casually set the empty glass on the counter before punching the man all the way to the door and throwing him out on calle Mayor.

Tánger paid for their meal and they left. The temperature was pleasant, so they strolled in the direction of the Murcia gates and the old city. There was a Marine standing motionless at the white door of the harbormaster's office—the same building, Tánger commented, in which the ship's boy of the *Dei Gloria* had been questioned. They also saw the blinking green lights of bored taxi drivers waiting at the Mariola theater, and people sitting around on café terraces. Every once in a while Coy saw a familiar face, exchanged a silent nod of the head, or said hi, see you later, without any intention of seeing anyone later, or ever, or even of getting an answer. He no longer had anything in common with anyone here. He saw a boyhood sweetheart, now a respectable matron with two children holding hands and one in a baby buggy, accompanied by a husband with gray, thinning hair, whom Coy remembered vaguely as an old schoolmate. As she went by, her face showed no sign of recognition in the glow of the postmodern streetlights that cluttered the sidewalks. But you know me all right, he thought, amused. LWUTSYWSYN: Law of Who Used To See You and Who Sees You Now. Me waiting at the gate of San Miguel, our hands brushing in the Café Mastia. That impromptu bash one New Year's Eve at your house when your parents were out of town: *Je t'aime, moi non plus*, couples embracing in the near dark as Serge Gainbourg and Jane Birkin held forth on the record player. The dark corner, and your brother's bed with a Madrid Atlético pennant pinned to the wall with thumbtacks, and the fit your father had when he returned unexpectedly to break up the party and found us all playing doctor. *Of course* you know me.

"The search phase," he said, "concerns me less than what happens if we do find the *Dei Gloria*. In that case, even if we mask what we're doing by coming and going, just being in that spot day after day will make us more suspicious." He turned to Tánger. "What I don't know is how long we can carry that off."

"I don't either."

They had gone up calle Del Aire as far as the Del Macho tavern. The steps of La Baronesa hill ascended toward the ruins of the old cathedral and Roman theater, past openings to narrow streets, few of which remained but whose layout was indelible in Coy's memory. Farther on were the barrios of the port workers and fishermen crowded together below the castle, with wash strung from balcony to balcony. The neighborhood was run-down now, occupied by African immigrants who stared at them, hostile or complicitous, from every corner. Good hash, lady. Jus' here from Morocco. Beneath old iron window grates filled with flowerpots, cats slipped along the walls like commandos on a night raid. From nearby bars came the mingled smells of wine and fried sardines, and a solitary whore paced like a bored sentinel beneath a little lighted niche containing a figure of La Virgen de la Soledad.

"In order to locate the bow and the stern, you'll have to take measurements of the wreck and compare them with the plans," said Tánger. "And then zero in on the place where the captain's quarters should be. Or what's left of it."

"And what if it's buried?"

"Then we'll leave and come back with the necessary equipment."

"You're the boss." Coy avoided meeting El Piloto's eyes, which he could feel boring into him. "Whatever you say."

The Del Macho tavern wasn't called that any longer, nor did it smell of olives and cheap wine, but the old bar was still there, along with the dark oak barrels and the look of an old wine cellar that Coy remembered. El Piloto was drinking Fundador cognac, and the naked woman tattooed on his forearm moved lasciviously every time his muscles contracted to raise his glass. Coy had seen those blue lines fade with the passage of time. El Piloto had it done when he was very young, during a visit of the *Canarias* in Marseilles, and then been down with a fever for three days. Coy himself had nearly been tattooed in Beirut, when he was serving as third officer on the *Otago*. He'd chosen a very pretty winged serpent from the designs the artist had exhibited on the wall. But once his bare arm was extended and the needle ready to touch his skin, he thought better of it. So he put ten dollars on the table and left with his arm untouched.

"There's another minor hitch," he said. "Nino Palermo. He's bound to have someone around here watching us. It wouldn't surprise me if he let us do the searching and then showed up the minute we locate the ship."

He drank a sip of his Sapphire gin and tonic, letting it slip, cool and aromatic, down his throat. He could still taste the salt from his nocturnal bath.

"That's a risk we have to take," she said.

Between her thumb and index finger she was holding a glass of muscatel she'd scarcely tasted. Coy watched her over the lip of his glass. He was thinking about the 357 magnum. He'd gone through her luggage, cursing in a low voice, without finding it. He was prepared to throw it into the sea, but all he found were notebooks, sunglasses, clothes, and a few books. As well as a box of tampons and a dozen cotton panties.

"I hope you know what you're doing."

He'd glanced at El Piloto before he spoke to her. It was best if the old sailor didn't know about the revolver, because he was not going to be happy about having weapons on the *Carpanta*. Not happy at all.

"I've done fine so far," Tánger replied glacially. "You two take care of finding the ship, and let me worry about Palermo."

She has a card or two up her sleeve, Coy told himself. The little bitch has cards up her sleeve that no one knows about but her. Otherwise she wouldn't be so sure of herself when it comes to that damn Dalmatian. I'll bet my boots she's already considered everything—possible, probable, and watch out! The problem is knowing which one I figure in.

"There's one other matter." There were only a few customers now, and the tavern keeper was at the other end of the counter, yet he lowered his voice before he spoke. "The emeralds."

"What about them?"

In El Piloto's eyes Coy read that his friend was thinking the same thing: If you decide one day to play poker, try not to play with her. Even if you've been playing a long time.

"Let's suppose they show up," he answered. "And that we find the coffer. Is it true what Palermo said? That you've thought about where to take them? That they'll have to be cleaned, or whatever? And that it will require a specialist?"

She frowned. She looked at El Piloto out of the corner of her eye.

"I don't think this is the time . . ."

Coy pounded his fist on the counter. His irritation was building, and this time he didn't bother to hide it.

"Look. El Piloto is in this up to his eyebrows, just like you and me. He's gambling his boat, and trouble with the law. You have to guarantee him. . . ."

Tánger lifted one hand. Mine tremble sometimes, Coy thought. In fact, mine are trembling nearly all the goddamn time. And look at her.

"What I've promised you justifies the risk for the time being. Later, with the emeralds, we will all be well compensated and happy."

She had emphasized the *all,* turning to Coy with a hard expression. He was once again wondering how many pieces she had used to construct her personality, as she lifted the muscatel to her lips, barely moistening them, and set it back on the counter. She held her head to one side, as if considering the advisability of whether to add something. Veronica Lake, Coy thought, admiring the asymmetrical curtain covering half her face. Tánger had mentioned *The Maltese Falcon,* but Kim Basinger in *L.A. Confidential* was more like it, a movie he had seen two hundred times in the video room of the *Fedallah.* Or Jessica Rabbit in *Who Framed Roger Rabbit.* I'm not bad. I'm just drawn that way.

"Regarding the emeralds," Tánger added after a minute, "I can only tell you that there is a buyer. I spoke with him, as Palermo told you.... Someone will come here to take charge of them as soon as we bring them up. With no further negotiations or complications." Again she paused and stared defiantly at them both. "With plenty of money for everyone."

It wasn't going to be easy, Coy sensed, looking at her freckles. Or, to be more exact, he *knew* it wasn't going to be easy. They were still on that island of knights and knaves, and the last knight had been dead and buried for centuries now. His preserved skull still showed the befuddled grin of a fool.

"Money," he repeated mechanically, little convinced.

He wrinkled his nose before looking questioningly toward El Piloto, who was listening with apparent indifference. After a moment he saw him half-close his eyes, agreeing.

"I'm getting old," El Piloto commented. "The *Carpanta* barely pays for herself, and I've never filed for Social Security.... I'd buy a little motorboat, and take my grandson out fishing on Sundays."

He almost smiled, and stroked his gray stubble. His grandson was four years old. Whenever they went out hand in hand around the port, the boy scrupulously kept count of the beers El Piloto drank, following his grandmother's orders, and then tattled when they got home. It was a stroke of luck that he'd only learned to count to five.

"You'll buy your boat, Piloto," said Tánger. "I promise you."

She grasped his forearm spontaneously. An almost masculine gesture of camaraderie. Precisely, Coy observed, on the faded tattoo of the naked woman.

LIKE the stutterings of a hoarse guitar, the first notes of "Lady, Be Good" stippled the lights of the city reflected in the ink-black water between the *Carpanta*'s stern and the dock. Little by little, the classic swing of bass chords was interwoven with the intricate entrances of the rest of the instruments—the trumpets of Killian and McGhee, the solos of Arnold Ross at piano, and Charlie Parker on alto. Coy listened to it all intently, headphones to his ears, watching the luminous dots on the water as if the notes flooding his head had materialized on that oily black water. Parker's sound, he decided, was saturated with alcohol, and shirtsleeves reeking of tobacco smoke, and vertical clock hands plunged like knives into the belly of the night. That melody, like the others, had the taste of a port of call, of women sitting alone at the far end of a bar. Of silhouettes reeling beside garbage cans, and red, blue, and green neon lighting the red, blue, and green half-faces of faltering, drowsy drunks. The simple life, hello and good-bye, with no complication but what the stomach and bowels could take, here I catch you and here I kill you. No time to court the princess of Monaco: Oh, my word, mademoiselle, how beautiful you are, allow me to invite you to have a cup of tea, I too read Proust. Which was why Rotterdam and Antwerp and Hamburg had porno movies, topless bars, mercenary madonnas knitting on the other side of sheer-curtained show windows, cats with a philosophical air observing Crew Sanders pass by, zigzag from sidewalk to sidewalk, vomit Black Label oil of turpentine, to kill time while waiting to return to vibrating steel plates, wrinkled sheets in your berth, and the ashen light of dawn filtering between the curtains at the porthole. Ta-da-da-dá. Dong. Ta-da-dá. The alto of Charlie Parker kept underlining the absence of commitment, the almost autistic nature of the theme. It was like the ports of Asia, Singapore and all the others, when you were outside the harbor, riding the anchor with the shore beyond the gunnel on which you're leaning, waiting for the launch with Mama San's girls and their lively, birdlike trills as they come on board, aided by the third officer, with Mama San chalking up accounts on the door of each cabin like a waiter on his marble bar: one x, one girl, two x's, two girls. Fragile, accommodating, satin-skinned girls, with malleable thighs and obedient mouths. No problem, sailor, hello and good-bye. You just haven't done it, the Tucumán Torpedoman once said, until you've done it here with three at a time. You never saw a depressed sailor when Asia or the Caribbean lay at the bow between the eyes of the hawseholes. But Coy had seen men crying like babies when headed in the opposite direction, simply because they were going home.

He looked up, focusing on something on the other side of the quay. The crew of a Swedish sailboat were having dinner in the cockpit, by the light of a lamp where nocturnal moths were circling dizzily. From time to time, despite the music, he would catch a few loud words, or a laugh. They were all blond and size XXL, with tiny children who tottered around the deck naked during the daytime, connected by harnesses to the manropes. Blondes like one he remembered, a pilot in the port of Stavanger whom he'd met when the *Monte Pequeño* spent two months there. She was the Nordic beauty you see in photographs and films, tall and substantial, a thirty-four-year-old Norwegian woman with the rank of captain in the Merchant Marine. She had confidently climbed the sea ladder from the launch in open water, leaving all the men on the bridge breathless, and then maneuvered the ship into the fjord in perfect English, directing the tugs with a walkie-talkie while don Agustín de la Guerra stared at her out of the corner of his eye and the helmsman stared at him. Stop her. Dead slow ahead. Stop her. A little push now. Stop. Afterward she drank a glass of whiskey and smoked a cigarette with the captain, before Coy, who at the time was a cadet of twenty-two, accompanied her to the gangway. An athlete in canvas pants and a heavy red anorak who smiled at him before she left. So long, officer. He ran into her three days later, while the crew of the tanker was going crazy over the dream-girl Scandinavians in the Ensomhet, a well-appointed and sad bar by the red houses on the Strandkaien dock, which was filled with men and women for whom a spree meant drinking for hours without saying a word, like stupefied tunas, until they tied on a 9 mm Parabellum drunk. He'd gone into the bar by chance, and she—there with a bearded, impassive Norwegian who looked as if he'd recently been demobbed from a Viking *drakkar*—recognized him as the young man from the gangway of the tanker. Hey, Spanish boy, Shorty, she said in English. Then she smiled and invited him to have a drink. An hour later, the impassive Viking was still leaning on the bar as far as Coy knew, while he, naked and soaked with sweat despite the early morning air blowing through a window open to the fjord and the snowy mountains towering over the sea, was making an all-out assault on the awesome broad-shouldered woman with muscular thighs, whose light eyes stared at him from the dark as her lips, when Coy's mouth left them free, emitted strange whispers in a barbaric tongue. Her name was Inga Horgen, and for the two months the *Monte Pequeño* was in Stavanger, Coy, envied by everyone from the boy in the scullery to the captain, spent every free minute with her. From time to time they drank beer and aquavit with the impassive Viking, who never objected when the woman stepped back from the bar with gleaming eyes and a slight imprecision in her walk, and Shorty, the "Spanish boy," took off in the company of that Valkyrie nearly nine inches taller than he was. With her he got to know the Lyse Fjord and Bergen, *koldtbord*, a few intimate words in Norwegian, and certain useful secrets about female anatomy. He even learned to think he was in love, and that not every woman takes the trouble, or the precaution, to fall in love first. He also learned that sometimes, when you get close enough and pay attention, the woman without her mask, whose half-open eyes wander absently across the ceiling as you open a way into her depths, wears the face of all the women who have inhabited the earth over the centuries. Finally, one night when there was a problem on board and he went ashore later than usual, young Spanish Shorty went directly to the house of black logs and white windows and there found the impassive Viking as drunk as he always was in the bar, the only difference being that this time he was naked. She was too, and she looked at Coy with a fixed and indifferent smile, hazy with alcohol, before speaking words that never reached his ears. Maybe she said "come," maybe she said "go." He slowly closed the door and returned to his ship.

BUM, bum. Bum. An exhausted Charlie Parker, who in the blink of an eye would be dead, had put his sax on the floor and was getting a drink at the bar, or, more likely, was shooting something in the men's room. Now, above the others, came the slap of Billy Hadnott's bass. In this last section he was again master of the melody, and it was at that moment that El Piloto came up from the cockpit to join Coy, taking the other teak seat attached to the stern rail. In his hand he had the bottle of cognac they'd brought from Del Macho's to finish on board. He held it out to Coy, and when he refused, shaking his head to the music dying in his ears, his friend took a swallow before setting it straight up in his lap. Coy pulled the headphones from his ears.

"What's Tánger doing?"

"She's reading in her cabin."

The San Pedro and Navidad beacons were flashing on the other side of the mole, marking the entrance to the port. Green and red, clusters of flashes every fourteen and ten seconds, familiar lights that had always been there for Coy, ever since he could remember. He looked up above the walls of shadows encircling the port. In the mountains, the lighted castles of San Julián and Galeras seemed suspended in the air, as in paintings from other centuries. The glow of the city outshone the stars.

"What do you think, Piloto?"

The clock in the town hall struck eleven before he answered.

"She knows what she's doing. Or at least she acts like she knows. The question is whether you do."

Coy wound the cord of the headphones around the Walkman. He half-smiled in the reflection from the oily water.

"She's got me back at sea again."

El Piloto kept looking at Coy.

"If that's an excuse, fine," he said. "But don't be talking nonsense to me."

He took another drink and handed Coy the bottle.

"I told you before. I want to count those freckles." He wiped his mouth with the back of his hand. "Every bloody one."

El Piloto said nothing, but reached out to reclaim the bottle. A night watchman walked down the quay, his footsteps sounding on the planks of the floating dock. He exchanged a greeting with them and went on his way.

"Listen, Piloto. We men go through life stumbling from place to place. Usually we grow old and die without really understanding what it's all about. But they're different."

He paused and stretched back, his arms extended. His head brushed the flag hanging limp from the mast, next to the mushroom-shaped antenna of the GPS. The night was so tranquil you could almost hear the screws in the bow rail rusting.

"Sometimes I look at her and think she knows things about me I don't know myself."

El Piloto laughed quietly, the bottle in his hands.

"My wife says the same thing."

"I'm serious. They're different. Clearheaded. So clearheaded that it seems almost like a sickness. You know what I mean?"

"No."

"It's something in the genes. It's even true of the stupid ones."

El Piloto was listening intently, with an open mind. But the slight tilt of his head was skeptical. Occasionally he gave a glance around at the sea and the lights of the city, as if in search of someone who would bring some sense to bear on all this.

"They're there. Not speaking. Watching us," Coy continued. "They've been watching us for centuries, you know? They've learned from watching us."

Then he and El Piloto lapsed into silence. From the Swedes' boat came the sound of voices as they cleared the table and got ready to go to bed. The town-hall clock tolled the first quarter hour. The water was so still it looked solid.

"This one is dangerous," El Piloto said finally. "Like that sea where ships get entangled and sit there until they rot."

"The Sargasso Sea."

"You told me she's bad. All I know is that she's dangerous."

He had passed Coy the bottle of cognac again. He held it without taking a drink.

"That's exactly what Nino Palermo said, Piloto. How about that. The day I talked with him in Gibraltar."

El Piloto shrugged. He waited, patient.

"I don't know what he told you."

Coy took a pull from the bottle.

"That we're bad because we're stupid, Piloto. Because we're dim-witted. We're bad because of ambition or lust, or ignorance. You understand?"

"More or less."

"I mean that they're different."

"They aren't different. They're just survivors."

That stopped Coy. He was surprised by how perceptive the comment was.

"Palermo said that, too."

Then he pointed at El Piloto with the hand holding the bottle, but said nothing. El Piloto leaned forward and took the bottle.

"Too many books."

After that he drank a last swallow, corked the bottle, and set it on the deck. Now he looked at Coy, waiting for him to stop laughing.

"What's she defending against?" he asked.

Coy raised his hands, evasive. How the hell, the gesture said, can I explain?

"She's fighting," he said, "for a little girl she knew a long time ago. A sheltered kid, a dreamer, who won swimming contests. Who grew up happy until she stopped being happy and learned that everyone dies alone.... Now she's refusing to let her disappear."

"And what's your part in this?"

"I get a hard-on like anyone else, Piloto."

"You lie. There are answers for that, nothing to do with her."

He's right, Coy told himself. When all's said and done I've had hard-ons before, and I never went around acting like a fool. No more than usual, at least.

"Maybe it's like ships passing in the night," he said. "Have you ever noticed? You're at the rail and a ship you know nothing about passes by. No name, flag, or idea where she's headed. All you see is lights, and you think probably someone's leaning on the rail who's seeing your lights."

"And what color are the lights you see?"

"What does the color..." Coy shrugged his shoulders, annoyed. "How do I know? Red. White."

"If they're red, the other ship has right-of-way. Hard to starboard."

"I'm speaking in metaphors, Piloto. Don't you get it?"

El Piloto didn't say whether he did or didn't. His silence was eloquent, and not very favorable to metaphors of ships, nights, or anything else. Don't screw up your compass, his unspoken words said. It's her pussy. Period. Sooner or later everything leads back there. The reason is your business, what makes me uneasy are the consequences.

"So what are you going to do?" he asked finally.

"Do?" Coy paused. "No idea. Be here, I suppose. Keep an eye on her."

"Well, you remember the old saying: With women and wind, act with caution."

After that El Piloto sank into another unsociable silence. His eyes were on the lights in the oily film.

"Shame about your ship," he added after a long silence. "Everything was going fine there. But on land it's nothing but problems."

"I'm in love with her."

El Piloto was standing now. He studied the sky, seeking a hint of what the weather would bring the next day.

"There are women," he said as if he hadn't heard anything, "who have strange ideas in their heads, like others have gonorrhea. And what they do is come along and give it to you."

He had bent down to pick up the bottle, and when he stood up the lights of the city gleamed in his eyes.

"So after all," he said, "maybe it isn't your fault."

With the wrinkles making shadows on his face, and his short gray hair turned to ash in the dark, he resembled a weary Ulysses, indifferent to sirens and harpies, to pubescent girls on beckoning beaches, to looks hazy with alcohol, "come" or "go," scornful or indifferent. Suddenly Coy envied him with all his heart. At his age it wasn't likely that a woman would cost him his life or his liberty.

XII

Southwest Quarter to South

This road differs from those on dry land in three ways. The one on land is firm, this unstable. The one on land is quiet, this moving. The one on land is marked, the one on the sea, unknown.

—Martín Cortés, BREVE COMPENDIO DE LA ESFERA

At dawn on the fourth day, the wind that had been blowing gently from the west began to veer to the south. Uneasy, Coy checked the oscillation of the anemometer and then the sky and the sea. It was a conventional anticyclonic day at the beginning of summer. Everything was calm in appearance—the water riffled, the sky blue with a few cumulus clouds—but he could see medium and high cirrus moving in the distance. And the barometer had dropped three millibars in two hours. After he'd woken up and had a quick dip in the cold blue water, he listened to the weather dispatch, noting in the log on the chart table the formation of a pyramidal center of low pressure moving across the north of Africa, not too far from a stationary high of 1,012 over the Balearic Isles. If the isobars of those two came too close together, the winds would blow strong out to sea, and the *Carpanta* would have to seek shelter in port and postpone the search.

He disconnected the automatic pilot, took the wheel, and brought the boat around a hundred and eighty degrees. The bow was again pointed north, toward the sunlit coast beneath the dark shoulder of the peak of Las Víboras. They were beginning to sweep sector number 43 on the search chart. That meant the Pathfinder had already covered more than half the area, with no result. The positive aspect of this was that they had eliminated the deepest areas, where dives would have been complicated and difficult. Coy looked toward Punta Percheles on the port beam. A fishing boat was casting nets so close to land that it looked ready to scrape the shells off the beach. He calculated course and distance, and concluded that they would not come too close, although the erratic behavior of fishing boats made them unpredictable. Then he glanced skyward again, connected the automatic pilot, and went below to the cockpit, where the monotonous drone of the motor beneath the ladder was more noticeable.

"Track forty-three," he said. "Heading north."

The sun was at the meridian, and it was hot despite the open portholes. Sitting at the chart table, near the echo sounder, the radar, and the repeater of the positioning system of the GPS satellite, Tánger was watching the screen like an overzealous student, jotting down latitude and longitude every time the surface of the ocean floor showed any irregularity. Coy looked at the depth indicator and speed: 118 feet, 2.2 knots. As the *Carpanta* followed the course set on the automatic pilot, the precise profile of the bottom was modified on the Pathfinder screen. They had taken enough turns there by now to be able to identify, without difficulty, the different shades the instrument assigned to features on the floor. Soft orange was sand and mud, dark orange was seaweed, and pale red indicated loose rock and shingle. Banks of fishes were reddish brown, shifting smudges with green streaks and blue borders, and important irregularities—large individual rocks, say, and the metal remains of an old sunken fishing boat already on the charts—were imaged as jagged hills of intense red.

"Nothing," she said.

Sand and seaweed, the screen said. The echo had turned blood red on only two occasions, tracing significant crests on the underwater relief, hard echoes at respective depths of 158 and 140 feet. They weren't capable of interrupting the run, so they noted the positions and returned very early the next morning, after spending the night, as usual, anchored between Punta Negra and Cueva de los Lobos. Coy was suffering the last effects of a cold, a minor souvenir of his night plunge, but they were enough to make it impossible for him to compensate for pressure on eardrums and sinuses. So it was El Piloto who got into his mended black neoprene wetsuit and jumped into the water, a compressed air tank on his back, knife on his right calf, and a hundred-yard line tied to a bowline at the waist of his self-inflating jacket. Coy stayed above, swimming at the surface with fins, snorkel, and mask, watching the trail of bubbles ascending from the old Snark Silver III demand regulator with dual rubber hoses that El Piloto still insisted on using because he didn't trust modern plastic. The old equipment, he said, never let you down. The echoes, he informed them when he emerged, were caused by an enormous rock that held tatters of tangled nets, and by three huge metal drums crusted with rust and algae. On one of them you could still read the word "Campsa."

Over Tánger's shoulder, Coy looked at the flat bottom the sounder was imaging. Her eyes never left the liquid-crystal screen. A silver pencil was in her hand, the graphed chart before her. Her freckled arms were exposed below the short sleeves of the white cotton T-shirt, her back wet with sweat. The rocking of the boat was rhythmically swinging the damp tips of her hair, which was kept in place with a kerchief tied around her forehead. She was wearing khaki shorts, and her legs were crossed beneath the table. Sitting at the rear of the cockpit, beside a porthole that cast an oscillating circle of sun on his short gray hair, El Piloto was tying a hook onto his fishing line, a crested lure he had just fashioned from a bit of old halyard. From time to time he looked up at them from his labors.

"We may get a change in the weather," Coy said.

Without taking her eyes from the screen, Tánger asked if that meant they would have to interrupt the search. Coy answered maybe. If a wind came up, or heavy seas, the sounder would give false echoes, and besides, they would be very uncomfortable bobbing around out here. In that case, the best thing would be to sit it out in Águilas or Mazarrón. Or go back to Cartagena.

"Cartagena is twenty-five miles away," she said. "I'd rather stay around here."

She was still focused on the Pathfinder and the chart. Although they took turns at the echo sounder, she was the one who spent the most time watching the curves and colors taking shape on the screen, hanging on until her eyes were bloodshot and she had to yield her post. When the motion became a little stronger, she would get up, looking pale, her hair stuck to her face with sweat, visible signs that the pitching and the constant roar of the gasoline motor were affecting her more than she admitted. But she never said anything, or complained. She forced herself to eat everything, out of discipline, and they would see her disappear toward the head, where she splashed water on her face before lying down a while in her cabin. Her package of Dramamine, Coy observed, was close to empty. Sometimes when they'd finished a series of sweeps, or when they were sick of the heat and continual noise, they stopped the boat and she dived into the sea from the stern, swimming straight out with a slow, steady crawl. She swam with the correct rhythm and breathing, not splashing unnecessarily with her kick, the palms of her hands cutting like knives with every stroke. Occasionally Coy dove in to swim with her, but she managed to keep her distance, in a way that was casual only in appearance. Sometimes he watched her dive between two waves, her arms pulling strongly, her hair undulating past schools of fish that parted as she passed. She swam in a flattering black one-piece suit with narrow straps, cut very low to reveal a V of coppery back. She had long slim legs, maybe a little thin—too tall and skinny, El Piloto had judged. Her breasts were not large, but they were as arrogant as Tánger herself. When she took off her bathing suit in her cabin, her body still wet, her nipples made damp circles on her T-shirt, leaving a residue of salt when they dried. At last Coy discovered what was hanging on the chain she wore around her neck—a steel tag with her name, national identification number, and blood type, O negative. A soldier's ID.

The echo sounder registered a change in the reddish tone of the floor, and Tánger bent closer to note the latitude and longitude. But it was a false alarm. She leaned back again in her chair at the chart table, pencil gripped in fingers with ragged nails that she was now chewing constantly. She still had the serious, focused expression of a model student that Coy so enjoyed watching. Often, seeing how absorbed she was in her notepad, the chart, or the screen, he tried to imagine her with blond pigtails, in a school uniform and white anklets. He was sure that before she used to hide in the bathroom to smoke cigarettes, before she became insolent to the nuns, before she dreamed of Red Rackham's treasure, of nautical charts and corsair booty, someone had tagged her as an exemplary little girl. It wasn't difficult to imagine her with a stubborn expression reciting *amo-amas-amat*, H_2SO_4, "In a village of La Mancha," and all the rest. And with flowers for the Virgin.

He leaned against the table at her side to look at the charted squares of search area. On the bulkhead the radio was sputtering on low volume, tuned to receive and transmit. A naval frigate was requesting dock hands to take their mooring line, but no one was appearing. From time to time, a Ukrainian sailor or Moroccan fisherman would reel off long paragraphs in his tongue. The master of a fishing boat was complaining that a steamer had cut his trawl lines. A patrol of Guardia Civil was blocked because of damage to a bridge in port Tomás Maestre.

"We may lose two or three days," Coy said. "But we have time to spare."

Tánger wrote something and then stopped, the pencil hovering over the chart.

"We don't have time to spare. We'll need every available hour."

Her tone was severe, almost reproachful, and once again Coy felt annoyed. The weather, he thought, doesn't give a shit about your available hours.

"If we get a strong wind, we won't be able to work," he explained. "The seas will be choppy and the echo sounder won't work efficiently."

He saw her open her mouth to reply, and then bite her lips. Now the pencil was drumming on the chart. On the bulkhead, next to the barometer, clocks marked local time and Greenwich time. She sat staring at them, and then checked the stainless-steel watch on her right wrist.

"When will this happen?"

Coy paused.

"Can't be sure . . . Maybe tonight. Or tomorrow."

"Then for the moment, we'll keep going here."

Again she concentrated on the screen of the Pathfinder, considering the matter settled. Coy looked up to meet El Piloto's eyes. You do it, said the lead-gray eyes. You make the decision. There was more than a little needling in that look, and Coy fled from it, excusing himself to go topside. There he studied the sky on the horizon, where high clouds unraveled into strings like white mares' tails. I hope to God, he thought, that it will get really bad, that we'll have fierce waves and a murderous easterly, and have to haul ass out of here. Then she'll run out of Dramamine, and I will get to see her hanging over the side, puking her guts out. The bitch.

HIS hopes were fulfilled, at least in part. Tánger didn't run out of Dramamine, but the next day the sun shone briefly amid a halo of reddish clouds that later turned dark and gray, and the wind veered to the southeast, kicking up whitecaps. By noon the seas were getting rough. The pressure had dropped another five millibars and the anemometer was indicating force 6. At that same hour, after the last position had been carefully noted on the graphed zone of track 56, the *Carpanta* was sailing toward Águilas with a reef in the mainsail and another in the Genoa jib, both hauled to port.

Coy had disconnected the automatic pilot and was steering manually, legs spread to counteract the list, feeling in the spokes of the wheel the tug of the rudder in the water and the force of the wind in the sails, along with the powerful pitching of the boat as she plowed the waves. They sailed southwest quarter to south on the compass, and with the large rock at Cabo Cope on the gray horizon. On the log, the anemometer showed 22 to 24 knots true wind. Sometimes the bow breasted a crest and spray showered as far as the cockpit, covering the windshield with spindrift. The air smelled of salt and sea, and the whistling in the rigging rose octave by octave, making the halyards chime against the mast with every plunge of the boat.

It was obvious that Tánger didn't need the Dramamine. She was sitting on the coaming of the cockpit, legs stretched toward the windward side, wearing the red foul-weather pants El Piloto had lent her. No one could doubt that she was enjoying the sail. To Coy's surprise, she hadn't protested too much when the wind forced them to interrupt the search. It seemed as if she had adapted better to the ways of the sea in recent days, accepting the fatalism inherent in the changing fate of the sailor. At sea, what couldn't be couldn't be; or was, in fact, impossible. Sitting there now—oversize pants, wide straps, T-shirt, kerchief knotted around her forehead, bare feet—she looked different, and it was hard for Coy to take his eyes off her and pay attention to the course and sails. Leaning against the cockpit, El Piloto was calmly smoking. From time to time, when he took his eyes off Tánger, Coy found his friend's eyes on him. What do you want me to say, he answered in silence. Things are what they are, not what you want them to be.

The anemometer soon showed 25 to 29 knots, and gusts hardened the feel of the rudder in Coy's hands. Force 7. That was strong, but not unmanageable. The *Carpanta* had weathered storms of force 9, with fierce winds at 46 knots howling in the rigging and short, quick, twenty-foot waves. Like that time when he and El Piloto had to run twenty miles with a following sea and no sail after the jib boom had split. Even with the motor, they passed the Cartagena inlet falling off, only fifteen feet from the rocks, and once they were tied up, El Piloto knelt down and very seriously kissed the ground. Compared with that, 29 knots wasn't much. But when Coy looked up at the gray sky above the swinging mast, he saw that high cirrus clouds were advancing from the left of the wind blowing at sea level, and that to the east a line of dark, threatening-looking clouds was beginning to form, low and solid. That's where the wind would be coming from soon. Better to keep an eye on it, he concluded.

"I'm taking in the second reef, Piloto."

As Coy said that his friend was looking at the mainsail, thinking the same thing. But on board El Piloto was the master, and that kind of decision was up to him. So Coy waited until he saw him nod, flick his cigarette to the lee, and stand. They started the motor to head the bow into the sea and wind, with the jib fluttering, a third of its canvas rolled in the stay. Tánger took the wheel, holding the course, and while El Piloto caught the boom in the center and then eased off the halyard of the mainsail, letting it drop, flapping, to the second reef, Coy stuffed some tethers in his pockets, held another in his teeth, and went to the base of the mast, trying in the violent pitching to keep from being sent into the sea a second time in one week. Bracing himself with his knees against the windshield of the cockpit, he fit the eyelet of the second reef onto the windward hook. Then when El Piloto held taut again, Coy moved toward the stern, adjusting as he went to the movements of the boat, and threaded a tether in each eyelet of the sail, knotting them beneath the boom to anchor the surplus. At that moment a heavy spray broke over the deck, soaking his back, and Coy leaped into the cockpit beside Tánger. Their bodies collided in the rolling, and to keep from falling he had to catch himself on the wheel, arms around Tánger, clasping her in an involuntary embrace.

"You can steer," he said. "Gradually let it fall to leeward."

El Piloto, coiling the main halyard, watched them, amused. She turned the spokes of the wheel to starboard, and the sails stopped fluttering. A little before the *Carpanta* picked up speed, the sea shook her abeam, whipping the mast, and making Tánger stagger within the circle of Coy's arms and chest, as he helped her effect the exact turn of the wheel. Finally the rock at Cabo Cope, standing gray among the low clouds, was again off the starboard bow, beneath the filled jib, and the needle of the log stabilized at five knots. A spray stronger than the previous ones broke over them, soaking their faces, hands, and clothing. Coy saw that the cold water had made Tánger's hair stand up on her neck and bare arms, and when she turned to face him, closer than they had ever been, she was smiling in a strange way, very happy and very sweet, as if for some reason she owed that moment to him. The shower of saltwater had multiplied to infinity the specks on her face, and her lips opened, as if she were going to speak words that certain men wait centuries to hear.

ON the terrace of the restaurant, a two-story open-air structure of wood, cane, plaster, and palm leaves rising high over the beach, the orchestra was playing Brazilian music. Two young men and a girl were doing a good imitation of Vinicius de Moraes, Toquinho, and María Bethania. As they sang, some of the customers sitting at the nearest tables were swaying in their chairs to the beat of the melody. The girl, a rather pretty mulatta with large eyes and an African mouth, was rhythmically drumming the bongos and gazing into the eyes of the smiling and bearded guitarist, as she sang *"A tonga da mironga do kabuleté."* On the table were rum and *caipiriña,* a heady Brazilian drink. Palm trees lined the ocean, and Coy thought how it could be Río, or Bahía.

He could see the beach through the open wooden railing, and beyond that El Piloto, sailing from the pleasure-craft port, whose forest of wood pilings rose from behind a small mole. At the back of that cove, on the high rock that protected the docks and fish market, Águilas castle was surrounded by a crest of gray stone that grew darker as dusk fell. At the entrance, the sea was breaking on the point and on the island whose shape gave its name to the port. But the wind had died, and a fine, warm drizzle left puddled reflections on the dark gray sand of the beach, where the water was calm. He saw the first beacon go on, its black-and-white-striped tower still visible in the uncertain light, and he counted the cadence until he could identify it: two white flashes every five seconds.

When he again turned to Tánger, her eyes were on him. He had been talking, just making conversation about the music and the beach. He had begun, rather tentatively, only to fill an uncomfortable silence after El Piloto drank his coffee and said goodnight, leaving the two of them with the music and the last ashen light slowly fading over the bay. Tánger seemed to be waiting for him to continue, but he had finished, and he didn't know what to bring up to fill the silence. Fortunately, there was the music, the voices of the girl and the other singers, its effect intensified by the proximity of the beach and the drizzle whispering on the palm-leaf roof. He could keep silent without seeming too unsociable, so he reached for his glass of white wine and took a sip. Tánger smiled. She was moving her shoulders slightly to the beat of the music. Not long before, she had shifted to the *caipiriña,* and it shone in the navy-blue eyes fixed on Coy.

"What are you looking at?"

"I'm watching you."

He turned back to the beach, uncomfortable, and poured more wine, though his glass was nearly full. The eyes were still there, studying him.

"Tell me," she said, "what it is that changed about the sea."

"I didn't say anything about that."

"Yes, you did. Tell me why it's different now."

"Not *now.* It was already different when I began to sail."

Her eyes never left him; she seemed truly interested. She was wearing the long, full blue cotton skirt and a white blouse that emphasized the tan of the last days. Her hair was silky and clean, like a sleek gold curtain; he had seen her washing it that afternoon. For the occasion she had replaced the masculine wristwatch with a silver bracelet whose seven links glinted in the light of a candle stuck in a bottle at one side of the table.

"Does that mean the sea doesn't do it anymore?"

"It isn't that either." Coy made a vague gesture. "It does. It's that . . . Well. It isn't easy anymore to get away."

"Get away from what?"

"There's the telephone, the fax, the Internet. You go to seaman's school so . . . I don't know. Because you want to go places. You want to know a lot of countries, and ports, and women. . . ."

His distracted eyes stopped on the mulatta singer. Tánger followed the direction of his gaze.

"Have you known a lot of women?"

"Right now I don't remember."

"A lot of whores?"

He turned to face her, irritated. How you enjoy your damned

little game, he thought. Now what he had before him were unblinking eyes the color of blued steel. They seemed amused, but also curious.

"Some," he answered.

Tánger evaluated the singer.

"Black?"

Coy gulped his wine, emptying half the glass. He slapped it down on the table.

"Yes," he said. "Black. And Chinese. And half-breeds . . . As the Tucumán Torpedoman used to say, the good thing about whores is that they want your dollars, not conversation."

Tánger seemed unfazed. She smiled pensively. Coy found nothing pleasant in that smile.

"How are black girls?"

Now her eyes were on Coy's muscular forearms, bare beneath rolled-up shirtsleeves. He contemplated her a few seconds and then leaned back. He was trying to think of something appropriately outrageous to say.

"I don't know what to tell you. Some have rose-colored cunts."

He saw her blink, and her lips part. For a moment, he noticed, perversely satisfied, she seemed taken aback. Touché, hot stuff. Then again the serene gaze, the sarcastic smile, the dark, blued steel reflected in the light of the candle.

"Why do you like to show off how gross and tough you are?"

"I'm not showing off." He drank what was left in the glass. He took his time doing it, then lifted his shoulders a fraction of an inch. "You can be gross and you can be tough, but still be a damn fool. On that island of yours, it all seems compatible."

"Have you decided whether I'm a knight or a knave?"

He waited, thoughtful, playing with the empty glass.

"What you are," he said, "is a witch. A goddamn scheming witch."

It wasn't an insult; it was a comment. The statement of an

objective reality, which she took without moving a muscle. She was staring so intently at Coy that he ended up wondering if she was looking at him.

"Who's the Tucumán Torpedoman?"

"Was."

"Who *was* the Tucumán Torpedoman?"

My God, he thought, how self-contained and clever she is. How bloody clever. Again he folded his arms on the table and shook his head, laughing almost to himself. A resigned laugh that swept away his irritation the same way wind dissipates fog. When he looked up, the eyes were still staring at him, but the expression had changed. She was smiling, but this time the sarcasm was gone. It was a frank smile. Nothing personal, sailor. And he knew deep down that was true; it wasn't anything personal. So he asked the waiter for a Sapphire gin and tonic, then made an expression as if he was trying to remember. A thoughtful Popeye with a drink in his hand. Those nights with Olive Oyl, et cetera, et cetera. And since that was exactly what it was about, and she was waiting, and he didn't have to invent anything because it was all there in his memory, he laid himself, the character of himself, out on the tablecloth, effortlessly spun from the taste of gin on his tongue. He talked about the Torpedoman, about Crew Sanders, about the merry-go-round horse they stole one night from a New Orleans amusement park, and about Anita's in Guayaquil, and the Happy Landers in El Callao, and about the southernmost whorehouse in the world, which was the La Turca bar in Ushuaia. And about the row in Copenhagen, and another with police in Trieste, and another time the Torpedoman and Gallego Neira had to run after they broke a patrolman's jaw—legs, don't fail me now—with Coy, as usual, dangling between the two of them, an arm around each, his feet running in the air without touching the ground, but they had reached the ship safely. And he also told Tánger, who was leaning forward and listening intently, about the most fabulous fight ever seen in any port in the world—the one on the tugboat in Rotterdam that was carrying sailors and stevedores from dock to dock and ship to ship, all of them seated on long benches, when a thoroughly trashed Dutch stevedore had tripped over the Torpedoman, and the fight spread like a flash of gunpowder. Viva Zapata! Gallego Neira had yelled, and eighty men filled with booze went at it tooth and fist in the main cabin. Coy went up on deck to get some air, and from time to time the Torpedoman would stick his head through a porthole, take some deep breaths, and then jump back into the melee. It all ended with the tug delivering unconscious and beat-up sailors, and stevedores reeking of alcohol off-loading them like cargo, dumping off bales here and there, each to his own dock and his own ship, like a pizza delivery service

Pizza delivery, he repeated. Then he sat back, a slight smile on his lips. Tánger was very quiet, as if afraid she might tumble a house of cards.

"What has changed, Coy?"

"Everything." The smile disappeared, and he took another drink, savoring the analgesic scent of gin slipping down his throat. "No such thing as a voyage today, almost all the real ships are gone. Now a ship is like an airplane. It's not a *voyage*; they transport you from point A to point B."

"And it used to be different?"

"Of course. A person could find solitude. You were suspended between A and B, and it was a long passage.... You carried very little baggage, and not putting down roots didn't matter."

"The sea is still the sea. It has its secrets and dangers."

"But not the way it used to be. It's like arriving too late at an empty pier and seeing the smoke from the funnel disappearing over the horizon. When you're a student you use the correct vocabulary, port and starboard, and all the rest. You try to preserve traditions, you trust a captain the way a child trusts in God. . . . But that doesn't work anymore. I dreamed of having a good captain, like MacWhirr on the *Typhoon*. Of being one myself some day."

"What is a good captain?"

"Someone who knows what he's doing. Who never loses his head. Who comes up to the bridge during your watch and sees a ship closing in on the port beam, and instead of ordering 'Hard to starboard, we're bearing down on her,' keeps his mouth shut and looks at you and waits for you to perform the correct maneuver."

"You had good captains?"

Coy grimaced. That was a real question. Mentally he turned the pages of an old photo album stained with drops of saltwater. And not a little shit.

"I had every kind," he said. "Miserable and drunk and cowardly, and some remarkable men too. But I always trusted them. All my life, until just recently, the word 'captain' inspired respect. I told you that I associated it with the captain Conrad describes: 'The hurricane . . . had found this taciturn man in its path, and, doing its utmost, had managed to wring out a few words.' I remember a bad storm, a nor'wester, the first of my life, in the Bay of Biscay, with huge waves that swept over the bow of the *Migalota* to the bridge. She was fitted with McGregor hatches that didn't fit right, and the ship was taking a beating. Water was coming in every time the seas broke over her, and the cargo was a mineral that shifts when it gets wet. Each time the bow plunged into the water and looked like it was never coming up, the Captain, don Ginés Sáez, who was welded to the wheel, would mutter 'God' very low, to himself. . . . There were four or five people on the bridge, but since I was standing beside him, I was the only one who could hear. No one else noticed. When he glanced my way and saw how close I was, he never opened his mouth again."

The three performers had finished their set and were taking their bows amid applause. The break was filled with canned music over loudspeakers installed in the ceiling. A couple got up to dance. "You're leaving because I want you to leave." Bolero. For a fraction of a second Coy was tempted to invite Tánger to dance. Ha. The two of them there, embracing, faces nearly touching. "I want other lips to kiss you," the song said. He imagined himself with a hand on her waist, stepping on her toes like a duck. Oh well, she was sure to be one of those women who jams an elbow between your body and hers.

"It used to be," he continued, forgetting the bolero, "that a captain had to make decisions. Now he's signing documents in the port; there's a difference of half a ton and he's telephoning the owner. Do I sign the papers? Do I not sign the papers? And in some office are three guys, three pieces of garbage in ties, who say, Don't sign. And he doesn't."

"And what's left of the sea? When do you feel you're still a sailor?"

When there are problems, he explained. When someone on board was hurt, or broke something, people tended to rise to the occasion. Once, he told her, the mother of all waves had torn the rudder blade off the *Palestine*, near El Cabo. They were adrift for a day and a half, until the towboats arrived. And for that time the crew were all true sailors. For the most part, they're nothing but truck drivers on the ocean, or union officials, but in crises they all work together. Shifted cargo, serious damage, bad weather, tempests. All that.

"That word sounds terrible: 'tempest.'"

"Some are bad and others are worse. The unpleasant time for a sailor is when he calculates his course and the course of a major storm, and there's a convergence. . . . I mean when the two get to the same place at the same time."

There was a pause. Some things he would never be able to explain to her, he decided. Force 11 winds off Terranova, walls of gray and white water boiling in a mist of foam blending into sky, waves pounding the bow, a shuddering, creaking hull, crew yelling with terror, tied to their bunks, the radio saturated with the Maydays of ships in distress. And a few men with calm heads on the bridge, or securing loose cargo in the hold, or below manning the engines amid boilers, turbines, and pipes, not knowing what was going on topside, tending to controls and alarm lights and orders, concerned about the sloshing of diesel in the tanks, about the split in the hull that was leaking water into the fuel, about damage in the burners that might leave them at the mercy of the sea. Sailors trying to save a ship, and with it their lives, accelerating in the downward slopes to maintain control, moderating just before the crests, searching for troughs between the largest waves to veer into when the ship could no longer take it head on. And the moment of anguish when, in mid-maneuver, a murderous wave strikes the hull dead abeam and the whole ship heels forty degrees while the men, clinging to anything they can, look at one another with frightened eyes, wondering whether the ship will right herself or not.

"At times like that," Coy concluded aloud, "things go back to how they used to be."

He was afraid he sounded too nostalgic. How could you long for horror? He was nostalgic for the way some men behaved facing horror; but that was impossible to explain at a restaurant table, or anywhere, for that matter. So he breathed hard, disturbed, looking around. He was talking way too much, he thought suddenly. It wasn't a bad thing to talk, but he wasn't used to telling about his life that way. He realized Tánger was the kind of person who chatted easily, the kind whose conversation consisted of asking the right questions and then leaving a silence so the other person could pick up and respond. A useful trick—you learn something and you come off well without giving up anything. After all, people love to talk about themselves. He's a brilliant conversationalist, they say later. And you haven't opened your mouth. Cretins. And he? Besides being a cretin, he was a blabbermouth, from truck to keel.

Nevertheless, even with all that, he realized that talking about those things, at the most basic level, with Tánger there and listening, made him feel good.

"Today," he said a moment later, "the kind of romantic sailing you dreamed of as a kid is reduced to a handful of small ships with strange registries that go around picking up coast trade, tubs with rusted hulls, the name painted over another, and greasy, poorly paid captains. I was on one of them just after I got my license as a second officer, because I couldn't find a berth anywhere else. She was named the *Otago*, and there weren't many times I was as happy as I was then. Not even on the ships of the Zoe line . . . But I didn't learn that till later."

Tánger said that maybe it was because Coy was young then. He thought about it a minute. Yes, he admitted, it was likely that he was happy then because he was young. But with flags of convenience, businessmen captains, and owners for whom a ship isn't much different from an eighteen-wheeler, the whole thing had gone to hell. Some ships were so short of crew that they had to get men from the port in order to dock. Filipinos and Hindus were now elite crew, and Russian captains filled with vodka stove in their tankers a little here and a little there. The one possibility for experiencing the sea *as* sea was on a sailboat. There everything was still a matter of it and you. But you couldn't make a living that way, he added. And a good example of that was El Piloto.

There was nothing but ice in Tánger's glass. Her fingers with those ragged nails were poking inside, rattling the cubes. Coy made a move to call the waitress, but Tánger shook her head.

"The other night, on the prow with the flare, you impressed me."

After saying that, she fell silent, looking at him. Her smile widened. Coy laughed quietly, again at himself.

"That doesn't surprise me. I was the one who was impressed, when I hit the water."

"I'm not talking about that. I was paralyzed as I watched those lights coming toward us. I didn't know how to react. But you went about doing things, one after the other, without even thinking. A kind of predisaster routine. You didn't lose your calm, your voice didn't change. Or Piloto's either. You both exhibited a kind of fatalism. As if it was all part of the game."

Coy bunched his shoulders modestly. He studied his own wide, clumsy hands. He had never imagined having to talk about such things with anyone. In his world, that is, the saltwater world from which he'd recently been expelled, everything was obvious. Only on dry land did they ask you to explain things.

"Those are the rules," he said. "Out there you assume disaster is part of the deal. Not willingly, of course. You pray and you curse, and if you have any class you struggle to the end. But you accept it. That's how the sea is. You can be the best sailor in the world, and the sea comes along and wipes you out. The one consolation is to do the best you can. I imagine that's how the captain of the *Dei Gloria* must have felt."

At the mention of the brigantine, Tánger's face darkened. Suddenly she tilted her head, distracted, her elbows on the table, her chin in her hand.

"That's not much consolation," she commented.

"It is to me. Maybe it was to him, too."

The lights that marked the outlines of the bay had come on, and the water near the shore shone yellow in the drizzle, scored by shimmerings, as if schools of tiny fish were swimming near the surface. The light of the beacon was more concentrated, and in the moisture its piercing beam seemed almost substantial as it circled again and again toward the inky blackness slithering across the sea.

"It must be very dark out there," she said.

Coy heard an involuntary tremor in her voice, and that made him look at her more closely. Her eyes were lost in the night.

"Falling overboard in the dark," she added after a few seconds, "must be terrible."

"It isn't much fun."

"You were very lucky."

"Yes, I was. When you go over like that, you don't normally get rescued."

Tánger's silver bracelet jingled as she put her right hand on the table, very near Coy's arm, but not actually touching. He felt his hair stand on end.

"I've dreamed about that," she was saying. "I've dreamed that for years. Falling into thick, dense blackness."

He searched her face, a little abashed by the confidential tone. And by the way she kept turning toward the shadows.

"I suppose it's about dying," she continued in a low voice.

She seemed almost frozen, staring with apprehension into the rain. She seemed, he thought, to be looking far beyond the shadowy sea.

"To die alone like Zas. In the dark."

She spoke those words after a long silence, in a tone that was almost a whisper, barely audible. Suddenly she seemed truly frightened, or moved, and Coy shifted in his chair, inhibited, as he shuffled through his emotions. He raised his hand to place it over hers, but dropped it back at his side without completing the gesture.

"If that ever happens," he said, "I would like to be around, to hold your hand."

He had no idea how that might sound, but he didn't care. It was sincere. Suddenly he saw a little girl who was afraid of the night, terrified of traveling alone through infinite darkness.

"It wouldn't help," she replied. "No one can accompany you on that voyage."

She had studied him closely when he said that about being around to hold her hand. Very serious and very intense, analyzing what she'd heard. But now, as if she didn't believe it, she was shaking her head with resignation, or defeat.

"No one."

After that, nothing. She was still looking at Coy so intently that he shifted in his chair again. He would have given everything he had—though he didn't have anything to give—to be good-looking, to be suave, or at least to have enough money to smile self-confidently before putting his hand on hers. Her protector. To say, I'll look after you, my dear, to a woman whom he'd called a goddamn scheming witch only a few minutes before, and suddenly he thought of the freckled little girl smiling in her father's arm in the framed snapshot, the champion of the swim meet, the winner of the silver cup that now, dented and missing a handle, was turning black on a shelf. But he was only a pariah with a seabag over his shoulder, aboard a sailboat that wasn't his, and he was so far from her that he couldn't even aspire to consoling her, or having the last hand that pressed hers before a hypothetical voyage to the end of the night. He felt a bitter impotence as she contemplated the distance that separated their hands on the table and smiled sadly, as if smiling at shadows, ghosts, and regrets.

"I fear that," she said.

This time, without even thinking, Coy reached out and touched her hand. Eyes boring straight into his, she slowly removed it. And he, flustered by his gaffe, his blunder, looked away so she couldn't see him blush. But after only half a minute he was struck by how life can produce unique situations that might have been choreographed or directed by the malice of a joker hunched down in eternity. Because at the precise moment he turned toward the railing and the beach, embarrassed by the sight of his clumsy, solitary hand on the table, he saw something that came to his aid so opportunely that he had to choke back his jubilation—a blind impulse, totally irrational, that tensed the muscles of his arms and back and filled his brain with a flash of incomparable lucidity.

Down near the lights bordering the beach, beneath the overhang of a closed little fish shop, he identified the small, unmistakable, and at this point almost perversely lovable, figure of Horacio Kiskoros, the ex-Argentine petty officer and Nino Palermo's hired assassin. The melancholy dwarf.

THIS time no one was going to steal the catch from his hook. So he waited thirty seconds and, using the excuse of a visit to the gent's, he ran down the steps two at a time, went out the rear door, past the garbage cans, and around in a direction that led away from the restaurant and the beach. He advanced cautiously beneath the palm and eucalyptus trees, planning his approach: one board to starboard and one board to port. The drizzle began to soak his hair and shirt, renewing the vigor that charged through his body, tense now with the acid pleasure of expectation. He crossed the road toward an open space, crept through the fennel growing in the ditch, and with the darkness behind him, crossed back, taking cover behind a trash barrel. I hear him breathing over there, he said to himself. He was windward of his prey, who, unaware of what was about to hit him, was smoking and protecting himself from the wet beneath the cane and board overhang. A car was parked near the sidewalk, a small white Toyota with Alicante plates and a rental-car sticker on the rear windshield. Coy skirted the car and saw that Kiskoros was watching the lighted terrace and the main door of the restaurant. He was wearing a light jacket and bow tie, and his brilliantined black hair gleamed. The knife, thought Coy, recalling the Guardiamarinas arch, I have to watch out for his knife. He shook his hands and closed them into fists, evoking the ghosts of the Tucumán Torpedoman, Gallego Neira, and the rest of Crew Sanders. His sneakers helped him take eight silent, fiercely stealthy steps before Kiskoros heard something on the gravel and turned to see who was coming. Coy saw the sympathy fade from the sympathetic frog eyes, saw them fly open and the cigarette drop from a mouth turned into a dark hole, the last mouthful of smoke spiraling through his precise mustache. He leaped, spanning the remaining distance, and his first punch landed right in Kiskoros's face, snapping his head back as if his throat had been cut. Then he slammed him against the wall of the building just below a sign reading La Costa Azul. Best octopus in town.

The knife, he repeated obsessively as he landed punch after punch, systematically, efficiently. Kiskoros, unable to stay on his feet before that onslaught, slid down the wall as he desperately tried to reach his pocket. But now Coy knew a few things about his opponent; he stepped back a little, built up steam, and the kick that landed on the Argentine's arm caused him, for the first time, to let out a long howl of pain, the howl of a dog whose tail has been run over. Then Coy grabbed him by the lapels and jerked him across the sidewalk in the direction of the sandy beach. He pulled, stopped to punch him, and pulled again. His victim, in agony, was emitting a series of muffled groans, struggling to get his hand to his pocket, but with each attempt Coy pounded him again. You're all mine now, he thought, all systems racing with that strange lucidity that occurs in the midst of rage and violence. I have you right where I want you; there's no referee, no witness, no police, and no one to tell me what I should or shouldn't do. So I'm going to lay it on till you're a sack of shit and your broken ribs nail your insides together, and you swallow your busted teeth one at a time and don't have the breath to whistle a tango.

Like a bull looking for a barrier to fall against, Kiskoros was barely struggling. His bow tie was twisted below his ear. The knife, which he'd finally got out of his pocket, had slipped from his unresponsive fingers and lay on the sand where Coy had kicked it. The light from the nearest street lamp gave density to the fine mist as Coy used his foot to roll the sand-coated Argentine over and over to the edge of the water. The last blows came when Kiskoros was already in the drink, splashing and moaning painfully as he attempted to keep his mouth out of the water. Coy waded in ankle-deep to deliver a last kick that rolled his target a few feet farther, and he watched as it disappeared completely beneath the yellow reflections and mirrored image of the shed on the black water.

He retraced his steps and sat down hard on the sand. The tension in his muscles began to relax as he recovered his breath. His ankles hurt from the kicks he'd delivered, and the whole back of his right hand, and up his forearm to his elbow, seemed tied in knots. Never in my whole life, he told himself, have I had such a good time beating up someone. Never. He rubbed his fingers to ease the stiffness, lifting his face a little so the rain could wet his forehead and closed eyes. Motionless, gasping through his open mouth, he waited for the galloping to still in his chest. He heard a noise and opened his eyes. Streaming water that made him glisten among the reflections, Kiskoros was crawling along the waterline. Coy kept his seat in the sand, watching his efforts. He could hear the jagged breathing and the dark grunts of a mauled beast, the clumsy splashing of hands and of legs incapable of supporting a body.

It was good to fight, Coy thought. Like cleaning out the bilges. It was stupendous for the circulation and gastric juices to pour all your anguish and bad humor and soul-rending despair into your fists. It was downright therapeutic for action to take your mind off your problems, and for atavistic impulses from days when a person had to choose between death and survival to claim their place in the game of life. Maybe that's why the world was the way it was today, he reflected. Men had stopped fighting because it was frowned on, and that was making everyone crazy.

He kept rubbing his sore hand. His rage was cooling. He hadn't felt so good in a long time, so at peace with himself. He saw the Argentine, on all fours, lift his body out of the water but then fall back, covered from the waist down. The yellowish light revealed hair and a mustache clotted with sand and reddened by streams of blood.

"Bastard," said Kiskoros from the water, breathless and moaning.

"Hey, shove it up your ass."

Then both were silent, Coy sitting and watching, the Argentine face down, breathing with difficulty, moaning quietly from time to time when he tried to move. Finally he pulled himself forward on his elbows, leaving a furrow in the sand, until he was clear of the water. He looked like a turtle about to deposit her eggs, and Coy watched dispassionately. His anger had nearly dissipated. He wasn't quite sure what to do next.

"I'm only doing my job," Kiskoros muttered after a bit.

"Your job's pretty dangerous."

"I was just shadowing you."

"Well, go shadow the bitch who birthed you out there on the pampas."

Coy stood up unhurriedly, brushing sand from his jeans. Then he walked toward the Argentine, who was getting to his feet with great difficulty, and stared at him a minute—until he decided to punch him again, this time a less impulsive and more businesslike punch, knocking him flat. Small, wet, stiff, and coated with sand, Kiskoros looked like a pitiful croquette. Coy bent over him, hearing his breathing—thousands of little whistles in his lungs—and methodically checked his pockets. A cell phone, a pack of cigarettes, and the keys to the rental car. Coy threw the keys and the phone far out into the water. The dwarf's billfold was huge, stuffed with money and papers. Coy walked over to the nearest light to take a look. A Spanish identification card with a photo and the name Horacio Kiskoros Parodi, other people's business cards, Spanish and English money, Visa and American Express credit cards. Also a color photocopy of a page from a magazine, which he unfolded carefully because it had been handled many times and was damp with saltwater. Under the heading "Our divers humiliate England" was a photograph of several British Marines with their hands up, guarded by three Argentine soldiers, faces blackened with grease, pointing submachine guns at them. One of those three was short, with a frog's bulging eyes and an unmistakable mustache.

"Hey, I'd forgotten. The hero of the Malvinas."

He put the identification and credit cards back in the wallet, added the clipping, kept the money, and dropped the billfold on Kiskoros's chest.

"So, talk to me. Come on."

"I don't have anything to tell."

"What does Palermo want? Is he here?"

"I don't ha . . ."

He stopped when Coy hit him again in the face. It was a dispassionate blow, almost reluctant, and Coy stood watching as the Argentine, who was holding his hands over his face, wriggled like an earthworm. Then Coy sat down on the sand again, never taking his eyes off Kiskoros. He had never treated anyone this way, and he was amazed that he didn't feel sorry for him. He knew, however, who that man on the ground was. He couldn't forget Zas, lying dead on the rug, poisoned, and he knew the fate women like Tánger had suffered at the hands of CPO Horacio Kiskoros and company. So as far as he was concerned, that sonofabitch could roll up his Malvinas clipping and carefully stick it up his asshole.

"Tell your boss that I don't give a fart about the emeralds. But if anyone touches her, I'll kill him."

He said that with unusual simplicity, almost modestly, as if he didn't want it to sound like a threat. It was merely information, absent any emphasis or overtones. A bulletin for sailors. At any rate, even the least attentive listener would have understood that, in Coy's case, such information was reliable. Kiskoros grunted darkly and turned onto his side. He groped for the wallet and put it in a pocket with clumsy hands.

"You are a fuck-up," he muttered. "You're greatly mistaken about Señor Palermo, and me. . . . And you are mistaken about her, too."

He paused to spit blood. He was looking at Coy through wet, dirty hair strung over his face. The frog eyes were not sympathetic now; they gleamed with hatred and hunger for revenge.

"When my turn comes . . ."

He smiled a horrible smile with his swollen mouth, but a fit of coughing left the threatening and grotesque words in the air.

"Fuck-up," he repeated with rancor, and again spit blood.

Coy kept staring at him as he got to his feet slowly, almost grumbling. I can't do anything more to him, he told himself. I can't beat him to death, because there are things I'm afraid to lose, and freedom and my life still matter to me. This isn't a novel or a movie, and in the real world there are police and judges. There's no boat waiting at the end to carry me off to the Caribbean to take refuge in Tortuga among the Hermanos de la Costa, and from there defy the English and take twenty prizes. Today those privateers have been recycled and are building condos, and the governor of Jamaica gets apprehend and arrest warrants by fax.

That was his state, frustrated and undecided, considering whether to punch Kiskoros in the face again, when he saw Tánger standing by the side of the road under a yellow street lamp. She was quietly watching them.

At the far end of the bay, the beam of the beacon was circling horizontally into the warm drizzle. The luminous intervals resembled narrow cones of fog as they swung around again and again, in each circuit picking out the slender trunks and motionless fronds of palm trees weighed down by water and reflections. Coy glanced at Kiskoros before setting off along the beach after Tánger. The Argentine had managed to reach the car, but he didn't have the key, so he was sitting on the ground, propped against a wheel, water-soaked and sandy, watching them go. He hadn't opened his mouth since Tánger appeared, nor had she, even when Coy, who was still a little revved up, asked if she didn't want to take the opportunity to send greetings to Nino Palermo. Or maybe, he added, she might draw pleasure from interrogating the g.d. *sudaca*. That's what he said—interrogate the goddamn South American—knowing that no matter how many kicks he gave him, no one was going to get a word out of Kiskoros. She started off down the beach. So Coy, after a brief hesitation, took one last look at the battered assassin and followed her.

He was furious not because of the Argentine, who had been a welcome target for pouring out the bile scalding his stomach and throat, but because of the way she seemed to turn her back, whenever it pleased her, to reality. Hello. I don't like this. So long. Any time something didn't fit into her plans—unforeseen appearances, difficulties, threats, the intrusion of reality into the daydream of her adventure—it was denied, put off, or set aside as if it never existed. As if the mere consideration of it was an assault on the harmony of a whole whose true dimensions only she knew. This woman, he concluded as he walked along the beach nursing his bad humor, defends herself against the world by refusing to see it. Although he was hardly the one to criticize her for that.

And yet, he thought as he caught up to her and grabbed her arm, whipping her around in the murky light, never in his whole damn life had he known eyes that saw so deep and so far when they chose. His grip on her arm was close to brutal, forcing her to stand there as he examined her wet hair, the reflections in her eyes, the drops of rain multiplying her freckles.

"This whole thing," he said, "is crazy. We'll never be able . . ."

All at once, to his surprise, he realized that she was frightened. Her half-open lips were trembling and a shudder shook her shoulders as the faint beam of the beacon slipped over them. He saw all that in the light, and a couple of seconds later the next flash showed that the warm drizzle had intensified to heavy rain, and she stood there trembling as the sudden downpour fell on her hair and face, pasting her wet blouse to her body and pelting Coy's shoulders and arms as, without even thinking, he opened them to take her in. Warm flesh, shivering in the night and the rain, came to the haven of his body, consciously and deliberately. Came directly to him and pressed against him, and for an instant Coy held his arms open, not yet enfolding her in them, more surprised than hesitant. Then he closed them, holding her softly against him, feeling her muscles and blood and flesh throb beneath the wet blouse, her long, firm thighs, the slim body shaking against his. And the parted lips, so close, lips whose quivering he calmed with his own in a long, long kiss, until they weren't shivering anymore and became warm and soft and opened wider, and then it was she who tightened her arms around Coy's strong back. He put his hand at the nape of her neck, a strong, square hand supporting her head, his hand beneath hair streaming water in the heavy rain. Now their mouths sought each other avidly, with unexpected ardor, as if starved for saliva and oxygen and life; teeth bumped together and impatient tongues touched and thrust. Until finally Tánger drew back to catch her breath, her wide-open eyes staring into his, untypically confused. Then it was she who threw herself on him with a long moan like that of an animal in pain. And he stood there waiting for her, squeezing her so tight he was afraid he would break her bones, and then staggered blindly with her in his arms until they realized that they had walked into the sea, that the rain was beating down, deafening, solid, erasing the outlines of the landscape, the drops popping as if the bay around them were boiling. Their bodies beneath wet, clinging clothes sought each other violently, collided in strong embraces, desperate, hungry kisses. They licked water from each other's faces, their mouths tingling from the taste of rain and wet skin on warm flesh. And she kept breathing into Coy's mouth the interminable moan of a wounded animal.

THEY returned to the *Carpanta* streaming water, tripping through the darkness, clinging clumsily to each other. Arms entwined, they kissed with every step, frantically, as they neared their goal, leaving a trail of water on the ladder and deck of the cabin. El Piloto, sitting smoking in the dark, saw them come down the companionway and disappear toward the stern cabins, and he may have smiled when they turned to the glowing ember of his cigarette to wish him a good evening. Coy was guiding Tánger, steering her before him, hands on her waist, as she turned with every step to kiss him greedily on the mouth. Coy tripped over a sandal she had managed to kick off, and then the other, and at the door of her cabin she stopped and pressed against him, and they embraced, crushed against the teak bulwark, hands stroking in the shadows, exploring bodies beneath the clothing they were undoing for one another—buttons, belt, skirt falling to the floor, unbuttoned jeans slipping down Coy's hips, Tánger's hand between jeans and skin, her warmth, the triangle of white cotton almost ripped from her thighs, the jangle of the metal ID tag. The lusty male vitality, rapt mutual appreciation, her smile, the incredible softness of bared breasts, silky, aroused. Man and woman, face to face, their panting close to challenge. Her inciting moan and his guiding her toward the bunk across the narrow cabin, wet clothes thrown everywhere, tangled beneath still-wet bodies, soaking the sheets, mutual invitation for the thousandth time, eyes locked to eyes, smiles absorbed, shared. I'll kill anyone who gets in the way now, thought Coy. Anyone. His skin and his saliva and his flesh were effortlessly entering flesh ever moister and more welcoming, deep, very deep, there where the key to all enigmas lies hidden, and where the centuries have forged the one true temptation in the form of an answer to the mystery of death and life.

Much later, in the dark, rain drumming on the deck overhead, Tánger turned on her side, her face buried in the hollow of Coy's shoulder, one hand between his thighs. He, half-asleep, felt the naked body plastered to his, felt Tánger's warm, relaxed hand upon enervated flesh still wet, still smelling of her. They fit so perfectly that it was as if they had always been looking for one another. It was good to feel welcome, he thought, and not simply tolerated. That immediate, instinctive alliance was good, a recognition that needed no words to justify the inevitable. That way each had led in his or her part of the journey, with no false modesty. Sensing the unspoken "do this," the intimate, wordless, panting, intense duel that had very nearly cleared away the bad times, equal to equal, with no need for excuses or justifications for anything. No who pays for this, no equivocation, no conditions. No adornment or remorse. It was good that finally all that had happened, exactly as it should have.

"If anything happens," she said suddenly, "don't let me die alone."

He lay quiet, eyes open in the darkness. Suddenly the sound of the rain seemed sinister. His state of drowsy happiness was suspended and once again everything was bittersweet. He felt her breath in the hollow of his shoulder, slow and warm.

"Don't talk about that," he murmured.

He felt her shake her head.

"I'm afraid of dying alone in the dark."

"That isn't going to happen."

"That always happens."

Her hand was still between Coy's thighs, quiet, her face in his shoulder, her lips whispering against his skin. He felt cold. He turned and buried his face in her wet hair. He couldn't see her face, but he knew that at that moment it was the face in the framed snapshot. All women, he knew now, had that face sometime.

"You're alive," he said. "I feel your pulse. You have flesh, and blood circulating through it. You are beautiful, and you're alive."

"One day I won't be here any longer."

"But you are now."

He felt her burrow closer against him. Her lips touched his ear.

"Swear . . . that you won't . . . let me die alone."

She said it very slowly, and her voice was barely a murmur. For a while Coy lay motionless, his eyes closed, listening to the rain. Then he nodded.

"I won't let you die alone."

"Swear it."

"I swear."

He felt her naked body swing astride him, her spread thighs gripping his hips, her breasts brushing against his chest, her lips seeking his. Then a hot tear fell onto his face. He opened his eyes, surprised, and saw a face made of shadows. Confused, he kissed the moist, open lips. Again he heard a slight sigh, and the long, suffering, female moan of a wounded animal.

XIII
The Master Cartographer

Erring due to the vagaries of the sea is not the worst thing.
Some err by using bad information.
—Jorge Juan, COMPENDIO DE NAVEGACIÓN PARA GUARDIAMARINAS

The *Dei Gloria* wasn't there. Coy was gradually coming to that conclusion as they swept the rectangle marked on the chart without finding anything. At depths from sixty-five to two hundred feet, the Pathfinder had imaged nearly the entire relief of the two square miles in which they should have found what remained of the brigantine. The days passed, each warmer and calmer than the last, and the *Carpanta*, to the incessant purr of the motor, was sailing along at two knots across a sea as flat and shining as a mirror, tacking north and south with geometric precision, and with continuous satellite position readings. Meanwhile, the beam of the sounder swept the floor beneath the keel as Tánger, Coy, and El Piloto, bathed in sweat, relieved one another before the liquid crystal screen. The colors indicating the composition of the ocean floor—soft orange, dark orange, pale red—marched by with exasperating monotony. Mud, sand, seaweed, shingle, rocks. They had covered sixty-seven of the seventy-four projected tracks, and made fourteen dives to reconnoiter suspicious echoes, without finding the least sign of a sunken ship. Now hope was fading with the last hours of the search. No one had spoken the ominous verdict aloud, but Coy and El Piloto were exchanging long looks, and Tánger, sitting obstinately before the echo sounder, was growing increasingly irritable and uncommunicative. Failure was in the air.

The eve of the last day they were anchored with one hundred feet of chain in twenty-three feet of water, between the point and La Cueva de los Lobos island. El Piloto stopped the motor, and the bow of the *Carpanta* slowly rode around the anchor and pointed west. The sun was hiding behind the dark, jagged mountains, illuminating clumps of thyme, palmettos, and prickly pears with tones of gold and russet. At the foot of the escarpment the sea was almost still, lapping softly on rocks and the narrow fringe of sand gleaming whitely amid tangles of seaweed.

"It isn't here," Coy said in a low voice.

He wasn't speaking to anyone in particular. El Piloto had just furled the mainsail on the boom and Tánger was sitting on the steps at the stern, her feet in the water, staring at the sea.

"It has to be," she replied.

Her gaze was unfaltering; she was focused on the imaginary rectangle where they had sailed, almost without respite, for two weeks. She was wearing one of Coy's T-shirts—so big it came to the top of her thighs—and was slowly kicking her feet, splashing like a child on the shoreline.

"This is crazy, all of it," Coy commented.

El Piloto had gone below to the cabin, and through an open porthole came the sounds of his dinner preparations. When he came back up on deck to open the chest that held the butane bottle and to connect the gas for the galley, his grave eyes met Coy's. This is your affair, sailor.

"It has to be," Tánger repeated.

She was still kicking her feet in the water. Coy was slouched against the binnacle, looking for something adequate to say, or do. Since he couldn't think of anything, he went to get a diving mask and jumped from the bow to check out the anchorage. The water was clean, warm, and pleasant, and the waning light allowed him to follow the line of the chain stretched across the bottom of sand and scattered rocks. The anchor, a fifty-five-pound CQR, was in the correct position, free of the seaweed that might have let it drag if the wind freshened during the night. He went down a little farther to see clearly, and then slowly came to the surface and swam to the sailboat on his back, paddling with his feet, unhurried, enjoying the water. He wanted to postpone as long as possible having to face Tánger again.

Once on board, he dried himself with a towel, contemplating the arc of the coast stretching eastward. Now totally red from the setting sun, it was the route of marble, Roman legions, and the gods. This time, however, he drew no pleasure from the view. He hung the towel to dry and went down into the well, where he sat on the last step of the ladder. El Piloto was busy with pots and pans in the galley, preparing a platter of macaroni, and Tánger was sitting in the cabin with the nautical charts spread out on the main table.

"There's no possibility of error," she assured Coy before he could say anything.

She had her pencil in hand and was pointing out the coordinates of latitude and longitude on various charts, determining miles on the scales in the margins, and transferring them with the compass onto the graphed rectangle, just as he had taught her to do.

"You checked the figures yourself," she added. "From Mazarrón to the headland of Las Víboras, to Punta Percheles, to Cabo Tiñoso." She was bent over, showing him the results, like a serious student trying to convince her professor. "37°32′ north of the equator and 4°51′ east of Cádiz on Urrutia's nautical chart corresponds to 37°32′N and 1°21′W relative to the Greenwich meridian. You see?"

Coy pretended to review the numbers. He had done that operation so many times that he knew them by heart. The charts were covered with annotations in his hand.

"There could be an error in the conversion charts."

"There isn't." She shook her head energetically. "I've already told you they came from Néstor Perona's *Aplicaciones de Cartografía Histórica*. Even that error of seventeen minutes in the Cádiz longitude relative to Greenwich on the Urrutia charts is corrected there. Every minute and every second is precise. It's thanks to these tables that they found the *Caridad* and the *São Rico* two years ago."

"Maybe the position the ship's boy gave wasn't accurate. In all the commotion, they may have made a mistake."

"No. That's not possible." Tánger kept shaking her head with the stubbornness of someone hearing what she doesn't want to hear. "It was all too exact. The ship's boy even talked about how close the cape was, to the northeast. . . . Remember?"

In unison they looked through the open starboard porthole toward the reddish mass outlined at the end of the semicircle of coast, beyond the bay of Mazarrón and Cabo Falcó. "Having already sighted the cape," the ship's boy had declared, according to the report.

"It may be," Tánger added, "that the *Dei Gloria* is buried in sand and we passed right over her without picking her up."

It was possible, Coy thought. Although not very likely. In that case, he explained, the sounder would at least have signaled differing densities in the composition of the floor. But it had been constantly indicating layers of sand and mud of seven feet, and that was deep not to show anything.

"Something would have to be there," he concluded. "Even if it was just the metal from the guns. Ten guns in one spot is a significant mass of iron. And to those ten you have to add the twelve on the corsair, even though they were scattered by the explosion."

Tánger was drumming her pencil on the chart, chewing the thumbnail of the other hand. The furrows in her forehead resembled scars. Coy reached out to touch her neck, hoping to erase that frown, but she was indifferent to the caress, focused on the charts. The drawings of the brigantine and the xebec were also where she could see them, taped to one of the cabin bulkheads. She had even estimated the dispersion of the corsair's guns on the localized charts, taking into account the explosion, drift, and distance to the bottom.

"The ship's boy," Coy offered, taking away his hand, "could have lied."

Another shake of the head as the frown lines grew more pronounced.

"Too young to come up with a deception of that complexity. He talked about the nearby cape, about a couple of miles of coast. . . . And in his pocket he had the penciled data on latitude and longitude."

"Well, I can't think of anything else. . . . Unless Cádiz isn't the right meridian."

Tánger gave him a somber look.

"I thought about that too," she said. "The first thing. Among other reasons because Tintin and Captain Haddock make a similar error in *Red Rackham's Treasure,* when they confuse the Paris and Greenwich longitudes."

Sometimes, Coy thought as he listened to her, I wonder if she's pulling my leg. Or if this isn't some childish adventure she dreamed up out of a comic book. Because it sure isn't serious. Or doesn't seem to be. Or wouldn't seem to be, he corrected himself, if it didn't involve that Argentine dwarf with his knife, dogging our shadows, and that boss of his, the Dalmatian. A little girl's dream of searching for sunken ships. With treasures and villains.

"But we know the meridians they used at that time," he said. "We have the position the ship's boy provided, and we can confirm it on the chart, along with where he was picked up after the ship went down. It can't be the Hierro meridian, or Paris or Greenwich."

"Of course not." Tánger pointed to the scale in the upper margin of one of the charts. "The longitude is definitely relative to Cádiz. With it, everything works out. The zero meridian of our search is the Guardiamarinas castle. That's where it was in 1767 and that's where it was in 1798. Old longitude from Cádiz to the wreck: 4°51′E. Present longitude, after the correction: 5°12′E. Relative to Greenwich, 1°21′W. No other meridian can situate the *Dei Gloria* so perfectly on Urrutia's and modern charts."

"That's all well and good. Perfect, you say. But we're missing the most important part—the ship."

"We've done something wrong."

"That's obvious. Now tell me what."

Tánger threw the pencil down on the table and got up, still studying the chart. Coy's eyes took in her bare feet against the deck planking, the long, freckled thighs and small breasts beneath the T-shirt. Again he caressed her neck, and this time she leaned a little against him. Her firm, warm body smelled faintly of sweat and salt.

"I don't know," she said, pensive. "But if there's an error, we're the ones who made it. You and me. If we finish the search tomorrow with no success, we'll have to start over."

"How?"

"I don't know. With how we applied the cartographical corrections, I suppose. An error of half a minute throws things off by half a mile. And while Perona's tables are extremely precise, our calculations may not be. All it would take is a slight miscalculation in the boy's latitude and longitude. That ten seconds would be scarcely noticeable in their system of positioning, but decisive when transferred to the chart. Maybe the brigantine is a mile more to the south, or to the east. Maybe we made a mistake in limiting the search area so strictly."

Coy took the deepest breath he could. That was all reasonable, but it meant starting anew. On the other hand, it also meant being with her longer. He circled her waist with his arms. She turned to face him and looked at him questioningly, her lips parted. She's afraid, he realized, resisting the temptation to kiss her. She's afraid that El Piloto and I will say we've had enough.

"We don't have forever," he said. "The weather may turn bad again. And up to now we've been lucky with the Guardia Civil, but they could start to hassle us any time. Questions and more questions. And then there's Nino Palermo and his people." He pointed to El Piloto, who was clearing the table to put on the tablecloth, acting as if he wasn't listening to the conversation. "And he has to be paid."

"Don't do that." Slowly, gently, she removed the hands clasping her waist. "I have to think, Coy. I have to think."

She smiled a little, distant but embarrassed, as if trying to soften her withdrawal. Suddenly she was miles away, and Coy felt a dark sadness slip through his veins. The void in the navy-blue eyes deepened as they turned toward the porthole open to the sea.

"But it's out there somewhere," she murmured.

She put both hands on the porthole and leaned forward. He rubbed a hand across his badly shaven face, feeling his own desolation. Once again she seemed isolated, solitary, self-absorbed. She was returning to the cloud from which they were excluded, and there was nothing he could do to change it.

"I know it's down there, somewhere close," Tánger added softly. "Waiting for me."

Coy said nothing. He felt a mute, impotent anger, like an animal struggling in a trap. He knew he would spend that night with Tánger lying awake in the dark in impenetrable silence.

NOW is when I make my appearance, although brief, in this story. Or when, to be more precise, we come to the more or less decisive role I played in the resolution—to give a name to it—of the enigma surrounding the sinking of the *Dei Gloria*. In truth, as some perspicacious reader may have noted, I am the person who has been doing the telling all this time, the Marlow of this novel, if you will permit the comparison—with the reservation that until now I hadn't thought it necessary to emerge from the comfortable voice I was using. Those are, they say, the rules of the art. But someone pointed out once that tales, like enigmas, and like life itself, are sealed envelopes containing other sealed envelopes. Besides, the story of the lost ship, and of Coy, the sailor banished from the sea, and Tánger, the woman who returned him to it, seduced me from the moment I met the protagonists. Stories like this, as far as I'm concerned, scarcely ever happen these days, and even more rarely do those protagonists tell them, though they may embellish the tale a little, as ancient cartographers ornamented the blank spaces of still-unexplored areas. Maybe they don't tell them because we no longer have verandas dripping with bougainvillea, where dark falls slowly as Malay waiters serve gin—Sapphire Bombay, naturally—and an old captain enveloped in pipe smoke spins his story from a wicker rocking chair. For some time now the verandas and Malay waiters and rocking chairs, even the gin, have been the province of tour operators—in addition to which it is no longer permitted to smoke, whether it be a pipe or any other goddamn thing. It is difficult, therefore, to escape the temptation to tell a story the way they used to be told. So, to get to the heart of the matter, the moment has come for us to open the next-to-last envelope, the one that brings me, with all modesty, center stage. Without that narrative voice, and this you need to understand, the classical aroma would be lacking. Shall we just say, by way of immediate introduction then, that the sailboat that entered the port of Cartagena that afternoon was a defeated vessel, as much as if instead of returning from a few miles to the southwest it was coming back—empty-handed, not with bags of gold—from an actual encounter with a corsair that had dispelled all dreams. On the chart table, the graphed area on nautical chart 4631 is covered with useless little crosses, like a used bingo card, disillusioning and worthless. As they arrived, there was little conversation aboard the *Carpanta*. Lying to facing the rusted superstructures of the Graveyard of Ships With No Name, its crew silently furled the sails, and then, under motor, made their way to one of the slips in the port for pleasure craft. Together they went ashore, unaccustomed to walking on solid ground, past the *Felix von Luckner*, a Belgian container vessel belonging to Zeeland, preparing to weigh anchor and set sail, and started out in the Valencia and the Taibilla, followed by the Gran Bar, the Sol, and the Del Macho, and ended their Via Crucis three hours later in La Obrera, a small tavern located on a corner behind the old town hall. That night, Coy would remember later, they looked like three good friends, three sailors come ashore after a long and perilous voyage. And they drank until things got hazy, one and another and then still another, followed by the next-to-the-last, all for one and no complexes. Alcohol distances events, words, and gestures. So Coy, aware of that, was attending the party, including the main show itself, with a perverse curiosity that contained both amazement and guilt. That was also the first and last time he had seen Tánger drink that much, and so deliberately and earnestly. She was smiling as if all at once the *Dei Gloria* was a bad dream left far behind, and she kept leaning her head on Coy's shoulder. She drank what he was drinking, gin with ice and a little tonic, while El Piloto accompanied them with eye-watering belts of Fundador cognac chased with beer. Watching them through amused, puckish, friendly eyes, he told brief and incoherent stories about ports and ships with that serious tone and slow, careful speech one uses when alcohol thickens the tongue. Sometimes Tánger laughed and kissed him, and El Piloto, cut short, would dip his head a little, always calm, or look at Coy and smile again, elbows on the worn Formica table. He seemed to be having a good time. As did Coy, who was rubbing Tánger's stiff waist and the slim curve of her back, feeling her body against his, her lips on his ear and his neck. Everything could have ended there, and it wasn't a bad ending for a failure. Because everything was grotesque and yet logical at the same time, Coy decided. They hadn't found the brigantine, but it was the first time the three of them had laughed together, without reserve, free of problems, unself-conscious and loud. It felt liberating, and in that state of mind they drank as if playing themselves, aware of the trite ritual the circumstances demanded.

"To the turtle," said Tánger.

She raised her glass, clinking it against Coy's, and emptied what remained in one swallow. That afternoon on the way to Cartagena, a mile south of Palomas Island, they had sighted in the distance something splashing in the water. Tánger had asked what it was, and Coy took a look through the binoculars—a sea turtle trapped in a fishing net. They had headed for her, watching the creature struggle to free herself. The netting was wrapped around her shell and bloody fins, strangling her as she fought to keep her head above water; she was on the verge of asphyxiation. It was rare to see a turtle in those waters, and the trouble she was in was a good indication of why. The net was one of thousands strung everywhere in the Mediterranean, a thousand feet of mesh held by plastic drums as floats, lethal labyrinths that trapped any living thing. The turtle would never be able to get free. Her strength was failing and her wrinkled eyelids were closing over bulging eyes in a death agony. Even if she got free of the net, her exhaustion and wounds had already sentenced her to death. But that didn't matter to Coy. Before anyone could say a word, blind with rage, he had jumped into the water with El Piloto's knife in his hand and was wildly slashing at the net around the animal. He hacked at the netting with fury, as if attacking an enemy he despised with all his soul. He would take a breath and dive in water blood had turned a rosy pink, and when he came up stare straight into the creature's desperate eye. He cut everything he could, roaring with outrage when he came up to breathe, then went back down to destroy all he could of the net. Even when the turtle was finally free and slowly drifting away, weakly moving her fins, he kept slashing, until his arm refused to respond. Then he took one last look at the turtle, whose dying eye followed him as he swam away toward the *Carpanta*. She didn't have much of a chance, exhausted and trailing blood that sooner or later would attract some voracious shark. But at least the end would come in the open sea, in accord with her world and her species, not a wretched death strangled in a tangle of cord woven by human hands.

In La Obrera they ordered more gin, more cognac, and more beer, and Tánger again rested her head on Coy's shoulder. She was quietly singing the words of a song, and from time to time she would stop, turn up her face, and Coy would seek her lips, cool from the ice and perfumed with gin, to warm them with his. No one mentioned the *Dei Gloria*, and everything was being played by the rules, by what the situation demanded, and by the roles that they—perhaps not El Piloto, or at least not consciously—were performing in that contemporary version of a timeworn plot. They had lived that scene a hundred times before, and it was soothing to lose the game in times when men were trained to see a certain kind of success evaporate before their eyes. At the bar, facing the tavern-keeper Coy remembered being there all his life in his apron and with a cigarette hanging from his lips, red-nosed drunks and steady clients with skinny, tattooed arms were putting down glasses of wine and goblets of cognac, turning from time to time to smile with complicity. They were old acquaintances of El Piloto, and now and again the three at the table would tell the tavern-keeper to serve a round for everyone. Your health, Piloto, and your buddies'. Here's to you, Ginés. And you, Gramola. You, too, Jaqueta. Everything was perfect, and Coy felt at peace. He was having fun playing his own character. All that was missing, he lamented, was the piano, with Lauren Bacall shooting sidelong glances as she sang in that hoarse, hushed voice, which in the original, subtitled version sounded a little like Tánger's. A little later, when they reached a certain point, the alcohol would transpose all images to black and white. Because after so many novels, so many films, and so many songs, there weren't even innocent drunks anymore. And Coy asked himself, envying him, what the first man felt the first time he went out to hunt a whale, a treasure, or a woman, without having ever read about it in a book.

THEY said good-night at the city wall. They had left the boat clean and secure, and that night El Piloto was going to sleep at his house in the fisherman's barrio of Santa Lucía. They stood watching him stumble off through the palm trees and huge magnolias, and then looked down toward the port, where beyond the seaman's club and the Mare Nostrum restaurant, the *Felix von Luckner* was casting off lines with her deck illuminated and her lights reflected in the black water. They had let the stern line go, and Coy mentally repeated the orders the pilot would be sending that moment from the bridge. Hard to starboard. A little forward. Stop. Rudder amidships. Engines half back. Cast off bowlines. Tánger was beside him, also watching the ship's maneuver, and abruptly she said, "I want a shower, Coy. I want to strip and take a really hot shower, boiling with steam, like fog on the high seas. And I want you to be in that fog, and not talk to me about boats or shipwrecks or any of that. I've drunk so much tonight that all I want is to put my arms around a tough, silent hero, someone who's returned from Troy and whose skin and lips taste like salt and the smoke of burned cities." She said that, and looked at him the way she sometimes did, quiet and very serious and focused, as if she were waiting for something from him. The blue steel of her eyes was softened by gin into shining, almost liquid navy blue, and she parted her lips as if the ice of the drinks she'd drunk made her mouth so cold that it would take

Coy hours to warm it. He wrinkled his nose and smiled the way he so often did, with that shy expression that lit his face and softened his rough features, the too large nose and chin almost always in need of a shave. Tough, silent hero, she'd said. On that particular island of knights and knaves, no one had spoken the magic words. Only I will lie to you and I will deceive you. Not even in that context of lying or betrayal had anyone yet said "I love you." At that precise instant, though with the world whirling around him and alcohol pumping through his veins, he was on the verge of being vulgar and saying it. He had even opened his mouth to say the forbidden words. But she, as if sensing it, put her fingers to Coy's lips. She came so close that the liquid blue of her eyes was sparkling and dark at the same time, and he smiled again, resigned, as he kissed her fingers. Then he took a deep breath, as he did before a dive, and looked around for five seconds before taking her hand and crossing the street, setting a direct course for the door of the Cartago Inn, one star, rooms with bath and views of the port. Special rates for officers of the Merchant Marine.

THAT night, enclosed by white tiles and thick steam, it rained on the shores of Troy as ship after ship set sail. It was, in fact, a warm fog, gray or shades of gray, in which all colors were washed out by that gentle rain falling on a deserted beach where signs of a denouement could be seen—a forgotten bronze helmet, a fragment of broken sword half-buried in the sand, ashes carried on the wind from some burned city out of sight but sensed, still smoking, as the last ships hoisted damp sails and sailed away. It was the *nostos* of Homeric heroes, the return and the loneliness of the last warriors coming home after the battle to be murdered by their wives' lovers or to be lost at sea, victims of cholera and the caprices of the gods. In that warm mist, Tánger's naked body sought Coy's, foam of soapy water on her thighs, smooth, freckled skin shining wetly. She sought him with silent determination, with intense purpose in her gaze, literally trapping him at the head of the bathtub. And lying back there, warm water to his waist and warm rain falling on his head and running down his face and shoulders, Coy watched her rise slowly, lift above him and slowly descend, decisive, slow, inch by inch, leaving him no escape but forward between her thighs, deep into that intense, desperate embrace, at the very edge of a lucidity draining away with his surrender and defeat. Never, until that night, had Coy felt raped by a woman. Never so meticulously and deliberately relegated to marginal status. Because I'm not me, he reasoned with the last bit of flotsam floating from the shipwreck of his thoughts. It isn't me she's embracing, it isn't anyone who can be assigned a face, a voice, a mouth. It wasn't for me those other times, when she moaned that long, sorrowful moan, and it isn't me she is imagining now. It's the tough, male, silent hero she was calling for before. Summoning him to the dream that she, all shes, have carried in their cells since the world began. The man who left his semen in her womb and then sailed for Troy on a black ship. The man whose shadow not even cynical priests, pale poets, or reasonable men of peace and the word who wait beside the unfinished tapestry have ever been able to erase completely.

It was still night when Coy awakened. She was not beside him. He had dreamed of a black, hollow space, the belly of a wooden horse, and bronze-armored companions who, swords in hand, slipped stealthily into the heart of a sleeping city. He sat up, uneasy, and saw the silhouette of Tánger at the shadowed window, against the lights from the city wall and the port. She was smoking. Her back was to him and he couldn't see the cigarette, but he caught the scent of tobacco. He got out of bed, naked, and went to her. She had put on his shirt but left it unbuttoned despite the cool night air blowing through the open window. The silver chain with the soldier's I.D. shone at her neck.

"I thought you were sleeping," she said, without turning.

"I woke up and you weren't there."

Tánger didn't add anything, and he stood quietly looking at her. She inhaled deeply, held the smoke in her lungs, then slowly expelled it. As she drew on the cigarette, the glowing tip lit her fingers with their ragged nails. Coy put one hand on her shoulder, and she touched it absently, distractedly, before taking another drag.

"What do you think happened to the turtle?" she asked after a while.

Coy shrugged. "By now she's dead."

"I hope not. It's possible that she made it."

"Maybe."

"Maybe?" She observed him out of the corner of her eye. "Sometimes there are happy endings, Coy."

"Sure. Sometimes. Save one for me."

Again that silence. She was gazing down below the wall at the empty space left at the dock by the departure of the Zeeland ship.

"Do you have the answer yet to the puzzle of the knight and the knave?" she asked finally, speaking very quietly.

"There is no answer."

She laughed very low, or he thought she did. He couldn't be sure.

"You're mistaken," she said. "There's always an answer for everything."

"Well then, tell me what we're going to do now."

It was some time before she replied. She seemed as far away as the wreck of the *Dei Gloria*. Her cigarette had burned down, and she leaned over to crush the butt on the ledge of the recessed window, very deliberately extinguishing the last ember. Then she dropped it out the window.

"Do?" She tilted her head, as if considering that word. "What we've been doing, naturally. Keep looking."

"Where?"

"Back on dry land again. You don't only find sunken ships in the ocean."

AND that was how I came to see them the next day in my office at the university in Murcia. It was one of those very bright days we tend to have, with huge parallelograms of sun gilding the stones of the halls of learning amid shimmering windowpanes and sparkling fountains. I had put on my sunglasses and gone down to the corner café for a cup of coffee, and on my way back, my jacket over my shoulder, I saw Tánger Soto waiting for me at the door—blond, pretty, full blue skirt, freckles. At first I took her for one of the students who at this time of year come to ask for help with their theses. Then I took note of the fellow with her, who was close but keeping a certain distance—I suppose you know what I mean if you know Coy a little by now. Then she—carrying a leather shoulder bag and with a cardboard document tube under one arm—introduced herself and pulled my *Aplicaciones de Cartografía Histórica* from her bag, and it came to me that she was the young woman my dear friend and colleague Luisa Martín-Merás, head of cartography at the Museo Naval in Madrid, had spoken to me about, describing her as bright, introverted, and efficient. I even recalled that we had had several telephone conversations about Urrutia's *Atlas* and other historical documents in the archives of the university.

I invited them to come in, ignoring the sullen students waiting in the corridor. It was exam period and work was piled on my desk in the lion's cage I have for an office. I took books off chairs so they could sit down, and listened to their story. To be more precise, I listened to her, because it was she who did nearly all the talking, and I listened to as much of the story as she was willing to tell at that time. They had come from Cartagena, only half an hour by car on the main highway, and the whole affair could be summed up as a sunken ship, the information that could make it possible to find it, a few previous unfruitful attempts, and exact coordinates of latitude and longitude that for some reason had turned out to be inexact. Same old story. I am, after all, accustomed to inquiries of this nature. Although for personal reasons I sign my articles and my books with the same name and modest title I use on my calling card—below the anagram, common in my profession, of a T inside an O: *Néstor Perona, Master Cartographer*—I have held the chair of cartography at the Universidad de Murcia for a long time. My publications mean something in the scientific world, and I must often respond to questions and problems posed by institutions and individuals. It is curious indeed that at a time when cartography has undergone the greatest revolution in its history—given aerial photography, satellite maps, and the application of electronics and informatics—and has progressed light-years beyond the rudimentary maps drawn by early explorers and navigators, scholars find it increasingly necessary to maintain the fragile umbilical cord that joins modern times to past eras of science, which are now little more than tested myth. Difficulties already existed in the fifteenth and sixteenth centuries, when advanced Flemish cartographers were faced with the daunting task of attempting to reconcile the contradictory lore left by authors of old with the new discoveries of Portuguese and Spanish navigators. And the process continued through successive generations. So today, without people like myself—you will forgive that minor, if legitimate, vanity—the ancient world would vanish and many things would lose their meaning in the cold neon light of modern science. Which is why, every time someone needs to look to the past and understand what he sees, he comes to me. To the classics. I consult with historians, librarians, archaeologists, hydrographers . . . seekers of treasure in general. You may recall the discovery of the galleon *São Rico* off Cozumel, the search for Noah's ark on Mount Ararat, or that famous *National Geographic* television special on locating the *Virgen de la Caridad* near Santoña in the Bay of Biscay, and the recovery of eighteen of her forty bronze guns. Those three episodes—although the quest for the ark ended in grotesque failure—were made possible by the correction tables developed by my team here at the university. And another familiar figure in this story, Nino Palermo, once paid me the dubious honor of consulting me—though the matter went no farther—when he was on the trail of 80,000 ducats that had gone down with a Spanish galley in 1562 near the tower of Vélez Málaga. Now, then. For more details, I refer you to my articles in the journal *Cartographica,* and to several of my books—the aforementioned *Aplicaciones,* for example, or my study on loxodromics, derived from the Greek *loxos* and *dromos*, as you are aware, in *Los enigmas de la proyección Mercator.* You may also consult my work on the twenty-one maps in the unfinished atlas of Pedro de Esquivel and Diego de Guevara, or my biographies of Father Ricci (*Li Mateu: The Ptolemy of China*) and Tofiño (*The King's Hydrographer*), the *Catálogo Hidrográfico Antiguo,* which I compiled in collaboration with Luisa Martín-Merás and Belén Rivera, and my monographs, *Cartógrafos jesuitas en el mar*, and *Cartógrafos jesuitas en Oriente*. All these works were written in my study, naturally. But certain things, such as boyhood dreams, must be visited in person, and only when you are young. In our mature years, postcards and videos are imprinted upon our senses, and we find ourselves in Venice, not in splendor but in humidity.

But back to the matter at hand. That morning in my office at the university, my two visitors laid out their problem. Rather, she laid it out while he listened discreetly, seated among the piles of books I had set aside so he could sit down. I must confess that I took an immediate liking to that quiet sailor. It may have been the way he listened in the background, or perhaps it was his rough good looks. In any case, he looked like a good man. I liked that frank way he had of meeting your eyes, the way he touched his nose when disconcerted or perplexed, the shy smile, the jeans and sneakers, the strong arms under the white shirt with sleeves rolled up to the elbow. He was the kind of man whom you sense, rightly or wrongly, you can trust, and his role in this adventure, his intervention in the puzzle and its unraveling, is the principal reason I am eager to tell this tale. In my youth I too read certain books. Besides, I tend to call on extreme courtesy—each of us has his own method—as a superior expression of scorn for my fellow man. The science to which I devote myself is a means as efficient as any other to hold at bay a world populated with people who on the whole irritate me, and among whom I prefer to choose with total impartiality, according to my sympathies or antipathies. As Coy himself would say, we deal the way we can. So for some strange reason—call it solidarity or affinity—I feel the need to justify this sailor exiled from the sea, and that is my motive for telling you his story. After all, narrating his adventure at the side of Tánger Soto is a little like a Mercator projection. In attempting to represent a sphere on a flat sheet of paper, you must occasionally distort surfaces in the upper latitudes.

That morning in my office, Tánger Soto gave me the general outline of the matter, and then set out the specifics of the problem: 37°32′N and 4°51′E on Urrutia's nautical chart. A ship had been sunk there during the last third of the eighteenth century and that location, after the proper corrections had been made with the help of my own cartographical tables, corresponded to the modern position of 37°32′N and 1°21′W. The question posed by the visiting pair was whether that transposition was correct. After brief consideration, I said that if the tables had been properly applied, then quite possibly it was.

"Nonetheless," she said, "the ship isn't there."

I looked at her with reasonable reserve. In these kinds of situations I always distrust absolute affirmations, and women, pretty or ugly, who are exceedingly clever. And many of them have passed through my lecture halls.

"Are you sure? A sunken ship does not go about shouting its location."

"I know that. But we have done exhaustive research, starting on land."

So perhaps they got their feet wet, I deduced. I was trying to situate the couple among the species I have catalogued, but it was not easy. Amateur archaeologists, avid historians, treasure hunters. From behind my desk, beneath the framed reproduction of Peutinger's *Tabula Itineraria*—a gift from my students when I was given the chair—I devoted myself to studying them carefully. Physically, she fit the first two categories, he the third. Assuming that archaeologists, avid historians, and treasure hunters *have* a specific appearance.

"Well, I don't know," I said. "All that occurs to me is the most elementary answer. Your original data are erroneous. The latitudes and longitudes are incorrect."

"That's unlikely." She shook her head with certainty, an action that caused her blond hair, which I observed to be cut with curious asymmetry, to brush her chin. "I have solid documentary evidence. In that sense, only a relative margin of error would be acceptable, and that will lead us to a second, and broader, area of search. But first we want to discard any other possibility."

I liked the lady's tone of voice. So competent and sure. Formal.

"For example?"

"An error on our part when we applied your tables. I would be grateful if you would review our calculations."

Again I looked at her for an instant and then glanced at him; he was still listening quietly, sitting still, his large hands resting on his thighs. My curiosity had its limits. I had heard many such stories of searches. But the students waiting outside my door were stifling, the day was too splendid for correcting exams, she was most uncommonly attractive—without being a true beauty because of her nose when seen in profile, although perhaps beautiful precisely because of that—and I liked him a lot. So, *pourquoi pas*? I asked myself, in the manner of Commander Charcot. This was not something that would take much time. The cardboard tube contained several rolled-up charts, which Tánger Soto spread out on my desk. Among them I recognized a fine reproduction of one of Urrutia's nautical charts. I knew that one, naturally, and studied it with affection. Not as beautiful as Tofiño's, of course. But magnificent drypoint scratched on plates of beaten and polished copper. Very precise for its period.

"We shall see," I said. "The date of the shipwreck?"

"1767. Southeast coast of Spain. Position from land sightings almost simultaneous to the moment of sinking."

"Tenerife meridian?"

"No. Cádiz."

"Cádiz." I smiled slightly, encouragingly, while looking for the corresponding scale of longitudes on the upper portion of the chart. "That meridian is enchanting. I refer to the old one, naturally. It has the traditional aroma of the vanished past, like Ptolemy the Elder's Hierro island. You know what I mean."

I put on my glasses to look more closely, and began to work before they could say whether they knew or not. The latitude was the first thing I established, and without difficulty. It was quite exact. In truth, as long as three thousand years ago Phoenician navigators knew that the height of the sun on the horizon, or of the stars near the north pole, measures the geographic latitude of one's location. Up to this point, child's play. A child with some notion of cosmography, of course. Well, and not just any child.

"You are fortunate that your episode occurred in 1767," I commented. "Only a hundred years before, you could have obtained the latitude with the same facility but the longitude would have left much to be desired. In 1583, Matteo Ricci, who was one of the great cartographers of the period, made errors of up to five degrees in calculating longitudes with respect to the Tenerife meridian. . . . It was fifteen hundred years before Ptolemy's globe shrank to size, and it happened very gradually.... I suppose you are familiar with Louis XIV's famous saying when Picard and La Hire moved the map of France a degree and a half: 'My cartographers have taken more land from me than my enemies.' "

I alone laughed at the tired anecdote, though Tánger had the courtesy to join me with a smile. This is a truly interesting woman, I told myself, observing her closely. I spent a while trying to place her more precisely, but soon gave up. A woman is the only creature that cannot be defined in two consecutive sentences.

"At any rate," I continued. "Urrutia refined things considerably, although we would have to wait for Tofiño, at the end of the century, for a Spanish hydrographic cartographer to address reality.... Let's see. All right. I believe that your estimated latitude is absolutely correct, my dear. You see? Thirty-two minutes north. It appears that the cartographer and the gentleman who took the latitude on his map are in agreement."

I said gentleman, and not lady, because I like to present myself to my female students as a reprehensible misogynist, although truly I am not one. I also wanted to test whether Tánger Soto was one of those women who have time to be offended by that kind of provocation. But she did not seem offended. She merely shifted slightly in her seat, toward her companion.

"This sailor is your 'gentleman.' "

Over my glasses, I peered at Coy with renewed interest.

"Merchant seaman? A pleasure. Your figures and mine are identical, in principle."

He did not respond. He smiled vaguely, slightly uncomfortable, and touched his nose a couple of times. Leaning over my desk, Tánger pointed to the scale on the upper edge of the nautical chart.

"Establishing the longitude," she said, "was more problematic."

"Of course." I leaned back in my professorial chair. "Until Harrison's and Berthoud's naval clocks were perfected, and that was well past the middle of the eighteenth century, longitude was the navigator's major problem. Latitude was obtained from the sun or the stars, but longitude, which any cheap wristwatch can provide us with now, could be calculated only by the imprecise measurement of lunar distances. When Urrutia compiled his charts, locating one's position on the ocean in reference to a meridian was still not totally resolved. They had pendulum clocks and sextants, but lacked a truly reliable instrument, a chronometer that would calculate those fifteen degrees in each hour of difference between local time and that of the prime meridian. That is why errors in longitude were more appreciable than those in latitude. After all, the true longitude of the Mediterranean was not established until 1700, and it was twenty degrees fewer than the sixty-two attributed by Ptolemy."

I granted myself a breath to observe Tánger Soto. She did not seem one whit impressed. Nor did Coy. It was likely that they already knew everything I was telling them, but I was a master cartographer, and they had come to my office to see me of their own free will. Each of us has his own character, and he plays the part as best he can. If those two wanted my help, they would have to pay the price. To my ego.

"That scarcely seems possible, does it?" I continued in the same tone, permitting myself to add a tender touch. "When I see a child coloring in his geography notebook, I think how men have studied land and sea from the beginning of time, calculating triangulations, lunar distances, and planetary eclipses, observing every feature of the terrain and measuring depths, to draw maps of what they have seen. 'The way of reaching here being so arduous,' wrote Martín Cortés, 'it would be difficult to make it understood with words or to write with the pen. The best description the ingenuity of man has devised is to paint it on a chart.' In this way man began to dominate nature, making explorations and voyages possible. With his talent, and with the rudimentary aid of the needle, the astrolabe, the quadrant, the forestaff, and the Alfonsine tables, man began to trace the line of the coasts; he marked its dangers on paper, and set lights and towers in appropriate places." I motioned over my head toward the *Tabula Itineraria*. It was not a paradigm of exactitude, with all those Roman highways and with geographic rigor sacrificed to military and administrative efficacy, but it was the gesture that counted. "And it was done with such imagination and efficiency, despite the logical imprecisions, that today satellites beam back landscapes described in almost perfect detail by men who explored and navigated them hundreds of years ago. Men who, above all else, spoke, observed, and thought.... Do you know the story of Eratosthenes?"

I told it to them, of course. From a to z, not omitting a single detail. A clever lad, that Cyreniac—director of the library of Alexandria, to give you an idea of who he was. There was a well in Asuan, the bottom of which was touched by the sun's rays only from the 20th to the 22nd of June. That placed the well in the Tropic of Cancer. Furthermore, the city of Alexandria lay to the north of that point, at a distance known to be 5,000 estadia. So Eratosthenes measured the angle of the sun at noon on June 21 and deduced that the resulting arc, approximately seven degrees, was one-fiftieth of earth's meridian. And for that meridian he calculated 250,000 estadia, which is approximately 28,000 miles. You must admit that isn't bad, eh? Considering that the true circumference of the earth is 25,000 miles. An error of less than fourteen percent in relative terms, which was extremely precise for a fellow who lived two centuries before Christ.

"And that," I concluded, "is why my profession delights me."

They still did not seem impressed, but I was in my element. And it is true that my profession delights me. With that point established, I decided to continue the consultation.

"Well," I said, after the appropriate calculations. "My congratulations. You have applied my tables correctly. Like you, I obtain a modern longitude of 1°21′ west of Greenwich."

"Then we have a serious problem," Tánger said. "Because there's nothing there."

I gave her a glance of condolence, again over my glasses, which have an irritating tendency to slip down to the tip of my nose. I also shot a sidelong glance at the sailor. He did not seem upset by the way I had one elbow on my desk, studying the blonde. Possibly his was a simple professional relationship, an unemotional give and take. I gathered hope.

"I fear, then, that you will have to revise the original position on the Urrutia. Or, as you foresaw, enlarge the search area. . . . The ship could have drifted from its last known position, or sailed a bit farther before going down. A storm?"

"Combat," she said, succinctly. "With a corsair."

How beautiful, I thought. How classic. And what a slim chance of success those two had. I put on a face befitting the circumstances.

Gravely, I offered my opinion. "Then between taking their position and reaching the place they went down, many things could have happened. . . . They must have been very busy on board as they took the sightings. I believe that places you in a difficult position."

They must have been aware of that before coming to me, because they seemed no more ruffled by my words than they had been when they arrived. Coy merely looked at her, as if expecting a reaction that did not come. And Tánger kept looking at me the way you do at a doctor who has disgorged only half the diagnosis. I took another look at the chart, hoping to find something good to report. Even a quadriplegic can still whistle a good tune, or paint with the toes of one foot. Or something of that nature.

"I suppose there is no doubt that the charts they were using were Urrutia's," I commented. "Any other chart would require accommodations in the theoretical position we are working with."

"No doubt at all." Listening to her I asked myself if that woman was ever in doubt. "We have the direct testimony of the crew."

"And you are sure it is the Cádiz meridian?"

"That's the only one it can be. Paris, Greenwich, Ferrol, Cartagena . . . None of them fits the general area of the shipwreck. Only Cádiz."

"The old meridian, I expect." A professional smile. Mine. In agreement. "You couldn't have made the error, which is more frequent than you might believe, of confusing it with San Fernando?"

"Naturally not."

"Right. Cádiz."

I was giving this serious thought.

"I realize," I said after a few seconds, "that you are telling me only what you feel free to tell me, and I understand that. I am familiar with circumstances such as these." Tánger maintained eye contact with supreme sangfroid. "However, perhaps you can tell me a little more about the ship."

"She was a brigantine sailing from the coast of Andalusia. Heading, northeast."

"Spanish flag?"

"Yes."

"And who was her owner?"

I saw that she was hesitant. If everything had stopped there, I would not have continued to question her, but would have bid them good-bye with all that courtesy I previously referred to. You cannot come to squeeze a master cartographer dry in exchange for only a pretty face, and on top of that, hide with one hand what you imply you are revealing in the other. She must have read that last thought in my face, because she started to say something. But it was Coy, from his chair, who spoke the magic words.

"She was a Jesuit ship."

I looked at him with affection. He was a good lad, that sailor. I suppose that this was the precise moment when he won me over to his cause. I looked at the woman. She nodded, with a slight, enigmatic smile, halfway between guilt and complicity. Only beautiful women dare smile that way when you are about to catch them in a fib.

"Jesuit," I repeated.

Then I nodded a couple of times, savoring the information. This was good. This was even stupendous. I imagine one becomes a cartographer to revel in moments like this. Taking my time, I studied the chart spread out on my desk, conscious of the two pairs of eyes on me. Mentally, I counted out half a minute.

"Invite me to dinner," I said finally, when I reached thirty. "I believe I have just earned a bottle of good wine and a stupendous meal."

I TOOK them to the Pequeña Taberna, a restaurant with Huerta cuisine, behind the San Juan arch near the river. I was luxuriating in the situation, like a torero with all the time in the world, relishing their eagerness to hear what I had to say, and doling it out with an eyedropper. Apéritif, a more than reasonable bottle of Marqués de Riscal *gran reserva*, a lovely *pisto,* a fresh vegetable omelette, blood sausage fried with onion, and broiled vegetables. They tasted scarcely a bite, but I did honor to the place and the menu.

"That ship," I said, once the proper time had gone by, "cannot be found at 37°32′ latitude and 1°21′ longitude east of Cádiz, for the simple reason that it was never there."

I asked for more *pisto*. It was delicious, and it made your mouth water to see it on the counter, displayed in large glazed earthenware tureens. It was also delicious to see their faces as I spun out my story.

"The Jesuits had a long tradition as cartographers," I continued, dipping bread in my sauce. "Urrutia himself counted on their technical aid in compiling his nautical charts. . . . After all, the scientific-hydrographic tradition of the Church goes back to antiquity. The first reference to a nautical instrument is found in the Acts of the Apostles: 'And dropping the sound, they found twenty fathoms.'"

That erudite touch did not have much effect. They were growing impatient, naturally. He made no attempt to hide it; his hands were planted on either side of his plate and he was looking at me with that when-is-this-imbecile-going-to-stop-dancing-around-the-mulberry-bush look. She was listening with an apparent calm that I dare qualify as professional. That cost her, I have no doubt. She showed little sign of anything other than extreme attentiveness, as if each of my meanderings was pure gold. She knew how to handle men. Later I learned just how well.

"The fact is," I continued, between mouthfuls and swallows of the *gran reserva*—"some of the most important cartographers were members of the Society of Jesus. Ricci, Martini, Georges Fournier, author of the *Hydrographie*.... They had their systems, their missions in Asia, their settlements in the Americas, their own routes, their fiefs of all kinds. Ships, captains, pilots. Blasco Ibáñez wrote a novel about them titled *La araña negra*, and in a sense he was right in referring to black spiders."

I continued with my meal and the details, still reserving the final lightning bolt. The Jesuits, I added, had their schools of cosmography, cartography, and navigation. They knew how important precise geographic knowledge was, and from the time of Ignacio de Loyola on they were charged with gathering all information useful to the Society. Even the Marqués de la Ensenada—I underlined my point with the asparagus impaled on my fork—during the reign of Philip V commissioned a modern and detailed map of Spain from them that was never published because of the minister's fall. I also recounted the Society's close relationship with Jorge Juan and Antonio de Ulloa, knights of Punto Fijo, who measured the degree of meridian in Peru. In matters of science, in short, the Jesuits were the parsley in every dressing. They had their friends and their enemies, naturally. Which is why they took precautions. In the course of my studies, I myself have come across documents that at times were difficult and occasionally impossible to interpret. Those men had a whole infrastructure devoted to what today—I smiled—we would call counterespionage.

"Do you mean that they used cryptographs and coded language?"

"Yes, my dear. That ship of yours was using a system of internal and secret codes. Like all the others belonging to the Society, it was traveling the world with charts that, like Urrutia's and others', indicated the scales of meridians and parallels necessary for navigation—Cádiz, Tenerife, Paris, Greenwich. . . ." I took a sip of wine and nodded my approval; the waiter had just uncorked a second bottle. "But theirs had a particular feature. You remember that the meridian is a relative concept used to find one's location on a map that imitates the surface of the earth by means of a spherical projection. . . . There are one hundred and eighty meridians, which are arbitrary in principle. The prime meridian, which some call zero meridian, can pass through any place one wishes, for there is nowhere in heaven or earth a fixed sign that obliges one to count longitude from that mark. Given the shape of the earth, all meridians are eligible to be considered the prime one, and any of them can be designated by that renowned and illustrious appellation. Which is why, until Greenwich was adopted as the universal reference, each country had its own." I drank another sip of wine and looked at each of them, dabbing at my lips with the napkin. "Do you follow me?"

"Perfectly." The dark steel eyes were fixed on me with extraordinary concentration, and I could not help but admire her composure. "In brief, the Jesuits had their own meridian."

"Exactly right. Except that I detest to say things in so few words."

Coy shook his head, slowly and wordlessly, a gesture of resignation and defeat. I saw him reach for his glass, and now he did take a long drink of wine. A very long drink.

"So," said Tánger, "the corrections we have been making with your tables should not be in respect to Cádiz."

"Of course not. They must be made in respect to the secret meridian the Jesuits were using in 1767 to calculate longitude aboard their ships." Again I paused and looked at them, smiling. "Do you see where I'm going?"

"Goddammit!" said Coy. "Just spit it out, will you?"

I gifted him with a look of affection. I believe I have told you that I liked this individual more by the minute.

"Do not deprive me of my moment of suspense, dear friend. Do not deprive me.... The meridian that you are seeking corresponds today to the present 5°40′ west of Greenwich. And passes precisely through the school of cosmography, geography, and navigation, as well as the astronomy observatory that the Jesuits administered until their expulsion in 1767, in what today is the Universidad Pontificia, the old Royal College of the Society of Jesus."

I made one last theatrical pause—abracadabra! Ladies and gentlemen—and pulled the rabbit from my hat. A silky white rabbit chewing happily on a carrot.

"A few feet," and now the precise news, "from the tower of the cathedral of Salamanca."

There was silence for at least five seconds. First they looked at each other and then Tánger said, "That can't be." Said it like that, quietly. That can't be. Looking at me as if I was a Martian. The words did not have the sound of an objection or of disbelief. It was a lament. In free translation: What a *fool* I am.

"I'm afraid it is so," I said softly.

"But that means..."

"That means," I interrupted, jealous of maintaining the lead role, "that at that latitude, between the Salamanca meridian and that of the Guardiamarinas college in Cádiz, on many maps of the period there was a differential of forty-five minutes longitude west. . . ."

As I was talking I appropriated a couple of forks, a piece of bread, and a glass to reconstruct an approximation of a coast. The glass was in the center, representing Cartagena, and the tip of the fork marked Cabo de Palos. It wasn't an Urrutia chart, but it wasn't bad at all. What more did one need? The checked tablecloth even resembled the parallels and meridians of a nautical chart.

"And you two," I concluded, counting squares toward the fork on the right, "have been looking for that ship thirty-six miles west of where it lies."

XIV

The Mystery of the Green Lobsters

Although I speak of a Meridian as if there were only one, there are actually many. All men and ships have their own meridians.

—Manuel Pimentel, Arte de Navegar

They were cutting through the dawn mist, sailing east along parallel 37°32′, with a slight deviation to the north in order to gain one minute of latitude. Screwed onto the bulkhead, the needle of the brass barometer tilted right: 1,022 millibars. There was no wind, and the deck cleats were shuddering with the gentle vibration of the engine. The mist was beginning to burn off, and although it was still gray behind the wake, dazzling rays of sun and golden color were filtering through ahead of the bow, and off the port beam, faint and very high, they could see the phantasmal dark gashes of the coastline.

In the cockpit, El Piloto was setting the course. And below, in the cabin, bent over her parallel rulers, compass, pencil, and gum eraser, like a diligent student preparing for a difficult exam, Tánger was superimposing the squares of a graph on chart 464 of the Naval Hydrographic Institute: Cabo Tiñoso to Cabo de Palos. Coy was sitting beside her, with a cup of coffee and condensed milk in his hands, watching her trace lines and calculate distances. They had worked all night without sleeping, and by the time El Piloto woke and cast off before dawn, they had established the new search area on the chart, with the center located at 37°33′N and 0°45′W. This was the rectangle that Tánger, under the light of the chart table, and with patience and careful allowance for the *Carpanta*'s gentle rocking, was now dividing into tracks of one hundred sixty-five feet in width. An area a mile and a half long by two and a half wide, south of Punta Seca and six miles to the southwest of Cabo de Palos.

"...But it happened that after the wind veered to the north, and having already glimpsed the cape to the northeast, upon putting on more sail in avoidance of the chase of which she was object, she had the bad fortune to lose her fore-topmast, while engaging in most lively combat almost yardarm to yardarm. Her foremast was lost and nearly all hands on deck dead or out of action by reason of the other's having raked them with shot and point-blank broadsides, but when the xebec was being brought alongside for boarding, the flames from one of her lower sails, as the deponent recalls having seen, jumped across to some cartridge of gunpowder, with the result that the xebec was blown up. The explosion also brought down the mainmast of the brigantine, sending her to the bottom. According to the deponent there were no survivors but himself, who was saved by knowing how to swim and finding the skiff the brigantine had launched as combat began, spending there the rest of the day and the night. At nearing eleven hours on the following day he was rescued six miles to the south of this place by the tartan *Virgen de los Parales*. According to the deponent, the sinking of the brigantine and the xebec took place at two miles from the coast at 37°32′N, 4°51′E, a position that matches the one written on a half-leaf of paper he was carrying in his pocket at the time of his rescue, the pilot having noted it once established on a chart of Urrutia, but having no time to log it because of the rapidity with which battle was joined. The deponent was quartered in the naval hospital of this city awaiting further proceedings. The most Excl Sr. Almirante requested the following day new investigations on certain points of this event, given the circumstance that the deponent had abandoned the environs of the hospital during the night, and there being until this moment no notice of his whereabouts. A circumstance about which the most Exce Sr. Almirante has ordered that a timely investigation be initiated without prejudice to the depuration of responsibilities. Dated in the Headquarters of the Seaport of Cartagena, eight February 1767. Lieutenant of the Navy Ricardo Dolarea."

EVERYTHING fit. They had discussed it inside and out, with the copy of the boy's testimony on the table, analyzing every turn in the exasperating posthumous joke that the ghosts of the two Jesuits and sailors of the sunken *Dei Gloria* had played on them and everyone else. With 464 spread out before him and compass in hand, the line of the coast in the upper portion of the chart—Tiñoso to the left, Palos to the right, and the port of Cartagena in the center—Coy had easily calculated the dimensions of their error. That night and predawn morning of February 3 and 4, 1767, with the corsair tight at her stern, the brigantine had sailed much faster and much farther than they had originally thought. At dawn, the *Dei Gloria* was not southwest of Tiñoso and Cartagena, but had already passed those longitudes and was sailing east. She was *southeast* of the port, and the cape glimpsed from her bow, to the northeast, was not Tiñoso but Palos.

Tánger had finished. She laid her rulers and pencil on the chart, and sat looking at Coy.

"For that they tortured Abbot Gándara for eighteen years.... They were looking for the ship in the location given by the ship's boy. They may even have gone down with divers and diving bells, but they found nothing because the *Dei Gloria* wasn't there."

Lack of sleep had left dark circles under her eyes, making them look bigger. Less attractive, more exhausted.

"Now tell me what happened," she said. "Your final version."

Coy looked at chart 464. It was lying above the reproduction of Urrutia's chart, which was also covered with penciled marks and notations. The dark brown line of the shore and the blue band of minimal depths followed the coastline, ascending in a gentle diagonal toward Palos point and the Hormigas Isles in the upper right corner of the chart. All the geographic features were represented, from west to east: Cabo Tiñoso, the port of Cartagena, Escombreras Island, Cabo de Agua, Portman cove, Cabo Negrete, Punta Seca, Cabo de Palos. . . . Maybe the wind from the southwest had been stronger that night than they calculated, Coy argued. Twenty-five or thirty knots. Or maybe Captain Elezcano had taken the risk of putting the rigging at jeopardy earlier, and had set more sail. It could also be that the wind veered to the north, blowing offshore long before dawn, and that the corsair, a ship able to sail close to the wind, thanks to the jib on her bowsprit and lateen sails on her foremast and mizzenmast, had got to windward and slipped between the brigantine and Cartagena to prevent her from taking refuge. There was also the possibility that in the course of some nocturnal maneuver intended to throw the corsair off the trail, the *Dei Gloria* had put herself in a perilous position by sailing too far from potential protection. Or maybe the captain, stubborn and holding to his instructions, gave strict orders not to enter any port but Valencia, to prevent the emeralds from falling into the wrong hands.

Coy tried to describe that first glimmer of morning—the still hazy coastline, the uneasy glances between the captain and the navigation officer as they attempted to recognize where they were, and their devastation when they discovered that the corsair was still there, giving chase, drawing closer, and that they had not lost her in the dark. At any rate, with that first light, while the captain kept looking up to the rigging, wondering whether it could tolerate so much canvas, sailing close-hauled as she was, the navigation officer went to the port rail and took land sightings to establish their position. Doubtless he obtained simultaneous bearings, situating Junco Grande at 345°, Cabo Negrete at 295°, and Cabo de Palos at 30°. Afterward he would have joined those three lines on the chart, and established the brigantine's position at their intersection. It wasn't difficult to imagine him with his spyglass and the alidade or bearing circle on the magistral, alien to everything other than the technical steps of his responsibilities, and the ship's boy at his side, paper and pencil ready to jot down the observations, glancing out of the corner of his eye at the sails of the corsair, red in the slanting rays of dawn and closer every minute. Then the officer, hurrying below to make the calculation on the Urrutia chart, and the ship's boy running back to the poop along the sharply listing deck, the paper with the bearings in his hand, showing them to the captain just at the moment when high overhead the topmast sprang with a crack and everything fell to the deck, and the captain ordered the crew to cut it free, throw it overboard, and ready the guns, and the *Dei Gloria* gave the tragic yaw that confronted her with her destiny.

Coy stopped, a quiver in his voice. Sailors. After all, those men were sailors like him. Good sailors. He could feel their fears and sensations as clearly as if he himself had been aboard the *Dei Gloria*.

Tánger was studying him.

"You tell the story very well, Coy."

Through the porthole he could see light struggling through the fog as the sun rose past the hazy gray circle. He also saw the bow of the corsair *Chergui* gradually bearing toward one of the open gunports of the brigantine.

"It isn't hard," he said. "In a way, it isn't hard."

He half-closed his eyes. His mouth was dry, sweat was running down his naked chest, and the cloth he had just tied around his forehead was dripping wet. Bent down behind a black four-pound gun in the smoke of the sizzling wick, he heard the breathing of his comrades crouched beside the gun carriage with rammer, sponge, and worm, poised to ease off the tackle, prime, and fire.

"Oh, well," he added after a few seconds, "I'm not saying that *is* how things happened."

"How do you explain the position of the ship's boy?"

Coy bunched his shoulders. The roar of the cannonade and shattering wood was slowly fading from his head. He pointed to a place on the chart before tracing a diagonal line southwest.

"Just the way we explained it before," he said. "With the difference that after the shipwreck, the wind pushing the skiff wasn't blowing from the northwest, but northeast. The offshore breeze could have shifted a few quarters to the east when the sun was high that morning and sent the boy out to sea, bringing him closer to the true bearing on Cartagena, a few miles to the south, where he was rescued the next day."

That wasn't hard to imagine either, Coy thought, looking at the line of drift on the chart marked with recorded depths. The boy, alone in this little drifting boat, dazed and bailing water. The sun and the thirst, the immense sea and the coast growing fainter and fainter in the distance. The restless sleep, face down so the gulls wouldn't peck his face, his head lifted occasionally to look around, then total hopelessness—nothing but the impassive sea and all the secrets stored in its depths. Up on the surface rippled by the breeze, he was another Ishmael floating on the blue tomb of his comrades.

"It's strange he didn't give the true position of the *Dei Gloria,*" Tánger said. "A boy like him couldn't have been aware of all the implications."

"He wasn't so young. I've mentioned before that boys went to sea when they were just kids, but after four or five years at sea, they matured in a hurry. By then they were men in their own right. True sailors."

She nodded, convinced.

"Well, even so," she said, "it's amazing how he kept his mouth shut. He was an apprentice, and had to know that the longitude didn't refer to the Cádiz meridian.... Yet he knew not to say anything, and he fooled the investigators. There's nothing in the report that indicates the least doubt."

It was true. They had been reviewing the documents, the rescued boy's declaration, and the official report, and there was not a single contradiction. The ship's boy had been firm about the latitude and longitude. And he had the paper in his pocket as proof.

"He was a fine boy," Tánger added. "Loyal as they come."

"So it seems."

"And clever. You remember his testimony? He talks about the cape to the northeast, but doesn't name it. From the position he gave, everyone believed it was Tiñoso. But he was careful not to correct them. He never said what cape it was."

Again Coy looked out at the sea through the porthole.

"I suppose," he said, "it was his way of carrying on with the fight."

The sun was well up by now and the mist was burning off. The dark outlines of the coast were becoming clear off their port. Punta de la Chapa emerged with its white lighthouse east of Portman Bay, the Portus Magnus of old, with the slag of abandoned mines on the old Roman highway and silt clogging the cove where ships with eyes painted on their bows had loaded silver ingots before the birth of Christ.

"I wonder what became of him?"

He was referring to the boy's disappearance from the naval hospital. Tánger had her own theory, which she sketched out, leaving Coy to fill in the blank spaces. In early February of 1767, the Jesuits could still rely on money and power everywhere, including the maritime district of Cartagena. It was not difficult to bribe the right people and assure the discreet removal of the ship's boy from center stage. All that was needed was a coach and horses and a safe passage to get past the city gates. No doubt agents of the Society arranged for him to leave the hospital before a new interrogation, taking him far away, out of reach, the day after his rescue at sea. "Unauthorized leave," was how it had been noted in the file, which was somewhat irregular for a very young merchant seaman being questioned by the Navy. But that "unauthorized leave" had later been corrected by an anonymous hand and replaced with "approved discharge." And there the trail ended.

It was easy, Coy thought as he listened to Tánger's story. It all fit together, and it took no effort to imagine the night. The deserted corridors of the hospital, the light of a candle, sentinels or guards, their eyes closed by gold, someone arriving, heavily cloaked and with precise instructions, the boy surrounded by trusted agents. Then the empty streets, the clandestine council in the city's Jesuit convent. A serious, quick, tense interrogation, and scowls that eased as it was ascertained that the secret was well guarded. Perhaps claps on the back, approving hands on his shoulder. Good lad. Good, brave lad. Then again the night, and people signaling from a shadowy corner; no hitch in the plan. The coach and horses, the city gates, the open country and star-filled skies. A fifteen-year-old sailor dozing in the coach seat, accustomed from boyhood to far worse jouncing, his sleep watched over by the ghosts of his dead comrades. By the sad smile of Captain Elezcano.

"However," Tánger concluded. "There's something... maybe interesting... maybe strange. The ship's boy was named Palau, Miguel Palau, remember? He was the nephew of Luis Fornet Palau, the Valencian outfitter of the *Dei Gloria*. Maybe it's only a coincidence..." She held up a finger, as if requesting a moment's attention, and then went through the documents in the drawer of the chart table. "Here. Look at this. When I was checking names and dates, I consulted some later shipping lists in Viso del Marqués, and I came upon a reference to the hoy *Mulata,* based in Valencia. In 1784 that ship had a battle with the English brig *Undaunted,* near the straits of Formentera. The brig tried to capture her, but the hoy defended herself very well and was able to escape. . . . And do you know what the Spanish captain's name was? M. Palau, the reference said. Like our ship's boy. Even the age is right—fifteen in 1767, thirty-two or thirty-three in 1784."

She handed Coy a photocopy, and he read the text. "Notice of the events of the fifteenth day of the present month, regarding the engagement between the hoy *Mulata* commanded by captain don M. Palau and the English brig *Undaunted* off Los Ahorcados island."

"If it's the same Palau," said Tánger, "he didn't give up that time either, did he?"

"It is reported before the maritime authority of this port of Ibiza that following a course from Valencia to this locality, when heading for the main channel of the straits at Formentera and in the vicinity of Las Negras and Los Ahorcados, the Spanish hoy *Mulata,* of eight guns, was attacked by the English brig *Undaunted,* of twelve, which had approached under false French colors and attempted to seize her. Despite the difference in size she sustained heavy fire but with great damage to both sides, and also an attempt to board by the English, who succeeded in getting three men aboard the hoy, there being then three dead heaved into the sea. The vessels separated and very bloody combat ensued for the space of half an hour, until the *Mulata,* despite an unfavorable wind, was able to pass to this side of the straits thanks to a maneuver of notorious risk, consisting of slipping through the middle strait, with only four *brazas* below and very near the reef of La Barqueta; a most uncommonly skillful maneuver that left the English on the other side, their captain not daring to proceed due to conditions of the wind and the uncertainty of the bottom, and the *Mulata* able to arrive in this port of Ibiza with four men dead and eleven wounded without further occurrence. . . ."

Coy handed the copy of the report back to Tánger. Years before, on a sailboat with minimal length and draft, he had passed through the middle strait at that very place. Four fathoms was twenty-four feet, in addition to which, depths diminished rapidly from the center to each side. He remembered well the sinister sight of the bottom through the water. A hoy fitted with guns might have a draft of ten feet, and a contrary wind would make sailing on a straight course very difficult; so whether the ship's boy Miguel Palau and Captain M. Palau were the same man, whoever was captaining the *Mulata* had very steady nerves.

"Maybe the name is just a coincidence."

"Maybe." Tánger was quietly rereading the photocopy before replacing it in the drawer. "But I like to think it was him."

She was quiet for a moment, and then turned to the porthole to focus on the line of the coast revealed by the rising mist, clean and free off the port bow, with the sun shining on the dark rock of Cabo Negrete:

"I like to think that that ship's boy went back to sea, and that he continued to be a brave man."

For eight days they combed the new search area with the Pathfinder, track by track from north to south, beginning at the eastern edge, in depths from eighty to eighteen meters. Deeper and more open to winds and currents than Mazarrón cove, the sea was rough, complicating and slowing their job. The bottom was uneven, rock and sand, and both El Piloto and Coy had made frequent dives—necessarily brief because of the depths—to check out irregularities picked up by the sounding device, including an old anchor that had raised their hopes until they identified it as an Admiralty model with an iron shank, one used later than the eighteenth century. By the end of the day, exasperated and exhausted, they would drop anchor near Negrete on nights with little wind, or, if sheltering from levanters and *lebeches,* in the small port at Cabo de Palos. The weather dispatches had announced the formation of a center of low pressure in the Atlantic, and if the storm didn't take a turn to the northeast its effects would take less than a week to arrive in the Mediterranean, forcing them to suspend the search for some time. All this was making them nervous and irritable. El Piloto went entire days without opening his mouth, and Tánger maintained her stubborn watch at the screen in a somber mood, as if each day that went by tore away another shred of hope. One afternoon Coy happened to see the notebook where she had been recording the results of the exploration. There were pages filled with incomprehensible spirals and sinister crosses, and on one the hideously distorted face of a woman, the lines scrawled so hard that in some places the paper was ripped. It was a woman who seemed to be screaming into a void.

Nights were not much more pleasant. El Piloto would say good night and close his door at the bow, and they would bed down, weary, skin smelling of sweat and salt, on mattresses in one of the cabins at the stern. They came together in silence, seeking each other with an urgency so extreme it seemed artificial, their union intense and brutal, quick and wordless. Each time Coy would seek to prolong the encounter, holding Tánger in his arms as they leaned against the bulkhead, trying to control the body and mind of this unknowable woman. But she would struggle, escape, try to hasten along their lovemaking, investing only breath and flesh, her mind far away, her thoughts unreachable. Sometimes Coy thought she was with him, as he listened to the rhythm of her breathing and felt the kisses of her parted lips, the pressure of her naked thighs around his waist. He would kiss her neck or breasts and hold her very tight, capturing her wrists, feeling the beat of her pulse on his tongue and groin, thrusting deep inside her, as if he hoped to touch her heart, to saturate it and make it as soft as the moistness he felt inside her. But she would draw back, a prisoner trying to escape his embrace. In the end she refused him the thought he was striving to capture. Her gleaming, remote eyes, boring into him in the shadows, would become absent, somewhere far beyond Coy and the ship and the sea, absorbed in arcane curses of loneliness and blackness. And then her mouth would open to scream, like the woman he had glimpsed in the drawing, a scream of silence that echoed in Coy's gut like the most galling insult. He felt that lament pounding through his veins, and he bit his lips, holding back an anguish that flooded his chest and nose and mouth, as if he were drowning in a viscous sea of sorrow. He wanted to cry the large, copious tears he had wept as a child, incapable of warming the cold shiver of such loneliness. It was a weight too heavy to bear. All he had done was read a few books, sail a few years and know a few women. He believed that was why he lacked the right words and the right moves, and he also believed that even his silences were sullen. But he would have given his life to get deep inside her, to filter through the cells of her flesh and slowly, softly, lick that center of her being with all the tenderness he could offer, to clean away the painful and malign tumor left there like ballast by hundreds of years, thousands of men, and millions of lives. That was why each night they were together, once she stopped moving and lay quiet, recovering her breath after the last of her shudders, Coy tenaciously insisted, forgetting himself and lashed by desperation, that he loved her more than anyone or anything. But she had gone away, too far away, and he did not exist; he was an intruder in her world and her instant. And that, he thought with pain, was how it would end. Not with noise, but with a nearly imperceptible sigh. In that moment of indifference, punctual as a verdict, everything in her died, everything was held in suspense as her pulse recovered its normal beat. Again Coy would be aware of the porthole open to the night, and of the cold creeping in from the sea like a biblical curse. He would fall into a desolation as barren as a vast, perfect, polished marble surface. A terrifyingly motionless Sargasso Sea, a nautical chart with names invented by those ancient navigators: Deception Point, Bay of Solitude, Bitterness Bay, Island of God-Help-Us-All. . . . Afterward she would kiss him and turn her back, and he would lie on his back, wavering between loathing for that last kiss and disgust for himself. Eyes staring into the darkness, ears tuned to the water lapping against the *Carpanta*'s hull and to the wind rising in the rigging. Thinking how no one would ever be able to draw the nautical chart that would allow a man to navigate a woman. And with the certainty that Tánger was going to walk out of his life before he possessed her.

IT was about that time that I heard from them again. Tánger called me from El Pez Rojo, a restaurant at Cabo de Palos, to ask me about a technical problem that involved an error of half a mile in longitude. I cleared up the question and inquired with interest as to their progress. She told me everything was going well, many thanks, and that I would be hearing from them. In fact, it was a couple of weeks before I had news of them, and when I did it was from the newspapers, leaving me to feel as stupid as nearly everyone else in this story. But I don't want to get ahead of myself. Tánger made the telephone call one noontime that found the *Carpanta* put up alongside the dock in that old fishing town converted into a tourist haven. The storm in the north Atlantic was still stationary, and the sun was shining on the southeast Iberian Peninsula. The needle on the barometer was high, without crossing over the dangerous vertical to the left, and that was, paradoxically, what had brought them to the small port that stretched around a wide black sand cove, dangerous because of the reefs just below the surface and presided over by the lighthouse tower rising high on a rock set out in the sea. That morning the heat had triggered the appearance of some anvil-shaped, gray, and threatening cumulonimbuses that were boiling higher by the minute. A wind of twelve to fifteen knots was blowing in the direction of those clouds, but Coy knew that if this cumulonimbus anvil kept building, by the time the gray mass was overhead strong squalls would be unleashed on the other side. A silent exchange of glances with

El Piloto, whose squint in the same direction deepened the wrinkles around his eyes, was enough for the two sailors to understand one another. El Piloto brought the *Carpanta*'s bow around to face Cabo de Palos. So there they were, on the whitewashed porch of the Pez Rojo, eating fried sardines and salad, and drinking red wine.

"A half a mile more," said Tánger, returning to her seat.

She sounded irritated. She picked up a sardine from the tray, looked at it a minute as if hoping to attribute some portion of responsibility to it, and threw it down with disgust.

"One damned half-mile more," she repeated.

From her lips, that "damned" was almost a curse. It was strange to hear her speak that way, and much stranger to see her lose control. Coy observed her with curiosity.

"It isn't all that serious," he said.

"It's another week."

Her hair was dirty and matted from saltwater, her skin shiny from too much sun and not enough soap and water. El Piloto and Coy, after several days without shaving, presented no better picture, and they were equally as sunburned and sweaty. They were all wearing jeans, faded T-shirts and sweatshirts, and sneakers, and signs of their days at sea were clear.

"One whole week," Tánger repeated. "At least."

She stared somberly at the *Carpanta,* still lit by the sun and tied up below them at the Muelle de la Barra dock. The gray anvil was gradually darkening the cove, as if someone were slowly drawing a curtain that doused the sun's reflection on small white houses and cobalt-blue water. She's losing hope, Coy thought suddenly. After all this time and all this effort, she's beginning to accept the possibility of failure. Where we're searching now it's deeper, and that may mean that the wreck will be beyond our recovery even if we find it. On top of that, the time allotted for the search is running out, and so is her money. Now, for the first time since who knows when, she knows the feeling of doubt.

He looked at El Piloto. The sailor's gray eyes were silently seconding his conclusions. The adventure was beginning to verge on the absurd. All the data had been verified, but the main thing was missing—the sunken ship. No one doubted it was somewhere out there. From the slight elevation of the restaurant they may even have been looking at the very spot where the brigantine and the corsair had gone down. Maybe they had sailed several times above where it lay beneath yards of mud and sand. Maybe the whole effort had been nothing more than a series of errors, the first one being that hunting treasure was not compatible with lucid adult rationality.

"We have a mile and half still to explore," Coy said gently.

The minute he had spoken those words, he felt ridiculous. Him, giving a pep talk? The truth was, all he wanted to do was put off the final act. Put it off, before going back to being on his own, an orphan clinging to Queequeg's coffin. To the skiff of the *Dei Gloria*.

"Right," she replied blankly.

Elbows on the table, hands crossed under her chin, she kept staring toward the cove. The gray anvil was above the *Carpanta* now, turning the sky black over its bare mast. The wind died, the sea flattened around the dock, and the sailboat's halyards and flag drooped limply. Then Coy watched as across the cove the reefs and rocks along the shore became streaked with white, lines of foam breaking as a darker color spread like an oil stain across the surface of the water. There was still sunlight on the restaurant porch when the first gust of wind rippled the water on the bay. On the *Carpanta* the flag suddenly stood straight out and the halyards cracked against the mast, jingling furiously as the ship tilted toward the dock, pushing hard against her fenders. The second gust was stronger, thirty-five knots at least, Coy calculated. The bay was filled with whitecaps and the wind howled, climbing the scale note by note around the hollow chimneys and eaves of the rooftops.

Now everything was somber and frighteningly gray, and Coy was happy to be sitting there eating fried sardines.

"How long will this last?" Tánger asked.

"Not long," said Coy. "An hour, maybe. Could be a little longer. It will be over by dark. It's just a summer storm."

"The heat," El Piloto added.

Coy looked at his friend, smiling inside. He feels as if he needs to console her too, he thought. After all, that's really what has brought us to this point, although El Piloto doesn't rationalize that kind of thing. Or at least I don't think he does. At that moment the sailor's eyes met Coy's. They were as tranquil and serene as always, and Coy had second thoughts. Maybe he does rationalize such things.

"Tomorrow we'll have to include that additional half mile," Tánger announced. "To forty-seven minutes west."

Coy didn't need a chart. He had 464 engraved on his brain from having studied it so long, and he knew the search area down to the last detail.

"Well, the good news," he said, "is that the depth decreases to between fifty-nine and seventy-nine feet on that side. Everything will go much easier."

"What's the bottom like?"

"Sand and rock, right Piloto? With clumps of seaweed."

El Piloto nodded. He took a pack of cigarettes from his pocket and stuck one in his mouth. Since Tánger was looking at him, he nodded again.

"There's more seaweed the closer you get to Cabo Negrete," he said. "But that area is clean. Rock and sand, like Coy says. With a little shingle where you find the green lobsters."

Tánger, who was taking a sip of wine, stopped, holding the glass to her lips, and focused on El Piloto.

"What is that about green lobsters?"

El Piloto was concentrating on lighting his cigarette. He made a vague gesture.

"Well, just that." Smoke escaped from between his fingers as he spoke. "Lobsters that are green. It's the only place you find them. Or used to. Nobody catches lobsters around here anymore."

Tánger had set her glass down. She placed it carefully on the cloth, as if afraid of spilling it. She was staring hard at El Piloto, who carefully knotted and wrapped the wick around his lighter.

"Have you been there?"

"Sure. A long time ago. It was good for fishing when I was young."

Coy remembered something. His friend had told him once about North African lobsters with shells that were green rather than the usual dark red or brown speckled with white. That had been twenty or thirty years ago, when there were still langoustine, clams, tuna, and twenty-pound groupers in those waters.

"They had a good flavor," El Piloto explained, "but the color put people off."

Tánger was following every word.

"Why? What color was that?"

"A kind of mossy green, very different from the red or bluish color of fresh-caught lobsters, or that dark green of the African or American lobster." El Piloto may have smiled behind the tobacco smoke. "They weren't very appetizing, which is why the fishermen ate them themselves, or sold the tails already cooked."

"Do you remember the place?"

"Sure." Tánger's interest was beginning to make El Piloto uncomfortable. He used the excuse of drawing on his cigarette to take longer and longer pauses, and to look at Coy. "Cabo de Agua abeam and the headland of Junco Grande around ten degrees north."

"What's the depth?"

"Shallow. Sixty-some feet. Lobsters are usually in deeper waters, but there were always a few around there."

"Did you dive there?"

Again El Piloto glanced at Coy. Tell me where this is going, his eyes said. Coy turned his hands palm up—I don't have the least fucking idea.

"Those days we didn't have the diving equipment we have now," El Piloto answered finally. "Fishermen set out reed traps or trammel nets, and if they got lost they stayed below."

"Below," she repeated.

Then she was silent. After a pause, she reached for her glass of wine, but had to set it down because her hand was trembling.

"What is it?" Coy asked.

He couldn't understand her mood or her trembling—nothing about Tánger's sudden interest in lobsters. It was one of the dishes on the menu, and he'd watched her pass over it without a flicker of interest.

She laughed. A strange, quiet laugh. A sort of chortle, unexpectedly sardonic, shaking her head as if enjoying a joke she'd just told. She put her hands to her temples—she might have been in sudden pain—and looked back toward the bay, now gray but lighter where choppy waves foamed under incessant bursts of wind. The filtered light outside accentuated the blued steel of her eyes. Absorbed. Or dazed.

"Lobsters," she murmured. "Green lobsters."

Now she was shivering, with a laugh too close to a sob. With a new attempt, she had spilled wine on the tablecloth. I hope she hasn't lost it, Coy thought with alarm. I hope all this shit hasn't pushed her over the edge, and instead of taking her back to the *Dei Gloria* we end up stopping by the loony bin. He dabbed at the wine with his napkin, then put a hand on her shoulder. He could feel her trembling.

"Calm down," he whispered.

"I am completely calm," she said. "I have never been more calm in my life."

"What the hell's going on?"

She had stopped laughing, or sobbing, or whatever she'd been doing, though her eyes were still on the ocean. Finally the shivering stopped. She sighed deeply and looked at El Piloto with a strange expression before leaning across the table and planting a kiss on the astounded sailor's face. She was smiling, radiant, when she turned back to Coy.

"That's where the *Dei Gloria* is! Where the green lobsters are."

RIPPLED sea, nearly flat, and a gentle breeze. Not a cloud in the sky. The *Carpanta* was rocking softly about two and a half miles off the coast, with her anchor chain falling straight down from the capstan. Cabo de Agua lay off the beam and Junco Grande ahead, ten degrees to the northeast. The sun wasn't high, but it burned into Coy's back when he bent down to check the pressure gauge on the cylinder: sixteen liters of compressed air, reserve above that, harness ready. He checked the valve and then fitted over it the regulator that would provide air at a pressure varying with the depth, compensating for increasing atmospheres on his body. Without that apparatus to equalize the internal pressure, a diver would be crushed, or would explode like a balloon filled with too much air. He opened the valve wide and then turned it back three-quarters. The mouthpiece was an old Nemrod; it smelled like rubber and talcum powder when he put it in his mouth to test it. Air circulated noisily through the membranes. Everything was in order.

"A half hour at sixty-five feet," El Piloto reminded him.

Coy nodded as he put on the neoprene vest, weight belt, and emergency life vest. Tánger was standing holding onto the backstay, watching in silence. She was wearing her black Olympic-style suit, fins, a diving mask, and a snorkel. She had spent most of the evening and part of the night explaining about the green lobsters.

She went over it backward and forward, questioning El Piloto exhaustively, making pen and paper sketches, and calculating distances and depths. Lobsters' shells, she had told them, have mimetic properties. As nature does with many other species, it provides those crustaceans with the ability to camouflage themselves as a means of defense. So they tend to adapt to their habitat. It had been proven that lobsters that live around sunken iron ships often acquire the rusty red hues of deteriorating metal plates. And the mossy green El Piloto had described coincided exactly with the color bronze acquires after long immersion in the sea.

"What bronze?" Coy had asked.

"The bronze of the guns."

Coy had his doubts. It all sounded too much like the Crab with the Golden Claws, or some other adventure. But they weren't living in a Tintin comic book. At least he wasn't.

"You said yourself, and we checked it carefully, that the *Dei Gloria*'s guns were iron. There weren't any great quantities of bronze on board the brigantine."

Tánger's expression was tranquil and superior, as at other times when she seemed to imply that he hadn't zipped his fly, or that he was an idiot.

"That's right. The guns on the *Dei Gloria* were iron, but the *Chergui*'s weren't. The xebec carried twelve guns—four six-pounders, eight four-pounders, and those four *pedreros*, remember? They had come from the *Flamme*, an old French corvette. And those twelve guns were bronze." She removed the plan of the xebec from the bulkhead and tossed it on the table in front of Coy. "That's in the documents Lucio Gamboa gave us in Cádiz. There are nearly fifteen tons of bronze down there."

Coy exchanged a look with El Piloto, who was merely listening, offering no objections. As for the rest, Tánger continued, it was obvious. The two ships had gone down in close proximity. Because of the explosion that finished the *Chergui*, it was likely that bits of the corsair were scattered around the main wreck. Since one of the components of the bronze guns was copper, the weapons had begun to take on that characteristic undersea coloration, which was then adopted by the lobsters that lived around the wreckage and in the mouths of the guns. There was an additional and very encouraging circumstance. The most important, really. If the lobsters had adopted the color of the bronze, that meant the area of dispersion was reasonably compact, and that the wreckage was not covered by mud or sand.

Coy heard a splash and saw that Tánger was no longer by the backstay. She had jumped into the water and swum around the stern of the *Carpanta,* wearing her mask and respirator. She wasn't going to dive with him but wait at the surface, watching the bubbles to keep track of his location. The radius within which he planned to explore was difficult to maintain while tethered to the sailboat with a safety line. Coy readied himself, knife on his right calf, depth meter and watch on one wrist and compass on the other, then went to the edge of the stern step. Sitting with his feet in the water, he put on the fins, spit onto the glass of his mask, and put it on after rinsing it in the sea. He lifted his arms so El Piloto could place the cylinder of compressed air on his back, and tightened the straps and put the mouthpiece in his mouth. Air whistled in his ears as it circulated through the regulator. He turned on one side, protecting the glass of his mask with his hand, and fell backward into the sea.

The water was very cold, too cold for the time of year. Maps of the currents indicated a gentle flow from northeast to southwest, with a difference of five or six degrees compared to the general temperature of the water. Coy felt his skin contract with the unpleasant sensation of cold water beneath his neoprene vest; it would take a few minutes to warm to his body temperature. He took a couple of slow, deep breaths to test the regulator. With his head half out of the water he could see El Piloto standing there over the stern of the *Carpanta.* He sank down a little, looking around at the blue panorama surrounding him. Near the surface, with the sun's rays lighting the clear, quiet water, there was good visibility. About thirty feet, he calculated. He could see the black keel of the *Carpanta,* with its rudder turned to port and the chain of the anchor descending vertically into the depths. Tánger was swimming nearby, with gentle thrusts of her orange plastic fins. Putting her out of his mind, he concentrated on what he was doing. He looked down to where the blue became darker and more intense, verified the position of the hands on his watch, and began the slow descent toward the bottom. The sound of the air as he breathed through the regulator was deafening, and when the needle of the depth gauge showed fifteen feet, he stopped and pinched his nose beneath the mask, to adapt to the increased pressure on his ears. As he did that, he raised the mask, relieved, and saw bubbles rising from his last exhalation. The sun had turned the surface of the sea into a ceiling of shimmering silver. The black hull of the *Carpanta* was overhead. Tánger had dived to swim slightly above him, and was looking at him through her mask, her blond hair floating in the water, her slim legs, extended by the fins, treading slowly to maintain her depth near Coy. When he breathed again, another plume of bubbles ascended toward her, and she waved her hand in salute. Then Coy looked down and continued his slow descent through a blue sphere that closed above his head, darkening as he neared the bottom. He made a second stop to compensate for the pressure when the gauge marked forty-six feet. Now the water was a translucid sphere that extinguished all colors but green. He was at that intermediate point where divers, with no point of reference, can become disoriented and suddenly find themselves contemplating bubbles that seem to be falling rather than rising; only logic, if in fact they retain that, reminds them that a bubble of air always rises upward. But he hadn't yet reached that extreme. Shapes began to emerge from the darkness on the floor beneath him, and moments later Coy fell very slowly onto a bed of pale, cold sand near a thick meadow of sea anemones, posidonias, and tall, grasslike seaweed enlivened by darting schools of ghostly fish. The depth meter indicated sixty feet. Coy looked around him through the half-light. Vision was good, and the mild current cleared the water. Within a radius of sixteen to twenty-three feet he could easily make out a landscape of starfish, empty seashells, large spade-shaped bivalves standing upright in the sand, and, marking the boundaries of the submarine meadow, ridges of stone with rudimentary coral formations. Small microorganisms floated past him, pulled by the current. He knew that if he turned on his light, color would return to all those monotone objects magnified through the shatterproof glass of his mask. He breathed deliberately several times, trying to adapt his lungs to the pressure and to oxygenate his blood, and checked his bearings on the compass. His plan was to move fifty or seventy feet to the south and then trace a circle around the *Carpanta*'s anchor, which was to the north, behind him. He began to swim slowly, with gentle movements of his legs and fins, hands at his sides, about a yard above the bottom. His eyes searched the sand, alert for the slightest sign of something buried beneath it—although the bronze guns, Tánger had insisted, had to be exposed. He swam to the edge of the meadow and peered into the seaweed and undulating blades. If there was anything in that thicket it was going to be difficult to find, so he decided to continue exploring the area of bare sand which, though it seemed flat, actually descended in a gentle slope to the southwest, as he confirmed with the depth meter and compass. He was inhaling and exhaling every five seconds, and the sound of air was interspersed with intervals of absolute silence. He concentrated on moving slowly, reducing his physical effort to a minimum. The slower the breathing rhythm, the less air consumption and fatigue, went the old divers' rule, and the more available reserves. And this was going to take a while. With lobsters or without them, this was like looking for a needle in a haystack.

Coy saw some dark patches on the sand and went closer to give them a look. Shingle and half-buried rocks covered with small seaweed. A little farther on he found the first object connected with life on the surface, a rusted tin can. He continued at a controlled pace, moving his head from left to right, and stopped when he calculated he had reached the edge of the radius of the circle he intended to search around the anchor. Then he oriented himself again and began to swim in an arc to his right. He was about to cross from the sandy bed to the rocks that marked the limits of the meadow when he spied a shadow a little farther away, almost at the edge of his field of vision. He went to it and found, to his disappointment, that it was a round rock covered with limy formations. Too round and too perfect, it occurred to him suddenly. He lifted it a little, raising a cloud of sand from the bottom, and the rock turned out to be surprisingly light as it broke apart in his hands, revealing a gray-green interior not unlike rotted wood. Astounded, Coy was slow to comprehend that it was exactly that—old, rotted wood. Maybe the wheel of a gun carriage. He felt his heart beating faster beneath the neoprene. His breathing was less tranquil now, and the rate rose to three mouthfuls every five seconds as he scratched in vain in the sand. The digging raised such a cloud from the bottom that he had to rise up a little to find clear water and continue looking. That was when he saw the first gun.

HE swam toward it, kicking very slowly, as if he feared that the large mass of bronze would deteriorate before his eyes like the wooden wheel. It was about five feet in length, and lay on the bottom as if someone had deposited it there with great care. It was almost entirely exposed, with a mossy film and a few incrustations, but the dolphin designs on the handles, the cascabel on the breech, and the heavy trunnions were all perfectly recognizable. It must weigh nearly a ton.

A little farther away he could make out the dark shadow of another gun. He swam to it and saw that it was identical, although in a different position. This one must have fallen almost straight down, diving mouth-first onto the ocean floor, its weight drilling it up to the trunnions in sand. There were also curious reddish stones around, which, when Coy cut them open, showed empty interiors like molds. Of course, he thought. When iron corrodes it leaves an imperfect copy of its shape in the limy formation that has covered it over time. Coy had to discipline himself not to shoot to the surface and shout the news. He had found the *Chergui,* or what remained of her. Instead, he fanned away sand, revealing wood fragments and objects better preserved because they were protected by the sand. He unearthed a bottle that appeared to be very old, its base intact but deformed. Melted, Coy was sure, by extreme heat. The corsair xebec, he concluded, had blown up precisely here, sixty-five feet overhead, and its remains were scattered over the bottom. A little farther on, close together, he found two more guns. They too had the green tone of bronze submerged for two and a half centuries, and were reasonably clean except for a few incrustations and the mossy coating. Now there was a lot of wreckage: wood protruding from the sand, metal objects in varying stages of corrosion, half-buried cannonballs, shards of clay, and shattered wood planking with iron nails. Coy even found a nearly intact wooden construction, which as he scooped away sand appeared to be larger and in better condition than he had thought at first sight. It looked as if it might be a sailmaker's table, with large deadeyes and bits of cordage that disintegrated as he touched them. And more guns. He counted nine, spread in an area some one hundred feet in diameter.

He was amazed at how clean everything was, and at the lack of more than a thin layer of sediment on the wreckage. The gentle, cold current flowing southwest might be one explanation; it had kept the site clear, emptying into a basin a little lower down and behind a low rocky ridge covered with anemones. Coy swam there to be sure, and could see that the depression, in the shape of a natural gully, drained off the sediment by directing it toward a series of terraces stepping down to deeper levels. An octopus, surprised in its den, skittered along the sand, its tentacles opened in the shape of an undulating star, shooting streams of ink to cover its retreat. Coy consulted his watch. It was getting more difficult to breathe, so he looked up toward the diffuse blue-green light above his head, pierced by silver bubbles. It was time to go back. He turned the valve at the base of the bottle to activate the reserve, and his lungs filled with air.

He was starting his ascent when he spotted the anchor. It lay at the edge of a second rocky, eroded ridge on the other side of the gully. It was large and it was old, its rusted iron flukes covered with crusts of lime. Both the anchor and the anemone-covered ridge held tangled remnants of old nets and rotted woven traps; over time, many fishermen had snagged their equipment here. But what caught his attention was that the anchor had a wooden shank, although the wood had rotted away and all that was left were a few splinters beneath the anchor ring. It was an anchor the xebec or the brigantine would have carried, and that encouraged Coy to cross the gully, swim around the ridge, and go closer, using the last minutes of his air reserve. On the other side of the rocks, sand alternated with a bed of shingle. The depression was more pronounced, varying from eighty to ninety feet in depth. And there, in the green darkness, looming in the depths like a ghostly dark shadow, was the *Dei Gloria*.

XV

The Devil's Irises

Everything found in the sea that has no owner belongs to the finder.

—Francisco Coloane, El camino de la ballena

In short, nervous musical phrases, the alto was improvising as no one had ever done. "Ko-ko" was playing, one of the themes Charlie Parker had recorded when he had invented everything he was destined to invent before rotting and exploding in a laughing fit. And in that order—first he rotted and then he died laughing, watching television. That had happened half a century ago, and now Coy was in his room in the Cartago Inn. The window offered a rainswept view of the port, and he was sitting naked in a rocking chair, a tray of fruit on the table beside him, listening to the digitalized recording of that old cut. Be-do-be-dooo. Toomb, toomb. Be-*bop.* Coy was holding a bottle of lemonade and watching Tánger sleep.

It was raining on the port, on cranes, docks, and Navy ships berthed two by two alongside the San Pedro dock, and on the rusting hulls in the Graveyard of Ships With No Name, where the *Carpanta*'s stern was tied up to the mole and her anchor dropped at the bow. It was pouring buckets because the storm had finally arrived. That had been arranged from the general headquarters of the low pressure system located over Ireland and spreading evilly outward in concentric, closely drawn isobars. Strong winds from the west were pushing successive fronts in the direction of the Mediterranean, weather maps were covered with black warnings and thunderbolts and signs of rain, and the coasts were pierced by arrows with wispy fletchings in the shaft, aimed at the heart of unwary ships. So that after three days of working at the site of the shipwreck, the crew of the *Carpanta* found itself obliged to return to port. Despite Tánger's impatience, she agreed that they could use the break to plan the last stages of the search, and to obtain the equipment they needed before a final assault on the secrets of that underwater tomb. The *Dei Gloria*'s tomb was now definitively situated two miles off the coast, at 37°33.3′N and 0°46.8′W, with her stern at eighty-five and her bow at ninety-two.

For several days, during which they lived with one eye on the sea and the other on the barometer, Tánger had directed the operation from the *Carpanta*'s cabin. Coy and El Piloto worked hard, taking turns below in spans of thirty to forty minutes, with intervals long enough to make long decompressions unnecessary. They had discovered in their earliest explorations that the ship was in good condition, considering the two and a half centuries she'd lain beneath the sea. She had gone down bow-first, losing one of her anchors on the rocky ridge before settling onto the bottom on a northeast-southwest axis. The hull, resting on its starboard side, was buried in sand and sediment to the waist. The deck was rotted and covered with marine life, but still intact at the stern. Toward the bow, the planking and deck beams were missing, and some of the frame protruded from the sand, recalling the ribs of a skeleton. When Coy and El Piloto explored the rest of the *Dei Gloria* on subsequent dives, they established that the back third of the ship was clear of debris, and that the damage would have been more major in other waters and in a different position. The waist seemed to be buried beneath a tangle of wood, clusters of iron powdery from corrosion, sand, and sediment that grew deeper as you approached the crushed and buried bow. It was obvious that the ten iron deck guns and all other heavy objects had shifted forward as the brigantine started down, and that over time the deck planking had caved in under their weight, disappearing beneath the sand. That was why the stern was a little higher and had sustained less damage, although many deck beams and ribs had yielded to the years, and sand had piled up in the rotten timberwork. They saw the stump of the mainmast, which had been blasted off during combat, as well as a pyramid of planks thrown together in a shape like a beach hut, two gun ports on the port gunnel, and the sternpost, to which the anchor was still attached, secured by mossy green pins and coated with fuzz and incrustations.

They were lucky, Tánger declared that first night as they rocked at anchor above the wreck. The three of them were grouped around Urrutia's chart and the plans of the *Dei Gloria* in the faint light of the cabin lantern, celebrating the find with a bottle of white Pescador that El Piloto had on board. They were lucky for many reasons, but the main one was that the brigantine went down bow first. That gave them better access to the captain's cabin, which was where valuable objects were usually stored for safekeeping. It was likely that the emeralds, if they were still on board at the time of the sinking, were either there or in the adjacent orlop reserved for passengers. The fact that the stern was not completely buried made their task much easier, because searching beneath the sand would have required suction hoses and more complex equipment. As for her state of preservation—optimum after so much time at the bottom of the sea—that was owing to the rocky ridge she lay behind, with natural channels and rocks protecting her from the action of the waves, marine sediment, and fishermen's nets. The gentle current of cold water flowing from Cabo de Palos had also lessened the work of shipworms, those wood-boring mollusks that find their most favorable conditions in warm waters. For all these reasons, the work that lay ahead would be exhausting, but not impossible. Unlike archaeologists conducting research on a sunken ship, they did not have to preserve anything; they could destroy anything in the way of their objective. They did not have the technical means or the time to move with care. So the next day, acting in compliance with Tánger's work on the plans spread out on the bulkheads and chart table, Coy and El Piloto spent one whole day in successive dives, laying a white halyard from bow to stern of the sunken vessel, following the apparent center line. Then, moving cautiously through shattered wood and limy growths that could cut like knives, they laid out shorter pieces of lead-weighted halyard in seven-by-seven feet squares, perpendicular to both sides of the longitudinal line. That divided the wreckage into segments corresponding to those Tánger had drawn with pencil and ruler on the plans of the brigantine, establishing rudimentary points of identification between reality and paper, locating the site of each part of the hull according to the 1:55 scale on the plans provided by Lucio Gamboa. The day that the barometer began to fall and the weather dispatches drove them to take shelter in Cartagena, they had already succeeded in calculating the position of the after part of the orlop, steerage, and the captain's cabin located beneath the poop. But what condition would they find Captain Elezcano's cabin in? Would the internal structure have withstood the pressure of sediment on rotting wood? And would it be possible to move around once they had discovered how to get inside, or would everything be so flattened and mixed up that they would have to begin at the top, breaking and clearing away debris until they came to the forty square feet near the stern gallery where the captain's quarters should be located?

The rain was still trickling down the windowpanes and Charlie Parker was fading from the landscape, cloaked on the road to eternal dreamland by the trumpet of Dizzy Gillespie. It was Tánger who had given Coy that recording, which she'd bought in a record shop on calle Mayor. They had been sitting by the door of the Gran Bar with El Piloto, after walking through the rain to the city's Museo Naval. Along the way they had gathered provisions in marine supply shops, supermarkets, hardware stores, and pharmacies. Tánger had withdrawn the money from an ATM—after two attempts that had failed for lack of available funds. I'm diving with my reserve tank too, she said sarcastically as she put the wallet into the back pocket of her jeans. They had been able to buy everything they needed, from hardware to chemicals, and the purchases were in bags beneath their chairs. The bar's canvas awning protected them from the warm drizzle, which had slicked the street, putting a melancholy face on the empty balconies of modernist buildings whose ground floors, which Coy remembered alight with cafés, had been turned into lugubrious banking offices. And there they were, the three of them, drinking apéritifs and watching raincoats and wet umbrellas pass by, when Tánger laid the local newspaper on the table—it was open to the page on ship arrivals and departures, Coy observed—got up and walked to a record shop opposite the Escarabajal bookstore. She came back carrying a package, which she put in front of Coy without saying anything. Inside were two double CDs with the master cuts of eighty pieces Charlie Parker had recorded for the Dial and Savoy labels between 1944 and 1948. Given the circumstances, he truly appreciated the gesture. This Parker was really a gem.

That same day Coy thought he saw Horacio Kiskoros. They were on their way back to the *Carpanta,* laden with their purchases. When they came to the walls of the old Navidad fort, next to the ship graveyard, Coy had turned and looked around. He did that often, instinctively, whenever he was ashore. Although Tánger seemed indifferent to Nino Palermo's threats, Coy still had them in mind; he hadn't forgotten the last encounter with the Argentine on the beach at Águilas. He was following Tánger and El Piloto toward the mole where the *Carpanta* was tied up when he saw Kiskoros at the foot of the old tower. Or thought he saw him. That was a path often followed by fishermen on their way to the breakwater, but the silhouette, black against the gray light, between the tower and the dismantled bridge of the *Korzeniowski,* did not look like any fisherman. He was small and dapper, with some resemblance to a full page ad for Barbour. In green.

"There's Kiskoros," he said.

Tánger stopped, surprised. She and El Piloto turned to look where he was pointing, but there was no one there. Anyway, Coy thought, LWLHMBM: Law of White, Liquid, and Homogenized, Must Be Milk. So Barbour, dwarfish and *there,* could only be Kiskoros. Besides, when bad guys hang around, sooner or later you're going to get a glimpse of them. He set the packages on the ground. It wasn't raining, but gusts of the warm southwest wind that had come whistling down the slopes of San Julián were rippling the puddles as his feet splashed toward the tower. There was no one there when he reached it, but he was sure he'd seen the hero of the Malvinas, and the abrupt disappearance reaffirmed his conviction. He looked around among the piles of blowtorched metal plate, the twisted iron staining the sand red, and stood still to listen. Nothing. There was a hollow clang of metal as he climbed the ladder of the scrapped bridge of the packet, staining his hands with rust. Runoff from the rain dripped from its roof, soaking the rotted wood of the deck; some boards yielded to his weight, so he tried to be careful where he stepped. He went down the other side and over to the split-open belly of the bulk carrier, its interior bulkheads filthy with caked black grease. This was a labyrinth of old iron, with junk piled everywhere. He skirted the base of a crane and went onto the ship by way of a listing passageway where water puddled against the hatchway coamings. His heightened senses absorbed the oppressive sadness of all that desolation, which was only intensified by the dirty light filtering in. On the far side of a stripped and empty cabin with all its cables pulled out and piled in a corner, he peered into the dark cavity of a hold. He dropped a piece of scrap and from the depths the sinister echo bounced back and forth between unseen metal plates. Impossible to go down there without a flashlight. Then he heard a noise behind him, at the end of the passageway, and he retraced his steps with his heart jumping in his chest. It was El Piloto, frowning and tense, with a foot-long iron bar in his hand. Coy cursed silently, caught between disappointment and relief. Tánger was waiting behind him, leaning against a bulkhead, hands in her jeans pockets, a somber expression on her face. As for Kiskoros, if in fact it had been he, he had disappeared.

Coy took off the headphones as the distant clock on the city hall struck seven. Its dong-dong-dong seemed to sound the last notes. Sipping lemonade, he continued to watch Tánger, asleep on the mussed bed. Gray light cast faint shadows on the sheet partially covering her. She was sleeping on her side, with one hand out from her body and the other between her pulled-up knees, her back to the uncertain light of dawn. The sweep of her naked hips was a slope of light and shadow on freckled skin, dimpled flesh, chasms, and curves. Motionless in the rocking chair, Coy studied the hidden face, hair falling onto wrinkled sheets that defined the shape of shoulders and back, the waist, the expanse of hips and inner line of thighs seen from behind, the beautiful V of flexed legs, and the soles of her feet. And especially that sleeping hand whose fingers lay between her thighs, very close to the intimation of pubic hair, golden and shadowed with darker tones.

Coy stood up and walked closer to the bed, to fix the image in his memory forever. The dresser mirror on the opposite wall reflected Tánger's other hand, resting on the pillow, the tip of a knee, and Coy himself integrated into the picture, a portion of his body reflected in the quicksilver of the mirror—one arm and one hand, the line of a naked hip, the physical certainty that the image belonged to him and no other, and that it was more than a play of mirrors in his memory. He regretted that he didn't have a camera to record the details. So he made an effort to engrave on his retina the half-waking, half-sleeping mystery that so obsessed him, the intuition of a mutable, all too brief moment that might perhaps explain everything. There was a secret, and the secret was in plain view, barely disguised in the obvious. It was another matter to isolate and understand it, though, and he knew he would never have enough time, and that in an instant drunken and capricious gods, unaware of their ability to create as they slept, would yawn and awake and everything would dissipate as if it had never existed. Possibly, he thought with desolation, that fleeting moment would never be repeated with such clarity, that flash of lucidity capable of placing things in their proper perspective, of balancing void, horror, and beauty. Of reconciling the man reflected in the mirror with the word "life." But Tánger began to stir, and Coy, who knew that he was on the verge of grasping the key to the enigma, felt that one-tenth of a second too late or too soon would distort the connection between scene and observer, like the fuzzy focus of an image impossible to decipher. And in the mirror, beyond the foreshortening of his own body and that of the woman lying on the bed, ships in the rain were once again reflections of black ships on a millenary sea.

Tánger awoke, and with her all the women in the world. She woke warm and lazy, her hair stuck to her face and her lips parted. The sheet slipped from her shoulders and back, uncovering the extended arm, the line of armpit to dorsal muscles, and the firm indication of a breast compressed beneath the weight of her body. The back tanned by the sun, lighter below the line of her swimsuit, appeared full length and, as Coy watched, the small of that back arched and Tánger emerged from sleep like a beautiful, tranquil animal, eyes squinting against the square of gray light in the window, discovering Coy's proximity with a smile first of surprise, then warmth. Suddenly, however, the eyes were serious and grave, aware of her nakedness and the scrutiny of which she was the object. Finally the challenge—turning, slowly and deliberately, onto her back before his eyes. Now her body was entirely free of the sheet, one leg stretched out and the other bent, one hand near her sex without hiding it, the other limp on the sheet, the lines of her stomach converging toward the inner face of her thighs like signals of no return. Motionless. And always the unwavering stare, the eyes fixed on the man observing her. After a few moments, she slid over to one side of the bed and rose to her knees before the mirror, showing him her naked back and hips. With her lips almost touching the glass, she breathed on it until it clouded over, and, without taking her eyes from the image of Coy, she left the print of her lips in the mist obscuring their reflection. Then she got out of bed, slipped into a T-shirt, and sat at the other side of the table, near the platter of fruit. She peeled an orange and began to eat it without separating the sections, biting into it, juice dripping from her lips and chin and hands. Coy sat down across from her. Tánger looked at him the same way she had when she was lying on the bed, but now with a smile. She held up her wrists and licked the juice trickling down to her elbows, and the shredded membrane and pulp in her fingers disappeared into her mouth. Coy shook his head as if he were refuting something. He sighed as if all his sadness and resignation were escaping in a moan. Very deliberately, he went around the table, took her hands, and just as she was, sitting there in a T-shirt barely covering her torso and with the taste of orange on her lips, he went in search of the road to Ithaca that lay on the other shore of the sea ancient and gray as memory.

THEY returned to the *Dei Gloria* as soon as the storm had passed, after the last clouds fled with dawn, streaking the horizon with red. Once again the sea was intensely blue and the sun blazed on the white houses along the coast, leading a gentle breeze by the hand. It was a shift for the better according to El Piloto. That same day, with vertical rays casting his shadow on the surface, Coy dived again, descending from a marker buoy—one of the *Carpanta's* lateral fenders—attached to an anchored one hundred-foot line that had a knot every ten feet. He touched bottom a short distance off the port beam of the sunken vessel, more or less at the waist, and swam along the hull to check whether the grid they had laid before the storm was still in place. Then he consulted the chart he'd brought down—wax pencil on a plastic tablet—calculated distances with the help of a metric tape, and began to clear away debris on the door of the companion, crusted with marine growth. Using an iron crowbar and a pick, he tore away rotted planking, which collapsed in a blinding cloud. He worked slowly, trying not to do anything that would increase his air intake. Occasionally he moved back a little to rest and let the sediment settle enough for him to see. He succeeded in breaking through the door, and when the water cleared he looked inside as he'd done the day before when he peered into the hold of the bulk carrier. This time he cautiously thrust in the arm holding the light and illuminated the chaotic innards of the brigantine, where fish disoriented by the brightness darted about madly, seeking ways to escape. The light returned the natural colors to everything, annulling the monotonous green of deep water. There were sea anemones, starfish, red and white coral formations, multicolor seaweed swaying gently, and the glittering scales of fish slicing through the beam like silver knives. Coy saw a wooden stool that seemed to be well preserved. It had fallen against a bulkhead and was covered with some green growth, but he could distinguish the carved spiral feet. Straight down from the opening he'd made was something that looked like a crusted spoon, and beside it was the lower part of an oil lamp, the brass clotted with tiny snails and half buried in a small mound of sand that had filtered through the rotted deck. Shooting the beam in a half-circle, Coy saw the remains of what looked like a collapsed cabinet in one corner, and in a heap of shattered planks he could identify coils of cordage covered with brown fuzz, and objects of metal and clay—tankards, jugs, a few plates and bottles, all of it covered with a very fine layer of sediment. In other aspects, however, the panorama was not very encouraging. The beams that supported the deck had collapsed in many places, and half the cabin was a jumble of wood and sand that had sifted in through the broken frame. The beam of light revealed openings large enough to enable him to move around cautiously inside, as long as the ribs and beams that supported the structure of the hull did not give way. It would be more prudent, he decided, to tear away as much of the poop planking as possible, and work from the outside, in the open, pulling away the timberwork with the help of air flotation devices that would reduce the effort involved. That would be slower, but it was preferable to having him or El Piloto trapped in the wreckage at the first careless move.

With great care Coy removed the tank of compressed air, lifting it forward over his head. He took a large mouthful of air and set the cylinder on the deck with the mouthpiece anchored beneath the valves. Then he pushed half his body through the open hole over the companionway, careful not to get hooked on anything, and moved toward the half-buried lamp until he could touch it. It was very light and came free from the bottom with little difficulty. At that moment he saw the eyes of a large grouper observing him openmouthed from an opening beneath a bulkhead. He waved a hand in salute and gradually worked his way backward until he was again out on the deck, careful not to release the last bit of oxygen, which he would need to clear the mouthpiece of the regulator and start taking air again. He clamped the mouthpiece in his teeth, exhaled into the bubbling regulator, and breathed fresh air without a problem. He slipped the cylinder back over his head and tightened the harness. On his wrist, El Piloto's waterproof

Seiko indicated he'd been down thirty-five minutes. It was time to go up, pausing at the knot that marked ten feet and waiting the seven minutes required by the decompression tables. He tugged five times on the line that was tied to a cleat on the *Carpanta* and began to swim upward, carrying the lamp in his hands, going slower than his own bubbles, seeing the water change from dark greenish shadows to green, and from green to blue. Before he got to the surface he stopped at the ten-foot mark, holding onto the knot in the line, with the black shadow of the motionless sailboat sitting overhead on a surface like polished glass. The glass shattered into foam as Tánger, wearing a diving mask, her hair flowing in the water, jumped in and stroked down toward Coy. She swam around him like an exotic siren, and the light filtering from above turned her freckled skin pale, making her appear naked and vulnerable. Coy showed her the lamp from the *Dei Gloria* and saw her eyes widen with wonder behind the glass of her mask.

For four days, taking turns, Coy and El Piloto tore away part of the brigantine's deck at the level of the captain's cabin. They stripped it away, removing rotted planks from top to bottom with crowbars and picks, taking care not to weaken the frames and beams that supported the hull beneath the poop. To lift large sections of wood they called on Archimedes' principle, using a volume of air equal to the weight of the object to be raised. Once the heavy planks were free, they used nylon line with floats resembling plastic parachutes, which they filled with compressed air from reserve bottles tethered off the side of the *Carpanta*. The work was slow and tiring, and at times the cloud of sediment was so thick that they were forced to rest until the water cleared.

They found human bones. They would come across them trapped in a tangle of planking or half-buried in sand, occasionally with fragments of what had been belts or shoes. Like the skull with an entry wound in a parietal that Coy found beneath a thin layer of sediment near one of the gun ports and quickly reburied in the sand, moved by an atavistic impulse of respect. The sailors of the *Dei Gloria* were still there, manning their sunken ship, and as he moved around amid the ruined wood of the brigantine, his only company the sound of the regulator, Coy could feel them close by in the green semidarkness.

There was an accounting every night beneath the midship cabin light, in meetings that resembled war councils, headed by Tánger with the plans of the brigantine spread out before her, and with Coy and El Piloto in sweatshirts despite the mild temperature, to offset the cold they still felt after so many hours in the water. Then Coy would sleep a heavy sleep barren of dreams or images, and the next morning start diving again. His skin was like soaked garbanzo beans.

On the third day, as he was ascending, ready to stop at the ten-foot mark to purge his blood of dissolved nitrogen, he looked up and felt a jolt. The dark silhouette of another hull lay beside the *Carpanta,* rocking in the increasing swell. He came to the surface without completing the decompression, with a stab of alarm that intensified when he saw the Guardia Civil patrol boat. It had stopped by to take a look, its crew curious about the *Carpanta*'s immobility. Fortunately, the lieutenant in command was an acquaintance of El Piloto, and the first thing Coy picked up when his head emerged from the water was a calming glance from his friend. Everything was under control. El Piloto and the lieutenant were smoking and talking, passing the wineskin back and forth between boats, while a pair of young *Guardias* dressed in green fatigues sent definitely unsuspicious looks at Tánger, who was reading on the stern deck in sunglasses, bathing suit, and baseball cap, apparently indifferent to what was happening. The story El Piloto had just finished telling in offhand bits and pieces was about these tourists who liked to dive and had leased his boat. For a lark they were searching for a fishing boat that had sunk a couple of years before in these same waters—the *Leo y Vero,* out of Torrevieja. His invention had sounded reasonable to the lieutenant, especially when he learned that the man climbing aboard the *Carpanta,* who looked vaguely surprised but gave him a wave after hanging his tank and harness on the stern ladder, was a native of Cartagena and an officer in the Merchant Marine. The patrol boat pulled away after the lieutenant perfunctorily checked Coy's diving license and recommended he renew it, since it had lapsed a year and a half before. As soon as the boat was half a mile away, at the end of a straight white wake, and Tánger had closed the book of which she'd been unable to read a single line, and the three of them had looked at each other with silent relief, Coy jumped back into the water with the bottle of compressed air, sank to the ten-foot mark, and stayed there, surrounded by white and dark medusas slowly drifting by in the current, until the nitrogen bubbles formed in his blood by the precipitous rise to the surface had dissipated.

ON the fifth day enough of the brigantine's poop had been removed to allow a first serious exploration. Almost all the deck planking was gone, and the naked structure of the hull at the stern revealed part of the captain's cabin, the remains of an intact bulkhead, and a passengers' locker in the steerage. Working from outside, Coy could undertake the search by sorting through jumbled objects, splintered wood, and residue that formed a layer nearly three feet thick. He dug with gloved hands and a short-handled spade, tossing useless material over the side, away from the hull, moving back again and again to let the sediment settle. He pulled out things that normally would have piqued his curiosity, but that now he simply discarded—assorted tools, pewter jugs, a candelabrum, broken glass and pottery. He came across the large bronze handle and enormous hand guard of a sword, with the nub of a badly corroded wide blade, a cutlass whose only purpose was to slash human flesh during a boarding operation. He also found a block of musket balls fused together in the shape of the box in which they'd sunk, though the wood itself had disintegrated. Buried in sand he found half a door, complete with hinges and a key in its lock, and also balls for the four-pounder, a clump of iron nails hollowed out by rust, and bronze nails that had fared much better. Beneath the loose boards of a cupboard, Coy found Talavera pottery cups and plates that were miraculously clean and intact, so perfect he could read the mark of their makers. He found a clay pipe, two muskets covered with tiny snails, blackened disks that were probably silver coins, the cracked glass of a sand clock, and an articulated brass ruler that had once traced routes on Urrutia's charts. For reasons of security, especially following the visit from the Guardia Civil, they had decided not to bring up any object that could raise suspicion, but Coy made an exception when he unearthed an instrument encrusted with lime. It had originally been composed of wood and metal, although the wood crumbled between his fingers when he shook off the sand, leaving only an arm with metal parts on the upper portion, and an arc below. Deeply moved, he had no difficulty identifying it as the brass or bronze metal parts corresponding to the index bar and the graduated arc of an ancient octant, probably the one the pilot of the *Dei Gloria* had used to establish their latitude. That was a good trade, he thought. An eighteenth-century octant in exchange for the sextant he had sold in Barcelona. He set it aside where it would be easy to find later. But what truly hit him hard in the gut was what he found in a corner of the locker behind the boards of a chest: a simple length of line, fuzzy with minute dark filaments but perfectly coiled, with a knot tightened in the last two hitches, just as it had been left by the expert hands of a conscientious sailor who knew his trade. That intact coil of line affected Coy more than anything he had found, including the bones of the *Dei Gloria*'s crew. He bit on his rubber mouthpiece to contain the bitter smile of infinite sadness he felt knot in his throat and mouth the closer they came to the sailors who had died in this shipwreck. Two and a half centuries before, men like him, sailors accustomed to the sea and its dangers, had held those objects in their hands. They had calculated courses with the brass rule, coiled the line, measured the quarters of the watch by turning the sandglass, and shot the stars with the octant. They had climbed to the yards, struggling against a wind fighting to tear them from the shrouds, and had howled their fear and humble courage into the oscillating rigging as they gathered canvas in stiff fingers. They had faced the Atlantic's northwesters and the murderous mistrals and *lebeches* of the Mediterranean. They had battled gun to gun, hoarse from yelling and gray with powder, before going to the bottom with the resignation of men who do their job well and fight bravely to the end. Now their bones were scattered amid the detritus of the *Dei Gloria*. And Coy, moving slowly beneath the plume of bubbles rising straight up into that shroud-like darkness, felt like a furtive grave robber violating the peace of a tomb.

LIGHT from the porthole was seesawing on Tánger's naked skin, a small square of sun bobbing up and down with the movement of the boat, slipping down her shoulders and back as she lifted herself from Coy, still breathless, gasping like a fish out of water. Her hair, which days at sea had faded almost white at the tips, was stuck to her face with sweat. Dribbles of sweat ran down her skin, leaving tracks between her breasts and beading on her upper lip and her eyelashes. El Piloto was eighty-five feet below them, working his dive. The nearly vertical sun had turned the cabin into an oven, and Coy, sitting on the bench beneath the ladder to the deck, let his hands slip down Tánger's sweaty flanks. They had made love right there, impulsively, when he had taken off his diving vest and was looking for a towel after his half hour at the site of the *Dei Gloria* and she walked by, brushing against him accidentally. Suddenly his fatigue was gone and she was quiet, looking at him the way she sometimes did, with that silent thoughtfulness, and an instant later they were locked together there at the foot of the ladder, attacking one another furiously, as if the emotion they shared was hate. Now he was leaning against the back rest, drained, and slowly, inexorably, she was withdrawing, shifting her weight to one side and freeing Coy's moist flesh. That small square of sun was sliding down her body, and her gaze, which was again metallic blue, dark blue, navy-blue, the blue of blued steel, was directed toward the light and the sun tumbling through the opening from the deck. From where he was still sprawled on the bench, Coy watched her walk naked up the ladder, as if she were leaving forever. Despite the heat he felt a chill crawl across his skin, precisely in those places that held a trace of her, and the thought came: one day it will be the last time. One day she will leave me, or we'll die, or I'll get old. One day she will walk out of my life, or I out of hers. One day I won't have anything but images to remember, and then one day I won't even be alive to reconstruct those images. One day it will all be erased, and maybe today is the last time. Which was why he was watching her closely as she climbed up the companionway and disappeared onto the deck, engraving every last detail in his memory. The last component in the image was the drop of semen that slid down the inside of a thigh, which, when it reached her knee, reflected the amber flash of a ray of sun. Then she was out of his field of vision, and Coy heard the splash of someone diving into the sea.

THEY spent that night anchored above the *Dei Gloria*. The needle of the wind gauge fluctuated indecisively atop the mast and the mirror-flat water reflected an intermittent spark from the Cabo de Palos lighthouse seven miles to the northeast. So many stars were out that the sky seemed right on top of the sea, so many it was actually difficult to see individual stars. Coy was sitting on the stern deck, studying them and tracing imaginary lines that would allow him to identify them. The summer triangle was beginning to rise in the southeast, and he could see tendrils of Berenice's hair, the last to disappear of all the spring constellations. To the east, bright above a landscape black as ink, the belt of the hunter Orion was very visible, and following a straight line from Aldebaran to him, above Canis Major, he saw light that had traveled eight years from Sirius, the most brilliant binary star in the heavens, there where the Milky Way trailed to the south toward the regions of the Swan and the Eagle. All that world of light and mythic images moved slowly overhead, and he, as if in the center of a unique sphere, was part of its silence and infinite peace.

"You're not teaching me the names of the stars anymore, Coy."

He hadn't heard her until she was at his side. She sat close but not touching him, her feet on the stern steps.

"I've taught you all the ones I know."

Water splashed as she put her feet in the water. At regular intervals the flicker from the lighthouse affirmed the hazy outline of her shadow.

"I wonder," she said, "what you will remember about me."

She had spoken quietly, her voice low. It wasn't a question, but a shared confidence. Coy thought about what she'd said.

"It's too soon to know," he replied finally. "It isn't over yet."

"I wonder what you will remember when it is over."

Coy shrugged. They sat in silence.

"I don't know what more you expect," Tánger added after a while.

From the midship cabin came the sound of the VHF radio. It was ten-fifteen and El Piloto was listening to the weather forecast for the following day. Tánger's shadow was motionless.

"There are voyages," she murmured, "we can only take alone."

"Like dying."

"Don't bring that up," she protested.

"Dying alone, remember? Like Zas. Once you told me that you're afraid that will happen to you."

"Don't say it."

"You asked me to be there with you. To swear it."

"Don't say it."

Coy leaned back until he was lying flat on the deck with the dome of the heavens above him. A dark shadow leaned over him, a black hole in the stars.

"What could you do?"

"Give you my hand," Coy replied. "Be with you during that journey, so you don't have to go alone."

"I don't know when that will happen. No one knows."

"That's why I want to be with you. Looking after you."

"You would do that? You would stay with me and look after me? So I wouldn't be alone when the time comes?"

"Of course."

The dark silhouette was no longer there. Tánger had moved to one side, away from him.

"What star is that?"

Coy looked in the direction indicated by the outline of her hand.

"Regulus. The foremost claw of Leo."

Tánger looked up, trying to see the animal sketched in the lights blinking high above them. A moment later she was paddling her feet in the water.

"Maybe I don't deserve you, Coy."

She said that so low he almost didn't hear. He closed his eyes and slowly let out his breath.

"That's for me to say."

"You're wrong. It isn't for you to say."

Again she was silent, the only sound her feet in the sea, stirring the black water.

"You're a good man," she said suddenly. "You truly are."

Coy opened his eyes, to fill them with stars and to bear the anguish radiating from his chest. All at once he felt helpless. He didn't dare move, as if he feared that the pain would be unbearable.

"Better than I am," she continued, "and everyone I've known. Too bad that . . ."

She interrupted herself, and her tone was different when she spoke again. Harder, and unemotional. And categorical.

"Too bad."

A long silence this time. A shooting star fell in the distance, to the north. A wish, Coy thought. I should make a wish. But the tiny streak faded before he could organize his thoughts.

"Where were you when I won my swimming cup?"

That she'll stay with me, he wished finally. But there were no shooting stars in the icy firmament now, he knew. The stars were fixed for eternity, and implacable.

"Living," he replied. "Getting ready to meet you."

He spoke with simplicity. There was a faint light on Tánger's dark face. A vague double reflection. She was looking at him.

"You *are* a good man."

With those words, the shadow moved toward him and he felt her moist lips on his.

"I hope," she said, "you find a good ship soon."

THE lead frame of a window still retained shards of glass. Coy moved away for a moment from the blinding sediment and then went back to work. He had come to a place in the cabin where sand quickly filled the space he had just emptied, and he had to make constant trips back and forth with the short-handled spade to throw what he had just dug overboard. It was exhausting work and it made him use more air than he wanted. Bubbles were rising at a much faster rate than normal, so he set the spade aside and swam to a jutting frame, holding onto it to rest and to convince his lungs not to demand so much. Beneath his feet was a cannonball and a piece of chain shot, one of those used to destroy the enemy's rigging, which El Piloto had unearthed during his last dive. It was in better than usual condition, thanks to the sand that had protected it for two and a half centuries. Maybe it had been fired from the corsair, and had ended its trajectory here after doing damage to the brigantine's rigging and sail. He bent down a little to get a better look—what men devise to destroy their fellows, he was thinking—and then, through an opening at the base of a bulkhead, he saw the protruding head of a moray. It was huge, nearly eight inches thick, and a sinister dark color. It opened its maw, angered by the intrusion of this strange bubbling creature. Coy prudently retreated from the open jaws that could take half an arm in one bite, and swam to get the harpoon from its place on the line with their tools and uninflated floats. He cocked it, stretching the elastic, and returned to the moray. He hated to kill fish, but it was not a good idea to work around rotted planking with the threat of those hooked and poisonous teeth clamping on the back of his neck. The eel was still standing guard beneath the bulkhead, defending the entry to its domestic refuge. Its evil eyes were fixed on Coy as he approached and pushed the harpoon before the open maw. Nothing personal, friend. Just your bad luck. He pressed the trigger and the impaled moray thrashed wildly, furiously snapping at the steel shaft protruding from its mouth, until Coy unsheathed his knife and cut the eel's spinal cord.

He went back to work in a pile of wood and debris in the corner of the cabin. Again and again sand filled the space his hands had dug. Snails and bits of ragged metal had shredded his gloves—this was the third pair he'd worn out—and his fingers were a pitiable mass of cuts and scratches. He found the barrel of a pistol, whose wooden butt had disappeared, and also a black and crusted crucifix that looked as if it might be silver and a nearly intact leather shoe. He pulled away some planks that broke in his hands, again thrust up above the swirling sediment, and when he came back saw a dark block covered with rusty and brown concretions. At first view it looked like a very large, square brick. He tried to move it, but it seemed to be stuck to the bottom. It's impossible, he told himself. Treasure chests have lids that open to reveal a glittering interior of pearls and jewels and gold coins. And emeralds. Treasure chests do not have the innocuous look of a rusty, lime-covered block, nor do they have the grace to turn up under an old shoe and splintered boards. So it is not possible that this thing I have before me is what we are looking for. Emeralds big as walnuts, Devil's irises, and things like that. Too easy.

He scrabbled at the sand around the encrusted block, shining the light directly on it to bring out the actual colors. It was about sixteen inches long, sixteen inches wide, and not quite that deep, and it still had bronze cornerpieces that had stained the agglomeration of tiny snails green. The rest of the block was covered with a hard, brittle crust, and splinters of rotted wood and rust-colored stains. Bronze, wood, and corroded iron, Tánger had said, and she had also said that in case they found anything matching that description, it must be handled with care. No hammering or digging into it. The emeralds, if it was the emeralds, would be stuck together in a calcareous block that would have to be dissolved with chemicals. And emeralds were very fragile.

Coy easily freed the block from the sand. It did not seem very heavy, at least in the water, but there was little question that it was a chest. For almost a minute, he didn't move, breathing quietly, releasing bubbles at a slower and slower rhythm, until he calmed down a little and his temple stopped pounding and his heart was beating normally beneath the neoprene vest. Take it easy, sailor. Chest or no chest, take it easy. Be Mr. Cool for once in your life, because nerves are not compatible with breathing compressed air at eighty-five feet under two hundred atmospheres of pressure. So after resting there a while, he removed one of the plastic floats, made a basket of sorts from some fine net, tied it to the parachute lines of the float, and secured the whole thing to a shackle with a bowline knot, then from his mouthpiece he fed a little compressed air into the float. Despite Tánger's instructions, he pried a little into the block with his knife point, breaking off a bit of the crust, without spotting anything notable. He dug a little deeper, and a chunk about the size of half his fist came loose from the rest. He picked it up to examine in the beam of the torch, and a fragment of the chunk broke loose and drifted slowly to the sand. It was an irregularly shaped, translucent stone with polyhedral planes. Green. Emerald green.

XVI

The Graveyard of Ships With No Name

Have you, as always, deceived and conquered that innocent with tricks?
—Appolonius Rhodius, ARGONAUTICA

They could see the city clustered beneath the castle in a mist of whites, browns, and blues heightened by light from the west. The sun was about to take its rest behind the massive silhouette of Mount Roldan when the *Carpanta,* on the port tack under jib and single-reefed mainsail, passed between the two lighthouses and beneath the empty gun ports of the old forts guarding the inlet. Coy held his course until he had the Navidad lighthouse and white heads of the fishermen sitting on the blocks of the breakwater on his stern fin. Then he turned the wheel windward, and the sails flapped as the boat luffed, slowing in the tranquil water of the protected dock. Tánger was turning the crank of a winch, gathering the jib, as he freed the clamp on the mainsail halyard and the sail slid down the mast. While El Piloto fastened it to the boom, Coy started the engine and set their bow for El Espalmador, toward the cut-up hulls and rusting superstructures of the ships with no name.

Tánger had just finished taking in the sheets and was looking at him. A long look, as if she were studying his face, and he responded with the hint of a smile. She returned the smile, and went to lean against the companion, facing the bow where El Piloto had opened the anchor well. Coy looked toward the commercial dock, where the *Felix von Luckner* was anchored beside a large passenger ship, and lamented that they had to be so secretive. He would have liked to fly a victory signal at the mast, the way German submarine commanders flew pennants on their conning towers announcing the tonnage they'd sunk. "Returning from Scapa Flow, mission accomplished." I announce that treasures exist, and that we are carrying one aboard.

The emeralds were on board the *Carpanta*. The block of limy accretions that contained them had been wrapped in several layers of protective foam, packed in an innocent-looking tote bag. They had cleaned their find carefully before wrapping it up, disbelieving what they saw before them, marveling at the accomplished reality of the dream Tánger had long ago as she studied a file of old documents—"Clergy/Jesuits/Varia n°356." It was as if they were floating on a cloud, so unreal that Coy hadn't dared tell El Piloto the approximate value the dirty, rocklike block rescued from the sea would bring on the international black market. El Piloto hadn't asked, but Coy knew him well, and he picked up an unusual excitement beneath the sailor's apparent indifference. It was a particular gleam in his eyes, a different kind of silence, a curiosity tempered by the self-restraint of men of the sea, who are at ease in their world but uncertain, timid, and suspicious of the traps and temptations of terra firma. Coy was afraid he would frighten him if he told him that those two hundred raw emeralds, even if badly marketed by Tánger and sold for a fourth of their value, would produce, at the minimum, several million dollars. An amount that El Piloto would never be able to picture in spite of his good imagination. At any rate, the plan was to wait while Tánger negotiated with the middlemen, and then split the profits—seventy percent for her, twenty-five percent for Coy, and five percent for El Piloto—which they would spread around discreetly to avoid suspicion. Tánger had already researched the appropriate mechanisms during the visit she had made months before to Antwerp, where her local contact had connections with banks in the Caribbean, Zurich, Gibraltar, and the English Channel Islands. Nothing would stand in the way, for instance, of El Piloto's later buying a new *Carpanta,* registered in Jersey, or Coy's collecting a salary from a hypothetical shipping company in the Antilles while he waited for his license to be reinstated. As for Tánger herself, she had replied to Coy's question—without looking up from the brush she was using to clean away the encrustation on the block of emeralds—that that was no one's affair but her own.

Under the chart-table light, they had discussed these matters the night before, after they had carefully hauled the Jesuits' chest aboard the *Carpanta.* They washed in it fresh water, and then, with patience, the proper instruments, and several technical manuals, Tánger went about removing the outer calcareous layer with chemical solvents in a plastic tub, while Coy and El Piloto watched with reverential respect, not daring to open their mouths. Finally they had seen a cluster of crystals—sharp protuberances and indications of hexagonal formations, still uncut and with their original irregularities—which in the cabin's light cast bluish-green reflections as clear and transparent as water.

They were perfect, Tánger had murmured, fascinated, working persistently, with the back of her hand wiping away the sweat beaded on her forehead. She had one eye closed and a jeweler's loupe held to the other, a small, slender ten-power loupe. Bent over the block, she was examining the interior of the stones at a distance of an inch or two, lighting it from various angles with a powerful Maglite torch. Translucent green, literally $Be_3Al_2Si_6O_{18}$, ideal in color, brilliance, and clarity. She had studied, read, and patiently asked questions for months to be able to make that announcement now. Raw emeralds, between twenty and thirty carats, with no inclusions or flaws, clean as drops of oil. Once they were studied for the most beautiful color and refraction, skillful jewelers would cut them into rectangular and octagonal facets, converting them into valuable jewels that ladies of high society and wives and lovers of bankers, millionaires, Russian mafiosi, and oil sheiks would flaunt in bracelets, diadems, and necklaces. They would never question their provenance nor the long road traveled by those unique formations of silica, aluminum, beryllium, oxides, and water for which men throughout time had killed and died, and would forever continue to do so. Perhaps, as happens, among a certain few initiates the word would spread that some of the emeralds, the very best, had been salvaged from a ship documented to have sunk two and a half centuries before, and the price of the best pieces, the largest and most beautifully crafted, would shoot up on the black market to the limits of madness. For the most part, the stones would again sleep a long sleep in obscurity, this time in safe-deposit boxes around the world. And someone, in a discreet workshop on a street in Antwerp, would quadruple his fortune.

Coy veered sharply to avoid the pilots' launch approaching on the starboard beam, on its way to one of the tankers waiting off the Escombreras refinery. He had been distracted for a moment, and from the bow he could feel the inquisitive look of El Piloto. In truth he was thinking about Horacio Kiskoros. He could sense the dwarf's presence nearby. And he was thinking about Kiskoros's boss. With the emeralds on board, the curtain was about to fall on the last act, and Coy could not believe that Nino Palermo would allow the drama to end this way. He remembered the Gibraltarian's warnings, his determination not to be left out of the deal. And the bastard was someone who would carry out his threats. Coy looked at Tánger, still leaning against the companion, motionless, eyes turned in the direction they were heading. She did not seem worried, but far away, immersed in the green glow of her dream. Coy felt a growing uneasiness, as when the sea is calm and the sky clear but a black cloud appears on the horizon and the wind in the rigging rises suspiciously. With apprehension he scanned the gray mole where they would be docking. When it came to Palermo, the question was simply *how* and *when.*

THE *lebeche* was blowing at a right angle to the mole, so Coy approached slightly forward and a little windward in the direction of its far end. At three lengths he put her dead center as the anchor manned by El Piloto fell into the water with a loud splash. When he felt it hold the bottom, Coy accelerated a little, turning the wheel as hard to starboard as he could, so the *Carpanta* would turn back over her anchor, with the stern to the berth. Then he set the wheel at straight, and reverse, and as he listened to the links of the anchor chain running out over the bow sheave, he backed, paying out chain toward the point of the mole. Within a half-length from the point he killed the motor, went to the stern, picked up the end of one of the lines tied to the cleats and jumped ashore to halt the gentle drift of the *Carpanta* toward the dock. While El Piloto took in a little chain to hold the boat in place at the other end, Coy secured the mooring line to one of the bollards—a small, rusted, antique gun sunk to the trunnions in concrete—then brought a second line to another. Now the sailboat was immobile, surrounded by old half-scrapped hulls and abandoned superstructures. Tánger was standing in the cockpit, and as her eyes met Coy's, he saw they were deadly serious.

"It's over," he said.

Tánger didn't answer. She was staring into the distance, toward the other end of the mole, and Coy turned his head in the same direction to glance over his shoulder. There, sitting among the remains of a shattered lifeboat, looking at his watch as if congratulating himself for arriving punctually at a meticulously planned appointment, was Nino Palermo.

"I HAVE to admit," said the hunter of sunken ships, "you've done good work."

The sun had just slipped behind San Julián, and shadows were lengthening in the ship graveyard. Palermo had taken off his jacket and folded it carefully over one of the broken seats of the lifeboat, and he had turned the cuffs of his shirt back a couple of times, exposing the heavy watch on his left wrist. They formed an almost cordial-looking group, the five of them there beneath the bridge of the old packet, conversing like good friends. And the number was five, because in addition to Coy, Tánger, El Piloto, and Palermo himself, there was Horacio Kiskoros. In truth his presence was decisive, because had he not been among them it was unlikely that the conversation would have been conducted, as in fact it was, in such a civilized vein. An additional influence may have been the fact that for the occasion Kiskoros had exchanged his knife for a chrome pistol with a mother-of-pearl grip, a pretty little thing that might have appeared inoffensive had the inordinately large eye of its barrel not been pointed in the direction of the *Carpanta*'s crew. At Coy in particular, for whose temperamental fits Kiskoros and Palermo seemed to harbor some resentment.

"I never thought you'd get it done," Palermo continued. "Really, you . . . My, my . . . Amateurs, eh? Well, you're really something. Well done, I swear to God. Well done."

He seemed sincere in his admiration. He bobbed his head to give emphasis to his words, shaking the gray ponytail and jingling the gold hanging around his neck. At times he turned to Kiskoros, calling on him as witness. Small, slicked-back hair, bandbox neat in his light checked jacket and bow tie, the Argentine seconded his boss while managing to keep an eye on Coy.

"You deserve a lot of credit," the treasure hunter continued, "for finding that ship. With the means at your disposal, it's really . . . Well. I underestimated you, señora. And this sailor here, too." He smiled like a shark circling live bait. "I myself . . . God almighty! I couldn't have done it better."

Coy looked at El Piloto. The gray eyes were alert, with the fatalism of someone waiting for the right signal to act, one way or another; to throw himself on these guys, running the risk of taking a bullet, or stand there and watch the bullets come, waiting for someone to decide. You deal the cards, that look said. But Coy thought he'd got his friend in too deep already, so he slowly closed his eyelids. Play it cool. He watched El Piloto close his in turn, and when he looked back at Kiskoros, it was obvious that the dwarf had been observing them, and that the barrel of the pistol was tracing arcs that paralleled the movement of his eyes. The hero of the Malvinas, Coy decided, wasn't born yesterday.

"I'm afraid," Palermo concluded, "Deadman's Chest is taking over the operation."

Tánger stared at him impassively. Cold as a lemon snow cone, Coy could see. The iron of her eyes was darker and harder than ever. He wondered where she had hidden her revolver. Unfortunately, not on her. Not in those jeans and T-shirt. Pity.

"What operation?" she asked.

Coy watched with admiration. Palermo raised his hands a little, taking in the scene, the boat. He almost seemed to include the ocean.

"The recovery operation. I've been watching you through my binoculars the last two days, from the coast. You get the picture? And now we're partners."

"Partners in what?"

"Come on. What do you think? The ship. You've done your part. . . . You've done it splendidly. Now . . . God almighty. This is a matter for professionals."

"We don't need any help from you. I told you that."

"You told me, that's true. But you're wrong. You do need me. Either I'm . . . God almighty. Either I'm in or I blow the whole thing for you and your two trained seals."

"That's no way to form a partnership."

"I understand your point of view. And believe me, I regret all this business with the pistol. But your gorilla . . ." He hooked his thumb at Coy. "Well, I swore he wasn't going to surprise me a third time. Nor does Horacio have very fond memories of the gentleman . . ." Automatically he turned his bicolored eyes on Coy with a mixture of rancor and curiosity. "A little too aggressive, don't you think? Too aggressive."

Kiskoros's mustache twisted into a smile that dripped vitriol. His sallow face still showed signs of the encounter at Águilas beach, and it was perhaps for that reason that he seemed less sanguine than his boss. The pistol moved suggestively in his hand, and Palermo smiled at the gesture.

"You see." Again that sharklike expression. "He's dying to put a bullet in your belly."

"I'd rather," Coy parried, "he saved it for the whoring mother. . . ."

"Don't be crude," the Gibraltarian interrupted. He seemed truly scandalized. "Just because Horacio is pointing a pistol at you, that doesn't give you the right to insult him."

"I'm talking about *your* mother. The whoring mother who brought *you* into the world."

"Well. I confess that now I wouldn't mind shooting you myself. But the fact is . . . Well. That makes noise, you know?" It seemed as if Palermo was sincerely interested in having Coy understand. "Noise is bad for my business. Besides, it might upset the lady. And I'm tired of all this squabbling. All I want is to reach an agreement. For everyone to get his . . . Can we do that? End this thing peacefully?" Palermo had picked up his jacket and was inviting them to follow him. "Let's go get comfortable."

He set off toward the hull of the half-scrapped bulk carrier without turning to see whether they were following. Kiskoros simply flipped the barrel of the pistol, indicating the direction they should take. So Tánger, Coy, and El Piloto began walking behind Palermo. They didn't have their hands in the air, and the Argentine's attitude was not particularly threatening. But when they reached the foot of the ladder that led to the quarterdeck, and Coy paused a moment, hesitating, and looked at El Piloto, in half a second Kiskoros was holding the pistol to Coy's head.

"You don't want to die young," he whispered very low, with intimations of the tango.

They went down wet, ruined passageways with cables hanging from the overheads and semidismantled bulkheads, and then past bare floor plates and keelson as they descended the ladder into a hold.

"Now we're going to have a long conversation," Palermo was saying. "We'll spend the night chatting, and in the morning we can . . . Yes. All go back there together. I have a boat with equipment waiting in Alicante. Deadman's Chest at your service. Absolute discretion. Guaranteed efficiency." He directed a mocking smile at Coy. "Oh, yes. My chauffeur is waiting there with the equipment. He sends his greetings."

"Go back? Where?" Coy asked.

Palermo laughed his canine snort.

"Don't ask stupid questions."

Coy stood with his mouth open. He looked at Tánger, who showed no expression at all.

"Is there another option?" she asked as if Palermo was selling encyclopedias door to door. Her voice sounded about five degrees below zero.

"Yes," Palermo replied as he switched on a flashlight. "But it would not be very pleasant for you. Watch your head. That's it. And put your feet here, please. Yes . . ." His voice rang hollow, echoing in the depths of the metal hold. "That option would be for Kiskoros to lock the three of you up here for an indefinite time. . . ."

He paused as he shone the flashlight on Tánger's feet to help her reach the bottom. The hold smelled of rusted iron and dirt mixed with the faint aromas of wood, grain, rotted fruit, and salt, cargoes it once held.

"Or," he added, "he can also put a bullet in your head."

Once everyone was down, with Kiskoros and his pistol trained on the three guests, the seeker of sunken ships used his gold Dupont to light the wick of an oil torch that flared into a stingy red flame. Then he turned off his flashlight, hung his jacket on a hook, and put the lighter back in his pocket before smiling around at the assemblage.

"Move away from the ladder. Everyone over there toward the back. That's it. Make yourselves comfortable."

In that instant, Coy understood everything. He doesn't know, he told himself. This asshole and his dwarf still don't know that the emeralds are already on the *Carpanta,* and that none of this monkey business is necessary, because all he has to do is go pick them up. Again he looked at Tánger, amazed at her cool. She looked annoyed at most, the way she would at the window of an incompetent clerk, waiting to make a deposit. This is ending, he thought bitterly. I don't know how the hell it will end, but it's ending. And here I am still admiring the stuff that woman's made of.

"Now we will have our little talk," said Palermo.

Coy saw that Tánger was doing something strange: looking at her watch.

"I don't have time to talk," she said.

The man from Gibraltar seemed nonplussed. For a count of three he was mute with surprise. Then he smiled artificially.

"You don't say." The white teeth stood out in the greasy light of the oil torch. "Well, I'm afraid . . ."

His expression changed. He was studying Tánger as if seeing

her for the first time. Then he looked at Kiskoros, El Piloto, and finally at Coy.

"Don't tell me that . . ." he murmured. "It isn't possible."

He took a few steps, put one hand on the ladder, and looked up at the small rectangle of fading light in the hatchway.

"No, it isn't possible," he repeated.

Again he turned to Tánger. His voice was so hoarse it didn't sound like him.

"Where are the emeralds? Where?"

"The emeralds don't concern you," said Tánger.

"Don't be stupid. You have them? Don't tell me you already have them! That's . . . God al*mighty*!"

The treasure hunter burst out laughing, and this time, instead of snuffling like a weary dog he let out a laugh that shook the iron bulkheads. An admiring, stupefied laugh.

"I take my hat off, word of honor. And I have to think Horacio is taking his off, too. I'm so damn stupid. . . . I swear to you . . . How *about* that? Well done." He contemplated Tánger with intense curiosity. "My respects, señora. Astonishingly well done."

He had pulled a pack of cigarettes from his jacket and was lighting one. The flame of the gas lighter dilated the pupil of the brown eye more than the green one. It was obvious he was giving himself time to think.

"I hope you won't take this the wrong way," he concluded, "but our partnership has just been dissolved."

He exhaled smoke slowly and regarded the three of them through half-closed eyes, as if trying to determine what to do with them. Coy realized, with desolate resignation, that the moment had come. That this was the point at which he would have to make decisions before others made them for him, and that whether or not they were his it was possible that a few minutes from now he would be sprawled face down with a hole in his chest. In any case, he shouldn't let that happen without testing his luck, without asking for another card. Hit me. Hit me again. LLC: Law of the Last Card. Until the hull is split open on the rocks or water covers the deck, you're still afloat.

"You can't win every time; you have to understand that," Palermo was commenting. "And there are times you never win."

Coy exchanged a glance with El Piloto, and saw the same resigned decision. I'm with you. We'll meet in La Obrera and toss down a few rums. Or somewhere. As for Tánger, from this point on there was nothing he could do except make it easier for her to get up the ladder to the deck. After that, everyone had to swim for himself. In the end she would have to manage without his hand when her turn came in the dark. He was going to cast off long before that. He was going to do that right now, backed by El Piloto, who he knew was waiting, ready for the fight.

"Don't even think about it." Palermo had guessed his intention and shot a warning look at Kiskoros.

Coy calculated the distance separating him from the Argentine, his pulse pounding and his stomach hollow. Two yards was two bullets, and he didn't know whether with all the ballast in his body he could reach the dwarf, or what condition he would be in if he did. As for El Piloto, Coy was sure Palermo wasn't carrying a weapon, but when the moment came, neither El Piloto nor Palermo would be his concern anymore. Tánger had said it beside Zas's body: We all die alone.

"We've wasted too much time," Tánger said suddenly.

To everyone's stupefaction, she started walking toward the companionway as if she had decided to leave a boring social gathering, ignoring Kiskoros and his pistol. Palermo's hand, which at that moment was raising the cigarette to his lips to take a drag, froze in midair.

"Are you crazy? Don't you realize . . . Wait!"

By now Tánger was at the foot of the ladder, hand on the rail, and there was no question that she was ready to take her leave. She had half turned and was looking around, ignoring Palermo, as if wondering whether she'd forgotten something.

"Stay right there or you'll regret it," said the Gibraltarian.

"Leave me alone."

Palermo raised the hand with the cigarette, motioning Kiskoros not to fire. The Argentine's face was a somber mask in the light of the oil torch. Coy looked at El Piloto and got ready to make his move. Two yards, he remembered. Maybe, thanks to her, I can cover those two yards without getting shot.

"I swear . . ." Palermo was saying.

Suddenly the words stopped, and the cigarette dropped from his hand to the floor. And Coy, who was prepared to lunge forward, felt his muscles freeze. Kiskoros's pistol had described a precise semicircle and was now pointed at Palermo. Palermo was stuttering a few indistinguishable sounds, something in the vein of, What the hell are you doing? and What the fuck is going on? without completing a single word, and then he stood inanely staring at the cigarette smoldering between his feet, as if it might provide an explanation, before looking back toward the pistol, prepared to confirm that it was all a trick of his senses, and that the weapon was pointing in the right direction . . . But the black hole of the barrel was still on a line with the belly of the treasure hunter, and he was looking at each of them in turn—at Coy, El Piloto, and last Tánger. One by one, taking his time, as if waiting for someone to clarify in detail what this was all about. Then he turned to Kiskoros.

"May I ask what the fuck you think you're doing?"

The Argentine did not change expression, elegant and fastidious as ever, not moving a hair, with the chrome and mother-of-pearl pistol in his right hand, his diminutive silhouette projected onto the bulkhead by the torch. His face was not that of an evil man, or a traitor or lunatic. Very decorous, very calm, with his slicked-back hair and his mustache, looking more dwarfish, more tango-world Buenos Aires, and more melancholy than ever, confronting his boss. Or, by all indications, his ex-boss.

Palermo again looked down the row, but this time he stopped on Tánger.

"Someone . . . God almighty. Can anyone tell me what's going on here?"

Coy was asking himself the same question, aware of a strange hollow feeling in his stomach. Tánger hadn't moved from the foot of the companionway, her hand still on the railing. Slowly it dawned on him: this wasn't a ruse, she was actually going to leave.

"What is happening," she said very slowly, "is that here is where we all say good-bye."

The void inside Coy spread to his legs. His blood, if in fact it was circulating, must have been moving so slowly that his pulse was imperceptible. Without realizing what he was doing, he gradually slumped down, until he was sitting on his haunches with his back against the bulkhead.

"Why you sonofabitching . . ." Palermo spit out.

He was looking at Kiskoros as if hypnotized. The reality had finally set in. And the more his legs trembled, the more contorted his face became.

"You're working for her," he said.

He seemed more astounded than indignant, as if the first thing to be denounced was his own stupidity. Still silent and unmoving, Kiskoros let the pistol pointed at the Gibraltarian confirm that view.

"For how long?" Palermo wanted to know.

He had asked Tánger, who in the reddish light of the torch seemed about to disappear in the shadows. Coy saw her make a vague gesture, as if the date the Argentine had decided to turn coat was of no importance. Again she consulted her watch.

"Give me eight hours," she said to Kiskoros in a neutral tone.

He nodded, his vigil of Palermo never relaxing, but when El Piloto made a casual movement the pistol moved and covered him as well. The sailor looked at Coy, stupefied, and Coy shrugged. The line dividing the two sides had really been clear to him for some time. On his haunches in the corner he was examining his feelings. To his surprise, he wasn't experiencing anger or bitterness, but rather the materialization of a certainty he had often sensed but ignored, like a current of icy water that penetrates the heart and begins to solidify in layer after layer of frost. It had all been there, he realized. It had all been clear from the beginning, in depth readings, coastlines, shoals, and reefs marked on the strange nautical chart of recent weeks. She had given him the information that should have prepared him, but he hadn't known how—or hadn't wanted—to interpret the signs. Now it was night, with the coast to leeward, and nothing was going to get him out of this.

"Tell me one thing," he said, crouched against the bulkhead, unaware of the others, his words for Tánger alone. "Tell me just one thing."

He asked with a calm that surprised even him. Tánger, who had started up the steps, stopped and turned toward him.

"All right, one," she conceded.

Perhaps I owe you at least one answer, the gesture said. I've paid you in other ways, sailor. But maybe I owe you that. Then I will walk up this companionway, and everything will follow its course, and we will be at peace.

Coy pointed to Kiskoros.

"Was he already working for you when he killed Zas?"

She didn't answer, merely stared at him. The dancing light of the oil torch cast dark shadows on her freckled skin. She turned, as if to leave without answering him, but then seemed to change her mind.

"Do you have the answer to the riddle of the knights and the knaves?"

"Yes," he admitted. "There are no knights on the island. Everyone lies."

Tánger considered that for an instant. He had never seen her smile such a strange smile.

"It may be that you arrived on the island too late."

Then she went up the stairs and vanished into the shadows. Coy knew that he had already lived that scene. A ray of sun and a drop of amber, he remembered. He saw Kiskoros's pistol, Palermo's desolate expression, and El Piloto's taciturn immobility before he again rested his head against the iron bulkhead. Now his certainty and his loneliness were so intense they seemed perfect. Maybe, he reflected, he was wrong after all, and the line between knights and knaves wasn't all that clear. Maybe, in her own way, she had been whispering the truth all the time.

ALL things considered, betrayal held a unique pleasure for the victim. He dug into the wound, relishing his own agony. And like jealousy, betrayal could be more intensely savored by the one who suffered its consequences than by the one responsible for it. There was something perversely gratifying in the strange moral liberation that came from being betrayed, or in the painful memory of noting the warnings, the perfidious satisfaction of confirming suspicions. Coy, who had just discovered all this, thought about a lot of things that night, sitting beside El Piloto and Nino Palermo with his back against the bulkhead in the hold of the half-scrapped bulk carrier, and facing the pistol of Horacio Kiskoros.

"It's a question of patience," the Argentine commented. "As a compatriot poet of mine said: With the dawn, every thief is with his aged mother."

Nearly an hour had passed. When his former boss had stopped insulting him and reproaching him for his deceit, the hero of the Malvinas had relaxed a little, and perhaps in memory of old times he had revealed a few confidences, speaking in a low voice, aided by the torch, the place, and the long wait. It wasn't, Coy decided, that he was so loquacious, but that like everyone else he had a certain need to justify himself. They learned how when Kiskoros had taken Palermo's first message to Tánger, she had changed the panorama of his loyalties with admirable skill and convincing reflection during a long conversation—man to man, Kiskoros emphasized—in which she expounded the mutual advantages of their working together. Palermo would be out of the picture, and thirty percent of the profits would go to the Argentine, if he agreed to act as a double agent. Because, as Kiskoros pointed out, life was a trade-off, et cetera, et cetera. And most of all, because hard cash is hard cash. Not to mention the fact that she was a real lady. She reminded him of another rebel he had met, in 1976, in the barrio of the silver moonlight of ESMA. After a week of the electric prod, they still hadn't got her real name out of her. Coy had no trouble imagining the scene. The military mustache of ex-CPO Kiskoros twisted in a grimace of nostalgia, and the stench of singed flesh mixed with the aroma of beefsteak around the corner at La Costanera, and the music of Viejo Almacén, and the girls of calle Florida. *Cajhe* Florida was how it came out in Kiskoros's Buenos Aires accent, as he stretched his suspenders mournfully. But that—he interrupted himself, not without effort—was another story. So, going back to Tánger—such a lady, he insisted—every time Nino Palermo sent him to watch her or put pressure on her, he actually passed on information. Beginning to end; subject, verb, object. And that included Barcelona, Madrid, Cádiz, Gibraltar, and Cartagena. Tánger always knew how close they were, and Kiskoros was punctually informed of every step she took with Coy. Well, nearly every step, he qualified delicately. As for Palermo, his assassin—supposedly *his* assassin—had kept him drugged with partial information, until the man from Gibraltar, fed up with pampas tunes, decided to take a look for himself. That very nearly threw a wrench into the works, but fortunately for Tánger the emeralds were already on board the *Carpanta*. Kiskoros had no choice but to ride along with Palermo. The difference was that now instead of Coy and El Piloto being alone in the hold, the treasure hunter was keeping them company. Three birds with one stone. Although, in that respect, Kiskoros was sure he would not have to throw it.

"This won't end here," said Palermo. "I will find you wherever. . . . Goddammit. Wherever you go. I will find her and I will find you."

Kiskoros did not seem to be overly concerned.

"The lady is totally in control, and she knows how to take care of herself," he replied. "And I plan to be far away. I may go back to my country—wrinkled and weary, as the tango says—and buy myself an estancia in Río Gallegos."

"Why does she want eight hours?"

"Obvious. To put the emeralds in a safe place."

"And leave you holding the bag."

"No." Kiskoros denied with the barrel of the pistol. "Our arrangement is clear. She needs me."

"That bitch doesn't need anyone."

The Argentine jumped to his feet, frowning. His bulging eyes shot sparks at Palermo.

"Don't talk about her like that."

The seeker of sunken ships stood staring at Kiskoros as if he were a green Martian.

"Don't shit me, Horacio. Don't . . . Come on. Don't tell me she's brainwashed you too."

"Shut up."

"This is a very serious matter."

Kiskoros took one step forward. The pistol was pointing directly at the head of his former boss.

"I told you to shut up. She is a total lady."

Ignoring the gun, the treasure hunter shot Coy a sarcastic glance.

"You have to admit," he said, "that skirt has . . . Well. Lots of appeal. Roping in you and your friend, I suppose, wasn't too hard. As for me . . . God almighty. That's a little tougher. But sucking up to this sonofabitch Horacio . . . You know? That's a piece of work."

He sighed, respectful. Then he reached for his jacket and took out his pack of cigarettes. He put one in his mouth and said thoughtfully, "I'm beginning to think she actually deserves the emeralds."

He looked for his lighter, absorbed in his thoughts. Then he smiled mockingly.

"We're idiots, all of us."

"Don't include me," Kiskoros demanded.

"All right. I take it back. These two guys and I are dumb. You're the idiot."

At that moment, the siren of a boat entering the inlet pierced the bulkhead—a hoarse, brief blast from the bridge warning a smaller vessel to clear the lane. And, as if that one toot were the culmination of a long process of reflection that had consumed Coy for the last hour—in reality, he had been thinking about it unconsciously much longer—he saw the rest of the game laid out in its entirety. He saw it in such clear detail that he almost blurted it out. Every one of the clues, suspicions, and questions he had been aware of during the last few days took on meaning. The part Kiskoros was playing at that moment, the eight hours, the selection of this hold as a temporary jail, all of it could be explained in few words. Tánger was getting ready to abandon the island, and they, betrayed knaves, were being left behind.

"She's leaving," Coy said in a loud voice.

They all looked at him. He hadn't opened his mouth since Tánger disappeared through the hatchway to the deck.

"And she's dumping you," he added for Kiskoros's benefit, "just like us."

The Argentine stared at him. Then he smiled, skeptical. A neat, slick-haired frog. A self-congratulatory dandy.

"Don't give me that shit."

"It's all so clear. Tánger asked you to hold us till daylight, isn't that right? Then you close the hatch, leave us here, and join her. True? At seven or eight in the morning at such and such a place. Tell me if I have it right so far." The Argentine's silence and expression said that in fact he did. "But Palermo is right. She isn't going to be there. And I'm going to tell you why. Because by that time she will be somewhere else."

Kiskoros didn't like that. His expression was as dark as the black hole of the barrel.

"You think you're very clever, don't you? Well, you haven't been so smart up to now."

Coy shrugged.

"Maybe," he conceded. "But even a fool can understand that a newspaper opened to a certain page, a certain kind of question, a postcard, a couple of trips, a matchbook cover, and information Palermo unknowingly provided some time ago in Gibraltar, all lead to one particular place. You want me to tell you, or shall I be quiet and wait for you to discover it yourself?"

Kiskoros was playing with the safety on the pistol, but it was obvious his thoughts were elsewhere. He frowned, uncertain.

"Go ahead."

Never taking his eyes from Kiskoros, Coy again rested his head against the bulkhead.

"We begin," he said, "with the fact that Tánger doesn't need you now. Your mission—play the double agent, keep Palermo in control, convince me that she was helpless and in danger—ends tonight, with you guarding us while she leaves. You don't have anything to give her. So what do you think she'll do? How can she get away with a block of emeralds? At airports they check the hand luggage with X rays, and she doesn't dare to risk destroying such a fragile fortune in a checked suitcase. A rental car leaves a paper trail. A train means borders and cumbersome changes. Does any alternative occur to you?"

He sat quietly, waiting for an answer. Saying those things aloud he had experienced a strange sense of relief, as if he were sharing the shame and bile he felt boiling inside. This night there's something for everyone, he thought. For your boss. For poor Piloto. For me. And you, blockhead, it's not all roses for you, either.

But the answer came from Palermo before Kiskoros could speak. He slapped his thigh.

"Of course! A ship. A goddamn ship!"

"Precisely."

"God in heaven. Clever as hell."

"That's my girl."

Stunned, standing at the foot of the companionway, Kiskoros was trying to digest the news. His batrachian eyes went from one to the next of them, wavering among scorn, suspicion, and reasonable doubt.

"That is too many suppositions," he protested finally. "You think you are intelligent, but you base everything on conjecture. You don't have anything to confirm a ridiculous story like that. . . . No proof. Not a single fact to hold on to."

"You're wrong. There is." Coy looked at his watch, but it had stopped. He turned to El Piloto, still quiet but alert in his corner. "What time is it?"

"Eleven-thirty."

Coy looked at Kiskoros with amusement. He was laughing quietly, and the Argentine, unaware that in truth Coy was laughing at himself, did not seem to appreciate the joke. He had stopped fiddling with the safety and was pointing the gun at Coy.

"At one o'clock this morning," Coy informed him, "the cargo ship *Felix von Luckner,* of the Zeeland line, sets sail. Belgian flag. Two trips a month between Cartagena and Antwerp, carrying citrus fruits, I think. She accepts passengers."

"Fuck," muttered Palermo.

"Within a week"—Coy's eyes never left Kiskoros—"she will

have sold the emeralds in a certain place on the Rubenstraat. Your former boss can verify that." He invited Palermo with a nod of his head. "Tell him."

"It's true," Palermo admitted.

"You see." Coy laughed disagreeably once again. "And then you also have the postcard she sent you."

This time the blow hit home. Kiskoros's Adam's apple bobbed wildly in a confusion of convoluted loyalties. Even swine, Coy thought, have a soft spot in their hearts.

"She never said anything about that." Kiskoros was glaring at Coy, as if he blamed him. "We were going to . . ."

"Of course she didn't say anything." Palermo was trying to light his cigarette. "Cretin."

Kiskoros's spirits plunged.

"We had a rental car," he muttered, confused.

"Well," suggested Palermo, "now you'll be able to return the keys."

He couldn't get his lighter to work, so the treasure hunter bent down toward the flame of the oil torch, cigarette in his mouth. He seemed to be amused by the splendid joke of which they all were the butts.

"She never . . ." Kiskoros began.

WE may just get there in time, thought Coy. As they scrambled up the ladder the night air struck his face. There was a multitude of stars, and the scrapped ships were ghostly in the glow from the port. Behind them, lying on the floor of the hold, the Argentine was no longer moaning. He had stopped moaning when Palermo stopped kicking him in the head, and the blood bubbling from his seared nose was blending with the rust of the floor and sputtering as it hit his smoking clothing. He had lain writhing at the bottom of the companionway, jacket blazing, screaming, after Nino Palermo, leaning forward to light his cigarette, had thrown the torch at him. The arc of flames whirred through the darkness of the hold, passed Coy, and hit Kiskoros dead in the chest, just as he was saying "She never..." And they never learned what it was she hadn't done or said because at that instant the oil of the torch spilled over Kiskoros, who dropped the pistol when a lick of flame touched his clothing and raced upward to engulf his face. An instant later Coy and El Piloto were on their feet, but Palermo, much quicker than they, had swooped down and picked up the pistol. The three of them stood there, looking at each other unblinkingly as Kiskoros twisted and turned, lost in flames and emitting bloodcurdling screams. Finally Coy grabbed Palermo's jacket and put out the flames, first slapping at them and then throwing the jacket over Kiskoros. By the time he removed it, Kiskoros was a smoking ruin. Instead of hair and mustache he had blackened stubble and he was braying as if he were gargling turpentine. That was when Palermo had landed all the kicks to the Argentine's head, in a systematic, almost bookkeeper-like fashion. As if in farewell he were laying money on a table for his indemnification. And then, holding the pistol but not pointing it at anyone, and with a not-at-all-amused smile on his face, he sighed with satisfaction and asked Coy if he was in or out. That was what he said—"in or out"—looking at Coy in the gleam of the last flames from the spilled torch on the floor, his face that of a night-prowling shark about to settle a score.

"If you hurt her, I'll kill you," Coy replied.

That was his condition. He said it even though it was the other man who had the chrome and mother-of-pearl pistol in his hand. Palermo didn't object; he just grinned that white-toothed shark's grin and said, "Okay, we won't kill her tonight." Then he put the pistol in his pocket and hurried up the ladder toward the rectangle of stars. And now the three of them—Coy, Palermo, and El Piloto—were running along the dark deck of the bulk carrier as across the cove, under the illuminated cranes and dock lights, the *Felix von Luckner* was preparing to cast off her mooring lines.

THE light was on in the window of the Cartago Inn. Coy heard Palermo's exhausted-dog, snuffling laugh beside him.

"The lady is packing her bags."

They were standing beneath the palms along the city wall, with the port below and behind them. The lighted buildings of the university shone at the end of the empty avenue.

"Let me talk with her first," said Coy.

Palermo touched the pocket that held Kiskoros's pistol.

"Not a chance. We're all partners now." He kept staring up, his smile somber. "Besides, she would find a way to convince you again."

Coy bunched his shoulders.

"To do what?"

"Something. Give her time and there's no question she'd convince you of something."

They crossed the street, followed by El Piloto. Palermo never lost sight of the window, and once inside the door of the inn he again patted his pocket.

"Does she still have that cannon she had at Gibraltar?"

His stare was intense. The green eye resembled cold glass.

"I don't know. She may."

"Shit."

Palermo reflected, then turned to Coy, as if reconsidering his offer to talk with Tánger alone.

"She has her reasons," Coy pointed out.

The man from Gibraltar half-smiled, cornered on that point.

"That's right. We all do." He motioned toward El Piloto, who was waiting behind them expectantly. "Even him."

"Let me talk to her."

Palermo thought about it briefly.

"All right."

The night clerk of the inn said hello to Coy, confirming that the señora was upstairs and that she'd asked her to prepare the bill. They crossed through the lobby and went to the second floor, trying not to make any noise. Framed prints of ships lined the walls and a statue of the Virgen del Carmen filled a small niche. The door of Tánger's room opened directly onto the landing at the top of the stairs. It was closed. Coy reached it first, followed by Palermo. The hall carpet had deadened their footsteps.

"Good luck," Palermo whispered, his hand in his pocket. "You get five minutes."

Coy tried the doorknob, turning it without difficulty. It wasn't locked. As he turned the knob, he realized how pointless it all was. The absurdity of his being there. Rejected lover, deceived friend, swindled partner. In truth, he suddenly knew that when he looked at things rationally, he didn't have anything to say. She was about to leave, but in fact she had left long before, setting him adrift, and nothing he could say or do was going to change the course of things. As for the emeralds, he was used to thinking of them as a chimera far beyond reach; they hadn't mattered to him before, and they didn't matter now.

Tánger was the person she wanted to be. She wanted freedom of choice, and from the beginning he had known she would always be that way. He had seen the old silver cup missing its handle and the snapshot of a young girl smiling in black and white. That was what was needed to understand that the word "betrayal" was out of place, regardless of what she did. In fact, Coy would have turned and walked away, walked past El Piloto and kept on walking to the *Carpanta,* with a stop at the nearest bar, had the door not already been opening. He felt no rancor, not even curiosity anymore. The door continued to open, revealing on the far wall the window overlooking the port, the half-packed suitcase on the table, the package of emeralds, and Tánger standing there in her dark-blue cotton skirt, white blouse, and sandals, her hair freshly washed, the asymmetrical tips still dripping water onto her shoulders. And her skin, freckled and tanned by the weeks of sea and sun, the navy-blue eyes wide with surprise, blued steel, metallic as the 356 magnum she had seized from the table when she heard the door open. Now Nino Palermo played his part in this series of betrayals. Without waiting the five minutes he'd promised, he slipped past Coy with the chrome and mother-of-pearl pistol glinting in one hand. Coy opened his mouth to shout "No! Stop!" That's enough, let's rewind this whole absurd story we've seen a thousand times at the movies, but her finger had already contracted and a white flash erupted at the level of Coy's hip, with a blast that reached him a millisecond after the impact below his ribs, a crack! that whirled him half around, throwing him against Palermo, who at that moment was firing back. This time the shot thundered close to Coy's ear, and he tried to throw a hand out to stop Palermo from firing a second time. But there was another flash behind him, and another roar shook the air, and Palermo leaped back as if jerked from behind, propelled toward the landing and down the stairs. It wasn't a bang! the way it sounds in films, but pumba, pumba, pumba, three times, very close together, and now an infernal cloud of smoke filled the room, a harsh, acrid odor . . . and absolute silence. When Coy turned to look, Tánger wasn't there. He looked more closely and saw why she wasn't standing. She was lying on the floor on the other side of the table, blood pouring out in a brilliant red, thick, pulsing stream, staining her blouse and the floor. She lay there moving her lips, and all at once she seemed very young and very alone.

So this was when Coy walked out. It was a perfect night, with Polaris visible in its prescribed location, to the right and five times the distance of the line formed between Merak and Dubhe. He walked to the balustrade of the wall, and stood there, pressing his hand against the wound in his side. He had felt beneath his shirt and found that the rip in his flesh was superficial, and that he wasn't going to die this time. He counted five weak beats of his heart as he contemplated the dark port, the lights on the docks, and the reflection of the castles high on the mountains. And the bridge and lighted deck of the *Felix von Luckner,* about to cast off her lines.

Tánger had spoken to him. Her lips were moving when he bent over her, as El Piloto tried to stop the hole in her breast through which life was escaping. She spoke so inaudibly that he had to lean close to understand what she was saying. It was too much effort for her to put words together; her voice grew weaker and weaker, and then faded as the crimson blood pooled beneath her body. Give me your hand, Coy, she had said. Give me your hand. You promised you wouldn't let me go alone. Her voice was silenced, and the remnants of her life seemed to have gathered in her wildly staring eyes, as if she saw before her a desolate, barren plain that held only horror. You swore, Coy. I'm afraid to go alone.

He did not give her his hand. She lay on the floor, like Zas on the rug of the apartment in Madrid. Thousands of years had gone by, but that was the one thing he could not forget. He watched her lips move a little more, pronouncing words he couldn't hear because he had got to his feet and was looking around with a dazed air. He saw the block of emeralds on the table, the black revolver on the floor, the red pool that kept spreading and spreading, and El Piloto's back, bent over Tánger. He walked across his own desolate plain as he went through the room and down the stairs, stepping past the corpse of Palermo, who was lying feet up and head down, his eyes neither open nor closed, the shark smile frozen on his face, and his blood running down the stairs to the feet of the terrified receptionist.

The night air sharpened his senses. Leaning against the wall he felt the blood from his wound running down his side. The clock in the city hall struck once, at which point the stern of the *Felix von Luckner* slowly began to move away from the dock. Beneath the deck's halogen lamps he could see the first officer overseeing the sailors on the forecastle by the hawseholes. Two men—undoubtedly the pilot and the captain—were on the flying bridge, alert to the distance between the hull and the dock.

He heard El Piloto's footsteps behind him, and felt him lean beside him against the balustrade.

"She's dead."

Coy said nothing. A police siren sounded in the distance, approaching from the city below. On the dock the last line had been cast off and the ship began to move away. Coy imagined the darkness of the bridge, the helmsman at his post, and the captain watching the last maneuvers as the bow pointed between the green and red signals at the mouth of the port. He could imagine the shadow of the pilot crawling down the rope ladder to the launch. Now the ship was picking up speed, slipping smoothly toward the black, open sea, its shimmering lights reflected in the wake. One last hoarse blast of her horn sounded a farewell.

"I held her hand," said El Piloto. "She thought it was you."

The police siren was closer now, and a flashing blue spark appeared at the end of the avenue. El Piloto lit a cigarette, and the flare of his lighter blinded Coy. When he opened his eyes, he could see that the *Felix von Luckner* was already in open water. He felt an intense longing as he watched her lights grow dim in the night. He could smell the coffee of the first watch, hear the captain's footsteps on the bridge, see the impassive face of the helmsman lit from below by the gyroscopic compass. He could feel the vibration of the engines belowdecks, as the watch officer bent over the first nautical chart of the voyage, newly unfolded on the table to calculate a good course drawn with rulers, pencil, and a compass, on thick paper whose conventional signs represented a known and familiar world ruled by chronometers and sextants that allowed a man to keep his distance from land.

Oh God, he thought, I hope they let me go back to sea. I hope I find a good ship soon.

LA NAVATA, DECEMBER 1999

If you enjoyed reading

The Nautical Chart,

look for these other titles by

Arturo Pérez-Reverte

The Fencing Master

0-15-600684-7

$13.00

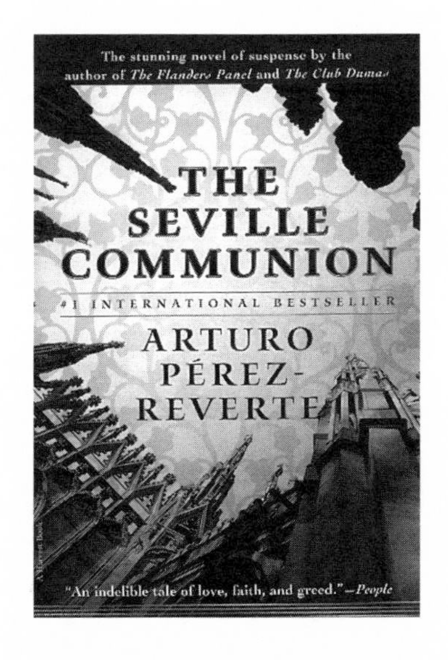

The Seville Communion

0-15-600639-1

$14.00